59x   469-469

HAD WE NEVER LOVED

Previous Novels by Patricia Veryan

Time's Fool
Logic of the Heart
The Dedicated Villain
Cherished Enemy
Love Alters Not
Give All to Love
The Tyrant
Journey to Enchantment
Practice to Deceive
Sanguinet's Crown
The Wagered Widow
The Noblest Frailty
Married Past Redemption
Feather Castles
Some Brief Folly
Nanette
Mistress of Willowvale
Love's Duet
The Lord and the Gypsy

HAD WE NEVER LOVED

Patricia Veryan

ST. MARTIN'S PRESS NEW YORK

Library of Congress Cataloging-in-Publication Data

Veryan, Patricia.
    Had we never loved / Patricia Veryan.
        p. cm.
    ISBN 0-312-07769-6
   PS3572.E766H3   1992
   813'.54—dc20   92-1010
                                                   CIP

First Edition: August 1992

10 9 8 7 6 5 4 3 2 1

Had we never loved sae kindly
Had we never loved sae blindly
Never met—or never parted—
We had ne'er been brokenhearted.

—ROBERT BURNS

HAD WE
NEVER
LOVED

PROLOGUE

The only light came from the steady flame of a candle on the solitary table in the centre of the room. The circle of light was feeble and left the corners of the room shrouded in blackness so intense that it was as if the candlelight shrank in upon itself and abandoned the uneven struggle to pierce the gloom. Although it was springtime, the room was chill and clammy, and the smell of mould permeated the air.

Six men were seated at the table. They were as so many graven images, each wearing a dark cloak, hood, and mask, so that only the gleams from the eye slits testified to the existence of life.

The man at the head of the table moved in his chair, and the candle flickered. Faint as it was, it drew sparkles from the miniature figures that were placed on the table, one before each man. Fashioned from jade or quartz, and about three inches tall, they were somewhat reminiscent of tiny gravestones with rounded tops. On each piece was carven the crude outline of a human face, this taking up most of the figure, with a suggestion of squat legs beneath. Scattered about the face were brilliant gems. Although identical in size, each figure was unique. One was of pink jade set with large rubies; another

———

was of lapis lazuli and sapphires. The pale green figure was jade also, enriched by the blue-green glow of emeralds; and there was a golden crystal inlaid with three topazes, and a glittering quartz studded with two fire opals. The figure at the head of the table was amethyst, lit by the cold fire of four superb diamonds, and it was the man seated there who now spoke, his voice thin and colourless.

"What is it that you judge to be foolish, Sapphire?"

The occupant of the lapis and sapphire position shrugged and said irritably, "All this drama and ritual. Damned nonsensical, was you to ask me. We know who we are well enough, Squire. Why the frippery masks and the elaborate secrecy? Like so many children playing poppycock!"

At the right hand of the man at the head of the table, a large individual toyed with the jade and emerald miniature before him. "You may *think* you could name us all, Sapphire," he said. "Though I fancy you'd be wrong in one or two cases."

"And even were you right," interposed the man with the ruby symbol, "how could you prove it, were you ever required to do so? Have you ever *actually* seen the face of any one of us while seated at this table? Could you swear in a court of law as to the true identity of any member our League?"

"Perhaps," said the man called the Squire, his voice very soft now, "Sapphire would prefer to come unmasked, so that the rest of us may be sure of *his* identity, at least."

There were some chuckles, and Sapphire drew back, disclaiming hurriedly, and saying he'd not looked at it in "just that particular way."

The Squire sprang to his feet and leaned across the table. "Then do so!" he snapped. "Far from being children at play, we are patriots, each one of us! Sworn, at great personal risk, to better this dear England and ensure her future well-being. Charles Stuart sought to seize the throne, and had he not been ill-advised and inexperienced, might well have succeeded. We *shall* succeed, because we aim not merely to rid ourselves of this German upstart who calls himself our king, but to do away with kings altogether and create a true republic."

"The people will be behind us, once we're ready," put in

the harsh voice of the Opal member. "They don't like German George above half! Who wants a king who cannot speak English? Who cares not a button for our land and would rather be back in Hanover, and who has made German the only language spoken at Court!"

The slight member with the Topaz symbol said, "We've done well. The Merriam and Albertson estates are safely in our hands and already being prepared."

Sapphire grunted. "We bungled the Rossiter business."

"Very true," said the Squire, sitting down again. " 'Tis well we have you among us, Sapphire, if only to keep us from becoming complacent. The member who—er, failed in that instance has paid the price. Else you, my dear friend, would not be here."

There was another burst of laughter, and Sapphire joined in, though rather uneasily.

Ruby said, "Sapphire reminds us, Squire, that young Rossiter and his unpleasant friends interfered with our plan, brought about the death of a valued member, and caused another to leave the country."

"We must expect casualties, apparently," said the Squire. "Even so, we achieved our objective, and Sir Mark Rossiter, one of England's great men, was disgraced and discredited."

"He has now been judged blameless," demurred Opal.

"By some, perhaps." The Squire gave a gesture of impatience. "But most people remember the bad and forget the good. Sir Mark's veracity has been tainted. When the time is right he will be judged just another thieving aristocrat."

"We all, I believe, are aristocrats," interjected Topaz in his soft voice.

"And will be the *only* aristocrats when we succeed," said the Squire. "Save that we shall be called Rulers, and our combined knowledge and expertise will prevail to guide this island and ensure that every common man has the opportunity to rise as far as his neighbour."

"And no further," murmured Ruby.

Over the burst of laughter, Emerald said, "Nonetheless, we

have a debt to pay, and time passes. Our enemies should be shown the error of their ways, Squire."

All heads turned to the man at the head of the table. Leaning back in his chair, he said thoughtfully, "Exactly so. The ringleader is now honeymooning in Europe."

"True, but Rossiter has, to an extent, already been punished," said Ruby.

"To . . . an extent," murmured the Squire. "Of his friends and allies, Lord Horatio Glendenning's loyalty to the throne is, to say the least, questionable, which could work very nicely to our advantage."

Sapphire said curiously, "Did the young fool really fight for Stuart's cause?"

"Very likely," said Topaz. "And is an obnoxious creature. What of this fellow Morris, Squire?"

"Lieutenant James Morris is of an old landed family, but there is no longer a title, and the estate is of no interest to us. He can be dealt with simply enough, but 'twill do little to advance our Cause. As to August Falcon—"

There were several scornful exclamations, and the Squire chuckled. "Half-breed he may be, but do not forget, gentlemen, he is as dangerous as he is wealthy, and Ashleigh is high on our list."

Sapphire's hand on the table clenched. "I've a long overdue score to settle with the Chandlers. When do we attend to them, Squire?"

"In due time, my friend." The Squire nodded to Emerald, who took a large folded document from a case on the floor beside him and spread it on the table. They all stood and gathered round. The rough map included a directional arrow pointing north, but in other respects it left much to be desired, for it lacked topographical detail and appeared to contain only large areas outlined in red, each having a neatly printed name and connected by lines to adjacent blue circles marked with initials.

"Do you know, gentlemen," murmured the Squire, tapping one well-manicured fingernail on the diamond emblem he held, "were we to proceed in the order of rank, and were we to handle the matter rather"—he laughed softly—"shall we say—deviously? We could chastise an irritating, but obligingly reckless young fellow, and in the process a most delectable plum might just chance to drop into our hands."

Below the mask his thin lips curved in response to the enthusiasm of his friends, and he leaned forward. The comments became a shout of endorsement as he set the diamond figure on one of the outlined areas on their abbreviated map. An area wherein two words were neatly printed: Glendenning Abbey.

CHAPTER I

Short Shrift was bustling, its single street crowded, most people afoot, but a few horsemen venturing cautiously among the boisterous throng. No less boisterous was the breeze that ruffled the chestnut trees, sent the ladies' skirts billowing, made mischievous snatches at wigs and bonnets, and flapped the many tents and awnings that had transformed the three-acre patch of turf known as the Village Green into a maelstrom of activity.

To designate Short Shrift a village was a matter of pride with the inhabitants and a topic sure to inspire scornful derision among the inhabitants of surrounding villages. Located in the beautiful rolling country west of Basingstoke, Short Shrift could boast only a baker's dozen thatched and whitewashed cottages. In response to sneers that it didn't even have a proper street, the inhabitants would point out that the lane curved "right pretty like" and, before their discreditors could add more insults, would unfailingly declare that Short Shrift was destined to grow. Rapidly. How could it fail? Already it had an "inn," which was (occasionally) a stop for the Oxford to Southampton Portsmouth Machine, or, as silly foreigners from London now called it, a "stagecoach."

It was in the stableyard of the Spotted Cat on this sunny

May afternoon that a horseman dismounted and glanced about for an ostler. On a normal day ostlers would have come running to take the splendid chestnut mare of this dashing young gentleman of Quality, but this was a far from normal day. The shabby old inn was crowded, and the host and his wife could scarcely run fast enough to accommodate the patrons who thronged the tap, pushed their way into the coffee room, and overflowed into the dusty corridor and dustier vestibule.

Therefore, the rider was neglected, and might with some justification have been annoyed. Horatio Clement Laindon, Viscount Glendenning, was an amiable young man, however, as the laugh lines at the corners of his green eyes attested. Of no more than average height, his lean figure and broad shoulders spoke of athletic pursuits, and although he fell short of being named handsome, his features were sufficiently good as to cause most female eyes to appraise him with interest.

There were female eyes upon him now. Brilliant eyes of dark brown set under slim brows. A purple scarf was tied about the night black hair of the young gypsy. The snowy low-cut blouse was amply filled and tucked into a long dark blue skirt. Sandals were tied about a pair of shapely ankles, and the little feet they protected were arched and slender.

Unaware of either the stare or the girl's attributes, Lord Horatio peered into the crowded stable. "Hey!" he called, without appreciable result.

"Look at him, Florian," murmured the gypsy girl, her red lips curling with scorn. "All beside of hisself 'cause six grooms and a ostler ain't come running to kneel at his feet. Proper helpless. Fair pathetic, ain't it?"

The gypsy lad beside her said softly, "The gentleman, perhaps. But the gry! Do you mark her? A rare prize, Amy."

His lordship was leading the mare into the stable. Watching the animal's silken movements, the girl whispered, "Aye. Oooh—aye!" She glanced up at her companion's finely boned young face and saw the glowing look in the beautiful eyes that were as dark as her own. "You think we could?" she hissed, tugging at his arm.

Suddenly appalled, he exclaimed, "Oh lor'! Never even dream of it!"

"But in a mob like this, 'twould be easy."

"Easy as death! You've maggots in your loft, girl!"

"I may be a girl, but I'd help, ye know that. Still . . ." She frowned thoughtfully. "Likely you're right and we'd swing on Tyburn Tree, the pair of us. Oh, well. We can think about the gry later. Now, you'd best go and help the poor Quality cove. He'll likely pay handsome. A nice mouth he's got. He'll be generous, I'll wager, and maybe toss you the price of one strand of that there wig he's got stuck on his noble nob."

Florian glanced at her in surprise. The tone was full of cynicism, but the words were unusually complimentary. "Here he comes," she added impatiently. "Go on, lump! Give a hand to Milord Rosy-and-Rare!"

He grinned. "You and your rhyming cant. He doesn't look like a nose-in-the-air to me. In fact—" He paused, his eyes widening. "Aiee! It's Lord Glendenning!"

"Know him, does ye? He's a pigeon for plucking if ever I see one. Go on!"

"Not me," he said, backing away. "He's no pigeon, Amy. Besides, he's a friend of Mr. Cranford. I'll not lighten his pockets, and no more should you."

His lordship turned in their direction. Florian melted into the crowd, and Amy Consett slipped into the shadow of the open stable door.

It had occurred to Glendenning that there were some decidedly odd goings-on in Short Shrift. On the few occasions he'd stopped here before, to glimpse more than a dozen people would have been remarkable. This afternoon the place was fairly mobbed. And mobbed by a most unusual crowd. The countryman he'd addressed, very politely, had rounded on him before he could say more than "Will you please tell me—?" Flourishing a handful of what looked like sheep's wool, the man had interrupted eagerly, " 'Ar—well 'ow long, master?" His astonished, "How the deuce do I know how long the stuff is?" had met with an indignant snort, and the obviously deranged individual had hurried off to wave his wool under the nostrils of a sturdy fellow in gaiters. Glendenning's second attempt had been even more peculiar. He'd readied his most beguiling smile to dazzle a pert young miss into chatting with him, and before he could say one word, she'd shaken a feather duster under his nose and asked in a shrill and alarmingly excitable manner what he would give for it. He had effected a hasty retreat, and now advised Flame, between sneezes, that if there was one article for which he had no use whatsoever it was a feather duster.

"Especially one that is blasted full of . . . dust!" he gasped, wiping tearful eyes after yet another sneeze.

As if endorsing his remarks, Flame whinnied and danced to the side. A shriek caused Glendenning to lower the handkerchief. He was aghast to see a gypsy girl sprawled on the ground practically under Flame's hooves. "Oh, Egad!" He fell to one knee and propped the girl, who appeared to be in a fainting condition. "I do beg pardon . . . miss . . ." His horrified utterance ceased. Her head had rolled back against his shoulder. The purple scarf had come loose, releasing a cloud of raven hair that rippled to her waist. He looked into an oval face blessed by high cheekbones, a delicately chiselled nose with the slightest uptilt at the end, a vivid, full-lipped mouth, and a firm little chin. Thick curling black lashes fluttered, and the bewildered eyes that blinked up at him were long and very dark. The swooping neck of her blouse had slid a little way over one white shoulder, leaving no doubt but that she possessed a remarkably handsome bosom. Somewhat dazed, his lordship had the fleeting thought that even Katrina Falcon would not outshine this beauty.

"You . . . hurt me . . . ," said she, in a husky, faltering voice.

Some sympathetic and indignant comments arose. Glendenning tore his gaze from the vision in his arms. A small crowd had gathered, and he was being regarded disapprovingly. "No, but— I—er— That is to say—was it my horse, mistress?" he stammered.

The dusky head nodded. The lustrous eyes closed. She sighed, and lay back again.

"Most improper!" remarked a stern-faced housewife, clad

in a plain grey gown and gripping a white parasol as though it were a bayonetted musket.

"It's these 'ere Quality coves, ma'am," whined a threadbare and cadaverous individual. "Much they care if their nags trample simple folk."

"You should be more careful, young fella," roared a large gentleman from beneath an awesome French wig. "Cannot go about trampling young females, y'know."

Red to the roots of his hair, Glendenning groaned and enquired if the "young female" could get up, or should he summon an apothecary.

Those great eyes were looking at him piteously again. "I'll . . . try," she said in a faint voice.

He practically had to lift her, and she clung to him weakly. There was a fragrance about her. A sweet, clean, natural fragrance.

A jeering shout broke through Glendenning's pleasant musing. " 'Ware the gypsies, me fine cove! Keep yer peepers on yer valleybles!"

His lordship snapped back to reality, and his eyes darted instinctively in search of Flame. Unperturbed by the several admiring children who were stroking her, the mare waited patiently, in the act of accepting the bullseye a small girl offered.

A loud and officious voice rang out. "Move aside, there! In the name of the law!" The crowd eddied and split. A man wearing a dark habit, a black tricorne set on his scratch wig, and with a sombre expression on his narrow face, pushed his way through.

Glendenning felt the yielding figure he held become tense. With a lithe twist the gypsy girl was out of his arms.

Springing forward, the constable seized her wrist. "Ho, no you don't!"

"Let me go, you nasty old cove!" Amy appealed to his lordship. "I ain't done nothing, has I, sir? Tell him I ain't done nothing, yer highness!"

"Indeed she has not," said Glendenning. "The shoe's on the other foot in point of fact. I—"

"I don't know nothing 'bout your shoes, sir," said the constable resonantly. "But there's been charges brought 'gainst this young woman." He added, over his shoulder, "Is this her, mate?"

A burly, red-faced young man, with a too-tight coat and a wig that made his lordship shrink, loomed up behind the minion of the law, and nodded. "That's 'er," he confirmed. "Stole me watch, she done!"

"Ooh! I never!" declared Amy, outraged. "Didn't yer ma never teach ye not to tell fibs, young man?"

"I, for one, am not in the least surprised," proclaimed the grey lady.

The large gentleman who had scolded Glendenning for not being careful now roared that it was only to be expected. "She's a gypsy, after all," he pointed out.

"I see you hanging on to this here gent," said the constable, tightening his grip on Amy's wrist. "You best check your pockets, sir. You'll be lucky if you still got your purse!"

"Ooh! What a wicked mind you got," said Amy, bursting into tears. "I never did nothing! You can search me from head to toe, you can, and you won't find that skinflint's cheap watch, nor the gent's purse, neither."

"Here! I ain't a skinflint," protested the red-faced young man.

"Yes, ye is," said Amy, scattering tears. "You promised me yer watch if I'd give you a kiss, and then you never give it me."

Ignoring the grey lady's shriek, and the outburst of laughter, the young man's face became redder than ever as he said indignantly that he couldn't give away what had already been stole. "Besides," he appended, "you never did give me the kiss!"

Glendenning, who had encountered a few gypsies during his eventful life, had been groping about in the deep pockets of his riding coat, just in case. He had not lost his purse, although it was now in the wrong pocket. He had, however, gained something. Keeping his features commendably bland, he informed the gathering with perfect honesty that nothing of his had been stolen.

"Ar, well it wasn't for want of trying, I'll wager," snorted the constable, and gave Amy's arm a tug. "You come along o' me, young woman, and—"

"No!" she wailed, casting an imploring glance at his lordship. "Oh, sir! Don't let him take me off and ruinate me. I ain't done nothing!"

" 'Pon my soul!" gasped the large gentleman. "He's not going to ruinate—I mean, he's an officer of the law, girl! Where ever did you come by such notions?"

"With a face like hers, you should know where she come by 'em," said the grey lady, all righteous accusation. "Men, is where! Men!" She waved her parasol about for emphasis as she expounded, and several of the onlookers were obliged to duck. "A pretty face, and they forget every moral value their poor mothers ever tried to inculcate into their lascivious minds! Men! Animals, more like. The lot of 'em!"

There was a brief awed silence, nobody venturing to contradict so fierce a crusader until someone braver than the rest (and well hidden) uttered a loud "Hee-haw!"

The large gentleman gave a shout of laughter. The grey lady turned on him in a passion. The crowd entered into the spirit of the argument, and his lordship, who rarely puffed off his consequence, drew the constable aside.

With cool authority, he said, "I am Lord Glendenning, officer. And I think you must know that you cannot arrest this lady without proof of an offense."

"Lady!" snorted the red-faced young man. "She ain't no more a lady than—"

His lordship snapped, "Careful, fellow. You speak slander!"

The alleged victim blinked at him. "What's that mean?"

"It means as she's gotta be searched," said the constable, adding a respectful, "ain't that it, your lordship?"

"Not by you, you dirty old—" began Amy.

Glendenning intervened hurriedly, "We shall find a respectable lady, Miss, er . . . ?"

"Lewis," lied Amy, smiling at him. "Alice Lewis, yer worship."

A timid little woman who had been selling nosegays was pressed into service. She took "Miss Alice Lewis" into a nearby tent and emerged some moments later to impart shyly that the young lady was "innocent as the day she was born."

The constable grumbled himself away.

The red-faced young man said sullenly that his lordship probably had his reasons for taking up for the thieving gypsy.

"And that will be enough from you," said the viscount. "I wouldn't doubt but that your watch is still lying where you dropped it when you were trying to take advantage of this lady. But if you can't find it," he clapped the victim on the shoulder, "buy yourself another. Go along now, and search for it, there's a good fellow."

The young man brightened when a gold sovereign was pressed into his palm, and with a leering grin departed.

Amy gave the viscount a limpid look, and edged closer.

Lord Horatio smiled into her dusky eyes, then exchanged a shilling for a nosegay, and offered it to her.

"You paid six times too much," she advised, smelling the violets.

"Yes, but the lady did us a favour." He slipped another shilling onto the little flower seller's tray and, brushing aside her transports of delight, led Amy from the continuing dispute between the grey lady and the large gentleman.

"You're very easy with yer better-or-worse, milor'," said Amy.

Her nose was still buried in the violets, and over the flowers her great eyes twinkled roguishly at him. She should, he thought, be taken at once to that fellow who had married Margaret Burr. What was his name? Oh yes, Gainsborough. He was quite clever with paints. Probably be very glad of a model like this enchantingly lovely gypsy lass. Something poked at his ribs, and Flame snorted uneasily. Looking up, Lord Horatio's dreaming gaze encountered a furled but aggressive parasol, and he retreated before two hard grey eyes under an austere grey bonnet.

"Shameful!" snorted the grey lady as she marched past.

And drifting behind her came the all-embracing denunciation "Men!"

Recalled to a sense of his obligations, Glendenning coughed and said, "Never mind about how easy I am with my purse, Miss Lewis. You *did* steal that poor fellow's watch, because it's in my pocket!"

She smiled at the violets. "Is it, sir? And where did a great nobleman like yerself learn that better-or-worse means purse?"

He thought of Enoch Tummet, and grinned. "I've come up against rhyming cant before. Matter of fact, the valet of a friend of mine—" He paused.

"Why d'ye frown, yer highness? Ain't he a friend? Or ain't the valet a valet?" Amy gave a ripple of laughter. "Straight, I never heard of no-one so grand as a valet what knew rhyming cant. That's what simple folk talk. Like me."

The viscount guided her to one side, avoiding a brawny labourer with a scythe slung over one shoulder. "The valet *is* a valet, I promise you," he explained. "And he *is* a simple— Er, I mean, he hasn't been a valet for long."

"What was he before, then?" Amy looked longingly at a stand where rows of toffee apples shone stickily in the sunlight. "A bishop, p'raps?"

Glendenning chuckled. "He was a guard. A—a sort of bailiff, actually."

"You mean what does executions in houses when folks can't pay what they owes and isn't allowed to move nothing out 'til it's all sold for debt? Cor! How'd the likes of him get to be a valet? That's *proper* grand, that is." Her eyes had wandered back to the apples again. "Why don't ye like him?"

His lordship edged through the crowd that surrounded the stand and bought two toffee apples, one of which he gave to Amy. She accepted it with pleasure, and he watched as her pink tongue was promptly applied to the toffee.

"I do like him," he said, answering her question and regarding his apple dubiously. "It's just that he don't work for my friend now, but for—er, another gentleman. None of which has anything to do with—"

14

"Oh," she interrupted, licking busily. "Then it's this here other gent what you don't like. Ain't you going to eat yer apple?"

It had been many years since Lord Horatio had attacked a toffee apple, and he approached it gingerly, but found it delicious. After a minute, he looked up to find Amy laughing at him.

"Don't be so ladylike, mate," she advised. "Forget as you're a squire, for once, and give it a good lick. Like this . . ."

'Ladylike!' he thought. But following instructions, gave it "a good lick."

"That's right," said Amy, encouragingly. "Have at it, yer highness. I knew as ye could do it."

It dawned on his lordship that the note to her voice, the gleam in her eyes, held a trace of mockery. He said, "And you properly turned me from the subject, didn't you? But now I want to know how it is that your kissing friend's watch found its way into my pocket."

Amy's lashes swept like two dainty fans onto her cheeks, and she said meekly, "I ain't a bad girl, yer worship. But sometimes, when I'm very hungry, the Devil he whispers in me earhole."

"Ear," he corrected. But looking at all the demure witchery of her, the very thought of her going hungry appalled him, and he had to struggle to add with severity, "And stealing people's watches is not the way to appease your appetite, Miss Lewis. You could have been transported had we not managed to bring you off. You would do better to obtain a position in—in a shop, perhaps."

She sighed and the dark silk of her hair swung as she shook her head. "I ain't got the proper gab fer it, milor'. And that young man with the red face, he was a rough bully. The kind a girl's got to look out fer. Deserved a lesson, he did, so I give him one."

"I see. And since I find that my purse has been moved, I presume you judged that I also deserved a lesson."

She darted a glance at him from the corner of her eyes.

"Still got it, ain'tcha? You been kind to me, yer honour. I don't forget folks what's kind to me. Someday, I'll pay ye back . . ." A far-away look came into her eyes. She said in a softer voice. "One o' these fine days . . ."

Curious, Glendenning asked, "What is it? Of what are you thinking?"

"That we'll meet again, milor'. Soon, I think . . . At the dark o' the moon, maybe."

He fought to repress a grin, but the side of his mouth twitched.

Amy saw, and bristled. "Think it's funny, does ye? A poor common gypsy girl don't go to balls and routs and the high and mighty opry, where she might meet someone so top lofty as yer lor'ship, eh? And anyway, I ain't good enough for ye to ever want to meet again, is that what you be sticking yer nose in the air at?"

A tall farm worker carrying a long-tined pitchfork, paused and looked with suspicion from the elegant young man to the gypsy girl.

Glendenning lengthened his stride, and said tersely, "Of course not. And I'm not sticking my nose in the air."

"Yus you is, and you got a long nose if ye want to know it. I wonder some blackbird don't fly down and sit on it!"

Glendenning, whose nose was described by kindly friends as showing strength of character, grinned. "Wouldn't you be surprised if one did."

"No, I wouldn't," she said crossly, and with a glance at his eyebrows, which were distinctly auburn, she added, " 'Sides, it looks to me like you got a red poll under that there wig. Red hair means bad temper. Always. So ye needn't think I'm making up to you or nothing."

"No indeed. Though I would be very flattered if you were. And 'tis kind in you to want to repay me for what little assistance I may have rendered. Especially since my hair is indeed red."

He had spoken with saintly meekness, and his green eyes were properly solemn. Very nice eyes, she thought. And he was truly a fine-looking man. But that telltale quirk hovered beside the humorous mouth again, wherefore, "You needn't try to turn me up sweet, Hoity-Toityness," she said, scowling.

"It isn't hoity-toity to know that stealing is wicked, Alice, and—"

"Me name's not Alice."

"Oh. But you said—"

"Never mind." A twinkle dispelled her wrath. She said mischievously, "And if you think stealing's wicked, then ye'd best shoot that pretty gry o'yourn, 'cause she's eating yer apple all up!"

Lord Horatio jerked his head around in time to see the apple disappearing between Flame's jaws.

Laughs went up as he shook his fist at the unrepentant mare, and told her she was a scamp. And clearer, sweeter, purer than all the rest was a silvery trill of mirth as Amy clung to his arm and pleaded that he not beat his gry.

"Well, I should," he argued indignantly. "Bless it, one might think—"

"Tio! Hello! Tio!"

Recognizing the musical voice, he turned, his eyes brightening. "Katrina!"

Miss Katrina Falcon's maternal grandmama, exquisitely beautiful, had been the product of a union between a Chinese mandarin and a Russian princess. Miss Falcon's ancestry was revealed only in her eyes which, although large and of a rich midnight blue, had a slight Oriental slant. If anything, this feature added mystique to a lady of rare loveliness, for Katrina was blessed with a clear if slightly olive complexion, her features were dainty, her rather tall figure slender and graceful. Now three and twenty, she had a gentle and affectionate disposition, and would have long since made a brilliant match save for two obstacles. One was her mixed blood, which was viewed with horror by much of the *haut ton*. The other was her brother, a deadly duellist who despised London's Society and declared contemptuously that he had yet to meet the man worthy of his lovely sister. Katrina was a considerable heiress and, despite her unfortunate birth, was much courted both by fortune hunters and by the many gentlemen who genuinely admired her. Mr. August Falcon dismissed them all. Often with a lack of tact that had led to several duels.

Aware of this, and aware also that the lady's deadly brother stood nearby, Lord Horatio was undaunted as he kissed Miss Falcon's outstretched hand. He acknowledged her beauty, he admired her amiable nature, but she did not touch his heart. He was fond of her, however, and was perfectly sincere when he exclaimed, "What luck that I should find you here! I'd fancied you to have gone down to Sussex after the Rossiter wedding."

"So we did," she answered merrily. "But I knew the Mop Fair would be held today, and—"

"And she could not resist it." August Falcon sauntered to join them. Her senior by six years, he was as handsome as his sister was beautiful, and so like her that there could be no doubt of their relationship. His eyes were not as large as hers, but of the same blue that was so dark as to seem almost black. In expression, however, they were very different; August's eyes were hard, and cold, and reflected a deep cynicism that was echoed in the uncompromising line of the thin lips. He offered a languid hand to Glendenning, and murmured, "A Mop Fair, God bless us! That I should have allowed myself to be bullied into mingling with such a sorry collection of yokels!"

"I did not bully," objected Katrina laughingly.

Glendenning asked, "What the deuce is a Mop Fair?"

"It is a day in which those seeking employment bring some tool of their trade and walk about hoping a prospective master will hire them," explained Katrina. "But if you did not know, then why are you here, Tio? I'd thought you were remaining in Town."

They moved out of the crowd and into the cool shade cast by a tent, and Glendenning answered, "I was, but— well it seemed rather dull after our little tussle with the League of Jewelled Men. So I decided to pop up and see how Mama goes on."

"Do pray alleviate our intolerable suspense," drawled Falcon. "How does dear Lady Bowers-Malden go on?"

Glendenning grinned. "Not a bit of use your trying to be obnoxious, Falcon. I know dashed well you like my mother. And I don't know how she goes on, because I haven't got there yet, as you see."

"I see," said Falcon, looking bored, "that your lordship is taking an extraordinarily circuitous route. Eton failed you, dear boy. Upon departing the Metropolis it is not necessary to ride through Basingstoke so as to reach Windsor. Not," he added dulcetly, "that it is any of my bread and butter."

One should know better, thought Glendenning, than to try and flim flam August Falcon. "Well, it ain't," he said without rancour. "But, if you must know, I thought I'd drop in on the Cranfords first."

"Whereby one assumes your mission to Glendenning Abbey is not an urgent one."

Lord Horatio tensed, his green eyes darting to Falcon's bland expression. "Why should it be?"

"Exactly so," replied Falcon obscurely. "To resume this enchanting tale, you detoured again to come to a fair you'd not known was in progress, eh?"

Katrina scolded, "Now August, you must not be such a tease. He likely decided to take luncheon here, is that not the case, Tio?"

"Yes, as a matter of fact." Glendenning smiled at her gratefully. "Although had I known 'twas like Bedlam, I'd not have come near the dratted place, I promise you."

"You surprise me," said Falcon. "I'd have guessed you'd— ah, hired that pretty piece you were flirting with just now."

"Jupiter!" Glendenning jerked around guiltily. "I quite forgot—" He broke off. Miss Alice Lewis was nowhere in sight. Her purple kerchief should be easy to find, but although he scanned the jostling crowd narrowly, there was no sign of her. He thought, 'Damnation!'

Watching him, Falcon chuckled. "Properly bewitched you and then tipped you the double, did she? You'd best look to your purse, my poor dupe."

"Nothing of the kind," said his lordship. "But I wish you might have met her, Katrina. She was the most enchanting little—" His earnest words ceased. He'd slipped one hand into his pocket, just to make sure. His purse and the red-faced man's watch were gone.

Falcon uttered one of his rare laughs. "An enchanting little female prig, eh? You may count yourself blessed that she didn't make off with your horse as I am very sure she longed to do." He patted Flame's glowing shoulder. "A damned fine animal you've got here. Did you find her at Tattersall's?"

"No. In point of fact, my brother gave her to me."

Falcon's flaring brows lifted. "Did he now? I saw Templeby last week." He added idly, "At the Cocoa Tree."

His lordship shrugged. "Michael's two and twenty. Old enough to be on the Town."

"True. And such a generous fellow. This fine mare to you; a diamond necklace for his sister, a tiara for Lady Bowers-Malden. Fowles tells me he's been on a winning streak."

Recalling Piers Cranford's veiled warning, Glendenning suffered another pang of unease, but he said with his pleasant smile, "I cannot allow my baby brother to outshine me. Come. I must find an ostler to take charge of Flame, and then I shall stand the huff for a magnificent luncheon at the Spotted Cat."

"How lovely," said Katrina, ever the optimist.

"Provided," murmured her brother, "Glendenning can reclaim his purse."

"Oh, Jupiter," groaned Lord Horatio, mortified.

Katrina laughed. "Poor Tio. Never mind, we shall take you to luncheon instead. 'Twill be our pleasure, won't it, dear?"

"Joy unsurpassed," grunted August Falcon.

CHAPTER II

Glendenning Abbey was an enormous house. The original pile, dating to the fifteenth century, had consisted of one long structure, now the rear wing. Subsequent owners had thrown up additional wings on each side, so that the modern abbey was in the form of a square with the south side left open, creating a huge entrance courtyard. Built of creamy-grey stone blocks, and a uniform two storeys in height, the abbey stood with dignity, if not warmth, amid gently rolling hills and lush meadows. It had a colourful history, and was widely admired. It was not, however, a comfortable house. To travel from the east wing, where were the bedchambers, to the west wing, which housed kitchens, sculleries, pantries, and the various breakfast parlours and dining rooms, took quite some time, unless one went outside and crossed the courtyard. Michael Templeby, the son of the earl's second wife, claimed that this rather irreverent procedure trimmed seven minutes from the journey, but the shortcut was impractical for much of the year, England's weather being what it is.

It had sometimes seemed to Horatio Glendenning that the very size of the vast pile had contributed to the fact that he had so little acquaintance with his sire. "The fact is, ma'am," he had once told his stepmother, whom he adored, "that I seldom can find the old—er, Papa. And when I do, 'tis an eagle to a ladybird I won't recognize him!"

The countess, a tall and statuesque matron, had uttered her booming laugh and advised the heir that he was being facetious. "This is a splendid heritage, Horatio, and one you should be proud of."

Glendenning had not voiced his deep regret that some ancestor had lacked the wisdom to add a fourth wing and seal off both the square and the mansion so that no one could get in, and had said rather hollowly that he was proud, of course. If he was proud, his pride was in his name and his lineage, but from childhood he had found the abbey ponderous, draughty, and dull, and he had escaped it whenever he could do so without distressing his stepmother.

Riding into the courtyard on this warm afternoon, he was met by racing stableboys and the head groom. He greeted his father's servants as warmly as they greeted him, and entered the main block with the intent of seeking out the countess and his sister. The butler, a small and wiry gentleman with bright birdlike eyes and an unfailing smile, frustrated this plan by informing the viscount that Miss Marguerite was out driving with her mama. "Mr. Michael," he added, "is in London, as your lordship is doubtless aware."

"Yes." Starting off in the direction of his suite, Glendenning paused, and turned back. "By the way, Darrow, has my brother been here recently?"

The butler moved closer and said in a cautious voice, "Last week, my lord."

"Out with it," said Glendenning, not standing on ceremony with this lifelong friend. "Trouble?"

"I—wouldn't say trouble exactly, sir. But Master— I mean Mr. Michael seemed . . . not quite himself. As if he was worrying at something."

'Likely he's been plunging too deep at the tables, the young fool,' thought Lord Horatio. "I'll have a word with my mother," he said. "Let me know when the countess comes home, if you please."

"Yes, my lord. But—er, the earl is expecting you."

"Egad! Now?"

"He knows you have arrived, sir. He wishes to talk with you, er—*before* you go up to change your dress."

"Blast! I'm in for it, am I Darrow?"

The butler made a wry face.

Sighing resignedly, the viscount turned about and commenced the long walk to his father's study.

Everything about Gregory Clement Laindon, the Earl of Bowers-Malden, was massive. He had a great frame that had not run to flesh and was all muscular strength; his head was leonine, his personality aggressive, and his voice a growl that could rise to a bellow that shook the windows and terrified the servants. He was of the same colouring as his son, and his strong face was not unhandsome and could at times take on a whimsical and surprisingly endearing grin.

Glendenning had seldom seen that grin, and, standing before his father's desk, enduring the long and detailed exposition of his faults, would have been hard put to it to remember that one existed. He remained respectfully silent while the earl dealt with his school years, but his nerves tightened when this sorry inventory was followed by a grim reference to the late tragic Uprising.

"And I know damned well," thundered Bowers-Malden, "that you fought with those bare-kneed Scots savages, so do not trouble to deny it."

The bushy eyebrows bristled; the green eyes shot sparks; and realizing he was to be allowed to answer, Glendenning said, "Mama is a Scot, sir, and—"

"By God!" roared the earl, rising from his chair as if a shell had exploded under it. "Do you say that because my wife was born a Comyn she has influenced you into treasonable activities?"

"No, sir! I merely point out that all Scots are not—"

The earl sat down again. "When I want your opinion of the inhabitants to the north of us, I shall request it, Glendenning. Not that it would be worth a damn, as you show by the example you set your brother! Oh, I'm aware of the rumours that you have been up to your ears in aiding Jacobite fugitives. Likely still are, dammitall! Your reasons, if you have any, are beyond me!"

With daring intrepidity, Horatio took up the gauntlet. "I find it exceeding difficult, sir, to condemn my fellow Britons for fighting to keep a *Briton* on the throne, rather than bending the knee to a Hanoverian prince who has no more desire to rule England than we have to be inflicted with—"

"And because you are so ill-informed, my lord," snarled the earl at his most menacing, "it pleases you to suppose that all the rest of us indulge the same bacon-brained notions as you do, eh?"

He was on his feet again, face flushed, eyes flashing, massive jaw outthrusting. Like many a man before him, it was all Horatio could do not to shrink back a pace before that formidable wrath, and although he managed to overcome the impulse he was momentarily struck dumb and stood in white-faced silence.

Incensed, the earl swept on. "Well, I thank God that most English gentlemen have the wits to prefer a German prince with a justifiable, however distant, claim to the throne. King George ain't the type of man I'd have chose, I grant you, but he follows our policies of parliamentary procedure, which is a sight more than we'd get from a hare-brained young Scot dedicated to the philosophy of Rule by Divine Right. Divine right, indeed! Much the Stuarts have brought us of divine anything! For nigh a century and a half they've been a plague *véritable,* a blasted great millstone round the neck of this nation! I wonder, my lord, nay, I am astounded, that it has not penetrated your alleged brain that your admired Scots who so repeatedly fell under the Stuart spell failed to learn from their mistakes! They were deceived, used, exploited, and *still* followed that forlorn cause. And what did their gallant but ill-advised loyalty earn for them? Tragedy, starvation, death, and persecution that continues to this day!" The earl sat down again, his great voice still grumbling, "*Stuarts?* Pah, I say, sir! Humbug!"

Battered but unbroken, Horatio found his voice and entered the lists again. " 'Tis precisely because of that brutal persecution and tragedy, Father, that many gentlemen do what they may to help Scots fugitives! There is no—"

"There is nothing to be gained from such mad recklessness save more death; more suffering! A man fights for what he believes, Glendenning, be he worthy to be called a man. But an he is defeated he must stand up bravely and take his punishment, not expect others to shoulder his burdens and share his risks. Certainly you know full well that to aid and abet a fugitive is punishable by death! One might think that what happened to your bosom bow, de Villars, would have cooled your ardour for the game. I'm told that reckless madman escaped these shores half a leap ahead of a troop of dragoons, and with a musket ball in his back!" Bowers-Malden interrupted himself to enquire interestedly, "Did he survive, by the bye?"

"Yes, sir. And married the Widow Parrish. I understand she is about to present him *un petit pacquet*." Taking advantage of this small thaw, Glendenning said quickly, "And I really do not think Michael is in the slightest sympathetic to the Jacobite cause, Papa."

"Well, if he ain't it's no thanks to you," boomed the earl, scowling as fiercely as ever. "The young fool idolizes you, and copies every blithering start you embark on! As if it was not bad enough that you must plunge into the Stuart fiasco, I'm told you made a confounded ass of yourself in the Rossiter business. What a'plague possessed you to fall into such a morass?"

Glendenning frowned. "Gideon Rossiter is my very good friend, sir. He came home from Flanders barely recovered of his wounds, and was abused beyond bearing."

"Unfortunate. But his father brought that about, ruining half the men in London with his financial caperings."

"Your pardon, sir, but Sir Mark Rossiter was the victim of a vicious conspiracy." Yearning to be able to tell the earl some details of that conspiracy, and of the fact that several of his friends considered it to have been only part of a far more complex plot, Glendenning was sworn not to speak of the matter. He therefore finished somewhat lamely, "It was my honour to help his son, insofar as I was able."

"Humph! And is it also your honour to frequent every gaming house and half the fancy houses in Town?" Overriding his son's indignant repudiation of this exaggeration, the earl swept on, "You are the eldest, Glendenning. I realize that Templeby is only your stepbrother, but I would expect you to set him a better example than to present him graphic lessons in—in treason, gambling, womanizing, and general irresponsibility."

Angry now, Glendenning said hotly, "My political beliefs do not march with yours, I am aware, sir. But I think my personal life is not yet sunk beneath reproach. Besides, my brother attained his majority more than a year since, and—"

"And you attained yours more than a decade since! I have no wish to see Templeby wind up ten years from today in *your* condition! 'Twould break his mother's heart." Bowers-Malden waved a large and impatient hand, again cutting off his son's indignant attempt to speak. "A man is known by the company he keeps! And only look at the men with whom *you* cry friends! You've run the gamut, Glendenning! From de Villars, who is a traitorous fugitive, to the Rossiters, to"—he sought his memory for the worst example, and bellowed in triumph—"to *August Falcon*! Faugh! The fellow is ostracized because he's a half-caste, which I don't hold with, mind you. His father—God help the poor fella!—says August has more in his head than hair, and from what the ladies tell me, he can be excessive charming. So does he use his brain to be conciliating? Or employ this alleged charm to win some friends? No, he does not! He has the tongue of an asp; he's forever fighting someone in an illicit dawn encounter; and as for his temper—! The man's an active volcano!"

Actually, August Falcon was not one of the viscount's closest friends, but they had recently engaged in a desperate adventure together, and he felt called upon to defend him. He pointed out that Falcon's disposition was not helped when most of London's gentlemen mocked him behind his back, and referred to him as the Mandarin. "Even his lovely sister—"

"Ah, now there's the horse of another colour," interrupted the earl, who thought Katrina Falcon a rare beauty. "And 'tis as well we've come to the subject of the ladies. You should have married any time these ten years, instead of risking your head in one stupid imbroglio after another. If only half of what I've heard about you is truth, you're damned lucky to be alive. But, soon or late, luck runs out for every man, and"— he had succeeded in frightening himself, and his voice wavered a little—"and I'd not see you dead because of your wildness, Horatio."

He had been addressed by his Christian name! Glendenning stared at his father in astonishment.

The earl coughed and went on irritably, "Well, fond as I am of young Michael, he ain't related by blood, after all, and cannot inherit."

"Oh."

" 'Tis past time," went on the earl, recovering his volume, "that you stopped frippering about Town, and wasting your life on useless studies and easels and drawing boards."

Glendenning's jaw tightened. "Sir, architecture is a fascinating art and not to be learned in a year or two, even—"

"A year or two! Zounds! You've been at it since you was at Eton, and what has it got you? Because a few of your bacon-brained friends with more money than sense have hired you to design houses for 'em, I fancy you'll be wanting to hang out a shingle, and go into business! *Egad!*"

Architecture had been the viscount's passion for as long as he could remember, and he was proud of the commissions that had come his way, and of the acclaim that had greeted his efforts. Stung, he said hotly, "You are unfair, Papa! I never met Mr. Patrington till he sought me out! Nor did I know Sir Giles Alkborough! And Lady Nola said that the cottage I designed for Mr. Dunsby was—"

"Yes, yes, well I'll own that was a nice little place, but the fact remains that you're a peer of the realm and have more important things to occupy you."

"Such as taking my seat in the House of Lords?"

"Well? You're a lord, aren't you? And a lord of your age should have a lady and have set up his nursery! There's plenty of 'em to choose among, Horatio. Shouldn't take you above a day or so if you put your mind to it. She don't have to be a woman of great fortune, though a young fellow with your breeding, background, and expectations would be a fool not to aim high. Still, family and a proper upbringing are all-important. I wasn't enraptured when you showed an interest in the Cranford gel, but she's a nice chit and pretty behaved, and had you not let her slip through your fingers, I fancy she'd have been a credit to you."

Glendenning, who had loved Dimity Cranford since she was a schoolroom miss, and had been shattered when she married Sir Anthony Farrar, clenched his hands, and said in a strained voice, "Perhaps you would wish to choose a wife for me, sir."

"Devil a bit of it! Although I've every right to have done so long since! I'm not one to give advice. If you can't find a suitable bride, Lady Nola will select one for you. You're not too bad looking a young fellow, and with your expectations I'll wager half the gels in London would jump if you dropped a hint. Just keep in mind that beauty don't last, any more than does love at first sight—which is a lot of poppycock. A sense of humour in a lady, however, is past price, for 'twill help you get over the rough ground of life, and sustain you when you're ninety." He cleared his throat, waited for some remark and, none being forthcoming, said, "Very well. That's all I have to say, so be off with you and change your dress. Your mama will be waiting to see you, I fancy."

He nodded in response to his heir's polite bow, and watched him march to the door, his head held as high as though he led a troop of dragoons down Whitehall. A faint grin curved the earl's mouth. Glendenning was properly seething with rage. Whatever else, he was a fine-looking rascal. And Lord knows, he'd sown some wild oats himself in his youth. A fellow wouldn't want a son who was a prissy miss. Still, there was a time to call a halt. By Jove, but there was!

"Don't forget," he called, as Glendenning opened the door. "I look forward to meeting a lady who'll make a worthy countess when your mama and I are gone. And keep away from firebrands like August Falcon! He'll come to a bad end, mark my words!"

It was as well, thought the viscount, as he stamped angrily towards his own apartments, that the earl was "not one to give advice"!

Whittlesey, the quiet and somewhat dour wizard who valetted Michael Templeby, was today assigned to Lord Glendenning. Having put off his riding coat, leathers, and top boots, Glendenning washed and was dressed in a coat of dark green velvet richly embroidered with silver thread; a waistcoat of green and silver brocade; and pale green satin unmentionables. A fine emerald pin was set amid the snowy Brussels lace of his cravat. His neat pigeon wing wig was replaced with one of the more elaborate French design he knew his stepsister admired, and his shoes with their high red heels made him seem taller. Despite this bow to fashion, Whittlesey knew better than to suggest paint or patches, and beyond murmuring that he hoped he saw his lordship well, he had little to say.

Glendenning had never quite fathomed why Michael had taken on this tall, middle-aged, and rather saturnine individual for his personal servant, but Whittlesey knew his trade, certainly. Surveying his reflection in the cheval-glass with justifiable satisfaction, he caught the valet watching him. He held those enigmatic pale blue eyes, and demanded, "Is my brother well?"

"To the best of my knowledge, your lordship."

"Why are you not in Town with him?"

"Because he did not desire it, sir."

"Have you displeased him, perchance?"

Very briefly, the suggestion of a smile lightened the grave mouth. "I trust not, my lord."

"What, then? No one knows a man like his valet, 'tis said."

"A wise valet does not betray his employer, sir."

Glendenning turned to face him. "Then you feel that to voice what you do know would constitute a betrayal?"

For a moment Whittlesey's eyes met his own. Then, they fell away. "It has been my experience, my lord, that when a gentleman goes off without his man, 'tis usually because he does not want his—er, activities to—er, become common knowledge."

"Profound," said Glendenning dryly. He started towards the door, and as Whittlesey swept it open, caught the bony wrist and held it firmly. "If anything should occur that you think would disturb the countess, and you are reluctant to speak of it to my father, you will come to me at once. Do you understand?"

The modestly but impeccably bewigged head was bowed. "I understand, milord."

Glendenning went into the corridor and made his way towards the front of the east wing and his stepmother's apartment. It was clear that there was more than mockery behind Falcon's remarks, and that Piers Cranford's careful words had indeed constituted a warning. Michael was in some kind of tangle. He frowned a little. God send the crazy boy had not really followed his example and become involved with Jacobites.

He reached Lady Nola's charming apartments and was greeted with warmth and affection. Emerging from that embrace he held her at arms' length and smiled at her fondly.

The countess was a large lady whose kind heart was hidden behind a regal and forbidding aspect. Born Nola Comyn, her stern Scottish parents had sent her to be educated at a Young Ladies Seminary in Harrogate, then married her, when she was barely seventeen, to John Templeby, a wealthy but reclusive Englishman thirty-five years her senior. She had given him a son, Michael, whom he had despised, since the little boy was sickly; and a daughter, Marguerite, in whom he had no interest whatsoever. Mr. Templeby had suffered a fatal slip on the ice when Michael was five and Marguerite three. Nola, who had the reputation of being outspoken, was not sufficient of a hypocrite to put on a great show of mourning, and had found it uncomfortable to be surrounded by people who expected such a display. An invitation to visit her dearest friend, Adelaide, by then Countess of Bowers-Malden, offered a welcome change, and the visit had opened a new world to the young widow. When she arrived, the youthful heir, Viscount Glendenning, was away at Eton, but both Lady Adelaide and the earl doted upon the timid Templeby children their father had scorned, and the widow was feted as an honoured guest. She had bloomed under such treatment, as had her children, and when thirteen-year-old Lord Horatio came home for the long vacation, he was delighted by the tall lady, and more delighted to play the worldly wise and sophisticated "college man" to the admiring junior Templebys. Some months later, Lady Adelaide fell victim to the inflammation of the lungs that swiftly claimed her life. Mrs. Templeby was a pillar of support to the stricken family, and by the end of the following year she had become the second Countess of Bowers-Malden.

Conscious always of the fact that he did not please his autocratic sire, Glendenning had soon fallen into the habit of taking his youthful troubles to his stepmother, and never failed to find kindness and understanding. Despite their differences, he respected his father and would have liked very much to win his love and approval, but although Lady Nola tried very hard to bring them together, the earl's impatience and Horatio's pride combined to make her task a difficult one.

Now, scanning her features, he rested one finger lightly upon the dark shadows under her rather protuberant blue eyes and said, "What's this, Mama? Have you been indisposed and not told me of it?"

"No such thing, my love. Am I really hagged? I am scarce surprised. We have had such a merry party here, Tio. Colonel and Mrs. Lathrop, Rudolph Bracksby, your Uncle Herbert and Aunt Hortense—"

"And cousin Ormond and his charming Monica," interposed Glendenning with a grimace. "Gad, what a gathering! If the Honourable Herbert was here I fancy Papa was up all night. Small wonder he was so testy. High stakes, love?"

"Not too bad, for Rudi is such a good soul, you know, and managed to keep your uncle to loo. But Bowers-Malden lost, of course. And Cousin Monica was— But I must not be uncharitable, for she doubtless cannot help being so— Oh dear," she sighed as Glendenning burst into a laugh. "I must not speak of the matter at all, or I shall be quite sunk. How handsome you look in that French wig, dearest. Marguerite will find you irresistible! Now come and sit down and tell me what you have been about, and does London still ring with the Rossiter scandal, and is it truth that poor Lennox Albritton has fallen into the clutches of That Porchester Woman?"

Chuckling, Glendenning followed her to the loveseat beside the fire that burned in her hearth during every month of the year except August and September. He told her about his visit with Piers and Peregrine Cranford, and confirmed that her old enemy, Estelle Porchester, had wed Colonel Lennox Albritton. "As for the Rossiters, Gideon and his bride are now honeymooning, and Sir Mark is busy as a dog with two tails. The shipyards are being rebuilt already, and with the funds they recovered from the embezzler, Sir Mark has repaid most of his investors."

Lady Nola shook her head regretfully. "Poor Rossiter. He lost so much in that trading company swindle, and then the dreadful shipyard fire, and the collapse of his banks. I am so glad he is getting back onto his feet again, but is there any hope he will ever be able to buy back his beautiful estate? Promontory Point has been in their family for centuries."

"Yes, and the loss of it grieves him—all of them—I am very sure. Perhaps they will recover it someday. Bracksby bought it, you know, and has told Sir Mark he may have it back whenever his finances permit."

"Then Rudi only bought it to preserve it for them? How very kind in him." The countess smiled, and said with a twinkle, "You will think me a proper gabblemonger, Tio, but I always suspected that Bracksby had a *tendre* for Collington's gel."

Glendenning looked at her incredulously. "Naomi Lutonville? No—really? I never heard of it. At all events, Rudi is too late. Naomi is no longer Lady Lutonville, but Mrs. Gideon Rossiter."

"True. I thought it odd that the earl did not appear at his daughter's nuptials. A strange man, for all his good looks."

Tightening his lips, Glendenning wondered what his stepmother would say if she knew that the Earl of Collington had been—perhaps still was—a member of the infamous group he and his friends referred to as the League of Jewelled Men. He returned a noncommital answer, however, and turned the conversation by asking her about Michael.

Invariably, to speak of the son she doted upon brought a glowing look to the countess. Today, however, she made a vague reference to the fact that Templeby was "in Town," and then asked for Court gossip.

He obliged her with as much as he knew, which was meagre and mundane. Still, she appeared fascinated, and had so many questions that at length, he patted her hand, and asked, "Mama, is there something you would like to discuss with me?"

She looked at him questioningly, then said with a short laugh, "Why, Tio! Has some gossip been filling your ear with fustian? What ill-considered flirtation must I vehemently deny?"

He tightened his hold on her hand. "I hope it is fustian. Perhaps you feel you cannot betray a confidence, but if Michael—"

"Tio!" With a squeal of joy, a slender girl with fair unpowdered curls and gentle hazel eyes ran into the room. The viscount jumped up to catch his stepsister and swing her around. Marguerite worshipped her "big brother," and said firmly that Mama's turn was done now, and Tio must give her his full attention.

He loved her dearly, but wished she had not come in at just that particular moment. Glancing at the countess, however, he saw that she was watching her daughter, her eyes fond. Her nature was straightforward. If something was really wrong, she would not have been able to conceal it from him. Relieved, he gave his stepsister the "full attention" she desired, and made up his mind to return to Town tomorrow.

The air was warm on this hazy afternoon, and the graceful summer-house in the gardens behind Falcon House offered a pleasant oasis of cool shade. There were several long wooden benches in the little open-sided house, designed to encourage the whiling away of an idle hour or so in comfort. However, the present occupant of the summer-house neither availed herself of a bench, nor was she idle. She was, in fact, sitting on the floor, a walking cane beside her, and her voluminous skirts spread in pale pink billows. She was small and fine boned, with light brown curls, blue eyes, and a rather wide mouth, and she hummed merrily to herself as she brushed a large and unlovely black hound. Admittedly, Gwendolyn Rossiter could not be classified as a beauty, but she was certainly not so unprepossessing as to warrant the scowl that darkened the face of the man who watched her.

When it became apparent that between her humming and her efforts she had not heard his approach, August Falcon propped one shoulder against a support post and said in his bored drawl, "Poor Miss Gwendolyn. You must find your visits with us very dull if that is the only source of entertainment my sister can provide you."

Gwendolyn Rossiter glanced around, the smile that lit her face earning only a continuance of Falcon's sardonic stare. "Don't be silly," she said blithely. "Katrina is writing to my new sister-in-law. And I do not find it in the least dull to brush poor Apollo. Still, I will gladly relinquish the task to you." She held out the brush, which Falcon ignored.

He wore a superbly cut grey riding coat and moleskin breeches tucked into topboots that shone like glass. His black hair was unpowdered, and the riband with which it was tied back had failed to subdue entirely its tendency to curl. She thought, 'The wretched creature does not even try to be elegant, but is the most elegant man I know. And so revoltingly handsome. What a pity he is such an appalling failure as a human being.' Waving the brush at him, she urged, "Is your duty, you know, for he is your dog."

"He *was* my dog," corrected Falcon, paying no heed to the brush. "And he was also a jolly fine watchdog before you ruined him."

Gwendolyn chuckled. Returning to hound and brush, she said, "He was a menace to anything on four legs or two, until I taught him how to play."

"Whereby he now welcomes any cut-throat, thief, or vandal, so long as they come equipped with stick in hand, and the word 'Fetch' on their lips! I hope you will be content when my father and sister are found murdered in their beds!"

At this, she burst into laughter. "Such a grump you are! I vow 'tis astonishing you are descended from Mrs. Natasha Falcon. I was looking at her portrait this morning, and—"

"I know. I saw you."

Rarely annoyed, Gwendolyn paused at this, and gave Falcon a steady look.

He had the grace to blush a little, and said with a shrug, "No, I was not spying to be sure you did not set light to the house."

Indignant, she exclaimed, "I would certainly do nothing that might harm Katrina or your aunt."

"Or my papa," he suggested dulcetly.

She opened her eyes at him. "Of course not. I am very fond of Mr. Falcon."

A quirk tugged at the side of his mouth. "Yes. Well now that I have been consigned to the flames, pray impart your invaluable assessment of my grandmama."

Apollo, stretched out blissfully, was jolted as the brush bit with unexpected violence into his throat, but Gwendolyn's voice was calm as she replied, "I thought her extreme beautiful."

"She was exquisite; the loveliest lady I ever have, or ever will, see."

"Loving her so deeply, I fancy you know a great deal about her background, which must be fascinating."

Falcon said coldly, "I was nine years old when she died, ma'am."

"But surely your mama—"

"My mama," he said, his eyes becoming increasingly grim, "was not proud of her heritage from Grandmama Natasha, and had little to say in the matter. Have you any more questions regarding my family, Miss Rossiter? I am sure you must be burning to know how grandmama died, or how it came about that a year later my mother's carriage overturned. You must not fail to make enquiries of my father. I am sure he could supply you more—gossip."

"Well, I shall do so," she said outrageously, determined not to be frozen. "But if it does not pain you too much, will you tell me what you thought of China?"

He blinked, and echoed in a rather stunned voice, "China?"

"Yes. In view of your devotion to your grandmama, you must surely have gone there? You would wish to discover something of her culture, which cannot fail to be dear to your heart and—" She broke off, for he had stalked up the steps and now bent over her. His face was very pale, and a nerve throbbed at his temple, while the look in his eyes caused her to draw back instinctively.

"Miss Rossiter," he said through his teeth. "You are a guest in my house, so I cannot box your ears as you deserve. It pleases you to use my mixed blood to taunt me. But I warn you—do not dare to—"

"Ah, so here you are, Lord Haughty-Snort. Good day, Mistress Gwendolyn. Breathing fire and smoke over you, is he?"

Falcon shut his eyes, and groaned.

"Hello, Jamie," called Gwendolyn, not sorry for this interruption. "He cannot help it, you know."

Lieutenant James Morris was a good-natured young gentleman who had fought with Gideon Rossiter in the War of the Austrian Succession. They had become friends while recuperating from wounds, and early in the spring had been sent home to England on the same ship. Still on inactive status, Morris wore civilian dress, and with his round boyish face and guileless expression, looked much too young to be the veteran of several desperate battles. He bowed to Gwendolyn, then dabbed a kerchief at his brow. "Beastly close this afternoon, ain't it, ma'am? Your servant, Falcon."

"God forbid!" Falcon enquired, "Come to discuss the weather, have you? I felt sure you must have good reason for paying a call. Or is it perhaps that you are ready to arrange— er, matters?"

Gwendolyn had been trying to make Apollo turn over, but at this she said in an irked way, "No, are you going to talk about duels again? Lud, but one would think you'd had sufficient of fighting in the Low Countries, Jamie. To say nothing of all the terrible things that happened after you and Gideon came home!"

"Not the least of which," growled Falcon, "was that I was mistaken for a highwayman and mercilessly shot down."

Morris said mildly, "It wasn't mercilesss, old boy. I didn't know you at the time."

Gwendolyn smothered a grin.

Falcon murmured, "What a very peculiar fellow I must be, to object when a blithering idiot puts a hole in my arm."

"Now, be honest," said Gwendolyn. "You know very well 'twas an innocent mistake. When Jamie and my brother came upon the hold-up and you rode at them with a pistol in your hand, how were they to know you were escorting Naomi's coach, and not one of the rank riders?"

"Miss Rossiter, I see no reason to discuss the matter with a female."

"I can see why. There was no cause for you to fight my brother—"

"Your brother and I engaged in a perfectly respectable duel—which you most improperly interrupted by dancing on my sword."

"I did no such thing! I merely trod on your sword when you dropped it, to try and stop you from slaying poor Gideon!"

"I had no intention of killing Gideon. I seldom put a period to the gentlemen I fight. Though"—he glared at Morris— "your friend may well drive me to it."

"He is your friend too, however you may pretend to dislike him." Under his breath, Falcon directed an exasperated and profane remark to the heavens, which Gwendolyn ignored as she went on, "At least, he is your comrade, because when Gideon was in trouble you both helped him. And gentlemen who fight together should not afterwards fight among themselves."

"Besides," put in Morris, "considering you are involved in a duel a week, Lord Haughty-Snort, I'd think you'd know that our seconds will arrange such details." He saw Gwendolyn's head turn towards him, and went on quickly, "If you must know it, I came—"

"To slither around my sister," interposed Falcon. "Damme, but I've warned you before. You are not the man for Katrina."

"I don't see that," said Morris doggedly. "I may not be her richest beau, but I ain't pockets to let. My family's not contemptible, I think. Miss Katrina is of age. And besides, you're not the head of your family, Mr. Neville Falcon is." He glanced to the side and said with a grin, "More company to depress your spirits, poor fella. Well met, Tio!"

Glendenning, wearing riding dress, was walking from the house. He waved cheerily, and Falcon's expression lightened very slightly.

Having shaken hands with the men, the viscount dropped to one knee and kissed Gwendolyn's fingers. She scanned his face and asked shrewdly, "Shall I go away, Tio?"

He smiled. "What, and rob us of your lovely presence?"

"I think you wish to talk gentleman talk. But if you mean to discuss duels, I shall sit here and listen to every word you say."

Morris said solemnly, "A watched pot never boils."

"Oh, Gad!" exclaimed Falcon. "Now see what you've done! He's at it again!"

"If you must know, madam, I came to talk about my brother," said Glendenning, laughing.

Gwendolyn lifted her hands. "Help me up then, if you please. I expect Katrina is waiting for me." Glendenning lifted her to her feet, and with a flourish Morris presented her cane. She thanked him prettily, and passed the brush to Falcon. "Here. You finish him."

Watching her limp away, Glendenning murmured, "What a darling she is."

"Sunny little thing," agreed Morris. "Pity she's—" He stopped, and his face reddened.

"Crippled?" Falcon said derisively, "Why choke over the word? She don't."

Irritated, Morris said, "Oh, brush your hound."

"I've no least intention of doing so." Falcon heaved the brush at him. "You do it. You're the one with the alleged heart of gold."

"Jove, Falcon!" exclaimed Morris. "That's the first nice thing you ever said to me!"

"I am feverish," muttered Falcon, feeling his brow anxiously. "I'd best go and lie down upon my bed!"

Morris grinned and threw the brush back to him. "Take this with you. You know damned well that brute would have my arm off did I dare touch him."

"Oh, yes." Catching the brush, Falcon glanced at Glendenning, who had sat down on one of the benches and was watching them with faint amusement. "What's to do, oh mighty peer? We have been bereft of your nobility and wisdom for several days."

"Had you need of either?"

Resuming the business of grooming Apollo, who had begun to eye Morris and show his teeth, Falcon replied, "I have managed somehow to survive."

Morris said thoughtfully, "My great uncle managed to survive till he was nine and ninety. Most foolish old duck I ever knew."

"Glendenning," said Falcon, "will you please tell us if the arrangements are made, and then take him away with you? He is lechering after Katrina again, and I'll not have it! I—er, presume you *did* come to tell us that you and Rossiter have set the date?"

"Well, I did, yes. But I told Miss Rossiter I had come to talk about my brother, so I'll keep my word and get that over first,

———

if you don't mind. I do not seem able to come up with Templeby. Crenshore told me he'd seen him with Piers Cranford, so I went to Muse Manor. Michael had already left there, but Cranford dropped the same hint to me that you did, Falcon."

Falcon shot a quick and faintly guilty glance at Morris.

Morris muttered glumly, " 'Wine sets a wise man singing.' "

Gritting his teeth, Falcon flung his hands over his ears. "Tell me when he's done!"

The viscount asked, "So you knew also, did you Jamie?"

"Heard he was making a cake of himself." Morris shrugged. "He's not a cloth-head y'know, and I would've blabbed to you, if I heard he'd gone in too deep. Though, mind you, I ain't cut from the same cloth as Lord Haughty-Snort. Don't like blabbing."

"Idiot," said Falcon succinctly. "About the duel, Glendenning?"

"Oh. Well, I'd a letter from Rossiter. Says he and his bride will be back in England on the twenty-fourth, and that we can schedule your meeting for Monday, the twenty-seventh, if agreeable. Have either of you objections?"

"Perfectly agreeable with me," said Morris.

Falcon nodded. "What about Cranford?"

"Piers is willing," answered the viscount. "Said he'd come and overnight with me on Sunday. I'll have to call on Kadenworthy, though."

Morris, whose thoughts had wandered, said, "I—er, suppose nothing more has been heard of our friend the Squire, and his merry reptiles?"

Glendenning frowned. "The League of Jewelled Men? I've not heard aught. Nor do I expect to."

"Why not?" argued Falcon, brushing Apollo's hair the wrong way. "We upset their applecart. I'd say they're not likely to forgive and forget."

Hesitating, Glendenning said, "True. If they're as devious as Rossiter suspects, they'll be hatching some nasty scheme again. But not yet, I'd think."

"Unless we've shut the barn door after the horse has fled," muttered Morris.

They both looked at him. Falcon said irately, "Deuce take it, if you have something to say don't go from Land's End to John o' Groats to say it!"

"Well, whatever I say, you'll make fun. But—that Albertson business did not seem just right to me."

Falcon said wearily, "Admiral William Albertson is in Newgate for defrauding the government by placing orders for supplies with companies he himself controlled. What in the name of all the gods and little fishes has that to do with a conspiracy to ruin Sir Mark Rossiter? Do not hesitate to dazzle us with your logic, mighty sage. We wait with bated breath."

Morris flushed, but persisted, "The admiral is one of Britain's greatest heroes. To the last he denied the charges brought against him, but he lost everything. Same as Sir Mark damn near did."

Falcon turned to Glendenning. "Do you see how faulted is his intellect? One gathers we are now to be suspicious of every scoundrel who is hauled before the courts. We'd as well investigate the man who beats his wife, or cheats at cards!"

"Yes, and there's another of 'em," said Morris triumphantly, ignoring Falcon's groan. "Look at that wretched Merriam business. Shot himself after being accused of cheating in the Cocoa Tree. Home and estates confiscated and sold for debt. Fishy, was you to ask me."

"Which, praise the Lord, we've no intention of doing," said Falcon. "No, for heaven's sake do not dignify his nonsense by looking thoughtful, Tio!"

"I don't know much about Albertson," said Glendenning. "But I'll own that Lord Merriam was the last man I'd have judged dishonourable. It might not be so far-fetched as you think." He stood. "After I find Michael, and drop in on Kadenworthy, it could bear looking into. Where is Kade, by the way? In Town?"

Standing also, Falcon said, "My sister heard he was down at Epsom for these new spring races they're holding. His country seat is nearby. Damned nice property."

Glendenning swore. "He would be in the country! Now I've

to go all the way down there! Well, I'd best get started. *Adieu, mes amis.*"

Morris said, "I'd go m'self, dear boy, but it wouldn't be the thing. Do you want us to scour around a trifle? For Templeby, I mean."

"I'd be grateful," called Glendenning over his shoulder. "If you find him before I do, keep an eye on him for me, would you?"

Morris waved, and the viscount walked briskly to the stables.

Deep in thought, Falcon and Morris started towards the house, Apollo escorting them, and growling sporadically at Morris' heels.

"The deuce!" said Morris.

Falcon muttered, "I wish to heaven I knew who it was."

"Eh? Oh—'tis another name for the Devil. I'd've thought you would know that."

"Not him, you clod! I mean I wish I knew who this damnable Squire is."

"Why should you be concerned? You hate England. What do you care if a lunatic threatens her?"

"I believe one may find a nation absurd, without hating it. And in case it has slipped your mind, Morris, I've already been dragged into this ugly business."

Morris frowned, and as they walked on together, stared at the ground in silence.

This atypical behavior wore at Falcon. "I hear rusty wheels turning," he murmured. "You must be thinking. Honour me by sharing your brilliant conclusions."

"All right," said Morris, looking up. "I think we should endeavour to find out who are the members of this League of Jewelled Men. And what the devil they're about."

Falcon paused to clap his hands. "Bravo! And—a simple question, forgive me it. Have you the least notion where we should commence this masterly scheme?"

"But of course," said Morris grandly. "In Windsor. You really must make a push to—just now and again—use that pumpkin on the end of your neck, poor fellow!"

CHAPTER III

Surrey was green and neat and lovely, as ever. The viscount reached Mimosa Lodge in late afternoon, and was received with courtesy by Lord Kadenworthy's aunt. Her nephew, she said, was down at the races and would likely not reach home until dark—if at all. "Hector," sighed the sweet-faced elderly lady, "so often is caught up in all the talk of horses and jockeys and weight and stewards that it is sometimes the wee hours of the morning before they are done, and then he stays with whomever he chances to be. This new business of a race meeting here, has properly caught the public fancy. If you would care to go in search of him you will see for yourself."

Glendenning had a soft spot for gentle old ladies, and having gratefully accepted a substantial tea, at which his hostess seemed equally grateful for his company, he did go in search of Kadenworthy, and he did see for himself. For the second time in as many days, he walked Flame through a noisy crowd. A different crowd this, in which the elegant and distinguished rubbed shoulders with dashing young Bucks and Corinthians, and were in turn jostled by humbler folk. It was a crowd in which predators roved, their shrewd eyes searching out the easy marks, and many a man carried a small pistol in his belt or in his pocket. Another race was to be run before sunset, and the air rang with the shouts of wagers offered and taken. This was to be an Owners to Ride race, and excitement was high.

Catching sight of Kadenworthy, astride a rangy-looking black, Glendenning's attempts to win through to him were unavailing, and he was obliged to dismount. A sudden disturbance arose near at hand, and he became part of a surging, neck-craning crowd. A dark-haired youth was struggling in the grip of a man dressed in a simple but well-cut green habit. Glendenning had an impression of a blandly smiling pink and white face, of hooded grey eyes, full lips, and a soft yet oddly resonant voice.

"You are a thieving gypsy, and will be dealt with as such. Now—put it down. At once."

The voice was not raised, the man showed no sign of ungovernable rage or violence, but the youth cried a desperate, "I did *not* prig it, sir! I swear—Ow! Do not . . . please! You'll break my arm!"

In his frantic efforts to escape, his head twisted, allowing Glendenning a full view of the convulsed features. He thought, 'Good God!' and called sharply, "What is the trouble here?"

The onlookers fell back before the authority in his tone. As usual, Flame evoked an immediate chorus of admiring exclamations. Someone said knowingly, "He'll be a rider, I reckons," and another man remarked, "Ar. Well, my money's on the mare, and the young gent looks as if he knows the difference 'twixt a tail and a hock!"

The man detaining the gypsy glanced up. His smile did not waver, but in the deep eyes for just an instant came a flash of something—surprise almost—immediately veiled. "Nothing I cannot deal with, sir," he said.

A bystander offered helpfully, "The gypsy tried to buy some currant buns, and the gent says as it ain't the lad's purse."

"I wish I may see the day a gypsy owns a purse like that one," smiled the man in green.

Following his eyes, Glendenning saw a familiar purse of silver mesh with an amber clasp. Stifling his astonishment, he said honestly, "He does not own it. I do. And I sent him off to buy my lunch. Perhaps you will be so good as to release my servant, sir."

A murmur of amusement went up. The green man's eyes shifted under Glendenning's cool stare, but he did not release the boy. Still smiling, he murmured, "An he is your servant, sir, you will certainly know his name. I—persuaded him to tell me it, just before you came."

The look that was slanted at him was gloatingly sly. The fellow was enjoying bullying his helpless prey. A strong sense of revulsion swept Glendenning. There was about this man the aura of things that dwelt in rotten trees: pallid things, dank, and crawling. His lip curling with contempt, he said cuttingly, "Of course I know his name. It is Florian." A ripple of laughter arose from the onlookers. There came a slight lessening of the green man's perpetual smile. The viscount stepped closer. "You have his name, sir, but I shall neither require yours, which I have no wish to know, nor shall I gratify you with mine own. I will however, advise you that if you give his arm one more twist, I shall apply my fist to your slippery eye. Let—him—go!"

For a moment he thought he was going to have to make good his threat. Then, the youth was released and his captor stepped back. "You are quick to take umbrage, sir," he said, his voice as soft, his smile as gentle as ever. "But you will own it looked suspicious. Had the lad explained—"

Florian was rubbing his right arm painfully. Glendenning said, "Now where is that baker? Come along, boy. I'm fairly starving!"

They blended into the amused crowd. Glendenning could feel those hooded eyes following. He said quietly, "That was an ugly customer. You see what you get for filching my purse, you young ruffian. I thought when Mr. Peregrine Cranford took you into his service, you had mended your ways. A fine return for his trust!"

"I didn't steal your purse, my lord. It was—" Florian bit off the words.

"You found it, perhaps?"

"Yes, my lord."

"In that pretty little thief's pocket, eh? Well, I mean to find *her*, and you shall take me to wherever she—"

"Tio! By all that's wonderful!" A slender young officer in military scarlet gripped the viscount by the shoulder. "Are you riding? I was prepared to put my money on Hector Kadenworthy till I saw your mare. What a beauty!"

Shaking hands, Glendenning said with a smile, "Best keep your bet where 'tis, Major, sir. I do not ride today."

Hilary Broadbent laughed, and cuffed him. "As well you show me some respect. How do you go on, you madman? And how is that scapegrace brother of yours? I hear you are seeking him."

Fighting not to betray the sudden fear that tightened his nerves, Glendenning said easily, "Do you? Dogging my footsteps, Hilary?"

"No, damn you!" Sobering abruptly, Broadbent added, "I hope I may never have to do so. Oddly enough I do not enjoy conveying my friends to the Tower, and I would purely dislike to see your ugly phiz on the end of a spike."

Meeting his eyes steadily, the viscount asked, "A warning, Major?"

"It wouldn't be the first time I've warned you, Tio. And if what I suspect is truth, you've paid me small heed." He grinned suddenly. "But I'll not stir old coals with the man who possesses so fair a sister. Tell me what has Templeby been up to? Women, cards, or the nags? He's of an age to sow some wild oats, you know."

"You know, and I know. My honoured sire, alas . . ."

Broadbent laughed. "What, did the earl send you after—" His gaze slipping past Glendenning, his pleasant face darkened, and he said in a changed tone, "Be damned! What's he doing here, I wonder?"

The viscount glanced around the sea of faces. "To judge by your expression you've not discovered a bosom bow."

"A cobra, more like. Though I'd not dare say so to his face, coward that I am!" Broadbent, a man not given to disparaging others, lowered his voice and said with bitter intensity, "'Tis Burton Farrier. No—don't look round, he's turning this way."

"Who the deuce is Burton Farrier? Never heard of the fellow."

"Be thankful for large mercies. He's military intelligence. Looks like a placid clergyman, and is the most dangerous man I know. He has an almost insane hatred for all Jacobites and I do believe would be delighted to personally cut the heart out of every living sympathiser." Broadbent frowned and added grudgingly, "Justified, to an extent, I suppose. His brother fell on the field of Prestonpans." He glanced to the side again. "He's a merciless hunter, and once put on a case hangs on like a bulldog. They call him 'Terrier Farrier.' "

"Charming. Is his life's work to destroy all Jacobites?"

"Oh, no. That's just a private hobby. He's usually assigned to very special cases, and so far as I'm aware is held in extreme high regard, because he has yet to fail. There—you can look now. And mark him well. A good man to avoid, Tio."

Looking in the direction his friend indicated, the viscount saw a well-built individual, not above medium height, clad in a green habit, and smiling beneficently at no one in particular.

Broadbent's words echoed in his ears. "A good man to avoid . . ."

The woods were dense, and the sun was almost gone, making it difficult to see through the dimming light, but the viscount rode on, guiding Flame carefully but with determination. Florian had vanished during his conversation with Hilary Broadbent, but he'd caught a glimpse of the youth just as he'd disappeared into these trees. He had recovered his purse, with surprisingly little missing, but while Lord Kadenworthy was busied with the closing formalities, he meant to find that larcenous gypsy lass. And he meant to discover why Florian was with her, instead of with the Cranford twins, who had so kindly rescued him from starvation and given him honest work.

Some distance ahead, the shrubs rustled. He shouted, "Florian? I want a word with you!"

A slim figure was briefly silhouetted against a solitary beam of roseate light before plunging into a tunnel-like gap between the trees.

Glendenning spurred in pursuit. Not until the last instant did he catch a glimpse of something thin and taut stretched above Flame's ears.

There came a mighty impact that tore the breath from his lungs and smashed him from the saddle. A violent shock; a fading sense of rage and pain. . . .

"Riding like the wind he were, I tell ye, and right on the lad's tail!" The male voice was sharp and querulous. "Another minute and he'd have been took. What then? Ar, you don't stop to think on that, does ye!"

Some misguided stonecutter was chiselling a hole in Glendenning's head, but he wanted to find out what was to do, and he tried to move. Another fool began to pound a white hot stake through his ankle. Fighting back a groan, he lost interest in the proceedings . . .

He was tormented by a fierce heat, and he could hear a woman talking. 'Mitten,' he thought. And if it was the lovely Dimity Cranford, then he must still be laid low from the musket ball that damnable trooper had lobbed at him . . . He wondered if they'd told Bowers-Malden that he was dying . . . And he could picture his sire's grief and shame when he discovered his heir had been carrying a vital Jacobite cypher when shot down . . .

An icy and refreshing coldness touched his face, and the voices became clearer. The man was talking again. He sounded very quarrelsome. ". . . should've been scragged, like

I said. A nob, ain't he? Perishers. They should all be scragged. Or topped!"

"You're talking foolish, Uncle Ab. Fair yearning to swing on Tyburn Tree, is ye?" The voice was lilting but neither cultured nor coarse. So it wasn't Mitten, after all. Puzzled, Glendenning listened as she said, "He can't help if he's Quality, poor cove. Now, what about his mare?"

"Flame!" exclaimed Glendenning, and sat up into a world that shivered to fragments and was gone . . .

A long time afterwards he was listening to bells. Not church bells, or a ship's bell; more like the little handbell that Mama kept on the chairside table in her private parlour. A tiny bell this, whose erratic chime was accompanied by a hissing sound. He wondered idly if it was a pet snake with a bell tied round its neck.

"Why do you frown?" asked the woman softly, and a cool hand stroked his temple.

If he dared open his eyes, the hammer in his head would probably break right through his skull. Not risking it, he lay still. The skin of her hand was rather rough, but her touch was gentle and comforting. "I was wondering . . . ," he began, and frowned again, because his voice sounded so far away.

"Yes? What was you wondering, poor cove?"

"Were," he corrected foolishly.

"Fiddle-de-dee! What *were*, then?"

"I was wondering . . . if snakes have . . . necks . . . ," he managed.

"Gawd," said the man's voice, querulous as ever. "Proper gone off his tibby, he has! Didn't I say it? Be kinder to put him out of his misery!"

The viscount was weak as a cat, and his head was pure hell, but be damned if he was going to lie here and let this rogue do away with him. With a great effort he took the risk, and forced his eyes open. Amid a scarlet mist he saw an extremely untidy scratch wig, under which there gradually materialised a fierce tanned face, all bushy eyebrows, glaring eyes, and out-thrusting chin.

"You slippery curst . . . horse thief," panted Glendenning. "What have . . . what have you done with . . . my mare?"

The screech that rang out reverberated shatteringly inside his head, and he fell back. Distantly, he heard the murderously inclined thief howling, "Didn't I tell ye? One foot in the grave, and he's ready to have me topped! Let me scrag him! Oh, you gotta let me scrag the perisher, Amy!"

Amy? Glendenning blinked, and another face appeared. A face that, even dimmed by the mists, was so delicately lovely that he was dazzled. He said weakly, "So your name . . . really isn't Alice . . ."

The soft lips parted. "I said it wasn't. I'm Amy Consett, and this is me Uncle Absalom Consett. And what's your name, mate?"

"You know . . . who I am."

"I forget. Remind me."

"I will if you . . . won't let him . . . kill me."

"All right. Then tell me."

He thought about it, but he was so weary that he fell asleep.

When he awoke, the mists were gone. The little bell was no longer chiming, but he heard another sound, a sort of faint and sporadic rattling. He began, gradually, to take stock of things. He lay on a rough but fairly comfortable bed. The mattress appeared to consist of straw and bracken piled on a wooden frame and contained by a sheet. Two coarsely woven blankets covered him, and, incongruously, his head was supported by a satin pillow. At first, he'd supposed he was in a cave, but he saw now that the room was built of stone blocks, and that sunlight was slanting through an opening high up in one wall.

He looked about curiously. Rough wooden packing cases were piled under the window, and beside them a large upended crate held a chipped water pitcher and bowl, a cracked mirror, and a hairbrush and comb. His wandering gaze was held by a picture that hung nearby. It depicted a goosegirl driving her flock across a field at sunset, with dark clouds building on the horizon, and it was another incongruity, because the artistry was superb, and the frame richly carven. 'Stolen, past doubting,' he thought.

He moved his head carefully, and was not punished by the immediate and savage stab of pain that had plagued him in earlier awakenings. He discovered a crude table, where the gypsy girl, Amy, sat on a three-legged stool. Her head was bent low over a curved strip of polished wood at which she worked with intense concentration. As he watched, she turned to a small open box on the table and began to poke about at the contents, this causing the rattling sounds he'd heard. She evidently found what she was seeking, because she selected a very small object, then bent to her work once more.

She had a charming way of tossing her hair back when it fell forward. Glendenning noticed how obediently most of the dark mass hung behind her, but one silken strand, as though unable to bear being pushed away, would slip stealthily across her snowy shoulder until it swung triumphant before her, only to be shaken back once more. He was waiting for it to start sliding again when she glanced at him.

Her face lit up. She exclaimed, "What, are you awake at last? And does you know who ye is, this time?"

"Yes, but—"

"Aha!" Standing, she approached the bed. "That sounds more like a man's voice, 'stead o' some poor ghost. Say it, then. All of it, mind!"

Vaguely irked, he said, "Horatio Clement Laindon. Viscount Glendenning. And I apologize if I've been a nuisance because I broke my head when you stole my mare."

"Broke it before, ain'tcha melord? Going to have a scar on both sides o' yer red nob."

He reached up instinctively and touched a bandage. They'd removed his wig, of course. He said ruefully, "I must look a proper sight."

She chuckled. "Well, yer hair's not so red as I'd thought 'twould be. Auburn, I 'spect they'd call it." She wandered closer, and touched his hair gently. "Starting to curl already, but I 'spect you'll whack it all off again, which is daft. Yer Irish-jig's not so nice as yer own hair."

He noticed, as he had before, that she had an odd way of sometimes pronouncing words correctly, and sometimes lapsing to a coarser version. " 'Irish jig'—meaning wig?" he asked, smiling. And when she nodded, he went on, "Why do you use rhyming cant? Sometimes you speak quite nicely, and you've a pretty voice."

"Well, ain't his lordship the generous one!" She dropped him a mocking curtsy. "Faith, but I scarce knows how to go on, I be that flattered!" He looked at her steadily, his lips tightening, and she laughed, then asked, "How'd ye get that there other scar? Wasn't too long ago, eh?"

His mind flashed back to a wild, stormy night, almost two years ago. A desperate ride, with troopers closing in all around, and the deadly Jacobite cypher in his pocket. Mistress Amy Consett obviously judged him a weak-kneed ne'er-do-well. He wondered what she'd think if she knew he was (rightfully) suspected of having fought for Bonnie Prince Charlie. "Oh—a duel, merely," he lied.

Her lip curled. "You Quality coves and yer duelling! What a stupid way to throw away the life the Good Lord give ye! Not that it's any of my bread and butter."

"Speaking of which . . ."

"Aha. Hungry, is ye?"

"And terribly thirsty."

At this, she ran to the table and returned to hold a cracked mug of water to his parched mouth.

"Not too quick, mind! There—that's enough."

He thanked her, and lay back with a sigh of thankfulness.

"I 'spect ye're wondering where you are, eh, melord?"

"Yes. And for how long I've been here, and—"

"One at a time, mate. One at a time. You been here—let's see—this is the fourth day. Took a woundy rap when you went down, and been out of yer head some of the time."

Glendenning stiffened, then said with forced lightness, "Egad! I trust I did not give away all the details of my lurid past?"

With a fluid and graceful movement she sat on the floor and leaned back on her hands. A lurking smile curved her vivid lips. "You got some funny friends, if that's what 'lure it' means. 'Jewelled men' you was a'gabbling of. And kidnapped ladies, all mixed up with 'blockheaded boys' and 'mama' and someone called Mitten." Watching his expressionless face, she laughed softly. "Wouldn't have ye, this here Mitten, would she, Quality cove?"

'Damn!' he thought, and said coldly, "And does that fact please you, Mistress Amy?"

She shrugged her soft white shoulders. "It's not such a bad thing when spoiled little rich boys find out as they can't have everything they want. Even if it's only once in their useless pampered lives."

His head was hurting brutally again. He blinked, and asked, "Is that why you stole my purse after I had lied to help you? Had you meant that I should be killed when I was knocked from the saddle?"

It was obvious that she had a deep hatred for the Quality, and he was surprised to see the flush that crept up her lovely throat to turn her cheeks bright pink.

With a flash of trim ankles she was on her feet and leaning over the bed, a small but deadly-looking knife gripped in one slender hand. "If I'd wanted that, gorgio rye," she said, biting the words out between her white teeth, "you'd be dead three days back!"

Glendenning jerked his head away as the knife flashed, razor sharp, under his chin. The quick movement brought pain lancing up his right leg, and he gave a gasp.

At once the knife disappeared, and with it Amy's fury. "Ah, but what a horrid girl I is!" she said remorsefully. "You've made me hurt ye! Is it yer head? Or yer poor foot?"

"My . . . foot."

She whipped back the bedclothes.

With a shocked yelp, he clutched them to him again. "Hey!"

"Oh, don't never be so daft." She tugged hard. "Who d'ye think has been tending it since you tumbled? I've seen yer legs before, melord! And very hairy they be, if you want to know it!"

It was Glendenning's turn to redden. He relinquished the blankets and lay back, breathing hard. The nightshirt he wore was voluminous. At least, he thought, he was decently covered. Amy's hands were busied with his foot, and another gasp escaped him as she cautiously unwound a bandage.

"Aye," she muttered. "I shall have to poultice it again."

He peered downward. "Is the bone broke?"

"Not as I can tell. But ye landed on some fallen branches, and one of 'em jagged through yer boot. I tried to clean the wound, but it got infected, and—"

"And we shoulda took his foot off. Like I told ye!"

"The devil you should!" argued Glendenning, frowning indignantly at the short but unexpectedly sturdy middle-aged man who had come into the room carrying a shallow wooden box and a steaming kettle.

" 'Fraid, is ye?" sneered the newcomer. "Not surprising. All Quality gents are cowards. Yellow as new chicks, and as puny. Here's the medicines you wanted, lass. Dunno why I give in t'ye. He ain't worth it. Ain't got sense enough not to gallop that fine mare through the trees at dusk, he's so eager to ride down a innocent lad. 'Twere the hand o' Providence that sent that there branch at his noble noggin."

"I'll show you how puny I am when I get up," promised Glendenning grimly. "And 'twas no branch that came at me, but the rope you'd stretched across my path. If you'd—"

"What?" Amy had been measuring some powder into a small bowl, but now jerked around with a look of horror. "Absalom Consett—you never did? Oh, and how silly I be! As if you could've knowed he'd come that way!"

"Ar," grinned her uncle. "Don't ye listen to this dainty dandy, my chick. Just trying to make trouble, he is. After all we done for him! Typical!"

Glendenning said firmly, "You knew I would go just that way, because 'twas the only clear path through the undergrowth. You likely keep that trap set for any troopers or constables chancing to venture too close to your camp, or whatever this place is."

"What a imagination," sneered Absalom, coming up to

peer at the injured ankle, but watching the girl out of the corners of his eyes. "Ain't it wonderful what they teach 'em at them universities, Amy?"

"T'will be easy enough to verify," persisted Glendenning. "Go out there and look, Mistress Consett. Like as not you'll find the rope still tied round one of the trees, and the rest of it concealed somewhere in the roots or the branches. Unless, of course, you do not wish to know."

She hesitated, looking troubled. Then she said with scorn, "D'ye think I'd take your word over his? Or care, if what you say is truth? When you go chasing humble folk, you deserve whatever ye gets!"

Absalom chuckled. "And if that don't put you in your place, Viscount Vanity, I dunno what—"

Whirling on him like a tigress, Amy said shrilly, "Let him be! And get away from me, fer I swear I could—I could fair box yer ears, if you wasn't me only uncle!" She sniffed, and added gruffly, "Which ye ain't."

The sturdy man looked devastated. "Now—now, Amy," he stammered. "Don't never turn on me! You would've done the same to protect Florian. Ye knows it."

"I knows as I wouldn't have done no such thing! I ain't all bone 'twixt me earholes. Lord Glendenning may be a peer, but he ain't a bad man. And what d'ye think would've come of it, if you'd broke his neck? No!" She gave a gesture of repugnance as he started to reply. "I don't want to talk to ye! I don't want to see ye! Go away and let me be."

Absalom stretched out a hand pleadingly. "But—Amy, lass. You never turned on me before. Don't let this gorgio—"

Springing up, she stamped her foot at him, and flung an arm imperiously towards the blanketed doorway through which he had come. "Go!" she commanded. "Now!"

His hand fell. He shot a venomous glare at the viscount, then went out, hanging his head abjectly.

As the blanket fell behind him, Amy suddenly crouched, and buried her face in her hands.

Horrified, Glendenning pulled himself to one elbow. "Don't cry. Please. I've no intent to bring charges 'gainst him,

I promise you. But I am very glad you were not a party to it, Mistress Amy."

She lifted a tear-stained face and stared at him for a minute in silence, then muttered, "Is ye?" She sniffed and dried her tears with the hem of her skirt. "Why? I be just a common gypsy girl."

Delighted by the glimpse of a shapely calf, he said, "You are a very beautiful girl, and—"

"And ye can get yer greasy eyes off my limbs," she said indignantly, restoring her skirt and gathering it about her. "Men! Absalom's right! Ye're all alike!"

Grinning, he said, "Yes, but Absalom's a man also. And you cannot expect any man to refrain from admiring so lovely a—"

"Oh, be still!" Scowling, she took up the kettle her "uncle" had brought in.

"But I would like to—"

"I can guess what you would like, lordship! And ye *won't* like it when I slap this here poultice on yer ankle. That I promise you!"

She began to add steaming water to the powder in the bowl. Watching her apprehensively, Glendenning said, " 'Tis very kind in you to help me."

"Stow yer gab, do!"

"That is ungracious, Amy. And your mouth is much too pretty to utter such crudities. I wish—"

"So do I," she interrupted, stirring the contents of the bowl rather savagely. "I wish that 'stead o' worrying about me limbs, and the way I talks, ye'd lie back quiet-like, and pull all yer courage together. If you got any. You're going to need it!"

Lord Horatio sighed and did as she suggested.

She was perfectly right.

Leaning back against the thick squabs of the large carriage, Katrina Falcon laughed, and said, "You know very well why Gwendolyn and I came, dear."

Beside her, Gwendolyn Rossiter nodded. "Had we not accompanied you, there would have been battle royal before you ever reached Windsor, much less before you returned home."

Falcon, seated next to James Morris, looked from his beautiful sister to the lieutenant's cheery face, and wondered if Trina would ever be so foolish as to consider the silly fellow. "Morris and I have made a pact," he said. "No matter how irksome he may be on this expedition, I'll not strangle him."

Katrina gave an indignant exclamation, but Morris, gazing out of the window at the might of Windsor Castle, appeared not to have heard the remark.

"Is there a special reason for your expedition?" asked Gwendolyn. "Or are we just visiting Glendenning Abbey?"

Katrina said, "I don't think we can be. Surely we should have turned off before this, August?"

"Oh, yes. If we were visiting Bowers-Malden. We are not." He hesitated. The ladies did not know the full story, but perhaps it would be as well if they were to an extent reminded. "You recall that Rossiter and Morris managed to get their hands on two of those jewelled figures?"

"How could we forget?" said Katrina. "Poor Naomi was kidnapped and her ransom was the return of the jewelled men. I only thank God that Gideon was able to rescue her!"

"No thanks to my brother Newby," sighed Gwendolyn. "When he decided that they must be worth a great deal of money, and took them to—" She looked up, her eyes widening.

Katrina put in nervously, "To an antiquarian who is an expert on jade, so that he might appraise their value. And the antiquarian dwells in Windsor! August—is it that dreadful Society again? The people you call the League of Jewelled Men? Is that why we came here? I thought that horrid business was over with!"

"It isn't over, is it?" demanded Gwendolyn, her eyes bright with excitement. "You think they're plotting again, so you've come to see what the jade expert can tell you!"

Dismayed, Katrina said, "Oh, never say so! The very thought of those evil creatures purely terrifies me."

"Then don't think of 'em, m'dear, for we've no reason to suppose they're at their tricks again. Morris was curious to meet the old fellow, is all. Another of his silly starts, but you said you wished to go for a drive, so I indulged him."

Somewhat reassured, Katrina settled back again.

"Truly, you are all generosity," said Gwendolyn, giving Falcon a speculative look. "What have you to say of it, Jamie?"

Morris glanced at her blankly, then gave a start. "Oh! Your pardon. I was just thinking. Probably dashed uncomfortable, y'know."

"For you, 'tis likely downright painful," agreed Falcon.

Puzzled, Morris said, "Me? I ain't got one."

"Everybody has at least one, my poor clod. Even you."

"D'you know, Falcon, considering you had a bang-up education, you're downright silly at times," observed Morris. "If that were so, there'd be no room in England for people!"

Falcon rolled his eyes at the roof. "I will not strangle him," he whispered. "I will not strangle him . . . I *hope* I will not—"

Laughing, Katrina interposed, "I believe my brother was referring to thoughts, Lieutenant."

"Well, there you are, then," said Morris. "Shows he's not paying attention. I was speaking of castles. Look at the size of that monstrosity. And I'll wager there's not a comfortable chair in the entire place!"

Gwendolyn leaned forward to scan the massive bulk of the castle. "Poor old thing. 'Tis going to rack and ruin. They should restore it."

"They'll do better to tear it down," said the ever practical Falcon. "No one in his right mind would want to dwell there. What use is it?"

Morris brightened. "I've an idea! It could be used to store ice in the summer time. Look at those walls. Likely six feet thick, at the least."

"I have heard," murmured Gwendolyn, pouncing on a

promising line of thought, "that there is a wall in China which is almost a thousand miles long."

"Nearer to fifteen hundred," corrected Falcon.

"Aha . . .," she said, turning from the window to smile at him.

His face flamed. He jerked his head away. Katrina met Gwendolyn's laughing gaze, and winked.

Morris said thoughtfully, "Why would anyone want—"

"Never mind!" growled Falcon. "We're coming into the town, thank God! You did give my coachman the direction, Morris?"

Morris confirmed this, and said that he only hoped Mr. Ellis might be at home.

The carriage jerked to a halt outside a small and rather rundown house distinguished only by a bright blue door.

Katrina asked, "Are we allowed to come in with you?"

"No," answered her brother. "He will speak more freely do Morris and I go in alone. The coachman can take you for a tour of this fascinating metropolis."

Katrina was disappointed, and Gwendolyn gave it as her opinion that the gentlemen were marplots, but Falcon was adamant.

Climbing the deep steps to the front door, he said, "Now don't forget, we know nothing. I don't want to colour any opinion he might have formed."

"Very well, but why shouldn't the ladies have come with us, I'd like to know? The old boy would likely be charmed by 'em, pretty creatures that they are."

"I'd think it might have occurred to you, since you so admire her, that Miss Rossiter would have a difficult time with these steps."

"By Jove! You're right! Jolly good, Falcon. Who'd have guessed you could consider anyone else?"

Fortunately, the door swung open before Falcon could reply.

The angular lady who came out onto the tiny porch was clad in shawl and bonnet and carried a large cloth bag. She was, she informed them, the housekeeper, and was going to the grocer's. Mr. Ellis could be found in the study. "Straight on back, sirs. Best knock loud, or he'll never hear, he gets that buried in his books."

She was titillated when Morris took her arm and assisted her down the steps, and she went off, flushed and smiling, eager to share the tale with her friends.

The carriage had only just started to roll away, and Katrina leaned from the window, and called softly, "Faithless!"

Morris blushed, grinned, and hurried back up the steps.

Gwendolyn met her friend's sparkling eyes and said, "He fairly worships the ground you walk on, Trina. Have you any affection for him at all?"

"I'll own I never thought I could have. But how can one fail to like him? He's such a gentle creature, and must be the most amiable man alive. I only hope . . ." Katrina broke off, her smile fading.

"What? Their silly duel?"

"Yes. I know the lieutenant drives my brother berserk, but if August should really hurt him . . . Oh, 'twould be dreadful!"

"Never worry. August has no intention of hurting him." Katrina looked at her curiously, and Gwendolyn chuckled. "You of all people should know that August doesn't dislike Jamie nearly as much as he pretends to do."

"True," Katrina said slowly, "but August can be deadly, Gwen, and sometimes Jamie—I mean Lieutenant Morris—does bait him, you know."

"Yes, he does. So do I."

"I have noticed you do. May I ask why?"

Gwendolyn hesitated. "Oh—'tis none of my affair, and I know I have not the right, but I think it so sad that he should allow foolish pride to—to spoil both your lives."

Katrina's smile was haunted. "He has his reasons."

"Yes, but when I see your father, and how blithe and merry he is, 'tis hard to comprehend they can be so unlike."

"Papa is not a half-caste."

"No more are you. What rubbish!"

"I wish August might believe it to be rubbish."

Looking back as they moved away, Gwendolyn said, " 'Tis fortunate they found the gentleman at home. I wonder what he will be able to tell them, or if he will even remember the pieces Newby took to him."

As it chanced, Mr. Ellis, a thin gentleman with an untidy wig, and dusty spectacles perched low on his nose, did remember the Jewelled Men Collection. He had, in fact, actually handled two of the pieces. Showing his unexpected visitors to chairs in his cluttered study, and peering at their calling cards, he said, "They were brought to me for appraisal some weeks ago, by a young man named—now, let me see . . . Ah! Mr. Newby."

"Mr. Newby . . . ," said Morris, with a sideways glance at Falcon.

"Yes." The antiquarian's shrewd brown eyes darted from the enigmatic elegance of the extremely handsome Mr. Falcon, who most certainly had some Oriental forbears, to the ruddy, good-natured, and easily readable face of the lieutenant. "Was it not his true name? I cannot say I would be entirely surprised. He seemed so nervous, you know, and fairly jumped each time my housekeeper opened the front door." He blinked over the tops of his spectacles and added anxiously, "I recollect now that a day or so later two other gentlemen made enquiries. I trust the icons were not—stolen property?"

"No, no," said Morris, with rather too much heartiness. "Devil a bit of it! They were friends of his, not Bow Street runners!"

Ellis looked even more alarmed. Falcon gave Morris an exasperated glance and said smoothly, "The jewelled figures have, in fact, been stolen and we are trying to help recover them. Neither my friend nor I actually saw the pieces, however, and we were hoping you might be able to give us a more accurate description than—er, Newby has done."

The old gentleman looked puzzled, and Morris inserted by way of explanation, "He's colour-blind, you see."

" 'Pon my soul! I'd never have guessed it. The other gentlemen were so kind as to take me out for a fine dinner." Mr. Ellis rested a wistful look on his callers.

Falcon said briskly, " 'Twould be our pleasure to do the same, sir. But we have two ladies waiting in the carriage. We shall, of course, expect to meet your professional fees for— say, half an hour's consultation. Could you perhaps sketch the figures for us?"

Ellis cheered up, and began to struggle with his desk drawer. It opened with a jerk, ejecting a shower of crumpled bills, pencils, printed tracts, handkerchiefs, a long clay pipe, and a quizzing glass, all of which shot onto the floor.

"Oh, I say," exclaimed Morris sympathetically. "Allow me, sir." He assisted Mr. Ellis in gathering up the items, on each of which he had some comment to make. One could never have too many pencils; the quizzing glass had a most intricate handle—pity the glass was cracked; and so on, until he said with great interest, "Jove, but that's a fine clay pipe! M'father smokes one that is very similar." This precipitated a discussion that turned from clay pipes, to the benefits of tobacco over snuff, the two men becoming quite involved with their debate and then laughing merrily over their efforts to cram the escaped items back into the drawer.

Fascinated, Falcon watched them. Recovering himself, he suggested somewhat tartly that they should not forget the ladies were waiting.

"Oh, begad, but you're right," said Morris.

Mr. Ellis blinked and looked bewildered, then rummaged through several more drawers, from one of which he at last extricated a rumpled sheet of paper. *Here* we are!" he said, pleased. Smoothing the sheet with questionable success, he dipped a quill pen into the Standish, and remarked that they must not waste time, this causing Falcon to grit his teeth.

"The icons," said Mr. Ellis, "were roughly three inches in height, and approximately an inch thick. Like . . . so." He drew two identical shapes, for all the world like miniature tombstones with rounded tops. "One," he went on, drawing busily, "was of lapis lazuli. The other was pink jade."

62

Standing, and peering over his shoulder, Morris prompted, "And they had faces."

Mr. Ellis looked up at him. "Ah. Then, you did see them, sir?"

"Why—er, I mean Rossiter said they had faces," said Morris, sitting down again and uncomfortably aware of Falcon's disgusted stare. "His brother, d'ye see?"

"Is that so? I had thought his name was Newby?"

"They are half-brothers," put in Falcon swiftly. "Can you recollect, by any chance, what the faces were like, Mr. Ellis?"

"Eh? Oh, yes, yes. I can indeed. They were only etched into the stone, and quite primitive. There. You see?"

"Jolly good!" exclaimed Morris. "I fancy you wouldn't recall just where the jewels were placed?"

Mr. Ellis wrinkled his brow. "I fear you have me there, Lieutenant. I believe they were scattered about haphazardly, as it were. I do remember however, that the lapis figure was set with six sapphires, and the jade with five rubies. All looking to be extremely fine stones. I can make a guess at placement, if you wish. But 'twould be only a very rough approximation."

At their urging, he did this, then handed over the sketch. "I was sufficiently interested to undertake some research on the figures, for I'd never heard of the existence of such a collection prior to this, but I was quite unable to discover any mention of them."

Falcon asked, "Was there anything in the craftsmanship to suggest where they were made? Anything at all outlandish, or incongruous?"

Ellis pursed his lips and considered. "Apart from the fact that they were very old, I would hazard a guess that they were carved in China, or by a Chinese artisan. I was privileged to see a piece from the Shang Dynasty which puts me somewhat in mind of—"

Falcon interrupted abruptly, "You are sure of that, sir?"

"No. Not by any means. It might possibly have been the work of a Greek or Italian. However, I'd be inclined, as I said, to suspect—"

"There was nothing else, then? Nothing that struck you as unique? Or that would give a clue as to what the pieces represent?"

Ellis said thoughtfully, "Could we see the complete set, we might learn more. The fact that there *is* a set would indicate a functional purpose. Like chess, or some Oriental game of skill. On the other hand, they might represent part of a group of mythical or religious figures. Have you a particular interest in the Orient, Mr. Falcon?"

"None whatsoever." Horribly aware of Morris' grin, Falcon's voice was chill, but the antiquarian appeared not to notice that one of his callers had retreated behind a wall of ice and murmured disappointedly that he had always longed to visit the Orient and liked nothing better than to discuss it with someone who shared his interest.

Falcon stood. "Thank you for your time. Good day, sir." He stalked out, leaving Morris to pay the antiquarian a good deal more than the humble fee he named.

As the front door closed behind them, Falcon drew Morris to a halt.

"You may take that smug smirk off your face. And I see no reason to mention Ellis' unfounded suppositions to the ladies."

Morris' grin expanded to a chuckle. "You know perfectly well that Miss Gwendolyn would be most interested. She'll likely start badgering you into researching Chinese myth—"

Through gritted teeth Falcon hissed, "An you say nothing, she will have nought to badger about, will she?"

"The only silent stream is at dead of winter," said Morris solemnly, but with his eyes full of laughter.

"Yes, and you'll be under it if you gibble-gabble to her, confound you!"

"Do you attempt to frighten me into compromising my honour by lying to the ladies?"

"I'd like to—"

Behind them, the door creaked open. Mr. Ellis said, "Ah, there you are! I do recollect something, gentleman. A very small thing. Foolish, no doubt, but—Oh, my! are you unwell, Mr. Falcon?"

"It's likely his liver," said Morris glibly. "Do not regard it."

"What a pity, what a pity! And so young a man. You do look rather flushed. Dear me! I trust 'tis not whirligigousticon. I hear that cases have been found in Brighthelmstone!" Stepping back a pace, he advised, "Try rhubarb, sir. Or, if you would steep the second rind of alder—"

Interrupting this well-meant prescription, Falcon said stiffly that he was perfectly well, thank you, and, affecting not to notice Morris, who had turned away and was wiping his eyes with his handkerchief, asked, "What is this small thing you have recollected?"

"Eh? Oh. Well, it is just my silliness, probably. But—the figures were so similar, you see. In size, I mean. Yet the weight was different. Not by very much, mind you. But—"

"I believe you said the lapis icon contained six sapphires," said Falcon, "whereas the pink jade only had five rubies."

"Just so, just so. But it would not account for— But there, 'tis an insignificant point, after all. Good day to you."

Morris thanked him and he stood watching as his two visitors walked to the luxurious carriage, and the footman sprang to open the door.

Morris called, "Hi, there! Coachman! Pray stop at a greengrocer's. We must purchase some rhubarb and—"

With a muffled growl, Falcon seized his arm and propelled him inside.

CHAPTER IV

"You're quite sure you are all right, sir?" Florian steadied Glendenning and peered into his pale, set face anxiously.

The viscount clung to the young gypsy until the room stopped spinning. "Perfectly fit, thank you," he managed breathlessly.

"Perfectly fit is just what you ain't, sir. Lor', but when Amy comes back she'll have my ears for shaving you and helping you to get up and dressed so soon."

"Well, it's done now, so she can't stop us. If you'll hand me that walking cane you brought, I'll try and get over to the table."

The cane Florian gave him was of oak, the handle cleverly carved into the shape of a dragon. It was a fine piece of work, and Glendenning wondered rather grimly if it had belonged to anyone he knew.

He felt much stronger this morning, although to thrust his bandaged foot into the riding boot had been beyond him. He refused Florian's help, however, and with the aid of the cane and some dogged determination he managed to hobble as far as the table and back. He was very glad then to sink onto the stool Florian pulled out for him, but he was also jubilant, and he panted, "Excelsior! What d'you think of that, you rogue?"

"I think you've got more pluck than wit, milord," said Florian with a grin. "But you're well enough that I can be on my way now, so long as you promise not to—"

"No such thing!" Glendenning hooked the youth's arm with the handle of the cane and pulled him back. "You will instead sit down and keep me company. And firstly, you can tell me why you're here, and what you know of Miss Consett."

Florian hesitated, then sat on a corner of the table, and said reluctantly, "I was with the tribe, milord. So was Amy."

This boy had always seemed to Glendenning to have a faintly foreign air. His features were delicately molded, as were Amy's, but his skin had a more olive cast than did hers. His dark eyes were large and bright with intelligence, and although his accent was not cultured, he enunciated his words clearly and his grammar was good. Intrigued, Glendenning demanded, "What d'you mean, you were 'with' them? Are you not a gypsy?"

The slim shoulders shrugged. "I don't know. Amy says I was brought into the tribe when I was about five years old."

"Then you are not related to her?"

"No, sir. But she has been as good to me as if I was her brother. The bigger boys made fun, because I was small and very frightened, and cried all the time. Amy was about seven then, and afraid of nothing, and she used to take my part when they beat me. After Absalom adopted her, she helped me whenever she could, but always I was in trouble, because I did not like to steal. I was very miserable and tired of their ways and their life. I knew Amy would be safe with Absalom, so I ran away. I lived in the cart, and if I sold one of my baskets, I bought food."

The words were quietly uttered, but the picture they conjured up appalled Glendenning. He muttered, "And then Mr. Cranford rescued you. Hmm. Do you remember nothing of your childhood before you were stolen?"

The youth considered, and said slowly, "I remember a big bed, and a dog, and a white pony. And a tall, very kind man, who told me stories at night. But . . . I do not think he spoke to me in English, sir."

"Do you know which language he did use?"

Florian shook his head. "But I could read English. Not much at first, but Absalom helped me. He is such a fine man. When I ran away he let me borrow his donkey and cart, but the tribe said I'd stolen them. I've got a horse of my own now, and I brought back Uncle Ab's donkey and cart." His eyes flashed. "As if I'd steal from *him!*"

"No, of course not. He would appear to have been a very good friend to both you and Amy. You said she would be safe with him. Safe from what? Did someone threaten her?"

"She started to grow up," said Florian simply. "And she was pretty. Absalom adopted her to keep them from selling her to a Flash House, but the *chals*—er, the young men, were always fighting over which one would buy her for his wife. She would have none of them, and she has her little knife, but Absalom was often away, and they gave her no peace. She caused much trouble, and by the law of the tribe, sooner or later she would have been forced to take one of them for her mate. So Absalom bought her out of the tribe and they came here to live."

"They *live* here?" Glendenning looked around at the stark chamber, the few pieces of rickety furniture, the single window high up in the cold rock wall. "Good God!"

The youth smiled mirthlessly. "This is a fine place for such as us, sir. It is dry, and there is another room we use for a kitchen, and where Absalom sleeps when he's here."

" 'Tis a blasted ruin! It was the cellar of some old house, I'll warrant."

"Yes. The main part of the house was on the hill. It burned down long ago, and was abandoned. Nobody comes here now because it is said to be haunted. But this cellar is partly below ground, and quite hidden away, and we built a fireplace, so it's not too cold in winter."

"And why are you here now? Did the Cranfords turn you off?"

"I hope not, milord. Amy can write." He said it as

though it rated a twenty-one gun salute, and, quite aware of the effort that must have gone into such an achievement, Glendenning said gravely that he thought that splendid. The youth beamed, and went on. "She sent a letter saying that Absalom was ill, and she couldn't manage. So I had to come. He is better now, and will be off, and I must go back." His teeth flashed in a white grin. "Mr. Peregrine Cranford cannot go along without me, you see."

Glendenning stared at him. "What d'you mean? Where will Absalom be off to?"

"He'll be off about his business," growled Absalom, coming in the door holding a bulging sack. "And you need not be thinking as ye can—"

"What's all this?" Following him in, Amy frowned. "You shouldn't be up so soon, lordship! Florian, I told ye plain—"

"You see?" said Florian, laughing. "Good-bye, milord. Good-bye Ab. I'm away!" He seized Amy, gave her a quick kiss, and was gone.

"Wait, ye young care-for-nobody!" Absalom thrust the sack at Amy, and hurried after Florian.

Amy eyed the viscount anxiously. "How are you this morning? You must be fair daft to—" She faltered, and smoothed her windblown hair, her cheeks becoming pink. "Why d'ye stare at me so?"

Yesterday, after she had dressed the infected wound above his right ankle, he had been exhausted and had slept most of the rest of the day away. With the instinctive reaction he'd developed when he'd been a hunted fugitive, at some time during the night a faint sound had jerked him awake. Moonlight had been flooding through the upper window, and by its soft radiance he had seen Amy creep in, wearing a long white nightgown daintily embroidered with tiny flowers and butterflies. Her long hair hung like a shining mantle about her shoulders, and she had watched him warily, very obviously ready to take flight if he showed any sign of wakefulness. Afraid of frightening her away, he had feigned sleep while she crept closer. He'd felt her cool fingers on his cheek, then she had cautiously pulled the blanket higher about him. When he'd opened his eyes, she was gone.

In his half-dazed state she had seemed as if surrounded by a glow, and he'd thought her angelically lovely. In the cold light of day, he decided that illness and moonlight had clouded his common sense. Amy was indeed beautiful, but there was little of the spiritual about her. She had a bold and challenging way of looking at one; her skirts were of a length Lady Nola would certainly judge vulgar, revealing as they did her ankles (very neat ankles one must admit); and what angel went with a knife in her garter and did not scruple to whip it out with not a vestige of modesty? And what an ungrateful wretch to be criticising her when she had cared for him!

"My apologies an I was staring," he said humbly. "You are very lovely, Amy. And you've been more than kind to me."

She smiled and began to remove the contents of the sack. "We prigged yer purse, don't forget. Look at this! Two fine hens for dinner!"

He glanced at the hens disinterestedly. They were plump birds, already plucked and dressed. "I retrieved my purse," he pointed out. "You had spent very little."

She took out a loaf of bread. "Didn't waste no time counting it, eh? Just as well. Never can tell what thieving gypsies will do!"

"Do not bristle. Certainly, I have caused you to buy more food. You must let me help with your expenses."

"Lor'," she said, her mouth curving scornfully. "Don't you never think o' nothing else? I don't want yer silly money!" She saw the amused upward twitch of his dark brows, and before he could make the obvious comment, she added, "I know what you're thinking, but I didn't know ye when I—borrowed yer purse. Besides, that were business. I don't take money from folks I knows."

"You mean from friends, which is quite proper. Even so, you must be sensible. You cannot afford to buy extra—"

"Extra—what? I ain't bought noth—anything."

He grinned. "Thank you. 'Anything' is better than 'nothing.' "

"Yes, 'tis. So ye can enjoy yer dinner, 'cause if I hadn't of prigged them cacklers you'd have nothing!"

"What? You never did?" Dismayed, he reached out and caught her wrist. "Do you know you could be transported for stealing two hens?"

She laughed and danced away, saying pertly, "They got to catch me first. Can't transport what ye cannot catch, eh, me noble lord?"

"Keep on like this and soon or late they *will* catch you! Surely you understand that, quite apart from punishment or whether or not they catch you, what you did is wrong. You took something belonging to someone else. Someone who may need it more than you do."

Her smile died, to be replaced by a stormy look. "La, how the aristo doth preach," she jeered, slamming the hens back into the sack again. "They couldn't need it more'n me, because they'd got it, and I didn't!" Taking up the sack, scowling darkly at him, her face flamed. "And don't you never look at me so high and mighty. Lor', but you'd think as I'd murdered someone!"

With her upbringing, poor chit, how could he blame her? "I suppose," he began, "you have never been taught—"

"Then you can s'pose again! And don't be thinking as I'm a iggerant gypsy trollop!"

"As if I would! Do not say such things!"

"You says I ain't been taught," she said fiercely. "Ye think I cannot do nothing—don't know nothing! Well, I *can* do things! All kinds o' things what *you* couldn't do! Like . . . like finding food when there ain't none. And getting fires to burn when the wood's wet. And how to turn a shirt so it'll last twice as long; and how much to pay them as asks five times what they ought for a loaf of bread!"

'Poor little creature,' he thought. 'What a dreadful life she has led.' And he asked gently. "How much would you pay them, Amy?"

At once the flashing eyes were softened by mirth. A dimple peeped, and she said mischievously, "Nothing, of course! I'd prig the loaf." Her amusement faded. "And there ye go, look-

---

71

ing down yer nose at me! Well, I'd like to see yer fine ladies go on living without no roofs over their heads, or if there wasn't no one to wait on 'em hand and hoof, and kiss their—" She saw Glendenning's covert grin and broke off, biting her lip. Before he could comment, however, she went on proudly. "I can write, too! Writ a letter I did! *And* sent it off! And I can read! Look here . . . !" With a swirl of skirts she ran to the piled crates where were her brush and comb and the little mirror. She pulled open a makeshift door on a lower crate, revealing several books neatly propped with a brick. She took out a much worn and dog-eared Bible and flew back to flourish it under Glendenning's nose. "Open it! Go on! Open it anywhere, and I'll read it!"

"Amy, my dear child, I did not mean—"

With an exclamation of impatience she opened the Bible, closed her eyes, and stabbed a finger at the page. "There! Now ye cannot say as I chose a bit I knows by heart." She bent her head and began to read slowly and with a painful care that he thought ineffably touching.

" 'Let him that stoled steal no more, but ray—ra-ther . . . let him . . . la-bour—' " Belatedly, the meaning of the words dawned on her. Moaning, she stopped reading.

Glendenning struggled to contain his hilarity.

Amy lay down the Bible, put both hands over her face, then peeped at him from between her fingers.

He was undone, and shouted with laughter. "If ever . . . I saw justice . . . meted out."

She tried to keep a sober face, but his mirth was contagious and soon her clear peals were mingling with his deeper laugh. How it came about, she could not have told, but somehow she was perched on his knee, his arm around her waist.

"Well now, Mistress Consett," he said. "And are you properly chastised?"

She smiled into his laughing face. "Ye won that hand, all right."

"Perhaps. But although you were hoist with your own petard, you proved your point, ma'am. You can read. Your uncle warrants a medal for teaching you so well."

Her eyes searched his face. She said with sudden desperate intensity, "Ye ain't a'mocking of me, lordship? Did I read it right?"

"You did indeed."

"Ah, but I made mistakes, didn't I?" She sighed, and said disconsolately, " 'Stoled' didn't sound just right, and I said 'rather' wrong at first."

"Yes. But you corrected yourself."

She sprang up, and said passionately, "If *only* I knowed how to read better!"

" 'Knew,' pretty one. Not 'knowed.' "

"There! You see! But 'tis cruel hard. There's so *much* to learn!"

"For all of us, child. Only look at me. You are perfectly right. I may know how to read, and—"

"And how to talk proper. And ye can talk other languages, I wouldn't wonder. Like—like French, and Latin?"

"Very little Latin, I'm afraid. And had I been obliged to face life's hard knocks as you have, much good would French and Latin have done me!"

"You're just being kind. You knows I'm iggerant."

Fascinated by her swift changes of mood, and by the vitality that seemed to radiate from her, he argued, "Nothing of the sort! You have a quick mind, that is very evident, and would learn quickly if—"

"Aye, if ye'd help me. Oh, sir! Would ye? Please? If I could speak nicer, I'd be able to sell me wares to better places. P'raps get a stall somewhere."

Curious, he asked, "What d'you mean, Mistress Amy? Do you sew, perhaps? I noticed that pretty night—" Too late, he cut off the words.

"Oh!" She stared at him in horror. "Ye *was* awake! And spying on me in me nightrail!" A wave of crimson swept up the white column of her throat, and pressing a tanned hand to her blazing cheek, she scolded, "Oh, but ye're a wicked young man, I think!"

Absalom came back in, saying stridently, "Ain't I told ye, lass? All the Quality coves be the same. Grinding folks like

73

you and me under their boots, and thinking as they've the right to bed any woman, be she decent or no, so long as she ain't one o' their own.''

"Stuff," said Glendenning, whose head was beginning to pound once more. "In the first place, I doubt you've ever been ground under anyone's heel—or God help him, you'd have properly stung him! In the second place, I never in my life knew of any well-bred gentleman—er, bedding a woman who was unwilling. And in the third place, you should not use such terms in front of your niece!"

"I'll use a few terms in a minute, I will," snorted Absalom. "Terms like—hop off, quick like!" He advanced on the viscount belligerently. "You think I ain't seen ye making sheep's eyes at my Amy? Go back to yer castles and yer hundreds o' servants what's waiting to grovel when ye snaps yer fingers! Yer perishing lordship ain't wanted here!"

"Now, Uncle Absalom," began Amy.

Glendenning clung to the edge of the table and dragged himself up. "If you imply that I would take advantage of Miss Consett—"

"I don't imply it, mate," snarled Absalom. "I *says* it. Straight out. Go back where—"

"He cannot go anywhere yet," interposed Amy. "See how ill he looks! Come, milord." She handed Glendenning his cane, and taking his other arm began to help him back toward the bed. " 'Tis no use grumbling, dear old Ab. He ain't really better yet, and if you keep quarreling with him, we'll likely have him in a fever again and he'll be here longer than ever."

Glendenning protested that he did not want to lie down again, but he was overruled, and he settled with inward relief onto the bed. He lay listening drowsily while Absalom argued that they should have left yesterday and that he wouldn't hear of leaving his little girl alone with the evil aristocrat. Fleetingly, it occurred to the evil aristocrat that he had neither contacted Hector Kadenworthy about the duel, nor run his elusive brother to earth. Thinking on those matters, he fell asleep.

Lord Hector Kadenworthy, having inherited great wealth at an early age, had been toad-eaten for most of his three and thirty years, and with few exceptions found his fellow man a dead bore. To those he loved he showed a lively sense of humour, kindness, and unfailing generosity, but those he loved were few, and he was more universally held to be a man of chilly demeanour and sharp tongue.

The latter qualities were in full force on this rainy afternoon as he sat at the desk in his study inspecting a pair of superb cannon-barrelled turn-off pistols, and ignoring the man who watched and waited and smiled.

As though suddenly recalling the presence of this patient individual, Kadenworthy raised his hard brown eyes and drawled, "Your pardon, Mr.—er, Farrier, but I fail to see why the theft of my mother's emeralds should be of concern to the Horse Guards."

Burton Farrier leaned back in his chair and rested the tips of the fingers of both hands together. "The Kadenworthy emeralds are famous, my lord," he said in his soft, purring voice. "That any of our noble families should be victimized by so daring a—er, robbery is, naturally enough, of interest to my superiors."

Replacing one pistol in its case, Kadenworthy took up the other and, admiring it, appeared again to forget his visitor.

Farrier watched him, eyes expressionless, smile unwavering.

After a long pause, Kadenworthy said idly, "You cannot know how relieved I am to learn that my government employs its best operatives to track down malefactors. In view of the number of rank riders upon the highways, your life must be a busy one. How many of the ruffians have you brought to book?"

"Alas, sir. I have given you a false impression. My work ceases when the missing jewels are—er, shall we say—found?"

Kadenworthy sighted along the silver-mounted barrel, turning the pistol until it pointed steadily between Mr. Farrier's eyes. "Shall we say you are aware that our gems were recovered?"

Undismayed by the aim of that deadly muzzle, Farrier separated his 'steeple,' then tapped it back together again. "We are aware that *some* gems were recovered, my lord."

Kadenworthy lowered the pistol. "I do not know what devious ploy brings you here, Farrier, but that you spend your time being of assistance to your countrymen I find as suspect as that damned grin of yours. Do you imply that the jewels we recovered are not the Kadenworthy emeralds?"

Mr. Farrier sighed, and looked sad. "Unhappily, my lord, it is believed the jewels your agents took from the fence may be very clever copies of your property." The smile reasserted itself. "Since I am expert in such matters, I have been assigned the task of confirming their authenticity."

His lordship replaced the pistol in its velvet-lined case, closed the lid, and rose. For a moment he stood there, looking at Farrier, who had sprung to his feet.

"Unless, of course," purred Farrier, "you would for some reason, object, sir?"

"I would have a perfect right to object, I believe."

"Oh, absolutely. People are usually quite anxious to be sure of the value of their belongings, however. The last estate I visited, Ward Marching— I believe you are acquainted with Sir Peter Ward?"

Not by a flicker did his lordship's expression change. He said coolly, "Sir Peter Ward is a friend of mine. Am I to infer he also has been robbed?"

"A thwarted attempt, fortunately. We had reason to suspect it might have been linked to the fact that an escaped Jacobite was known to be in the vicinity of Ward Marching a year or two since . . ."

Standing very still, Kadenworthy said nothing, but one eyebrow lifted in faintly bored enquiry.

"For a while, in fact," went on Farrier, "the traitor was thought to have broken into the house. Ah, but how forgetful I am! I tell you what you already know, for you were among the guests that night, no? You and . . . Trevelyan de Villars."

How benign the smile. How soft the voice. But his lordship's nerves tightened, and his neatly powdered head lifted a trace higher. He raised his quizzing glass and through it directed a level stare at his visitor. "And a couple of hundred other guests. Damme, Farrier, but one might almost suppose you to have been sticking your nose into my appointment book. If you knew of my presence at the Ward Marching Midsummer Ball, you must also be aware that Mr. Trevelyan de Villars and I went out the previous year, and that he came curst near to killing me."

"I'd heard he is a deadly man with a sword. Thank heaven you survived the encounter, my lord. And may I remark that one can only admire you for later treating him with such magnanimity. A most admirable example of, ah—restraint."

"If you imply that my 'restraint' stretched to assisting de Villars to escape to France, you—"

With patent horror, Farrier raised both hands. "Good gracious me! As if I could think such a thing! De Villars is known to have helped countless Jacobites elude justice. He is a foul traitor to his king and country! I would be a fool indeed to suspect that a loyal gentleman such as yourself, a peer of the realm, would willingly breathe the same air with such—vermin! Much less be of aid to him."

Smiling faintly, Kadenworthy murmured, "I have heard of you, Farrier. It appears that rumour did not exaggerate."

Farrier bowed. "You are too kind, sir."

"Oh, no," said his lordship blightingly. He walked past and flung open the door. "This way," he called over his shoulder.

For just an instant, Mr. Farrier's grin slipped, but when he followed Hector Kadenworthy along the hall, it was as bland as ever.

"You're damned crusty today," observed August Falcon, occupying a deep chair in Kadenworthy's spacious withdrawing room.

"The rain does not appear to deter unwelcome callers," grunted his lordship, strolling over to the credenza and unstoppering a decanter. "I no sooner get rid of one noxious pest than you arrive. I presume you're here about your confounded duel. I do not scruple to tell you, Falcon, that 'twill be a great day for England when you cease whittling down the population."

A derisive smile lit August Falcon's lean face. "Much you care about the population."

"I care about it when I am constantly bamboozled into seconding you. Madeira or sherry?"

"Madeira, if you please. Prepare yourself; I may call out Glendenning next. I assumed you'd not object, but he should've had the common courtesy to let me know."

Kadenworthy carried a glass of Madeira to his guest, then sat down on a black and gold brocade sofa. "Not object to what?"

Jerking the glass back from his lips, Falcon splashed some of the wine on his blue velvet coat, and swore lustily. He dabbed at the stain with his handkerchief and asked, "Has Glendenning not yet reached here?"

"He came last week and took tea with my aunt. Said he wanted to see me, but I was racing that day. We had quite a large turn-out. I presume Tio decided to return at a more convenient time."

"*More convenient time?*" Falcon spluttered, "Good God, man! The duel is for Monday morning!"

"The hell it is! The twenty-seventh, d'ye mean? Well, of all the shabby set outs! Is everyone else agreed?"

"Yes. And if you tell me you must cancel, I'll likely shoot Morris out of hand and be done with it! This is the second time we've arranged this damned meeting, and each time we postpone, the clod has an excuse to come mooning around Katrina again!"

Watching the handsome features darken with rage, Kadenworthy grinned, and added fuel to the fire by remarking that he rather liked Morris. "Be curst if I can remember why you're fighting."

"Well, I'm not likely to forget, I promise you! 'Twas when our coach was held up and I pursued the filthy rank riders."

"Ah, yes. And when you returned, poor Morris mistook you for a highwayman."

"*Poor Morris?* The devil! You'd not think him so poor had he shot *you* down by mistake! Stupid blockhead! When I think—"

"Pray do not! I've no least desire that you should explode in here! My house has been sufficiently contaminated today. Oh, never breathe fire and smoke, I'll second you, dammit. I gave my word. I'll come up on Saturday and stay at my club."

Falcon thanked him gruffly, took another swallow from his glass, then asked, "Who was your other contaminant? Or do I presume too much?"

Kadenworthy scowled and said a clipped, "Burton Farrier."

"Zounds! What treachery have you been about to bring that wart down upon you? I'd not thought you were for our royal Scots dimwit."

"Charles Stuart was ill advised, but he's no dimwit. Nor is Farrier, blast him! He was full of sly innuendoes about my acquaintanceship with Treve de Villars."

Falcon rubbed his wineglass thoughtfully against the end of his nose. "You are a hard-hearted man, Kade, and I have no love for you, but if you need safe passage to France . . ."

"*Merci beaucoup, mon cher ami,* but my only brush with the Jacobites was a brief one. It was chancy, though. And that idiot de Villars was very much involved."

"So the Horse Guards have set the Terrier to sniff you out, eh? Did he accuse you, or let you sweat?"

"He pretended to doubt the authenticity of my mother's emeralds. I allowed him to inspect 'em, and he oozed away. I sent him off with a flea in his ear, I can tell you."

"Don't flatter yourself he noticed it. I fancy the dolt's ears are fairly crowded with fleas. An he really had some proof, Kade, you'd be en route to the Tower at this very minute. He's sent a score of fine gentlemen to their deaths."

They looked at each other.

Repressing a shudder, Kadenworthy muttered, "I fairly

panted to plant my fist in his smile. The fellow makes my skin creep!"

"Yes. I sympathize. Still . . ." Falcon frowned. "I wonder what he was really after."

The Countess of Bowers-Malden stood at the window of her private parlour, watching a raindrop dodge and wriggle down the glass. "I should have guessed," she said, a very faint tremor to her usually resonant voice, "when you gave us all such splendid gifts. That beautiful tiara for me, the dressing case for your father—"

The young man sprawled in the chair by the fireplace put a slim hand over his eyes, and interrupted wearily, "The fault is entirely my own, Mama. I was a blind fool not to see that they were letting me win only so as to—to lure me into larger wagers. But they were all fine gentlemen, and I did not dream . . ." The words faltered, and ceased.

The countess turned to gaze at the tall, scholarly boy who was her so beloved son. Michael was crushed with despair. Her heart wrung, she went over and touched his thick light brown hair tenderly. "Never worry so, dearest. We'll find some way to pay them. If Papa knew—"

"No! I beg you! An he knew he would surely blame Tio. He blames Tio for everything! And he would fix me with that terrible look of contempt." The hazel eyes, usually so carefree, were frantic. He clasped her hand. "I deserve that you *should* tell him, I know, ma'am. But—I could not bear it!"

She sat on the chair close to his, and said soothingly, "Then, of course, we must not consider it. Have you told your brother?"

The fair head ducked once more. "I couldn't find him. Would to God I had. Tio would rip me up, I don't doubt, but he'd help, just the same. Then, I wouldn't have had to bother you with it all."

She said gravely, "*Have* you bothered me with it all, darling?" His eyes flew to meet hers. She said, "I think you have only told me part, yes? You were invited to play cards with three gentlemen, and over two evenings of play, you won two thousand pounds, which—like the generous creature you are—you spent on some very lavish gifts. The next night you played at Mrs. Alvelley's house, and you won again, to the tune of three thousand."

He said bitterly, "And two nights later I had lost ten. 'Fore God, Mama, I don't know how it chanced. Tio warned me never to drink heavily when I played, and I thought I was careful, but"—he shrugged—"the widow is a beautiful lady and—and—"

"And flattered and encouraged you, I do not doubt," put in the countess with wrathful indignation. "Such women should be whipped at the cart tail, and would have been in grandmama's day! But that is neither here nor there. You have returned the tiara and your sister's necklace, and with what I could raise we have repaid six thousand. Somehow, we must find the rest, although one week allows us very little time. I have given you all the funds I had. To get more I would have to ask Papa, and to approach him for such a sum would certainly raise his suspicions." She wrung her hands. "I could appeal to my friends, or some of our relations—Lord knows, they could afford it. But sooner or later Papa would be sure to hear of it."

Flushing darkly, he said, "And how splendid it is that I must take back the gifts I had bought you. I am truly a deplorable villain. And now—God forgive me!—I've to ask if . . . if we might perhaps borrow 'gainst your jewels?"

She saw how tightly his hands were clenched, and knew very well what that plea must have cost him. She loved him dearly, but she took a deep breath and said with quiet finality, "I will be honest, Michael. I dare not. I have never told you this, because Bowers-Malden's first wife was my very best friend, and I do not care to speak ill of poor Adelaide. Gregory was wild with joy when she told him she was in a delicate condition again, some months after Tio was born, but she was not a strong woman. She suffered miscarriages with that babe and the one which followed, and the physician told her there would be no more children. Gregory had longed for another son, and Adelaide was heartsick. She sought solace in gaming. It became an obsession, and she not only lost a great deal of money, but some exquisite diamonds that had belonged to Gregory's great grandmama. I was staying here then. I have never seen him so enraged. Always he has been passionately opposed to gambling in any form. He loved Adelaide, but he felt that she had betrayed his trust. I think that was the final blow to her health. When she died, he reproached himself bitterly for having scolded her so."

Michael's sensitive heart was touched. "Good Lord!" he muttered. "What a tragic thing."

"Yes. So you see, I would not—I *could* not put him through such a nightmare again. And, alas, the only jewels I have that are of real worth are those he gave me. Oh, if *only* Tio would come back."

He looked up sharply. "Come back? He was here?"

"Yes, and asking for you. The dear soul sensed that I was worried. I had my work cut out not to tell him, but you had my promise, so I managed to convince him all was well. If that wretched widow means to hound you, however, you must go to him, my love. He can lend you the four thousand, I've no doubt, and then—" She paused, alarmed by his anguished expression.

" 'Tis not four thousand, dear Mama." He stood and faced her squarely. "I had not the courage to tell you the whole. When I'd lost the ten thousand, I was half out of my mind, I think. Mrs. Alvelley was all kindness and understanding. She convinced me that my luck must turn, and agreed to take my vowels. I won, and won again. I was overjoyed, and everybody said this was—was my winning streak. Oh, God! I *must* have been mad, but I could not seem to lose, and the—the end of it was that I staked it all on the turn of a card!"

Scarcely daring to ask, she said hoarsely, "How much n-now, Michael?"

He wrenched away and strode to the hearth. With his back to her, he gripped the mantelpiece and bowed his head onto his hands.

"Michael?"

He turned, his face deathly pale. "Twenty-two . . . thousand," he croaked. "Twenty-two *thousand!*"

Lady Nola sat very still and, after a moment, said in a failing voice, "What a merciless harridan, to so ensnare a young fellow!"

"If the young fellow is as foolish as I, he deserves it! At all events, it now transpires that Mrs. Alvelley is but a figurehead as it were, and does not actually own her—establishment. Her patron is a Major Trethaway. He is quite the man about Town, but I think you are not acquainted. He allowed me a month to make good the debt. I sold everything I could, and with what you gave me I was able to take him eleven thousand. But he is charging a very high rate of daily interest, and much of my payment was swallowed up. And now, he says he has suffered heavy reverses and must have the entire balance at once, or he will . . . will have me thrown into Debtors Prison."

The poor countess closed her eyes for an instant, then quavered, "But what good would that do? Surely, he would be better advised to wait a little while until we can raise the funds?"

"I—*begged* him, Mama!" Driving a fist into his palm, Michael swung around and began to pace up and down. "If you had but seen how I humbled myself to the dirty—" He broke off, and ran a hand through his disordered locks, then said harshly, "He says my father will pay up sooner than face the disgrace of having a m-member of his family thrown into the Gatehouse."

With a muffled sob, Lady Nola buried her face in her hands.

Michael ran to kneel before her. His own eyes tearful, he groaned, "Poor, dear Mama! I am so sorry! I am so *sorry!* If only Marguerite still had that old plaid pin that belonged to Grandmama Comyn, we might come about, but—"

Lady Nola's head jerked up. "What plaid pin? Michael—you never mean that hideous great thing with the amethysts and all those odd inscriptions?"

"Yes. It was very old, I believe, and Trethaway is most

---

interested in antique jewellry. He asked if I had anything of the kind. I described the pin to him, and he said he thought he knew the piece and that 'tis listed in several catalogues and of considerable value. I thought I was saved! But when I asked Marguerite she said she lost it years since, and never dared tell you for fear you would be angry.''

The countess gripped her hands together. "Thank heaven! Your sister did not lose it, my dearest. I took it away from her after I found it pinned on one of her doll's dresses and left to lie in the rain."

"Mama!" His haggard face lighting up, he gasped, "Do you say you *have* it?"

"Yes, dear! Yes! I tucked it away for safe keeping, and had quite forgot the ugly thing!" She stood, her eyes radiant.

Elated, he took her in his arms and whirled her around. "Hallelujah!" he shouted joyously. "Oh, Mama! How wonderful you are!" He gave her a smacking kiss, and she laughed and wept, and wiped tears away. Holding her at arms' length then, he said earnestly, "I have been a weak fool, my dear, and have caused you great anxiety. I swear to you I shall never do so again. I'll take your brooch to Trethaway, but with Tio's help I shall redeem it for you. I give you my word!"

She kissed him fondly. "I do not doubt you will, my love. Meanwhile, we must be grateful. Most gentlemen gamble, after all, and it could have been so much worse! Praise God, we have found a way out!"

"Amen to that," said Michael fervently.

CHAPTER V

"I tells ye I won't! And that be that! I sold her. 'Twas me right! And we needs the dibs, ye knows that. What _____ it is, Amy, that there perishing Quality cove has addled yer female brains! D'ye think he'd give you a second look if it wasn't that he's knocked up for a day or two? Ha!"

"Much I'd care if he did. But I won't prig from a man what—who saved me from the nubbing cheat, or being transported. You do like I say Uncle Ab, else—else I'll coil rope!"

The angry voices disturbed Glendenning's midmorning nap. 'Nubbing cheat,' of course, was cant for the gallows, but he wondered drowsily what 'coil rope' meant. After a pause, he had his answer.

Absalom said in a tone of disbelief, "Ye'd *slope*, gal? After all the years I kept ye safe, is that the thanks I get? You'd really go off and leave me?"

Another pause, then the girl's voice, shaky but defiant: "I'm grateful, Uncle Ab. I allus will be. But—there's some things— What I means is—I got me pride."

"I saved you from the *chals*! All the fights and the argifying! And I bought you outta the tribe. But never mind about me. Don't even think what yer life woulda been like today if I hadn't of brought you here. You don't owe *me* nothing. Not

so much as you owes *him,* 'cause he's young and good looking, and full of fancy Quality gab."

"Oh . . . Uncle Ab . . . !"

Glendenning lifted his head and blinked at them. The blanket was tied back, and he could see into the kitchen. Morning
sunlight streamed through the open outer door, touching the
scarf tied about Amy's glossy hair and making of it a blaze of
scarlet. She stood by the table, holding a string bag full of
onions clasped to her bosom, and looking distressed as she
faced Absalom's truculent glare.

"What'll you do," snarled Absalom, "if he's after ye the
minute I goes? And he will be, certain sure."

"You just said he wouldn't give me a second look."

"No more he will. Not a decent look, any rate. The most
you'd ever get from the likes o' him would be a guinea—if he
was feeling generous. So if you're thinking as you'll be offered
a slip on the shoulder, you're giving of yourself airs, gal."

"Which shows how much you know," said Glendenning,
raising himself to one elbow. "I would be very pleased to give
Amy a slip on the shoulder!"

She whirled to face him, her mouth very round. "Oh!" she
exclaimed. "You don't mean it! Ye're just sick and—"

"I'm much better." He sat up with a grin and held out his
arms. "Come, pretty one. I'll take good care of you, and
proudly, for you're the loveliest—"

A strange sound issued from her shapely lips. She ran to
him, her arm swung, and the bag of onions slammed against
his jaw, smashing him back onto his pillow.

As from an echoing distance he heard Absalom's shrieks of
laughter interspersed with Amy's lengthy and singularly un-
complimentary assessment of the Laindon forbears.

Dazed, he gasped out, "But . . . I thought you wanted . . ."

"Wanted to be your fancy piece?" she shrilled, bending a
flushed countenance above him. "What d'ye think, yer worship? That the world's made up of only two kinds of females?
The high and mighty ladies you mustn't touch till they be
safely wed? And the gutter bred, like me, who dream of the

day they can have the high honour of being ruinated by lechers like you?"

Feeling his jaw gingerly, he muttered, "There's no such word as ruinated. And furthermore, I'm not . . . a lecher, and would have seen to it that you were well provided for and lived in the lap of luxury for so long as—"

"As long as I pleased you. And when I wasn't so young and pretty no more, then 'twould be a kiss and a kick out the door, eh?"

"I made you a perfectly well-intentioned offer," he said, annoyed. "I think you could do worse than live under my protection, and if you've broke my jaw, my girl—"

"I ain't yer girl," she raged, baring her white teeth at him. "I've read the Bible, *noble*man! You just show me the part where it says as it's all right with our Lord if a woman sells herself to a lecher without no wedding ring!"

"Egad!" gasped the viscount, staring at her. "You expect me to *marry* you?"

Absalom, who had been listening thoughtfully, said, "Lookee lass, there's something to what he says. You can't really think as—"

Half sobbing with hurt and fury, she said, " 'Course I don't! D'ye think as I'd want to be a hoity-toity countess, even if I could?" She dragged a hand across her eyes fiercely. "But that don't mean as I'm a loose woman! I'd sooner be—be boiled than marry a useless thing like a viscount. Besides, there's other men! Better men than him, as would be glad to wed me!"

Absalom pursed his lips, regarding Glendenning speculatively. "I dunno, Amy. You could do worse. You ain't always going to have me to protect you. And this here viscount would likely set you up nice in some flat in London—eh, milord?"

"Not if I'm to be battered with bags of onions," grumbled Glendenning, struggling to his feet, and reaching for the cane.

"Ye'd best stow yer clack, Uncle Ab, and go!" Amy hoisted her pungent bag high. "You ain't managed to sell me off today!"

"Now, don't whack me, lass! I was only thinking—"

"I know what you was thinking. What ye all think! That a woman's good for nothing but to be a doormat and a bedmate for a man! You'd as well know now—both of ye—that I'll die a old maid 'fore I sell meself to any cove who wants to have me—without loving me enough to give me his name! You gotta be better born than what I am to sink so low! For shame that you could think so bad of me, Uncle Ab! Now go! 'Fore I do something I'll be sorry fer!"

"But—lass! I can't leave ye alone with—"

"With what? This poor apology for a gentleman?" She slanted a scornful glance at the tight-lipped viscount. "Don't you never worry about him. If he comes the ugly, I'll tickle his ribs with me little woe-and-strife. 'Sides, he's well enough to go back where he belongs! And good riddance to bad rubbish!"

Absalom looked from the flushed and rebellious girl to the white and stiffly silent man. Shaking his head, he left them.

Amy turned to Glendenning. "Well?" she demanded belligerently. "If you got something to say, say it!"

He was leaning on the cane, but not so heavily that he was unable to offer a polite bow. His eyes green ice, he replied, "You have said all that needed to be said, and a great deal that did not, ma'am. Be assured that you will have no cause to resort to your—er, woe-and-strife, which I presume means knife. Though," he added with a gratifying flash of inspiration, "I'd think it might better be used in the place of 'wife.'"

"Would you now. Well, 'wife' is 'trouble-and-strife.' And I'll resort to *what* I want, *when* I want. So you just take care, lordship."

"I shall also relieve you of my unwanted presence at the earliest possible moment."

"Good!" And with her head held very high, and her little nose tilted upward, she took herself and her onions away, jerking the blanket closed as she went.

Left alone, Lord Horatio sat down and struggled with his boots. He had to use his pocket knife to slash the seam of the right boot before he could endure to pull it on, and was obliged to rest a little when that unpleasant battle was won. Sitting there, he took stock of the situation. He could not recall ever having been more infuriated. This slip of a gypsy; this child of the gutter who lacked all breeding and background, who had not a particle of the refinement or manners of a lady; this utter *hoyden* had dared to question his honour! He took up the cane again, and limped to the makeshift chest of drawers. She had stolen his purse. She'd been responsible for his damn near breaking his neck. (Gad, but this blasted ankle was a nuisance!) Evidently she had sold Flame. And she had *dared* to name him a "useless thing!" 'Twas past belief!

At this point he reached the crates and with a sigh of relief put his full weight on his left foot while he rummaged about. His belongings were in one of the lower boxes. His wig, neatly combed, was draped over a round white teapot from which the spout was missing. The pert Mistress Consett had stuck a long carrot in the triangular gap, presumably in lieu of a nose, and had painted two demurely downcast eyes, and a very prim mouth. He had a lively sense of humour and at another time he would have laughed, but today he was in no mood to be amused. Gritting his teeth, he snatched up the wig, then paused, catching sight of his reflection in the little mirror. She'd said his hair was nicer than his wig. It would soon need a barber's attention if— Lord, but he looked like a ghost with his colourless face and the shadows that were for all the world like bruises under his eyes.

'There's other men . . . better men than him . . . !'

Small wonder she should think that, if she had judged by his present appearance. But his inherent honesty forced him to admit that was not so. She'd judged by his behaviour, which admittedly had not— But most gentlemen had mistresses, and what difference did it make what the chit thought of him? Impatient with himself, he slammed his wig on, quite forgetting the injury to his head. The resultant pain was blinding. He clung to the crate and waited it out, breathing jerkily, his knees like water. He was sweating when the room stopped tilting, but he managed to straighten his wig. There. Now he looked more like a gentleman.

'This poor apology for a gentleman . . .'

Damme, but the vixen had a vicious tongue! Well, he would soon be gone, and she could forget such "useless things" as viscounts, and find herself some gypsy *chal* to make an honest woman of her and, hopefully, beat her regularly. He retrieved his purse, took out two guineas and put them under the offensive carrot. Not that he need feel obliged, Lord knows. They'd taken Flame from him. And Michael had given him Flame. Michael! He should have found the boy before this. And there was the duel. Gad, but Falcon would be breathing fire and smoke!

Taking up the cane, he limped to the door and swung the blanket aside. The "kitchen" was small, and very clean, with a coziness about it. The outer door stood wide, letting the sunlight in. A table in the centre of the room was brightened by a handleless mug that served as vase for a colourful bunch of wildflowers. The table, which was round and nicely made, also held a bin of flour, carrots, an onion, a cooking knife, and long-handled spoon. Of the cook there was no sign.

He went inside and looked about curiously. A fire burned on a raised brick hearth above which was hung a formidable-looking blunderbuss. A large kettle on an idle-back sent a thin spiral of steam drifting up. On the other side of the hearth was suspended a covered iron pot, in which something was starting to sizzle and smell so divinely that he realized he was very hungry. Shelves, looking as new as the hearth, had been put up from floor to ceiling along one wall, and were crammed with all manner of articles. His mildly curious glance discovered Absalom's shaving utensils, a hammer and saw, boxes of nails, candles, pots and pans, a heterogeneous collection of chipped and cracked dishes, a glass jar of what looked like salt, and various shapes and sizes of closed tins and boxes. String bags of onions, garlic, and potatoes hung from ceiling hooks, and several nicely framed pictures of rural scenes alleviated the starkness of the walls. His boot touched a narrow and neatly made-up bed on the floor, and he suffered a guilty pang, because Amy had given up her bed to him, and must have slept here. 'Well,' he thought defiantly, 'she can sleep in her own bed tonight!'

Walking with as much dignity as he could muster, in case he encountered Her Majesty the Gypsy, he proceeded to the outer door.

Opposite, shallow steps cut into the hillside led up to a small clearing, shut in by trees and shrubs. The air was rather chilly, and the pale sun, being directly overhead, provided no help in determining his direction. Still, whichever way he went, he was scarcely in the wilds of Africa, and there being no lions or man-eating cannibals loitering about, he should soon be able to command a vehicle and get back to Town. His ankle jabbed at him spitefully when he toiled up the steps, but he'd known worse and with the aid of the cane could contrive to walk. He took out his pocket watch, which by some miracle had been wound but not purloined and was ticking busily, presumably showing the correct time of day. A quarter past twelve. He put it away again, and started off resolutely. By two o'clock, at the latest, he would be well on his way home.

Shortly after one o'clock he at last found something approaching a path through the dense woods, but half an hour later, it petered out.

At three o'clock he was sitting with his back propped against a tree trunk, his eyes closed against the vindictive pangs that seemed to reverberate from his head to his ankle. He was desperately tired, but if he rested just for a little while, he'd feel better and could go on . . .

It was half past five when he awoke. Shocked, he scrambled to his feet. Sleep had eased the pain in his head, but his ankle throbbed and felt swollen inside the ravaged boot. Common sense warned that he should have swallowed his pride and stayed till he was stronger, instead of rushing out in a huff. But how could a gentleman stay with a girl who considered him a lecher? He started off, swore, and clutched the tree, then started off again, his thoughts turning to Danielle. The widow of an army colonel, she was a poised, delectable creature, with all the refinement that a governess and a charming family could bestow. After her husband's death, she could have married any one of several well-circumstanced gentlemen, but had preferred to become his *chère amie*. And although she'd had not a sensible thought in her pretty head and had left him for a wealthy cit old enough to be her grandfather, she'd not screamed at him, nor hurled a bag of onions at his head. Above all, she'd not named him a *lecher!* He swore, gripping his right leg, which seemed to become more painful with each step. A *lecher!* The girl was simply too ignorant to realize he had done her honour! What other titled gentleman would be willing to set up a common gypsy for his peculiar?

He checked, and stood gazing at a tree trunk, conscience nagging at him. 'Titled gentleman indeed! Since when have you found it necessary to flourish your title about?' And much good it might do him if the authorities ever proved what they obviously suspected: that he had fought for the dashing Bonnie Prince Charlie! The "common gypsies" would have the last laugh then, watching, as he was dismembered, disembowelled, hanged, and decapitated. Such ghastly punishment had been meted out to many "better men" than he.

Chilled, he stumbled on. Was there no end to these confounded trees? He should have come out of the woods hours ago. One might think he was in the New Forest! Unless—was he perhaps going in circles? He glanced up, and was puzzled to see the sky covered with clouds. That was odd. He'd thought it was sunny. It was getting quite cold, too.

After a long period of effort that he feared had not taken him very far, he was short of breath, and lowering himself cautiously onto a large root again looked at his watch. Half past six? It *couldn't* be! But it was. And there was no arguing with the fact that after six hours of painful struggling, all he had achieved was to become thoroughly tired, cold, and thirsty. With a sigh, he acknowledged that he was beaten. He'd have to go back. Amy might forgive him, was he very humble. Surely, she would at least let him stay there while she made arrangements for his friends to come and fetch him. That was it; he would go back. But his leg throbbed so, and his head was worse than ever, so he'd rest here for a minute or two. No longer, because if it got dark he'd never find his way . . .

Hands were tugging at him. He thought fuzzily that she had come. She'd found him, bless her—

"Wake up, mate! Whatcher doing 'ere?"

A man's voice. A Londoner. Glendenning peered through the gathering dusk. There were four of them, looking down at him with varying degrees of amusement and not a trace of compassion in their predatory faces. He sat up. Jupiter! 'Twas almost dark. Managing to sound firm and assured, he said, "So you've found me at last. Did my father—"

"Hey!" exclaimed a big man wearing a florid and greasy waistcoat under a too small frieze coat. "D'you hear that there fancy talk? We got a nob 'ere, my coves!"

There was a concerted laugh, but another man, with a thin face and crafty black eyes, put up his hand for quiet. "Are you in some difficulty, sir?" he enquired respectfully.

Glendenning knew men, and recognized savagery when he saw it. They were four, and he was alone and incapacitated, but it would be fatal to show any sign of weakness. He said coolly, "I was thrown. I've been trying to find my way out of these confounded woods, but—"

"Bin tryin' fer a day or two, aintcha, your highness?" sneered a rosy cheeked youth, a grin twisting his loose mouth. "Someone give you a hand, eh? Look here, Sep."

Glendenning glanced down. His sagging right boot allowed a glimpse of bandages. "I hurt my leg, and—"

The polite man, whose name was evidently Sep, interrupted. "Then we must help you, sir." He jerked his head. "Have a look, lads."

"No!" said Glendenning sharply. "If you'll just—" His words were cut off as he was seized and his right boot wrenched off. This sent him into a hazy world, through which their voices echoed dimly. He roused to the bite of brandy in his throat, and blinked up at them, coughing. They must have decided to stay, because a small fire had been started. By the light of the flames they looked even more dirty and unkempt, and it became unpleasantly evident that they were not in the habit of bathing.

The one they called Sep said with an unctuous leer, "Good thing some kind soul bandaged your ankle s'nice for you, sir. Still, it's a ugly cut. Just tell us which way to go, and we'll carry you back to your friends."

Glendenning damned him faintly but thoroughly. "Get me to a posting house, and I'll make it . . . worth your while."

"A posting 'ouse, 'e says," jeered Greasy Waistcoat. "Ain't it a pity there ain't no such thing fer miles 'n miles."

Sep, who appeared to be the leader, smiled and agreed it was a sad fact. "We'd best take you back to the people what helped you, sir. Which way might that be?"

"I've not the remotest notion," answered Glendenning truthfully.

"P'raps we can help you remember," offered a lean individual with straggly greying hair. "Let's have him up, boys."

They jerked Glendenning to his feet. He clung to a tree, their grins reinforcing his awareness that he was in very bad trouble. "What the hell," he demanded angrily, "do you want of me? If 'tis my purse, take it and be damned! But 'twill go hard with you if—"

"If—what?" interrupted the grey-haired ruffian. "If we slit yer noble throat? They couldn't hang us no higher fer that than fer bashing you about, Quality cove."

"Billy Brave!" Sep threw up his hands in mock horror. "What a unkind thing to say!"

There was a concerted laugh at this sally, and Greasy Waistcoat thrust his face at Glendenning and demanded, "Where's yer friends? You must have some idea which way you come."

The viscount was contriving to stand very straight and hold his head proudly, but the thought of these animals discovering that a young and beautiful girl was all alone in the woods sent a debilitating wave of fear through him. "I told you, I don't know." A remark of Florian's came to mind, and he went on: "But I'd as soon get out of these woods. They're said to be haunted."

This dreadful assertion gave them pause. Greasy Waistcoat

crooked the first two fingers of his right hand, just to be on the safe side; the cherubic youth drew a horse pistol; Billy Brave tugged at his grey hair nervously; and even Sep was silent. Witches and warlocks were known to frequent woodsy places at the dark of the moon, and tonight was dark indeed. Furthermore, since several highwaymen had been hanged on the great gibbet which stood at the crossroads on a nearby hill, the presence of a ghost or two was very probable.

Billy Brave glanced about uneasily. "I heered that, too," he muttered. "This is a bad place, Sep. This nob's not no good to us. Let's get out."

The youth recovered his nerve. "I got a pop here'll put paid to any ghost. Don't be scared, Billy."

"Just shut yer jaw," growled Septimus, his careful pronunciation slipping. "He's been helped, ain't he? So who helped him? Mebbe him as we're looking for." Seizing the viscount by the arm, he added, "We ain't got all night to waste, and you don't look to be in good point, mate. A 'pothecary's what you need, and we'll fetch one, soon's we get you into shelter. Where's the harm in telling us who tied up yer leg?"

If he was sure of where he was, thought Glendenning, he could point them in the opposite direction. The devil was in it that he might very well send them straight to Amy. "I shall be perfectly all right here," he said haughtily. "Just be—"

Greasy Waistcoat cursed, and shoved with brutal force.

Glendenning went down hard. His head smashed against a root . . .

Some indefinable time later, he could hear them talking and making a great deal of noise as they tried to construct a rude shelter from the rain.

". . . and if it's them, they're prob'ly close by." The voice of Sep. "This dog's meat gent couldn't have come far with that leg."

"No. And we ain't going to get far tonight." That cantankerous growl would be Greasy Waistcoat. "Prop it up with this 'ere branch, Billy. That's right. It's perishing dark, Sep. Even if the nob do know the way, he'd never find it now."

"He knows it! So I says we wait till light, then make him

show us. With that hole in his leg, it'll be easy to persuade him to do what he's told!"

"*What?*" wailed Billy Brave. "Is you saying we gotta stay here *all night*? Why don't we just tie him to a tree and gag him? We can find a tavern and come back in the morning."

The youth said contemptuously, " 'Cause he might get loose, a'course, or someone else might find him 'fore we got back. 'Sides, the Squire says—"

Abruptly, Glendenning's misery was forgotten. He stiffened, listening intently. The *Squire?* Were these crude varmints referring to a simple country squire? Or was it possible that they spoke of the murderous leader of the League of Jewelled Men? No, that was ridiculous. More likely some local squire had sent them out after poachers. Clearly, they thought he'd been aided by someone they sought. That Amy and Absalom could have any connection with the business was out of the question. Unless . . . Amy *had* admitted stealing those confounded chickens. Was she being hunted down for that crime? It was not impossible, but on the other hand, would any squire send four men to track down the purloiner of two fowl? Whatever the case, there was no doubting what would happen if rogues of this stamp got their filthy hands on her. He tightened his jaw and made some grim resolutions. He might be a "lecher," and "a poor excuse for a gentleman," but, by Jupiter, he'd die before he'd lead them to—

"What you whispering about?" demanded Sep.

Billy Brave's voice shook. "I—thought I—heered something."

"Of all the perishing—" began the youth scornfully.

"Stow yer gab," snarled Greasy Waistcoat. "There it is again!"

There it was, indeed. A low moan that set the hairs lifting on the back of Glendenning's neck. A moan that rose into a hideous wheezing, then ended in an unmistakable *hee-haw!*

Sep laughed shakily.

The youth said in mixed relief and disgust, " 'Tis nought but a perishing moke!"

Greasy Waistcoat's voice had a shrill edge as it sliced

through their half-embarrassed exclamations. "Listen! Pox on you! *Listen!* That ain't no dang ass!"

Silence, as they all strained their ears. There came a soft chuckling, gradually increasing in volume until it became a scream of insane laughter that died away, leaving a hushed yet throbbing quiet in its wake.

"Oh," whimpered Billy Brave. "Oh! My Gawd!"

The youth asked threadily, "What the . . . hell . . . was *that?*"

"They do say," quavered Greasy Waistcoat, "as Old Nick likes to change his shape! He appears first as a beast, and then—"

"Shut up," ordered Sep fiercely. "Likely 'twere nothing worse than someone's donkey what's strayed and woke up a stupid owl. Any rate, it's gone now, so—"

But it hadn't gone. Sep's harsh words were in turn rudely interrupted. If anything, the chuckling was closer this time, and Glendenning's blood ran cold, for it echoed upon itself, as no earthly voice might do.

"*Look!*" Billy's voice squeaked with terror. "Holy Christ! *Look!*"

With an effort, Glendenning managed to turn his aching head. He gave a gasp, and lay rigid.

An eerie glow was drifting through the trees. As it came nearer he discerned a long white robe, one abnormally long arm waving menacingly, and, tucked under the other—a human head. A ghastly, glowing, blood-streaked head, with a gaping mouth, and dark hollows for eyes. And ever, as it came, that horrible, bubbling chuckle came with it.

The youth uttered a choking sob of terror.

Made of sterner stuff, Sep jerked a long-barrelled pistol from his pocket. The night was reft with an instant of glaring fire and an ear-splitting retort followed by a brief and oddly musical sound.

The apparition paused. Its head was gone, but now both those long, handless arms rose to the sides. A piercing howl of rage rang out, and the nightmarish thing surged toward the petrified little group.

A shriek was closely followed by another. Four bold thieves fought tooth and claw in their frantic efforts to be first through the only other break in the dense shrubs that surrounded them.

Faint with horror, the viscount tried to drag himself up, but the thing was almost upon him. Crowding into his mind came memories of terrible tales of headless queens in the Bloody Tower; of vengeful ghosts and phantoms that at school had been gleefully related by senior boys to shivering new boys; the reports of foul fiends and witches so often recounted in hushed voices in London coffee houses and country taverns. The sounds of flight, the terrified shouts, were fading. He was all alone, and his bones were like water. He could do no more than throw up one arm to protect his head, and shrink back against the tree trunk, waiting in helpless dread for those unearthly glowing arms to touch him.

Silence.

He peeped from under his trembling fingers. Dear God, how hideous it was! Floating above him; those handless arms waving about, and a faint indeterminate odour emanating from it.

A high-pitched nasal wail pronounced, "Your sins has found ye out, evil one! Do ye repent of your vile scheme to ruin a innocent young girl?"

Dizzy and sick, Glendenning gasped out, "I—I do . . ."

"And does ye solemnly swear never to put your wicked hands on her no more?"

An illiterate bogle this, but one did not quarrel with so fearsome an apparition. Through chattering teeth, he declared, "I does— I do! N-never!"

Slowly, the arms sank. If only it would go away! 'Please, God! Make it go, and I'll . . . nevermore . . .'

By all the saints! It was—it was folding in upon itself! Becoming smaller and smaller! Glendenning could bear no more. He was going to faint . . . like a girl. . . . Perhaps because his eyes were closing, the odour was clearer. *Fresh baked bread!*

His eyes shot open.

The ghost had melted into a glowing pile on the ground, and was being gathered up by—

"Amy!" he croaked.

She looked down at him. "Can you get up?"

"No," he declared, humiliation very quickly replacing his superstitious fears. "Do you know you dam-dashed near caused me to have a seizure?"

With a muffled giggle she said, "I might've knowed I wouldn't get no thanks."

He said in sudden anxiety, "Have they hurt you? That shot—"

"It broke me head. The one I had under me arm, lucky fer me." She bent and took his hand. "Come on."

With her help, he struggled to his feet. Dazed but persistent, he panted, "But, you . . . *glowed!* How, on earth—"

"D'ye want to wait about here and gab like a fool till they come back? Or would you as soon live a bit longer? Come *on!*" And then, in a kinder voice, "Oh, crumbs. You can't can ye? Poor lordship. A fat lot of good you done by running away."

"I . . . wasn't running . . . away."

"Not running, anyways," she said, with a jeering laugh he thought most insensitive. "Lucky I brought Lot. You can ride him. It won't be the Lord Mayor's Coach, y'r honour. But it'll have to do."

There was so much he wanted to say, so much he wanted to ask. But it was all he could do to lean against the tree where her strong hands had propped him, and, when she returned, to drag his protesting body onto the donkey's back and be carried, most unheroically, to safety.

"All I said," repeated Enoch Tummet, adjusting the black bow that tied back his temporary employer's thick hair, and regarding it with approval, "was as it struck me as a odd thing. O-d-d odd." He peered critically at the haughtily handsome face in the mirror, and reached over to loosen a lock of hair too tightly drawn back above the flaring right eyebrow.

"Devil take you!" snarled August Falcon, slapping his hand away. "Don't do that!"

Tummet's bright brown eyes twinkled in his square and rugged countenance. "Makes you look 'uming, mate," he said irreverently. "Don't please the females if a gent looks like a froze codfish."

"One," said Falcon, his own midnight blue eyes glittering, and his voice dangerously quiet, "for the five hundredth time, do—not—call—me—*mate!* Two, since I appear still to live and breathe, I suspect I am sufficiently human—not necessarily a desirable trait. Three, I have no cause to believe the ladies are either displeased, or that they regard me as in any way 'frozen.' "

"Right ye are, guv," said Tummet agreeably. "Orf, I was. Ain't nothing froze about yer." He turned away and, under his breath, muttered, "A perishing volcano, more like it!"

Falcon, the possessor of excellent hearing, murmured, "I only pray that someone, someday, will explain to me how I was so fortunate as to inherit you to impersonate my valet."

"Easy, ma— sir. Me guv'nor, Captain Rossiter, went orf 'crost the water on 'is 'oneymoon. And I don't like boats."

"Ships."

" 'Swhat I said. And then yer valet's pa come down ill, so 'e left yer. And, bang-and-slam, 'ere I am."

Falcon shuddered. "I think my mind is failing me. Logical enough. Between you and Morris, there's—"

"Which reminds me. 'E's waiting. Dahnstairs, mate. Sir mate!"

Falcon's cold gaze slanted to him, and Tummet offered his broad engaging grin.

"Do I dare to hope your legal employer has returned with him?" enquired Falcon.

" 'Ain't no 'arm in 'oping, is there?" But Tummet saw the dangerously thin line of the mouth, and added hurriedly, "The lieutenant come alone."

Falcon rose, slipping a great sapphire ring onto his slender hand. "He shouldn't be here, when we're engaged to fight tomorrow morning! Damme, but the man has as much breeding as—" He directed a simmering glance at his pseudo valet. "As me, eh guv? Lord love yer, I ain't got no breeding, and I knows it. Don't worry me none. What I see of them as got breeding, they're always running about losing all their rhino— that's money to you, mate—or shooting of each other if one looks at the other sideways, or being bored and miserable. Now—take me on the other 'and; I lives a very jolly life. I can—"

He was interrupted by one of Falcon's rare laughs. "I don't doubt you can, you accursed hedgebird. Get out my coli-chemarde and check the blade. Morris has likely come to tell me that Lord Kadenworthy is agreeable and our meeting will take place tomorrow, as scheduled."

Tummet pursed his lips. "The lieutenant should've let 'is seconds come and tell yer that, guv."

Falcon grunted, and strolled to the stairs thinking that James Morris was perfectly aware of the correct protocol to be observed in an *affaire d'honneur*. It would be astonishing if the pest was here for any other purpose than to moon over Katrina.

His suspicions were borne out when he entered the morn-ing room to find his beautiful sister laughing merrily with the lieutenant, and holding a great bouquet of pink and white roses.

"What the devil are you doing here, Morris?" demanded Falcon. "I would think I've made it plain that you are not welcome in my house."

"Oh, now, August," said Katrina, smiling at him. "How can you scold, when Lieutenant Morris has brought me such lovely flowers?"

"We've a garden full of flowers, and I fancy our gardener is not become too aged and decrepit to pick you some!"

His eyes dreamy, Morris said, "Miss Katrina looks like a bride, don't she?"

"Which she will become when a worthy gentleman asks for her hand!"

Morris sighed. "Dished again," he said mournfully.

"Always supposing I care for the worthy gentleman." Katrina spoke quietly, but she seldom voiced any opposition to her autocratic brother, and Morris brightened.

Falcon was both irritated and disturbed by this glimpse of insubordination. He scolded, "You should know better, ma'am, than to receive Morris alone, and—"

"Besides," put in Morris, picking up an earlier thought, "it ain't your house. Belongs to y'father."

"Who is here in all his glory." Mr. Neville Falcon's elegantly bewigged head appeared from around a deep chair, and his whimsical grin was levelled at his son. "Wherefore, Katrina and Lieutenant Morris are properly chaperoned, dear boy, so do not be flying into the boughs."

August crossed at once to shake his father's hand and utter a polite greeting. "I had thought you was in Sussex, Papa. What brings you back to Town?"

"Boredom, of course." With a little difficulty, Mr. Falcon extricated himself from the chair. "I know you thought I was safely tucked away for a month or so, but I can stand just so much of sylvan solitude and then must again inflict myself upon you. However naughty I may have been."

August looked irritated. Katrina gave a trill of laughter. Morris was considerably shocked. This plump little gentleman, with his merry good humour and mischievously twinkling eyes, was the last type he would have expected to have sired such a volatile individual as August, or such a ravishing beauty as Katrina. One could only assume that his children had taken after their mama's family. Certainly, Mr. Falcon had neither his heir's looks nor his fiery temperament. In fact, that last speech might give one the impression that Neville Falcon was the son, and August the stern parent. As for Mr. Falcon's attire, Morris could scarcely keep from staring.

Neville Falcon wore a pigeon wing tie wig, but the solitaire attached to the bow at the back was not the customary thin black riband, being instead a bright scarlet, continuing around the throat above the white stock. The lacy jabot was exceptionally full, foaming out from his chest, and causing the gentleman, in Morris' opinion, to resemble a pouter pigeon. His coat was impeccably tailored, but the deep purple velvet made a poor blend with the lavish scarlet embroidery on the great cuffs of the sleeves and down the front panels. No less garish was his puce waistcoat adorned with silver flowers; and although his unmentionables were an inoffensive pale blue satin, they did nothing to improve matters.

When Morris first arrived he had been somewhat stunned by this sartorial extravaganza, but his full attention, as usual, had been upon Katrina, exquisite in a dainty green muslin gown. Receiving again the full effect of the father's glory, Morris blinked and glanced at the son, the epitome of good taste, in a blue coat whose very simplicity emphasized his dark good looks.

"Sir," said August, frowning, "I fear your remark will give our—guest—a wrong impression."

"Oh, no," argued Morris. "Not in the slightest, sir. Assure you. 'Nature never put the heart of a hen into a tiger!' "

Mr. Falcon stared at him blankly. August closed his eyes for a second. Suppressing a giggle, Katrina said she must put her flowers in water, and with a smile that devastated her admirer, left the gentlemen alone.

August turned at once to Morris. "Well?" he demanded curtly.

Morris tore his eyes from Katrina's graceful walk. "Ross is in Town."

"Never put the heart . . . of a hen . . . ," murmured Mr. Falcon in an abstracted way.

"Then we are able to proceed," said August.

"We—ell . . . ," demurred Morris.

"What the hell d'you mean? And for God's sake do not be prating any nonsensical rural aphorisms. Just say it. Plain and simple."

"Can't say anything while you keep tossing jawbreakers about."

"Into a . . . tiger . . . ," murmured Mr. Falcon, striving.

August took a menacing step toward the lieutenant.

Morris grinned. "Found one of my seconds. Lost one of yours. Tio's hopped off."

Roused by his son's blast of profanity, Mr. Falcon blinked

at Morris, then laughed and clapped him on the back. "So you think I'm a tiger, do you my boy? Honesty compels me to admit I ain't. But—I've had my moments." He slanted a sly glance at August and said *sotto voce*, "Tell you a few jolly tales, one of these days."

"God forbid," snapped August.

Mr. Falcon chuckled, wandered to the credenza, and poured three glasses of Madeira.

August demanded, "Do you say we have to postpone again? Dammitall! He gave me his word! Where did the block hop to?"

"Which block?" asked Mr. Falcon, carrying a glass to Morris.

"Tio Glendenning." Morris accepted the glass with a murmur of thanks. "A good enough fellow, y'know. Must be, or he'd never agree to second— Oh—er, your pardon. But he tends to do it, y'know. Vanish I mean. Did the same thing about this time two years since. Everyone thought he'd been—" He cut the words off hurriedly.

Mr. Falcon settled himself into a gold velvet chair that inevitably clashed with his garments. "I must have a word with that young rascal. One of the reasons I come to Town."

Retrieving the third glass, and still fuming, August looked at his father narrowly, then said, "Nothing to do with his brother, I hope, sir?"

"Do you?" said Morris, surprised. "Didn't think you liked Templeby."

"Very perceptive, for I think him a proper knock-in-the-cradle," responded Falcon acidly.

Morris grinned. "We all was at two and twenty. Except you, of course. You probably never was two and twenty. Went straight from short coats into middle-age. Mr. Falcon, was he ever—"

"I do not consider the light side of thirty to be middle-aged," said August, his eyes flashing. "Now be so good as to either leave, which would be preferable, or refrain from jabbering nonsense. Papa—about Templeby?"

Mr. Falcon, who had enjoyed this by-play, sobered, and

said thoughtfully, "Don't know nothing about Michael Templeby. It's Burton Farrier."

The two younger men exchanged taut glances. Morris asked, "Friend of yours, sir?"

"Be damned if I don't resent that," said Mr. Falcon, showing an unexpectedly quelling hauteur.

"My apologies, but you said—"

"I neither have the acquaintance of Mr. Farrier, nor have I the least desire to cultivate it! I merely wanted to warn Glendenning."

"Warn him?" said August. "Is the Terrier sniffing around Tio's reputation, sir?"

Mr. Falcon twirled the wine in his glass and watched it reflectively. "He's sniffing around a good many of our finer families. Looking for something, I think."

"Do you say, Papa, that Farrier is after *any* fine family? Or only those families having Jacobite connections?"

"Egad!" exclaimed Morris. "D'ye think he knows that Tio—"

"Careful!" hissed Falcon, with a glance at the open door.

Mr. Falcon said in a lowered voice, "Nobody *knows*, Lieutenant Morris. Not with certainty. But—there are rumours abroad, no doubt of that."

August nodded. "Farrier was at Hector Kadenworthy's place in Surrey. Slimy as hell. Kade trod carefully, I can tell you."

"Very wise," said Mr. Falcon. "Ain't healthy to step on snakes."

"Is that it, sir?" asked Morris, troubled. "D'you think that miserable hound is after Tio?"

Mr. Falcon said slowly, "I hope not, my boy. I like young Glendenning."

CHAPTER VI

It was ridiculous, thought Glendenning, that he should feel so happy this morning; almost as if he had come home. He glanced up from the small cracked mirror, lowering the razor as he looked around at the stone walls and crude furnishings. This was poverty. Certainly, there was nothing here to make him so light-hearted. It was, he told himself, relief; plain and simple gratitude that he was alive. A trifle stiff, perhaps, and his ankle bothersome, but, considering the hectic events of the previous day, feeling remarkably well. The diagnosis, however, did not quite satisfy his remorseless introspection, and he stared soberly at his own reflection, seeing it not at all. His mind's eye saw instead a dark woodland glade and the flickering flames of a fire that played on four cruel faces. If Amy had not come . . .

"Breakfast! Hurry up, slugabed!"

He smiled faintly as that lilting call rang out. "I'm coming. And I shall expect some answers, my girl, so prepare yourself."

She made no reply, but he heard her low chuckle, and smiled again as he resumed the business of shaving. Last night she had refused his weary attempts to question her, and he'd been asleep almost before his head touched the satin pillow so incongruously placed on the crude straw bed. Today, he promised himself, would be the day of reckoning!

He finished shaving and reached for his wig. The teapot was gone, and the wig was propped irreverently on a head of cabbage. "Of all the . . . !" he muttered, snatching it up and inspecting the inside for unwanted residents. Still holding it, he seized the cane and limped into the kitchen. "Where is my teapot?" he demanded.

Amy, busied at the hearth, spun around. The door was wide open, allowing sunlight to splash into the room and revealing the lush green of grass and trees outside. Birds were carolling industriously, and the air smelled deliciously of frying bacon and coffee. Yet the heart of my lord Horatio quickened not to these delightful things, but to the sparkle in a pair of mischievous dark eyes, the curve of two vivid lips, the dimple that came and went in a petal soft cheek. Today, her snowy blouse was tucked into a full dark skirt on which pink rosebuds were embroidered here and there. Her thick dark hair was bound into two fat plaits tied with pink ribands, and she looked very young and enchantingly pretty.

Meeting his stare, Amy was thinking that his auburn hair curled charmingly, and that the laugh lines at the corners of his green eyes found an echo in the set of the humorous mouth. "*Your* teapot?" she teased.

He had quite forgotten the teapot, and murmured, "Amy, do you know how very lovely you are?"

Her cheeks became as pink as the ribands, and she turned away quickly.

He thought, 'I'm being a lecher again!' "You know very well what I mean," he said. "My wig is not accustomed to being supported by a head of cabbage!"

"Oh, I don't know . . . ," she said provocatively, then squealed, and danced to the far side of the table, as he laughed and made a lunge for her. "Behave," she warned, "or your breakfast will go to Lot. He's waiting, as ye see."

Sure enough, the little donkey stood at the door, looking in with great hopeful eyes.

"He deserves a reward, certainly," acknowledged Glendenning, hobbling over to the shelves and appropriating a carrot. "May I?"

She nodded. "And then sit down, and leave off that silly wig. I like what there is of your curls."

"Why do you call him Lot?" he asked, feeding the carrot to the donkey.

" 'Cause Lot's wife was turned into a pillar of salt, and that's what he does, sometimes."

"You mean he becomes recalcitrant?"

"Cor," she said, staring at him in awe. "What a jawbreaker. What's it mean?"

"It means to be obstinate and refuse to move."

"That's Lot, all right." She clapped her hands and said exuberantly, "Oh, wait'll I throws that at Uncle Ab. Recassy— how does it go?"

"I'll teach you how to say it properly. After you've told me what happened to my teapot."

She added fried eggs to the bacon and toast on a large plate, and carried it to him. "Ye saw what they done—did to it. Now eat."

With belated comprehension he exclaimed in horror, "No! Was my teapot your extra head, then? And they shot it from under your arm? My dear God! You might have been killed!"

He had turned quite pale. Touched, she shrugged. " 'Twas a lucky shot, is all. Nothing to get in a garden-gate about."

"I'd say it was something to get into a *proper* gar— er, state about," he contradicted. "You were holding it under your arm! An inch or so either way . . . !"

The thought that her gallant rescue might so easily have resulted in her own death brought a cold sweat starting on his skin. He seized her hand and pressed it to his lips. "How shall I ever thank you? To think you would take such a risk for my sake! Amy, were you not terrified?"

She jerked away from his clasp and for a long moment stood quite motionless, gazing down at her hand. Then, "Nah!" she said with a curl of the lip. "I ain't no airy-fairy fine lady swooning in the parlour when she's sure there's a gent ready to catch her!"

"You certainly are not!" For some obscure reason the glance he received upon thus agreeing with her was decidedly unfriendly, and he regrouped hurriedly. "What I mean is, you're incredibly brave. I wonder you were not cut!"

"I was, just a little." Her eyes softened. "Now don't be getting all aside o' yerself. 'Twere just a small cut."

He sprang up. "Oh, Lord! Why didn't you tell me? Is it your arm?"

"No, it ain't." She poured ale into his mug, and went on roughly, "And ye'd as well sit yerself down again, 'cause it ain't where you can tend it, so don't waste yer breath argle-bargling! Why don't ye eat? If what I cooked ain't good enough, I'll give it to Lot."

He sat down, and said in a frigid voice, "I was waiting for you, ma'am."

From under her lashes she looked at his proud averted face. A tiny smile curved her lips and, after a minute, she said, "I can't afford to snore in bed all day, mate. I et hours ago."

"I see." He took up a slice of toast and glared at it.

Amy bustled about, singing softly. When she glanced at him again, he was watching her, his face stern, his breakfast untouched. She demanded, "What's the matter with it?"

"I find I am not hungry, thank you."

"Hoity-toity," she jeered, hands on hips. "Now what's got the noble gent all bristly?"

He had decided to be coldly indifferent, but the sight of her standing there like the spirit of the morning, with the two plaits swinging and her glorious eyes full of mischief, made indifference an impossibility. He said angrily, "Why must you always think the worst of me? I was distressed to learn that you had cut your, er—self. Is it a crime that I should worry for you? If I asked about your hurt, 'twas not because I sought to— That is, I had no thought to look at your—" Aware that he was making a hopeless botch of this, and that the mischief in her eyes had become mirth, he said irritably, "By Zeus, madam, you are perfectly safe with me, I promise you! I've never yet sunk to—to abusing a helpless girl!"

She retaliated with a triumphant, "No, and you can't now,

109

can ye, Lord Quality? The ghost made you take a vow last night, and you took it, all shiversome as you was."

Reminded of his craven terror, he flushed, but seeing the peep of the dimple, said with a reluctant grin, "You little wretch! I knew all the time 'twas you!"

"Fibber! Oho, if you could've but seen yer face! I thought you was going to faint!"

"You make a joke of it, Amy, but the truth is that you did risk your life to help me. I promise I mean to do whatever I may to repay—"

Her amusement gone in a flash, she said stormily, "Oh, stow yer gab! Can't ye think of nothing else but paying me off?"

"Dammit!" Again he jumped up and, disregarding the immediate lance of pain through his leg, seized her wrist. "I didn't mean that! Always, you twist what I say, and—"

"Aye, I does," she cried, her voice shrill as she fought and clawed at him. "Let me go! Leave me be, ye dirty . . ."

He released her at once, and stepped back.

She crouched before him like a wild creature at bay, her little knife a glittering upraised menace.

A tense pause. Then he said very gently, "My poor child. How terrible your life has been."

"I ain't your child," she panted. "And much . . . you know o' life." Despite the scornful words, her eyes searched his face in a strangely desperate fashion. Suddenly, she hurled the knife from her, put both hands over her face, and burst into tears.

"Please do not," he begged, horrified. "Amy—please don't cry." He touched her silky hair cautiously, and her sobs seemed to become even more wracking. "Oh, Lord," he groaned. "I'd best go, if I make you so very unhappy."

"Well . . . ye does," she gulped, dragging the back of her hand across her eyes.

"Why? What have I done?"

She sniffed. "You—you won't—eat the breakfast I made ye."

He laughed, limped over to pick up her knife, and presented it with a flourish. "There, madame. Now you may be safe. Amy—please won't you sit and talk to me?"

She hesitated, then smiled through her tears, and bent to restore the knife to its garter sheath. "Oh, all right, then," she said, drawing out the other stool and perching on it. "But I ain't got all day." She dried her eyes on the hem of her petticoat. "You wants to ask yer questions, is that what it is? Go on then, only— *Now* what is you all crimp-faced about?"

This was not the moment, decided the viscount, to explain that a lady should not pull up her skirts in front of a (relatively) strange gentleman. "My apologies," he said humbly. "I expect 'tis just that I'm very hungry."

"Well, *eat*, then!"

Obeying, he attacked succulent toast, bacon that was tangy and crisply delicious, and eggs cooked just the way he liked them. "First," he said, spreading damson jam on a slice of toast, "why did you bother to follow me, and how did you know where I was?"

"I follered 'cause . . ." Amy became intent upon adjusting the position of the butter saucer. "Oh, 'cause ye went off with Uncle Ab's favourite cane. I'd give up, and was on me way home when those silly great bullies started tearing down branches and making noise enough fer ten, trying to build that shelter—what would've come down at the first puff o' wind. You must've goed round in circles, lordship, 'cause ye was close by. So I run home quick, and made our ghost."

Glendenning looked at her over a forkful of bacon. "However did you do it? I never saw such an eerie sight." And struck by a sudden thought, he asked, "What d'you mean *our* ghost? Have you used it before?"

She nodded, her expressive face saddened. "When the *chals* come after me. It keeps 'em away." She grinned. "Frightens most folks away, to say truth."

"So I would suppose. But—"

She raised a hand. "One at a time, melor'. It ain't me what makes the ghost so scary. Uncle Ab does. He calls it 'phossy,' and when he puts it on a old sheet or something—well, you saw how it shines." She hugged herself, chuckling gleefully.

111

"Did you hear how me voice echoed-like when I moaned and laughed at first? That's 'cause I talked into a broken old tin. I couldn't use it after I come out, 'cause then I had to use me hands to hold up the sticks and make me arms longer."

He chuckled, remembering the weird echoing of her laughter, and how those long arms had waved about. "You were truly a magnificent apparition. But where does Absalom get this 'phossy?' What is it?"

"I dunno, lordship. He's a clever one, Ab is." She glanced to the door and leaned closer, whispering, "Promise ye won't tell, but—he's a wizard. A little bit."

How big and solemn were her eyes now; how sweet and fresh the fragrance that hung about her. And how, he wondered, could one be "a little bit" of a wizard?

"He makes it," she confided, "but he won't never let me see, nor tell me how he does it. He says it's a old, old secret, what he learned from some other wizard in exchange fer a picture he made him. And that he swore a awful oath not to tell no one."

Glendenning had never put too much faith in wizards. Witches, everybody knew about, but one heard very little of wizards. Perchance their club was more exclusive. A wizard, however, even a "little bit" of a wizard, might be a tricky customer, and best handled with care. Preoccupied, he chased the last piece of bacon around the plate. Three times, it fell off his fork.

"Oh, for goodness' sake!" exclaimed Amy. "Pick it up, mate, do!" She leaned forward, retrieved the elusive morsel, and popped it into his mouth. "Like that!" Laughing at him, her fingertips lingered for just an instant on his lips, and leaning across the table thus, the neck of her blouse dipped. Enchanted, he gazed at the rich, snowy swell of her breasts, then, with a hissing intake of breath, wrenched his eyes away. "What," he croaked, "kind of picture?"

She drew back, watching him steadily. After a pause, she said in her most scornful voice, "Ye got eyes, aintcha?"

All too aware of that fact, he met her gaze for a brief, guilty moment, and mumbled that he did not take her meaning.

With a contemptuous snort she slipped off the stool. "No!" he exclaimed. "You're cross again, and I am behaving—er, trying to behave properly. Please don't go."

She moved with her graceful swinging walk into the bedroom, saying over her shoulder, "You be just a man, poor thing. And I'm just a gypsy."

Her words threw a shadow over this beautiful morning. Glendenning stared glumly at the empty plate, reliving the touch of her soft fingers on his lips. 'And I'm just a gypsy.' The most beautiful gypsy ever created, but . . . Sighing, he knew it would not be wise to remain here much longer.

"Wake up, Sir Lordship!"

Amy stood in the doorway, holding the painting that hung in the bedroom. "Didn't ye never rest yer peepers on this here?"

Incredulous, he stammered, "Why, yes—but—Jupiter! Do you say *Absalom* painted that?"

"Didn't carve it out with his knife, mate. But he's got one. A big one!"

His face was hot. Ignoring the scornful tone, and the implication of her words, he took up his cane and limped over to inspect the painting.

Almost, the goosegirl seemed alive; almost, one could hear the geese complaining as she hurried them home through trees touched with the fiery blush of sunset. He muttered, "Of course I saw it, but I thought—"

"You thought we'd prigged it, I suppose." She swung the picture away and marched back into the bedroom.

Following, he said, "Amy, I do wish you would try not to be angry with me all the time."

"Then don't look at me so daft," she said ungraciously, struggling to raise the heavy frame. "All soft and sweet one minute, and sneery and top lofty the next."

He dropped the cane and reached up to take her burden and hang it. Turning, he pounced to seize her by the shoulders. "When did I sneer at you, Miss Consett?"

Her teeth flashed in a snarl of fury, and something sharp dug at his ribs.

113

Really angry now, he said, "Strike, then! But if you don't kill me, you'll have to nurse me again, so be sure you strike truly."

She said in a choked voice, "I hate ye, I does! With yer—yer silly red hair, and yer evil eyes."

"I've never treated you in an evil way. Be honest, and own it."

"Green as grass, they is," she evaded, blinking tears away. "And that's bound to be evil. Certain-sure, you *thinks* evil thoughts. Always saying we prig—"

Relenting, he tilted her chin up. "Steal," he corrected, smiling down at her. "And if I judge you, child, 'tis only because of what you've told me yourself."

She wrenched away, and dabbed at her tears with her petticoat. "Always making me blubber. And I never cries! *Never!*"

"I'm sure you don't, for you're the bravest lady I ever met, and—"

"And there ye goes again! Don't do it! Don't!"

The eyes that turned up to him, pleaded. And he knew exactly what she meant, and that he must indeed leave here. While there was yet time. And yet, knowing that, after a breathless moment, he heard himself pleading in turn. "Can we not cry friends, at least? A truce, Amy? For just a little while?"

She swung her head away from his wistful gaze, and stared at the curtained doorway.

Glendenning tugged one thick plait gently. "You've had my given word, and I rate my honour high. Don't fear me. You are as safe as though Absalom stood beside me. You have been so good, and I want to know more of you—both. I want to help."

"Help?" She unwound his fingers from her plait and walked back into the kitchen. "How?"

Retrieving the cane, he hobbled after her. "You asked me to help with your grammar."

"Oh. I thought you was going to offer yer gold, again."

"I won't. I promise. Now, tell me, if Absalom paints so

magnificently, why do you live here in poverty? He must be a great master. He could be—"

"Transported," she interposed, carrying several small boxes to the table.

"Why? You said— Then—he *did* steal the painting?"

"No, he did not! That picture *is* a original. 'Cept"—the dimple flickered—"it's a copied original."

"Absalom *copies* great masterpieces?"

She nodded. "He don't like to, 'cause it's chancy and takes him a awful long time, but—sometimes . . . Like, if he gets took ill, or I do. Or if his teeth gives him pepper—his teeth can't abide him, he says—well, then, there ain't much choice."

"But the man has enormous talent. Why run the risk of arrest and imprisonment? Why not paint his own pictures?"

She crossed to the shelves and came back carrying the long curving piece of wood she had been working over when he'd first arrived. He moved quickly to pull out the stool for her, and she gave him a faintly wondering look as she sat down.

"Who'd buy em? A picture painted by an unknown gypsy? Cor! You *are* green, yer viscountship! Poor Uncle Ab would be lucky to get sixpence fer it. And paint's dear. When, a' course," she added sardonically, "we don't prig it."

"Now be a good girl, Miss Consett, or I won't tell you that you should say 'of' course, not 'a' course. And you must forget that 'cor,' 'prig,' or 'ain't' ever sullied your ladylike ears."

She pulled back a glossy plait and asked eagerly, "*Is* they ladylike, melor'?"

He ran the tip of one finger lightly around the delicate curve of the ear thus revealed, and murmured, "They are perfection."

Amy shivered.

Recovering himself, he said briskly, "Er, yes! Now tell me, who does buy Absalom's copies? Is he well paid?"

"He once got a guinea," she said, turning her attention to the piece of wood. "But I don't know who bought that one. It was of a man wearing a funny-looking helmet. Not a pretty picture, like the one in the bedroom. I wanted that one so much, Uncle Ab give—gave it to me for Christmas last year.''

"The man with the funny-looking helmet," he probed. "It wouldn't—it couldn't have been a *golden* helmet by any chance?"

"Yes, matter o' fact." She rummaged in one of the boxes.

"Jupiter!" he said under his breath. "One trusts Mr. Rembrandt don't put a curse on him!"

"What did you say?"

"Oh, nothing of importance. What are you about now?"

She sat straighter, so that he could see her work. It was the top bar of a chairback, beautifully carven, and inset with gold leaf, enamel, and stones, to form an intricate design. "They wanted a extra chair," she explained, selecting a piece of mother-of-pearl from one of her little boxes. "So Ab built it, and I'm making the top to match with the rest. It's about done."

"Why, how clever you are! Are you given much of this type of work?"

"No. But sometimes I fixes the lids for dressing cases—things like that. Depends what Uncle Ab can find fer me. He goes to a lot of shops what sells—*that* sells to the nobs. This don't pay much, but"—she twinkled up at him—"every little helps, eh?"

"Yes. Absalom taught you, I collect?"

"Mmm. He does the carving. Like that there cane. You should see some of the things he makes. A jeweller told him he's got the hands fer it." She placed the mother-of-pearl fragment into one spot, then tried another.

Watching interestedly, Glendenning said, "He seems to have taken good care of you, I'll own. But—this isn't much of a home for you."

"I'm safe," she said, bristling at once. "He's kept me safe from the *chals*. You shoulda seen that, last night!"

"They weren't *chals*," he argued. "They were Londoners. They said something about having been employed by a squire." He eyed her narrowly. "Is there any reason why a country squire would seek you?"

Her head flung up and her eyes glittered. "Why not? Absalom broke into the squire's mansion and stole his butler, and sold the poor cove to the king of Lilliput. And the silly arse of a squire ain't been able to open his front door since, so—"

Glendenning's shout of laughter interrupted her.

"Oh, Amy! What a delightful puzzle you are! But how *ever* are you to become a lady if you use such terms?"

"I might surprise ye," she said, twinkling at him.

"You constantly surprise me. How did you contrive to read Gulliver?"

"A fine lady in a carriage throwed it at her husband and it—" She hesitated, then said carefully, "*Came*—through the window. So I picked it up and run."

"Ran, Mistress Consett."

She sighed. "I can't get 'em right all the time."

"You've a quick ear. You'll do splendidly, I don't doubt."

Brightening, she said, "That's what Uncle Ab says. 'Sides, he heard a duchess talking once, and she swore something dreadful, so I'm going the right direction, ain't—isn't I?"

He smiled. "Perhaps. But I'd rather hear you speak like a gentlewoman, m'dear."

"Oh. All right. I'll try. Still," she appended, beaming up at him, "how many gentlewomen ever made ye laugh like that?"

It was a home question.

The Countess of Bowers-Malden held the calling card at arms' length and said without warmth, "You are on the staff of General Underhill, Mr. Farrier?"

Standing before her chair in the richly appointed red saloon at Glendenning Abbey, Burton Farrier bowed.

She viewed his sober grey habit disparagingly. "Yet you do not wear uniform."

He bowed again, and the countess' thought that she did not care for his persistent smile was strengthened.

"There are some matters, ma'am," he said with an apologetic gesture. "Matters of a . . . sensitive nature, one might say, that are better handled in civilian dress."

She observed coldly, "You mean you are a spy."

Up went both white hands in horror. "I'faith, no, my lady! Nothing so vulgar."

"What do you want with my son?"

"I came on a matter which need not disturb a lady. 'Tis why I had asked to see Mr. Templeby."

"Mr. Templeby is in London."

"Ah. And Lord Bowers-Malden, I am told, is in Ireland. Perhaps—Lord Glendenning?"

Lady Nola wondered if that smile might be amputated. She said, "The viscount visits friends."

"In company with his brother, perchance?"

"Not to my knowledge. Nor do I see how Lord Horatio's whereabouts need concern you, Mr. Farrier."

Another bow. A faintly wounded air. "If I am concerned, dear ma'am, 'tis only that because of the apparently dire emergencies that have called your husband and sons from your side, I am forced to—"

"I do not recollect," she interrupted glacially, "that I described the absences of my menfolk as being due to 'dire emergencies.' "

"Oh, dear me. How I offend. I humbly apologize. It just seemed odd, you know. That *all* your gentlemen would leave you, my lady. But then, perhaps I am overly protective where the fair sex is concerned."

Her sense of danger was strong. She said, "I have little time to spare, Mr. Farrier. You will do better to overcome your protective impulses and say whatever it is you have come to say. Pray be seated."

He thanked her, and sat watching her, his smile positively benign. "It is, my lady," he said in his soft voice, "in the matter of a jewel thief. A very clever fellow who conspires with a servant in some fine house, removes a piece of great value, copies it, and returns the copy in place of the original."

"Indeed? We have had nothing stolen, sir. But I thank you for the warning."

"Ah, but ma'am, how would you know? This, you see, is why I am sent to you. I am expert, and can detect a copy in an instant. The general was most anxious that your valuables be verified as authentic, for you have some pieces he holds in high esteem."

"I suppose that *might* explain why a general in His Majesty's service would feel called upon to investigate the activities of a common thief."

Farrier laughed softly, and clapped his white hands. "Ah, but you are too clever for me, my lady. Rumour hath spread its wings, I see. How astonishing that word of the list should have reached you so swiftly!" He leaned forward. "But *you* have nothing to fear, ma'am. So loyal a family as the Laindons are not suspect, I do assure you."

Lady Nola experienced the sensation that a cold wind had breathed upon her. 'Tio!' she thought. 'This horrid creature is come after Tio!' Trying to sound calm, and dreading lest she had turned pale, she said, "List? What kind of list, sir? And how does it concern us?"

"It does *not*, my lady! Of that there can be no doubt. But I will explain, in the fervent hope that you will not be too provoked with me for having twisted truth's tail, as they say. 'Twas required of me in the course of duty, and from no wish of mine own." He looked at her soulfully, and receiving no response save for her steady stare, went on: "There has come to light, madam, a list, drawn up by the traitor Charles Stuart."

The countess felt quite breathless, but she managed to keep her gaze fixed unwaveringly upon this serpent and his grin.

"You will have heard, I feel sure," Farrier continued, "of the treasure that was donated by the Jacobites to finance their treacherous cause?"

"I heard," she acknowledged, "that much was given by ill-advised supporters, but was received too late to be of help to the prince. And that nothing is known of what became of it."

"Very true. Egad, but I cannot fail to admire so well-informed a lady! At all events, there was a list made of everything the Jacobites received. Each donation was given a number and, on a separate sheet, another list contained the names of all those who contributed. Beside each name were noted the numbers of the appropriate items on the first list, so that after the war, restitution could be made. Ah, I see you are shocked, ma'am."

"Indeed, I am," she said, struggling to command her voice, and wondering if the name of her beloved but exasperating stepson was on that accursed list. "I am shocked to think that loyal Englishmen would indulge such folly!"

"The point exactly, ma'am. They are *not* loyal! But they are about to be unmasked, for—the list is in our hands now!"

The room seemed to swim before her eyes. She said, "Then you can arrest them all."

The lady had become very white, noting which Mr. Farrier looked down to hide the triumph in his eyes. Spreading his hands, he sighed, "Would that we could. Alas, we have only the first list, which describes the *articles* contributed. The names—ah, if we had that!"

"You will pardon my obtuse brain," said the countess, able to breathe once more. "But I fail to see what all this has to do with the activities of a thief."

"Ah, well, that was my little subterfuge, ma'am. One does not wish to distress ladies unnecessarily. And I am sure that in your case it would be unnecessarily."

A terrible premonition began to hover at the edges of Lady Nola's mind. She said, "Do you say, Mr. Farrier, that you believe *this* family has donated articles to the cause of Charles Stuart?"

He sprang to his feet, and with a hand over his heart said, "Heaven forfend, ma'am! The very *thought* that the threat of imprisonment; the confiscation of all the earl's properties; the horrors of questioning and execution for High Treason! That such terror might come upon so splendid a family!" He took out a lace-trimmed handkerchief and mopped his brow. "Faith! It quite unmans me!"

"Mr. Farrier," said the countess, rising and looking down on him from her commanding height, "you weary me. I take it that you wish to ensure that certain valuables are still in our possession and have not passed into the hands of Bonnie Prince Charlie. Shall you require a complete inventory? Or have you a specific area of interest? Deeds of Trust? Livestock? Silver? Strong box? Antiques?"

Again, he looked grieved. "You are vexed. How should I blame you? I am desolate to so offend. But—the general, ma'am. I have no choice, alas, and must do as I am bid. Forgive, but—if I might just be allowed to see your jewellery?"

With regal steps despite her trembling knees, the countess walked to the door.

Farrier leapt to open it and bow her out. As he accompanied her along the hall, she asked, "May I know if there is any particular piece that interests the general?"

He said apologetically, "You will laugh, ma'am. You will snap your pretty fingers in my stupid face. But—you own, I believe, a very ancient plaid pin?"

CHAPTER VII

Glendenning reached for the cane, then stood staring down at it and turning it slowly in his hands. His head seldom troubled him now, and his ankle was sufficiently healed for him to dispense with the cane. It was eleven days since he'd come crashing into Amy's life, and he acknowledged guiltily, that he should have gone home before this.

He doubted that Lady Nola would be worrying, for it was not uncommon for several months to elapse between his visits to the abbey. But quite often Michael would appear at his flat, or they'd run into each other somewhere about the Metropolis. And Samuels, his head groom, who doubled as his man when he was in Town, was a regular mother hen since he'd been shot down while carrying that Jacobite cypher. Remembering, Glendenning's grip on the cane tightened involuntarily. That had been damned close. Except for Dimity, he'd not be alive today. Dimity—who was now Lady Anthony Farrar . . . He closed her out of his mind hurriedly. And then there was Falcon, who would be beside himself, for the date they'd set for his duel with Morris had come and gone!

Sighing, he propped the cane against the wooden crates and limped into the kitchen. These past three days had been an oasis of peace in his rather hectic life. He had begun to help Amy with her tasks, as well as to correct her grammar. She responded eagerly to his instruction and was quick to learn not only the correct usage, but also the cultured accent. Each sentence correctly spoken became a small triumph for her, and her delight when he praised her was touching.

He had insisted upon accompanying her when she drove the donkey cart into Epsom to deliver her completed chairback. Afterwards, they'd gone shopping, and he'd been angered to note how the eyes of the men followed her. She had been radiant that day, and had danced for joy in her spontaneous way when he'd bought her a bright silken scarf and blue ribands for her hair. Small things, he thought rather sadly, to have thrown her into such transports.

Always, she was full of questions about London life and fashions, and the Court. He'd done his best to gratify her curiosity, often coming to grief when attempting to describe the gowns and coiffures of the ladies, so that she would dissolve into peals of laughter and tell him he was a great silly, who wouldn't know warp from weft—whatever that might mean. In the evenings, he chatted with her lazily, watching her quick light movements as she bustled about at her cooking, or tidied the rooms, or worked at some task for Absalom. Sometimes, while listening to the quaint songs she sang, he would meet her eyes across the room, and smile at her. At first, she'd returned his smile cheerfully, but of late he noticed that the thick curtain of her lashes would sweep down, and she would avoid his eyes. She seemed also to revert to her coarse ways of speech and for no apparent reason would take him in strong aversion. Suspecting that she was tired of the extra work he caused, he'd tried to be of more help, but his efforts seemed to exacerbate her ill humour, and she would tell him ungraciously to sit down and stop getting underfoot. Fortunately, she soon got over these odd fits, and would be as bright and light-hearted as ever, drawing his attention to the shape of a cloud, or the wonder of a blooming weed, or the patient crawl of a caterpillar, so that he marvelled at her ability to find beauty in the most commonplace things, and envied her passionate zest for life.

So had the golden days drifted past, and for the first time in a very long while, he'd been content. 'When Absalom comes back,' he'd told his niggling conscience. 'When Absalom comes back, I'll go.' But Absalom had not come back. Several times he made up his mind that the farewells must be said, but then he would recollect the expression in the eyes of men who had ogled her in Epsom, until his fierce glare had sent them off. And he thought of the louts who had tried to make him lead them to her, and of the *chals* who lusted after her. Wherefore, increasingly aware of her vibrant beauty, he was afraid to leave her alone in the ruined house in the deep woods.

She was singing now. A rather plaintive song today. Her voice was exceptional only because of the feeling she imparted to the words, and the pathos of this particular melody disturbed him, so that he went outside to find her. She had set up a small table in the little clearing at the top of the steps, and was busily arranging battered knives and forks and positioning the cracked and ill-assorted plates with as much care as any superior butler might do.

As if she sensed his presence, she stopped singing and turned around. The new scarf was draped across her shoulders, the blue ribands were wound among the plaits that were arranged into thick coils beside each ear, and her eyes were bright and happy. "Surprise!" she called. "We're going to have breakfast out here, Tio." She spread her arms, as if to embrace the sun-splashed trees and the blue sky. "Oh, ain't— isn't it a glorious day? Look! Look! There's old Bill!" She tugged at his hand, pulling him to the edge of the trees and pointing to where a rook perched on a limb, his black garb shining in the sunlight. After a brief glance at the bird, Glendenning looked down at her again, and thought smilingly that she seemed as the spirit of this bright morning, all purity and youthful exuberance.

"Watch," she commanded. "And stand very still, mind." She whistled a lilting little rill, and the rook tilted its head, then sang the same rill. Amy threw the viscount a sparkling glance and went to break a piece off the loaf and toss it in the air. With a whirr of wings the bird zoomed down, caught the bread before it struck the ground, and zoomed away again.

"There!" exclaimed Amy proudly. "I taught him how to sing for his share. Ain't he the clever one?"

"Yes," he agreed, not wishing to spoil the moment by correcting her lapse. "And lucky to have such a lovely lady teach him how to beg."

Her eyes shot to him, the stormy look in full force. "Sit down, and I'll fetch yer breakfast," she muttered.

"I'll help." He followed her into the house, but he still could not walk without limping, and she was carrying out a plate of cold sliced pork and a board of bread, butter, and pickles before he had a chance to pick up anything, her movements so swift and forceful that he knew she was angry.

The smell of coffee in the open air was delicious, but she slammed his mug down so hard that he had to jerk back his hand to avoid being scalded. He said nothing, wondering what he'd done, and confirmed in his belief that women were the most unpredictable of creatures.

Stirring sugar into his coffee, he asked cautiously if she was not feeling well.

"Yes, I is."

"Why do you say 'is' when you know it should be 'am'?"

" 'Cause I'm iggerant."

"You are not ignorant, but I think I have angered you. What have I done?"

"Nothing," she said sullenly, reaching for the pickle jar.

He took it up and offered it, and perversely she pulled back her hand and gazed at the cellar wall in such a way that he wondered it did not catch fire.

"You know you crave a pickle," he said, trying to make her smile.

Lightning swift, she snatched the jar, speared a pickle and waved it at him ferociously. "So now I got one, ain't I!"

Without waiting for the musical invitation Old Bill swooped, snatched the pickle, then dropped it in the dirt.

With a squeal of wrath, Amy threw her fork after the bird, and shouted, "Sneak and snitch, you son of a"—she glanced at Horatio from the corners of her eyes, reddened, and finished awkwardly—"witch."

Glendenning gripped his lips tightly in an effort to preserve a solemn countenance. She ignored him, but the dimple hovered. He extracted another pickle, went to her side, and dropped to one knee. He recited,

> *"I have here a gift for a lady fair,*
> *Who's sweet, petite, beyond compare."*

Amy laughed, and blushed a deeper pink. "Get up do, you silly great creature!"

> *"With the kindest of smiles,*
> *And such glorious hair."*

He paused, gazing at a glossy tendril of that same hair, and thinking that it was indeed glorious.

Amy peeped at him from under her thick lashes, and asked in a very soft voice, "Are you done with your foolishness, Lordship Tio?"

"Eh? Oh—no." He felt oddly muddled. "Let's see now . . .

> *"Yet her passion, alas,*
> *Must all females be fickle?*
> *It burns not for me,*
> *But for this lowly pickle!"*

She clapped her hands, and her merry peal of laughter rang through the clearing.

Glendenning waved his offering under her nose. "Now that I have charmed you with poesy, you must forgive mine offense, dear lady. And do not be looking a gift pickle in the mouth."

Still laughing, she accepted his "gift." "Get up now, or you'll hurt your poor ankle."

"What? No word of thanks? No vows of undying gratitude? Then I shall claim a kiss in return for my efforts!"

She was suddenly very still, almost as if she had ceased to breathe.

Glendenning took up her hand and kissed it, manoeuvreing around the pickle. "Hmm," he said, struggling to his feet again. "Your dainty fingers are somewhat briny, m'dear, but—" And he stopped, because she was gazing up at him with a look he had never seen before. An awed, almost reverent look. He said, "Why . . . Amy," and touched her cheek wonderingly. Always, she was quick to draw away if he attempted to so much as hold her hand, but now she did not evade that simple caress.

The breeze tossed the leaves gently, the warm air was heavy with the scents of honeysuckle and woodsmoke, and the sun struck fiery gleams from the auburn hair of the man and painted the shadow of a small wayward curl upon the girl's smooth cheek. And for a long moment, neither of them moved.

Old Bill was the villain who shattered that brief enchantment, seizing his opportunity to swoop down again and appropriate a morsel of bread.

Amy gave a start and looked at the pickle as if she could not understand how it came to be in her hand.

Glendenning limped around to sit at the table again, and stare at his plate blankly.

In a hurried, breathless fashion, Amy said, "Ye'll never be saying you made that up? Out of empty air?"

"It was worthy of the Bard—no?"

"Get away with you! *Did* you make it up?"

It seemed difficult to collect his thoughts. "I—er—"

She managed a chuckle. "Ye doesn't remember?"

"Of course I do." Recovering himself, he boasted, "It had the power of Chaucer, the brilliance of Shakespeare himself! And to think 'twas composed by"—he bowed—"your very humble, obedient."

"Humble, is it!" Smiling, she forked some pork slices onto

his plate. "Still, 'twas very nice, and here is your reward, clever lordship."

"Most gratifying. I'm famished! This looks jolly good, Amy."

"I bought it from a farm wife this morning."

"This morning!" He looked up, frowning. "I wish you'd not go off without telling me."

"Does ye, indeed?" Carving a piece of bread, she offered it on the end of the knife. "I went about alone before you co—came. And I'll do the same after you goes, so don't get into a garden-gate."

"Go," he corrected absently. What she said was truth, of course. But if he was getting into a state, he felt his concern justifiable. He would have a word with Absalom. "Jupiter!" he exclaimed, hunger taking command. "Was there ever such a smell as newly baked bread?"

Amy sank her white teeth into a crusty buttered slice, and said a rather indistinct, "Never!"

They ate in silence for a while, bathed in the peace of this brilliant morning. But at length, Glendenning asked, "Why were you so cross with me just now?"

She did not reply for a minute, then with the flirt of one white shoulder said, "Reasons."

"What reasons?"

"Just . . . reasons."

"That is *un*reasonable, Amy, and a typically feminine evasion."

"Well? I'm a feminine, ain't I?"

"You are not. You are a female. And that's another thing. Why do you always allow your speech to lapse when you are vexed with me?"

"Reasons."

He gave an exasperated groan, and she giggled and told him to eat and not talk so much. But a moment later she murmured, "Did you write lotsa poems to your Mitten?"

His breath was snatched away. He feigned a laugh. "Good Lord, no! Do not be fancying that London is littered with my—ah, masterpieces."

Despite the light tone, he was watching her intently, aware of which she adjusted the shining coil of one plait, and murmured, "It's none of my bread-and-butter, so there ain't no call to fib, lordship."

"Nor," he said, annoyed, "do I make a habit of telling falsehoods."

"No? Then you must've dreamed it all, I suppose."

"I do not take your meaning, ma'am."

"You talked about it that first day. I told you."

"You said I mentioned Mitten, but—"

"There's iggerance fer ye. I musta used the wrong word, 'cause it was a sight more'n a mention, sir. Fairly raved about her, you did. And a poem you'd give her. And a lotta gab about Charlie somebody."

'God save us all!' he thought. He must have been delirious, and babbling of the Jacobite cypher he had carried! " 'Twas a private—er, poem, Amy. I would be glad if you'd not speak of it to others."

"Would you?" Standing, she began to gather up the plates. "You must've liked her if you wrote her a poem."

Irritated, he snapped, "I did not write her a poem. Exactly. 'Twas—"

"Lor', but ye're ruffled up. Why? 'Cause she wouldn't have you?" She laughed tauntingly. "That there poem didn't do ye much good, did it?"

He stood, and said at his haughtiest, "You are perfectly correct. The lady would have none of me. And besides being a very poor sentence, your remark was unkind."

"Much I care," she stormed, and flounced into the kitchen with her plates.

Seething, he made up his mind. He would leave today! She very obviously—He heard a crash then, and ran.

In the bedroom, Amy knelt on the floor weeping heartbrokenly. One of the crates had fallen, and lay beside her, the contents scattered about.

He rushed to draw her to her feet, and put his arms about her, stroking her hair, trying to comfort her. "There, there,

129

never weep so. Oh, Gad, what a brute I am to have again upset you!"

"Yes, you is," she confirmed brokenly. "But . . . but why shouldn't you be? All ye thinks o' me is that I . . . I'm just a iggerant thieving gypsy what . . . what goes about . . . *begging!*"

"Of course I don't think such stuff," he said, kissing her forehead tenderly.

Clinging to his cravat, she wailed, "Yes ye does! You—you said I'd taught Old Bill how to *beg!*"

The last word was scratchy, but uttered with such loathing that he comprehended how deeply he had wounded her with his clumsiness. Remorseful, he said, "Dear little soul—may I be accursed if I meant to imply—"

Her fingers flew to cover his lips. Her eyes, very wide, looked up at him fearfully. "Oh, don't ye never invite no curse, Tio! Don't ye!"

He appropriated her hand and pressed the soft palm to his lips. "I' faith, but I deserve it for being so thoughtless. How could I think evil of you, when you very likely saved my life? Don't you know how much I respect your courage, your unfailing ingenuity? Only think what good comrades we've been. I've helped you with your grammar, and you have taught me so much!"

She sniffed, and murmured wistfully, "What have I taught you, Lordship?"

"Why—how to peel a potato, for one thing, and—"

"Oh." The dark screen of her lashes lowered, and she gave a shaken laugh. "You peeled it all away!"

"The first one, perhaps. But I did better with the second. Come now, own it."

"You did so much better that dinner was late because I had to bind up your thumb."

"Yes. Er, well then, I learned how to bargain with farm wives, and—"

"And how to prig cacklers," she teased, the twinkle coming back into her dark eyes.

He laughed, grateful that the tears had ceased. His arm was still about her. It was warm and quiet in the old cellar, only bird songs and the rustling of leaves breaking the silence. Suddenly, he was very aware that he stood in a bedchamber, with a beautiful girl in his arms. Her red lips were slightly parted, showing the tips of the even white teeth. He felt drowned in the great velvety eyes upturned to him. Her lovely body was so soft . . . so inviting. As one in a dream, he bent to her mouth.

His kiss was very gentle, and her lips responded with a sweet and tentative innocence. He kissed her again, harder, and when she tried to draw back, his arms crushed her closer.

Fear came to Amy. She fought to get away, but desire was in his green eyes, and he was much stronger than she had realised. She wrenched her head away, but his lips were on her cheek, sliding down her throat. Between kisses, he murmured husky promises, tender words of endearment.

"No," she gasped, struggling. "No! Let me be!"

He scarcely heard her. She had kissed him back. She wanted to be loved just as much as he yearned to love her. He slid the blouse aside and began to kiss the warm softness of her shoulder. "I won't hurt you, my beautiful. Don't be frightened."

"I ain't frightened," she lied, sobbing, and straining to push him away. " 'Cause I've got the word of—a gentleman!"

That home truth seemed muffled and distant in Glendenning's ears. She was afraid, that's all it was. But, he wanted her. Oh, how he wanted her! And he would take care of her, always. It wasn't as though he meant to abandon her once she had given herself to him. He tightened his arm, his hungry mouth seeking lower.

Amy screamed shrilly, "Don't! Tio—please, *don't!* Is that—is that all yer honour's worth?"

It was as if a sword had slashed through the mists to reveal stark reality. His word of honour . . . He had given his word of honour to protect her. He'd sworn that she would be safe in his care. Good God! Had he lost his mind? He was a gentleman, and he was violating the Code that he had been taught to revere since childhood. The Code of Honour, unchanging, unassailable, by which a man was judged, and which decreed that above all else, the word of a gentleman must be inviolate. How terrified she looked. Horrified, and with a wrenching effort, he flung her from him and stumbled away, to stand with head down, fists clenched at his sides.

Trembling, Amy watched him, and saw that he also was shaking. She crept up behind him and, very softly, one fingertip touched the cuff of his sleeve.

Unaware of that gesture, despising himself for what he almost had done, and how his mind had sought to justify such a betrayal, he realized that she was saying something, her voice full of sadness.

". . . head has broke off, and Ab made it for me. If you hadn't got me so cross, I wouldn't of kicked the crate."

Breathing hard, he fought for self-control. She was offering him an escape from a contretemps a gentleman of honour should not have allowed to happen. He had never forced a woman in his life. Especially a girl so far beneath his own station in life, and to whom he owed so much. He could well imagine what Papa would have to say of such disgraceful conduct. Turning, he found that she was kneeling again, holding two pieces of a broken figurine. She looked so small and so daintily vulnerable. She had trusted him, and he, sworn to protect her, had almost—He muttered shamefacedly, "Amy, I do not know—"

"Only look," she interrupted, holding the pieces up for his inspection. "It's ruined."

He held her eyes levelly. "I don't deserve that you should be so forgiving. I behaved despicably."

"I know," she agreed. "But—you're just a man, ain't ye. Even if you is—Quality."

He flushed scarlet. "I can only beg your forgiveness."

She said nothing, and for a long moment he stood with head downbent, mute and wretched.

Amy gave a little tug at his coat. "You stopped," she pointed out kindly. "There's lots as wouldn't have. Now look at my poor deer. It was so pretty."

Pulling himself together, he raised his eyes to the pieces she held, and was not surprised that she should be so distressed. The small deer had been most beautifully carven from white marble. The head, itself a work of art, had broken off. "Good heavens!" he muttered, taking the sections from her. "Is there no end to your uncle's talent?"

"He does all sorts of things, my Old Ab. He can mend broke pots, and statues and arty things like this. He was making a swan for a lady's garden when you first came, but I told him to stop, 'cause I thought the noise was troubling you."

He remembered the sounds that had puzzled him that first day, and that he'd thought to be the chiming of a little bell. Intrigued, he asked, "But how can he afford to make you such a gift? Surely, this type of marble must be—Now do not fly into the boughs! I am not accusing him of—prigging!"

To hear that word on his lips drew a tremulous laugh from her. "It was left over," she explained. "Sometimes rich folk let him keep whatever he don't use for their things. And he gets bits from jewellers now and then, when they've got something that needs mending. I think it's 'cause they don't know how to fix it theirselves—" She threw up a hand imperiously. "Don't say it! *Them*selves." She was relieved to see his faint grin, and went on: "Ab says sometimes their customers is in a hurry and they can't get things done quick enough to please 'em, so they call on him."

Glendenning turned the little deer in his hands. Pleased by his obvious admiration, Amy asked, "Would you like to see Ab's drawings? He likes to sketch out what he's working on. I'll bring them in the kitchen, and you can look at them while I tidy up."

He was only too willing to do whatever she suggested, so he sat and looked through Absalom's sketches, and the more he saw, the more impressed he became. The man was a master; an extraordinarily talented craftsman. "Small wonder the jewellers hire him," he said. "But they take advantage of the poor fellow. With skills such as these, he should at least be able to afford a better way of life."

Amy put the left-over pork in a stone bowl and covered it tightly. "You think they're good, then?"

"Good! They're absolutely—"

"Here! What you a'doing of?" demanded Absalom, stamping in at the door, the picture of belligerence.

Glendenning scarcely heard him. He was staring, frozen with astonishment, at the sketch of a squat, primitive figure. It was shaped rather like a small gravestone, but with the outline of a face on the front so that the figure seemed all head, with a suggestion of stubby legs beneath. The accompanying measurements indicated a height of three inches, and scattered about the grotesque "face" were five small circles with at the side a notation: rubies here.

"My dear God!" he whispered.

"Oh! What is it?" cried Amy, alarmed by his expression. "Whatever's the matter now?"

He could not at once answer her, and continued to stare in disbelief at the sketch he held. The figure portrayed was of one of the icons carried, apparently for identification, by members of the secret society that he and a small group of friends believed threatened England. The powerful, fanatical, and deadly band they had named the League of Jewelled Men.

The heat of the afternoon was alleviated to an extent by a bustling wind; a pranksome wind, which set Gwendolyn Rossiter's many lace-trimmed petticoats fluttering, and snatched at the pages of her book. Wandering across the lawns toward the summer-house, with Apollo panting at his heels, August Falcon paused to watch with a grin as Gwendolyn attempted to subdue petticoats and pages. Absorbed, she did not notice him, and would have been astounded had she known what was in his mind.

She was an annoyance in his life. A prickly pest whose constant presence here irked him. But there could be no doubt that Katrina missed her dearest friend, Naomi Lutonville—now Mrs. Gideon Rossiter—and that Rossiter's crippled sister had done much to fill the void. Falcon loved only two people in the world, one of whom was Katrina, and he could not thoroughly dislike anyone who made her happy.

Gwendolyn Rossiter, with her quick wit, her merry sense of humour, her outspoken candour, delighted, and was delighted by, Katrina.

Regrettably, Miss Rossiter had also embarked upon a crusade to reform one August Nikolai K. Falcon, and lost no opportunity to pinch at him, so that, however he strove to control it, he invariably lost his temper with her. He had no least desire to be reformed. He was a confirmed cynic, a loner, an arrogant, autocratic, bad-tempered care-for-nobody. And he was also selfish and rude. All of which she had informed him, and with which he, for the most part, had no quarrel. But not content with pointing out his faults, she wanted to make the sinner into a saint, which was irritating and a bore. The simplest way to deal with the vixen was to avoid her like the plague, yet somehow the very sight of her was a challenge, drawing him inexorably into their next battle of wits.

Just at the moment she presented a rather charming picture, with the sunlight gleaming on her unpowdered light brown ringlets, and the great blue skirts billowing about her. The ankle that the wind obligingly revealed was neat and trim. Should a gentleman of limited intellect chance to come upon her seated thus, he might judge her to be quite pretty.

Falcon's musings were interrupted as a heartier gust made off with the wide-brimmed hat that had been loosely tied to hang behind Gwendolyn's shoulders, and she dropped the book so as to catch the hat.

"Maledictions, and confound you, wind," she exclaimed. "Now you've made me lose my place!"

Amused, Falcon retrieved the book, and riffled idly through the first few pages.

"I might have guessed," she moaned. "You *would* come just in time to hear me swear!"

Looking at her, his face darkened. "And I might have guessed you would bring such rubbishing stuff here so as to taunt me again."

"*Au contraire,* kind sir. If it is rubbishing stuff, 'tis your own, for I borrowed it from your book room. As for taunting you—I'll admit that, initially perhaps, I had hoped to awaken your interest in—"

"The other side of my—heritage?"

"Just so. Did you know that when you sneer like that, your lip curls up?"

"But how fascinating."

"Oh, no. And there it goes again. However, what I started to say was that I am myself becoming most interested in—you will forgive if I say the word?—China. 'Tis surprising that I knew so little about such a very big country. This gentleman"—she reached out to reclaim the thin volume—"was a missionary in Peking, and he writes that one of their first emperors discovered how to awaken a flame when he watched a bird make sparks as it pecked at—"

"At his foolish head? 'Tis scarce to be wondered at. But an you are not come to tease me, ma'am, nor to admire my curling lip, why are you here? Faith, but one might think you mean to move in with us."

"Scarce surprising, Mr. Falcon," said she, refusing to be flustered by such rudeness, "when your papa and your dear sister are so very kind to me."

"Whereas I am *unkind*." He strolled to sit on the steps and stretch out his long legs with the fluid grace that characterized all his movements. "Is that what I am to deduce from your saintly rejoinder?"

She considered, then said thoughtfully, "You are kind to your sister. And—sometimes—to your papa." He gave a smothered and contemptuous grunt. "Out of all the world," she appended.

" 'Tis a sad and sorry world, Miss Rossiter."

"To the contrary, the world is beautiful, sir. Mankind brings the sadness and sorrow."

He glanced at the cane lying beside her. "And what of womankind? You have not been gently dealt with. Do you really find the world beautiful?"

"Exceeding beautiful. Only look around you."

"Thank you—no. You would rave of the glories of Nature. I would point out its cruelty, and in striving to open your eyes to plain truth, would merely waste my breath. I shall deny you the opportunity to counter common sense with puerile platitudes. Sad to say, you've spent so much time with Jamie Morris you have memorized some of his idiocies."

"Since the poor young man has so little time left, 'tis as well that somebody should benefit from his wisdom."

"Wisdom! 'Fore heaven, ma'am, he must be a skilled necromancer to have so thoroughly gulled you. The man is a veritable blockhead! And what do you mean by saying he has little time left? Are we to be blessed by his departure at last? Is he called back to active service?"

"Not to my knowledge. But I had understood 'tis your mission in life to fight him."

"Oh. Yes. Well, as you know, we have had a—er, quarrel. For too long!"

"And for a silly quarrel you mean to kill him." She clicked her tongue condemningly.

His shoulders lifted in a bored shrug. "You should be grateful that I am willing to remove such a blot from your beautiful world."

That angered her, and she said sharply, "I think my beautiful world would miss him very much. I know *I* would."

"Such admirable loyalty." He slanted one of his mocking glances at her. "And only because he is your brother's friend. Or—can it be that you nourish a *tendre* for the bumpkin?"

Gwendolyn took up her hat, and with no little difficulty restrained the impulse to fling it in his face. "Alas, but I am unmasked," she said lightly. "Before I die of unrequited love, I shall go and cheer up my rival."

He scowled. "An you refer to my sister, your mission of mercy is unwarranted. She is not despondent."

"No. But she is often lonely."

"Nonsense. She has her family, and is widely admired."

"And isolated."

He began to inspect Apollo's paw for fleas. "Say protected, rather."

"Certainly not. You do not protect. You suffocate. And 'tis a misplaced persecution because—"

"Persecution? Now, damme if—"

"—because your papa is the head of— There's one! There's one!" She gave a squeal of excitement as Falcon caught the parasite and despatched it.

He stifled a grin. " 'Tis past time that you should appreciate my accomplishments. The next honours to you, ma'am. And as for my papa—he has other interests to command his time."

"I know," she agreed outrageously, peering without great enthusiasm at Apollo's neck. "I've—Ugh! It hopped! I've seen some of his—er, interests."

Shocked, he exclaimed, "If ever I heard a lady make such a vulgar remark! And you cannot kill the brutes by looking them to death, Miss Rossiter. The way to do it is—" Irritated by this lapse, he said austerely, "I think my sire's behaviour is none of your affair."

" 'Tis my affair because Katrina is my friend. And were you not entirely too high-in-the-instep"—his angry gasp caused her to rush on before he could voice his indignation,—"you would stop making it your life's work to offend everyone, besides bullying Katrina. But for you, she would be happily wed by now."

"Yes, to some stupid clod like—" He frowned to a sudden suspicion. "Speaking of which, an you came to see my sister, why are you not with her?"

She had been anticipating this question, and said demurely, "Because she went into the house. For a moment."

"Oh." He looked mildly embarrassed, but he had learned not to underestimate this frail-seeming girl, and asked, "Did Ross—I mean, did your brother drive you here?"

She said mischievously, "You have my permission to call him Ross, sir. Many of his *friends* do so. No—do not fly into the boughs. Jamie brought me."

At once inflamed, he sprang to his feet.

"Wait!" Starting up also, she moved too fast and, lacking the support of her cane, she stumbled and fell.

Perforce, he had to help her, but said, seething, "You did that deliberately!"

She fastened a death grip on his arm. "Now, August, for

mercy's sake! Give Jamie a moment with her. She has a kindness for him, I do believe. And he adores her, and is such a
good man. What harm—"

"A *good man* is it? He is an idiot, madam! He has not two
brains to rub together, his family is of mediocre background,
and his prospects are insignificant! When I find a man worthy
of Katrina—"

"You never will," she gasped, clinging like a limpet as he
tried to break free. "In your bitterness and pride, you will
demand a prince of the blood. And—and even did you ever
find one, he'd likely prove to be the very man to make her
*un*happy!"

"If any man—ever—makes Katrina unhappy—" he began
through gritted teeth, then paused as her eyes slipped past
him.

Mr. Neville Falcon, glorious in green and mauve, was hurrying towards them. " 'Pon my soul, August," he panted,
mopping his heated brow. "How you peck at me because I
love the pretties, and here you are, fondling Miss Gwendolyn
where all the servants can goggle. How de do, m'dear?"

His son's finely chiseled jaw sagged. Releasing Miss Rossiter as though she were white hot, he uttered faintly, "Fondling . . . ?"

It was too much for Gwendolyn. She went into such
whoops of laughter that Apollo became alarmed and, rushing
to her side, began to growl at the most likely culprit.

Neville retreated at speed, calling over his shoulder, "I
cannot deal with it, m'boy. Weeping women! Ghastly! I'm a
coward, I know, but . . . there you are." And he vanished
through the gate and into the alley.

Two words broke through August's stupefaction. *Weeping
women.* "Katrina!" he whispered, and sprinted to the house.

He entered through the large dining room, and at once
heard Morris' voice, an odd note to it, coming from the red
saloon. "Damn the swine," growled August, and racing on
with murder in his heart, plunged into the room and stopped
abruptly.

The Countess of Bowers-Malden was seated on the gold

velvet chaise-longue, handkerchief in hand, and head bowed. A pallid Lieutenant James Morris hovered over her, holding a wineglass and looking petrified.

"But he was not at the Cranfords," the countess was explaining in a quavering voice. "So I went up that dreadful Snow Hill to Sir Mark Rossiter's house, but . . . they had not seen him. I could not speak to—to Newby, you know." She looked up at Morris pathetically.

"No, no," he gulped, shoving the wine at her. "All straw and no grain, what?"

Grinning, Falcon backed away.

Gwendolyn hurried up to peep around him, and gave him a little shove. "Well, go on! Go on!"

"Devil I will," he whispered, ducking into the hall and easing the door to. "It's that awful Bowers-Malden dowager."

Indignant, she argued, "But the poor lady sounds distressed."

"So would I be an I went in there!"

"Lieutenant Morris is likely terrified, but at least *he's* trying to help." The Crusading Look came into her blue eyes and her lips pursed up.

Unmoved, he hissed, " 'Tis what comes of being a fatuous and noble block. But you, of course, will be eager to offer him your equally fatuous support. *En avant, mes enfant!*"

Pleased with that snide little speech, he started off.

Gwendolyn grabbed the skirts of his coat. "So here you are, Mr. Falcon," she shrilled at the top of her lungs. "Lady Bowers-Malden has come to see you!"

At once Morris could be heard galloping across the room. Falcon turned a bared-teeth snarl on Gwendolyn, who put one finger under her chin and curtsied.

Morris flung open the door. "Thank G-God!" he stammered, seizing Falcon by the arm with the desperation of a drowning man. "Here he is, my lady!"

"Damn you," hissed Falcon, tearing free. "An that treacherous Glendenning ever appears for our duel, you'll pay for this!"

Her ladyship had risen, and she reached out appealingly.

Falcon had no recourse but to himself '*en avant*,' and bow over her hand.

"I would not have come to you," she said, her face haggard with strain, "for I know you are not a—a close friend of Horatio's but—"

Gwendolyn ran to put an arm about her. "Poor dear lady," she said, all tender sympathy. "Of course you should have come. My brother will be so sorry he was not in London when you needed him, but he has taken Naomi down to Devonshire for a few days. How fortunate that the lieutenant and Mr. Falcon are here, for you know they are only too glad to assist any lady in distress."

Yearning to wring her neck, Falcon said nothing.

Of a far more gallant nature, Morris took up the wineglass once more, and muttered staunchly that he would "be honoured."

Falcon led Lady Nola back to the chaise-longue. "Perhaps you will tell us the nature of your difficulty, ma'am," he said, very obviously bored. "I have obligations, alas, which may forbid I be of service, but I feel sure that my father—"

"Pray do not be foolish, August," said her ladyship, too distraught to temper her notorious tendency towards outspokenness. "Neville is a dear soul, but 'twould be as well to pit a mouse 'gainst the Minotaur."

Morris stared at her uncertainly.

Falcon's chin went up and his eyelids drooped. "You must tell us which Cretan has offended," he drawled, watching the swing of his quizzing glass.

Gwendolyn gave him a sizzling glare, relieved Morris of the wine, and carried it to Lady Nola.

My lady took a sip, the glass trembling in her hand. "A man—came to see me," she said. "He is—is called . . . Burton Farrier."

"Oh! Great jumping Jupiter!" exclaimed Lieutenant Morris.

CHAPTER VIII

Sitting at the kitchen table beside Glendenning, Amy said worriedly, "But he says they wasn't *chals*, Ab!"

Absalom glowered down at the sketch in his hands, and gave a scornful grunt. " 'Course they was. Been after us since I got you outta the tribe, ain't they? 'Sides, they likely want to get their hands on young Florian and that donkey and cart they say he stole, and they'd think as he might be along of us. Don't be listening to what any Quality cove tells ye, my lass." He shot Glendenning a look of burning resentment. "Tricky as a barrel o' monkeys, every last one. Oughta be done away with, says I, or put where they can't—"

"Have done!" Glendenning's voice fairly cracked across that bitter flow. Amy jumped, and Absalom's mouth hung open with surprise. "An I am right," Glendenning went on grimly, "you and Amy are in real peril. And not from *chals*. I have heard more than enough of your rantings, Consett, and I've held my tongue because you've been kind to Amy. And also because I respect genius, and 'tis very clear that you are a brilliant artist whom the world has ignored for too long."

Amy gave a squeal of excitement and hugged her uncle impulsively.

Absalom flushed brick red. Dumbfounded, he tore off his

scruffy wig and wiped a purple kerchief over his shaven head. "Be jiggered," he muttered.

"We may all be jiggered unless you answer my questions," said Glendenning.

"Ask then. But be danged if I can see what—"

"When you took Amy away from the tribe, did the *chals* follow you here?"

"What, d'ye take me for a flat? They follered, but I give 'em the slip, proper."

"Then nobody in the tribe knew you had moved in here?"

"Not nohow. For why? 'Cause we hadn't found it. Not for half a year, about, eh lass?"

Amy nodded, her gaze anxious again, and fixed on Glendenning's stern face. "And they didn't find us fer a long time after that, Tio," she explained. "They must've seen us at one of the fairs, or when we was on the roads, and follered us. But when we set the ghost after 'em, I thought we'd frightened 'em off for good."

"I rather suspect you had." Glendenning lifted a hand as they both began to talk at once. "Consett, I want you to be very sure about this. You say that you had made some small repairs for a jeweller in Canterbury, and that you were in his shop one day when two gentlemen brought in a little figure"—he took the sketch from Absalom's hand—"'like this."

"Aye. 'Twas very old, and valuable, they said. But some fool had dropped it and a piece broke off, and two of the stones had fallen out."

"Did you speak to these gentlemen?"

"Lor'—no! More'n I'd dare do! Mr. Shumaker—he was the jeweller, dead now, poor cove—he didn't want none of his customers to know he didn't do all the work hisself. No, mate. I was hid away in the back."

"And when they'd gone, the jeweller asked you to repair the figure?"

"Right ye are. Poor old Shumaker was afraid of 'em, and didn't dare offend, but he says he couldn't get the work done so soon as they wanted. It was a tricky business, mind yer, and took time, and he had some other gents already complaining 'cause they was having to wait. Rich folk," said Absalom, fixing Glendenning with a hard stare, "allus think their work should be done first."

"Were you able to complete it in time?"

"By the skin o' me teeth." Reminded, Absalom shook his head glumly. "Me poor teeth, what hates me! Still, I got it done at last, and a funny little thing it was, eh, Amy?"

"Yes, in fact— *Now* what's the matter?"

Glendenning steadied himself. "*You* saw this figure, Amy?"

" 'Course she did. I done the work right here, mate."

"Yes . . . You said that the jade was broken."

"So 'twas, but— Hey! It don't say nothing here 'bout it being jade. How'd you know that?"

"I held it in my hands, sometime after you repaired it, I believe." They both stared at him, and the viscount added, "It didn't look to have been broken."

Amy said proudly, "When Uncle Ab does a job, it's done right."

"Thankee, lass. But that were a funny sorta job. Pink jade's rare, but the gents found some. And *particular?* I never see the like of it. They'd got one of the rubies what was lost, but Shumaker had to find another just the right size, and, what with the repair to the jade—cor! I wasn't sure I could do it. Not so exact as they wanted."

Glendenning asked intently, "How exact?"

"To measure the same, to the last fraction of an inch, as it was before it was broke. And to weigh not a featherweight more nor less than what they'd writ down. Phew! When I took it back to poor Mr. Shumaker, we neither of us dared hope I got it right. But 'twixt his giving me three rubies to choose among, and me allowing for the weight of the glue— well, we done it. Though what in the world that's got to do with them bullies what grabbed you in the woods, is more'n I can see."

"I think," said Glendenning, frowning, "it may have every-thing to do with it. Tell me now, and think carefully, when was the last time you scared the *chals* away?"

They looked at each other, and finally agreed it had been about two years.

"We thought 'twas over at last," said Amy ruefully. "But just recent they started creeping about at night, so we knowed—knew we'd have to get our ghost out again soon."

"And this new outbreak of searching for you began before, or after, you worked on the little figure?"

Absalom gasped. "Why—'twere after. You'll mind, Amy? About the same time we heard poor Mr. Shumaker's shop had burned down and him in it, rest his soul!"

She nodded. "Early in April, Tio. But—why?"

General Underhill had warned them all, Rossiter, Falcon, Morris, and himself, that they were not to speak of the conspiracy they suspected. Glendenning chose his words with care. "I believe they think you know something, and they want you dead, so you'll not speak of it."

Amy sprang up and clung to Absalom, and he slipped an arm about her. "You're frightening my girl," he said severely. "If this be some kind of joke, I don't like it."

"Good God! D'you think I would joke about such a thing? Now—one more question, if you please. You said two gentlemen brought the figure to Shumaker's shop. Did you see them? Even from the back?"

"No, sir." Absalom checked, biting his lip in chagrin that the courtesy title had escaped him. Glendenning gave no sign of having noticed the slip, and Absalom went on quickly, "I see their shadows, and that's all. They was both tall men. Taller'n you. One bigger built than t'other."

"What about their speech? Any lisp, or accent—or something of the kind?"

Absalom shook his head. "Gents. Talked fancy—like you." He considered, then added, "Only other thing I recollect was that one of 'em hummed all the time." He looked sheepish. "Silly thing to even mention, but—"

"No, no. What kind of tunes did he hum, do you recall any?"

"Not many to recall, mate. Just one. Over and over, like. Goes like this . . ." He hummed a melody.

"Oh, I knows that," exclaimed Amy excitedly. "But I don't know what it's called."

"I do," said Glendenning. "Though 'tis likely of no significance. It's an old marching song called Lillibulero, and—" He checked as a loud bray rang out. "Was that Lot? I never heard him sound like that."

Amy said uneasily, "He only does it when he's afraid o' something."

"Likely jealous," said Absalom with a grin. "Don't like that there high-bred mare looking down her nose at him."

Amy clapped her hands delightedly.

Incredulous, Glendenning said, "You found my mare?"

Absalom scowled. "Worst day's work I ever done. Had to buy her back. And I wouldn't have got her then, if I hadn't scared the poor cove by saying the rightful owner had sent special constables after her, and he'd get took and topped if he was caught with her."

Amy hugged him hard. "I knowed—knew ye could do it, dear old Ab!"

He smiled at her fondly. "More'n I dare do to come back without her, after the way I was sent off." He scowled at the viscount. "Said she'd leave me, my girl did, if I—" He stopped, frowning as Lot complained again. Putting Amy aside, he said, "Best get out there and harness the old fool to the cart, love. And keep quiet about it, just in case."

She nodded, and ran outside.

Absalom went to the hearth and lifted down the blunderbuss.

Glendenning asked, "Is my pistol still in my saddle holster?"

"No it ain't. More's the pity."

Glendenning swore, but this was not the time for recriminations. Limping into the bedchamber, he took off his coat and slipped his swordbelt over his shoulder, then went back into the kitchen and stood where he could watch the clearing while he adjusted the position of the scabbard.

Amy came back in, out of breath. "I didn't hear nothing, Ab."

Glendenning said tersely, "That doesn't mean the coast is clear."

Having checked the priming of the formidable blunderbuss, Absalom said, "We'll be ready, if they does come, but you won't need that pig-sticker, milor'." He held out the blunderbuss. "See what's writ round the muzzle?"

Glendenning read aloud, " 'Happy is he that escapeth me.' Very true, but the trouble with guns is that they only give a fellow one shot."

"One shot from this little friend will clear the whole—"

Not too far distant, a twig snapped.

For a second they all stood motionless. Then, Absalom said in a low urgent voice, "Get in the bedroom, Amy! And keep out of sight. If—"

"No," interrupted Glendenning sharply. "If we're knocked down, she won't be able to get out. Keep behind this door, Amy. I'm going to have a look round."

His voice scornful, Absalom said, "What—*you*, milor'? D'ye know aught of fighting?"

Glendenning smiled faintly. "I've been out a time or two."

Amy stared at him, and Absalom's bushy brows went up. "Well, now," he muttered. "Then—tell me quick, 'fore ye goes. If there *is* something bigger'n a rabbit creeping up on us, and if they're not *chals*, who are they?"

Glendenning's hesitation was brief. "Suffice to say they're enemies of England." Amy gave a shocked gasp. Absalom's hands stilled, and his jaw dropped. "They must have discovered that you know of the existence of the jewelled figure," added Glendenning, "which is, for some reason, of great importance in their schemes. More than that I cannot say, but I do know that they are ruthless. They destroy anyone they judge to be a threat to them—even their own people. If trouble starts, get your niece clear."

Amy was beside him, clinging to his arm. "Take care, Tio. Oh, do take care!"

He smiled down at her, then went outside. The air was beginning to feel sultry, and a few great clouds were sailing up the sky. The breeze, which had been rising gradually, was now

quite strong, and the trees were tossing about, which might
have resulted in the noise they'd heard. Certainly, the clearing
was quiet and there was no sign of life. Still, they could take
no chances. He crouched, and sprinted to the nearest tree as
rapidly as his ankle would allow. Halting, he pressed back
against the trunk and stood very still, listening. No sound to
cause alarm. He peered around and saw Flame, still saddled,
tethered in the shade beside the ruins. Nearby, Lot grazed
placidly. Another quick scan of the clearing. A gnarled old
oak some thirty feet away would offer an easy climb and a
good and well-screened vantage point. He started for it, then
whipped back as a leg came into view, groping downward
through the leaves.

It didn't seem possible that the climber could have missed
seeing him, but the man was coming down backwards, and
must have been turned away in those few seconds he had run
across the clearing.

A rustling in the shrubbery announced the arrival of a thin
individual, with a cunning face. Glendenning drew in his
breath. Sep! And the fellow coming so clumsily down the tree
had lank grey hair. If Sep and Billy Brave were here, likely the
other two ruffians were somewhere about.

Sep called softly. "Well?"

"They're inside," answered Billy Brave, in a hoarse whisper. "Three of 'em. The old goat and that gent we caught
Saturday. And—a mort." His tone changed subtly. "A ripe-
un. I want her."

Glendenning's hand tightened on the grip of his sword.

Sep gestured a warning, and both rogues melted into the
trees.

"Good day, friend. And what might you be wanting?"

Glendenning jerked his head round. Absalom stood in the
open doorway, smiling amiably at the largest member of the
unlovely quartet. In an apparent attempt to allay suspicion,
Greasy Waistcoat had a pack slung on his back. He said
ingratiatingly, "I be just a poor cove on the padding lay, mate.
And, lor' bless you, I don't want nothing." He wandered

closer. " 'Cept a drink, maybe. Warmish today. Very warmish."

"Keep your distance!" Absalom took a step forward, blunderbuss at the ready.

Greasy Waistcoat uttered a yelp and backed away. "What
a unkind soul! Here comes I, wanting only to spread the milk
o' human kindness, and—"

Glancing up, Glendenning saw something move on the
roof. It was the cherubic youth, a large boulder held in both
hands, and his intent clear.

"The roof!" roared Glendenning, whipping sword from
scabbard. " 'Ware the roof!"

The youth sent the boulder whizzing down. Absalom
sprang back, but he was a fraction of a second slow. The rock
caught the muzzle of the blunderbuss and smashed the
weapon from his grasp. He made a grab for it, but the youth
leapt down, sending him sprawling. Simultaneously, Greasy
Waistcoat rushed to join the youth, while Billy Brave and Sep
started for Glendenning. A pocket pistol appeared in Sep's
hand and was aimed with smooth expertise. There would,
Glendenning knew, be no warning, no demand that he drop
his own weapon. He hurled himself to the side, heard the
shattering retort and felt the ball pluck at his hair. A corner
of his mind registered the dispassionate awareness that the
man must be a crack shot to have aimed for the head. The
echoes of the shot were augmented by the terrified brays of
Lot, and Flame's shrill neighing.

Sep came on with eager savagery. Billy Brave paused to hurl
a heavy dagger. His aim was excellent. Crouched and ready,
Glendenning barely had time to duck before the razor sharp
blade skimmed across his shoulder. Sep still held a long knife,
and having missed with the dagger, Billy Brave snatched up a
hefty branch which he flailed at Glendenning's sword. Glendenning jumped aside, then ran in under the branch and
thrust hard. The blade caught Billy Brave's side, and he
screamed and retreated. Sep seized the opportunity to dart up
behind Glendenning and send the knife plunging at his back,
but Glendenning was already whirling about, and the knife

only ripped through his shirtsleeve. His colichemarde darted, and Sep cursed, grabbed his arm and fled from the range of that deadly blade.

Billy Brave must not have been badly hurt, because he bored in again, with a longer and heavier branch this time. Sep had moved off to the right, but was edging closer, so that they had the viscount between them. Whatever else, these assassins knew their trade and, apart from their fear of ghosts, they were not cowards. Glendenning backed away from Billy's continuing swipes. From the corner of his eye he saw Sep moving in and, desperate, jumped aside. Billy Brave sprang at him, the branch flying in a murderous arc that tore the sword from his grasp and sent him to his knees. Not for nothing had Glendenning fought beside his loved Scots: his reaction was lightning fast. He snatched up a handful of earth and flung it in Billy Brave's face. The ruffian dropped his branch and halted, cursing furiously, and clawing at his eyes. Sep was running in for the kill. Glendenning rolled, snatched up the branch, and was on his feet again. He swung the branch with all his strength. Sep, arm upflung to strike, had no time to adjust to the new weapon. The branch thudded home, sending him soaring back to land in an ungainly and motionless heap.

Distantly, Glendenning heard Amy scream. He whirled about. His branch had snapped with the force of the blow, and he was unarmed. Billy Brave was upon him, face contorted with rage, the sword a deadly glitter flying at his throat. Glendenning hurled himself to the side, the sword missing him by a hair. Billy Brave recovered his balance and whipped the weapon into a sweep that would certainly have decapitated his helpless opponent, but Glendenning was already leaping to grip a low hanging branch and swing himself upward. The sword flashed under his feet. Hanging by both hands, he kicked out hard. His boot caught Billy Brave solidly under the chin. The exultant grin vanished from the man's face as his feet left the ground. He crumpled to earth without a sound.

Glendenning's one thought was to get to Amy. Panting, he retrieved his sword and tore in a hopping uneven run to the ruins. Absalom was struggling gamely with Greasy Waistcoat.

Leaping over them, Glendenning ran into the kitchen in time to see Amy swing the iron kettle at the youth, who laughed and dodged aside, then sprang at her, his knife upraised. Glendenning jumped between them. His sword flashed, and the youth howled and melted to the floor. Kettle in hand, Amy rushed past. Glendenning ran after her, snatched Greasy Waistcoat's wig from his head, and bowed politely. Amy swung the kettle up and then down. The big man stopped strangling Absalom and collapsed beside him.

Amy dropped to her knees, caressing Absalom's purpling face. "Dear old Ab," she said frantically. "Are you all right?"

Panting, Glendenning bent and extended a hand, and Absalom hauled himself to a sitting position. "I . . . am now," he gasped out. "Did ye scrag him . . . lass?"

She glanced in belated horror at Greasy Waistcoat's inanimate bulk. Glendenning kicked him onto his back. He was breathing stertorously.

Amy sighed with relief. "I'd best run and look at them others."

"Never mind, me duck." With the viscount's assistance, Absalom clambered to his feet. "Our noble friend don't mess about. They won't give us no more trouble, certain sure."

She stared at Glendenning, her eyes very wide.

Also watching him, Absalom said, "I see some nobs at their duelling, milor'. Proper polite and neat, they was. But the only man I see fight like you just done was a Reb. No holds barred, and to the death. Not as I could blame the poor fella."

Glendenning met his gaze steadily.

"Then it's true," said Absalom. "What I heard about you."

"You'd have your work cut out to prove it."

"Don't never mean to try." Absalom shook his head wonderingly. "And I asked if ye knew aught of fighting. Cor!"

Amy cried, "Oh! Tio! Your arm!"

He glanced down. A wet crimson stained the slash in his shirtsleeve. "Jove," he muttered. "I never even felt it."

"Come inside and let me—"

"Sep? Where be ye?"

"Hey—Billy!"

The shouts were not far off, and were echoed by others. Amy whispered, "There's more of 'em!"

Absalom said, "Lor', did they send out a regiment?"

"Too many for us to handle, at all events," said Glendenning. "We'll have to make a run for it."

Absalom started towards Flame.

Glendenning sheathed his sword and snatched up the blunderbuss. "If we can reach a main road—"

"Not with that lot between it and us. I'll lead 'em off."

Glendenning hesitated, then threw the blunderbuss. "Take this, then."

Absalom caught it, but threw it back. "You'll need it, pal. Take care of my Amy!"

"No!" cried Amy. "Ab—"

Glendenning clapped a hand over her mouth.

Making no attempt at concealment, Absalom rode out.

Glendenning pulled Amy around to the side of the cellar and they crouched amongst the shrubs.

Someone yelled. "There they go!"

"Where's Sep and the others, then?"

"You lot—find out. The rest o' you—come on!"

The rapid thud of many hoofs. A glimpse of racing figures. Amy gave a muffled sob, and Glendenning hissed, "Quiet!"

Five men rode into the clearing. They were a very different type to Sep and his cohorts. Neatly, if inelegantly dressed, they were uniformly well built and rangy. They spread out as they came from the trees. No words passed between them, but one dismounted and bent first over Sep, then sprinted to peer at Billy Brave. He gestured with his hand, thumb pointing downward, and walked forward, pistol in one hand, reins in the other, to join a companion who bent over Greasy Waistcoat.

Glendenning began to ease away through the shrubs. A sound behind him. Something soft and warm nudged the back of his neck. He froze, then spun around to encounter a trusting expression and two long ears.

"Lot," whispered Amy. "Can we take him?"

"I wish we could, but they'd hear—"

Without warning the donkey uttered an ear-splitting bray. Glendenning knew that bray now, and at once he flung Amy to the side. A shout, and a dark shape hurled at him from the roof. He was smashed down, but in a quicksilver reaction he rolled, avoided the kick that would have crippled him, and used the blunderbuss as a cudgel. His attacker sprawled motionless. The struggle had alerted the others, however, and they came on the run.

Glendenning sprang up, but stumbled as his ankle buckled, and the shot aimed at his heart burned instead across Lot's flank. The donkey gave a scream of pain and shock, and bolted. The rogues were advancing, tightly bunched until the panicked donkey joined them, the cart sending their mounts into a frenzy as Lot plunged about in wild confusion.

Watching the rout, Glendenning grinned, but knew the respite would be brief. "Call him, or they'll shoot him!"

Amy whistled, and prayed that for once Lot would obey.

Perhaps from a sense of a job well done, or perhaps because he was tired, Lot came trotting to them, leaving chaos in his wake.

Glendenning handed Amy into the cart and sprang in behind her. She snatched up the reins and slapped them on Lot's back. "Giddap!" she cried urgently.

Lot sat down.

"Oh, *Gad!*" groaned Glendenning. "Keep low, Amy!" He crouched, aiming the blunderbuss over the tail of the cart.

The tangle of men and horses was straightening out. A bullet zinged over Glendenning's head.

The sound evidently reminded Lot of another bee that had recently stung his flank. He stood up very fast, and went off at top speed.

The four rogues charged in pursuit, but the path only allowed room for them to ride two abreast, and since none was willing to yield, they suffered an embarrassment that gave Glendenning and Amy a brief lead. Lot knew these woods, and the cart rocked and rattled as he plunged unerringly through the trees. If they could just reach a main road, thought Glendenning, they might have a chance. The ruffians were coming up again, but it

---

was dim under the trees; exposed roots and the thick carpet of twigs and shrubs made the ground treacherous, and the rising wind whipped the branches about, so that their progress was less rapid than it might have been.

Keeping himself between Amy and their pursuers, Glendenning held the blunderbuss levelled. Amy called a warning of low branches. He ducked, and a minute later shouted with delight as one of the men was torn from the saddle. Only three now.

He grabbed for the side as they rocked around a great oak and, jerking himself up again, saw the lead rider aiming a pistol. "Stay back!" he roared, and levelled the blunderbuss, his finger tightening around the trigger. The sight of that yawning brassbound barrel inspired the ruffian to rein aside and fire from cover, but his shot went wide.

It began to rain as they came out onto a lane. The surface was narrow but comparatively level, and there were no trees now to protect them and hamper their pursuers. Had there only been some other riders or vehicles about, the ruffians might have been obliged to give up the chase, but there was no sign of travellers. Glendenning's heart sank as he darted a glance at Amy, so bravely urging Lot onward. God help her, if he was knocked down!

Even as he had the thought, another shot rang out, and the ball whanged into the cart inches from his hand. The lane was widening. If their pursuers spread out, his chances of disabling them with one blast from the blunderbuss would be gone. It was now or never. He took aim, and fired. The roar was deafening. The recoil sent him reeling. Howls of rage and pain, and the shrill neighing of horses rang out, but when he looked back, all the hacks were standing, and only one man lay motionless. Although his two comrades were bloodied, they were mounting up again, and the fellow who had earlier been unhorsed by the tree limb, was galloping to join them. The viscount thought bleakly that a high price must have been set on their lives.

Over the outpouring of rage and profanity, someone

shouted, "The bastard's done! He only had that one Betsy! He's good as dead!"

"Not the gal," came another howl. "We don't want *her* dead!"

The cart lurched wildly, and Glendenning was sent tumbling. The wheels sang a smoother song as he scrambled upright again. They had turned onto a proper roadway. Their pursuers were almost upon them. The sight of their bestial exultant faces sent his eyes flashing to Amy's gracefully swaying figure as she urged Lot onward. Her head turned to him. A smile trembled on her lips, but as her gaze slipped past, he saw fear in her eyes. Rage sustained him. He seized the heavy blunderbuss by the muzzle and began to whirl it over his head. The group of ruffians reined back a little. The leader urged them on, glancing back to scream, "He can't knock us all down, boys! Come—"

The blunderbuss caught him squarely across the neck, and he flew out of the saddle.

Glendenning smiled grimly, and whipped out his sword. With luck, he'd hold off the other two until—

Amy shrieked, "Tio! Look!"

He risked a quick glance around. Praise God, they were coming into some traffic. At last!

A carriage shot past, and then a stagecoach, the passengers staring in astonishment at the plunging donkey cart and its occupants. Some following riders slowed, and one shouted,"Hi! Ain't that Glendenning?" Another man brandished his tricorne. " 'Tis, by Jove! Hold up, Tio!"

Instead, he waved them on, and they reined around and followed.

"I say, Glendenning!" called a good-natured young dandy named Sir John Dark. "What's to do? Is't a race?"

"Yes. Only they ain't playing fair! Lend us your escort, Johnny!"

It was all these sporting-mad young bucks needed. With whoops of excitement they closed in around the cart, and became an enthusiastic part of the odd procession galloping along the country road.

155

Gradually, the thwarted would-be murderers fell back and were at length lost from sight.

"I believe my command of the English language is fair enough," said the viscount angrily. "But I will repeat my wishes since your hearing is evidently impaired. I require two rooms. One for me and one for the lady. And—"

Stifled giggles arose from the maids peeping around an inner door. The tavern keeper, a large individual with a round red face that seemed to rise neckless from a foaming cravat, interrupted with a contemptuous, "You will do better to try elsewhere, my good man. The Black Gander caters to the gentry, not to the likes of you, and your"—he darted a stern look at Amy—"young woman."

Glendenning's hand shot out to close in the host's cravat and jerk hard. The host, propelled forward across his rickety old desk, uttered a strangled roar.

"I think you meant to say 'young lady,' " said Glendenning through clenched teeth.

Both maids were screeching; a stout matron approaching the desk turned to fling her arms about her diminutive husband and implored him to protect her; and two brawny young men ran up and wrenched the viscount back.

Amy had begged Glendenning not to seek shelter at this wayside tavern after his friends had left them, for she had anticipated just such a reception. She belaboured the viscount's attackers with fists and feet, while demanding at the top of her lungs that his lordship be freed.

Displeased when one of his men was launched at speed across the desk, the host raged, " 'His lordship,' is it?" He snatched up a hefty cudgel. "I'll lordship him!"

"You will unhand Viscount Glendenning at once, fellow!" The command, uttered in a stern cultured voice, was reinforced by a sharp crack as a malacca cane slammed down on the desk.

The uproar quieted. Mine host, turning infuriated eyes on

the brilliance of Mr. Neville Falcon, was given pause, and looked at Glendenning uncertainly.

The first brawny young man, who was picking himself up from the floor, muttered with grudging admiration, "He don't look like no viscount what I ever see, but he's got a left, surely!"

Glendenning had already freed himself, and was shaking hands with Falcon.

Convinced, the host mumbled a reluctant apology.

A small crowd had gathered to gawk from the windblown gypsy girl to her coatless, dishevelled, and bloodstained young champion. Their stares passed quickly to Mr. Falcon, and lingered on his magnificence. A vision in red and yellow, he demanded a suite, and settled for a bedchamber with small private parlour. Once upstairs, he ordered wine, tea, and cakes, winked at the rosy-cheeked maid and accompanied her to the door. A faint squeal sounded. He closed the door and turned a bland smile on his companions.

Somewhat apprehensively, the viscount performed the introductions. To his relief, the seldom predictable Neville Falcon bowed politely. Amy curtsied with a grace and dignity that surprised both men, then hurried to pour water into the washstand bowl, while commanding that the viscount roll up his sleeve. This was easier said than done, and Glendenning sat at the parlour table and attempted to detach his shirtsleeve from the cut.

"This is a grand coincidence, sir," he said gratefully. "You'll never know how glad I am to see you!"

Amy hurried to his side. "Don't pull at it! Ye'll start it to bleeding again. Now—just let me." She went to work gently and with an expertise that spoke of much practice.

"There is nothing in it of coincidence, Horatio." Falcon pulled up a straight-backed chair and laid hat and cane aside. "In company with half London, it seems, I've been searching for you. In heaven's name, boy—what have you been about? Your mama is worried to death. My son is out with Lieutenant Morris even now, trying to find you."

Glendenning stared. If Jamie Morris and August Falcon,

157

who barely tolerated each other, had joined forces, there must be a very large roach in the rum. "Ow!" he exclaimed as Amy at last coaxed the sleeve free. Her eyes flew to his face in quick anxiety, and he grinned reassuringly at her.

Watching them, Mr. Falcon complained, "There's the devil to pay and no pitch hot, and here you are cavorting about with this pretty creature, carefree as a colt in buttercup pasture." He scanned Amy through his glass, and admitted with a chuckle, "Not that I can fault you for that. Jove! Where a'plague did you find her?"

"Say rather that to my great good fortune Miss Consett found me. After I'd—parted company with my horse."

"Thrown, were you?" Mr. Falcon, who was notorious for his ability to fall from the saddle even when his mount was standing perfectly still, said grandly, "Well, it happens to the best of us. I remember when I'd wagered Seldon I'd race him to Oxford. Don't know if you've his acquaintance. Zachary Troy's sire. Splendid fellow. I hear he's getting leg shackled, by the bye. To Octavia Aynsworth. What a Toast *she* was in her salad days! Not but what your little beauty here couldn't have given her a run for her money. Now where was I? Oh, yes. At all events, there was Seldon and I tearing down the pike road, when I spotted a dairymaid with a crate of eggs fallen off the tail of her cart. Most shapely little filly you ever laid eyes on! I pulled up so sharp I went tail over head. Landed in the curst eggs. Jove, how we laughed the pair of us! And later on—"

"Your pardon, sir," Glendenning intervened hurriedly, "but you were going to tell me about my mama and some kind of trouble."

"Burn it, so I was! What a fellow I am! And the devil's in it that I can't give you many facts. Thought it was you at first, Horatio. But now I'm inclined to think it's Templeby he's after."

Startled, Glendenning raised his eyes from the long gash Amy was bathing with gentle hands. "My brother? What's he been about? And who is after him?"

"Been plunging devilish deep, I can tell you. Surprised you ain't heard."

"I knew he'd been playing at the Cocoa Tree, but—"

"And at the alluring Alvelley's."

"The deuce he has! I'm damned sure they load the dice at her house. Has she got her hooks into him, then?"

"Very likely. Don't know to what extent, mind. But it must be serious to bring your mama to Falcon House in tears."

"*What?* Lady Nola turned to you? Why on earth—?"

"No call to shout, dear boy. She turned to August, not me. And she didn't really *turn* to him, exactly. Came to Town hoping to find you."

"Damnation!" Glendenning's clenched fist pounded at the table, causing the water to slop over the side of the bowl.

Amy said, "Tio, how can I bandage this nasty cut if you keeps jumping about?"

He subsided, but declared fiercely, "My mama never weeps! She is one of the bravest women I know. What did she tell you, sir?"

"Not a word, I promise you. Her la'ship frightens me to death when she's *slightly* put out. In *tears?* God bless my soul! I ran like a rabbit!"

"Fiend seize it! Of all times to have dropped out of sight, just when she needed me!"

"I agree. But you really should curb your language in front of your pretty piece, Tio. And—"

"Miss Consett is *not* my 'pretty piece,' " said the viscount, bristling.

"Whatever you say, dear lad." Mr. Falcon laid one chubby finger alongside his nose and winked conspiratorially. "But *I* think she's very pretty indeed, and if you don't want her, I'll—"

Glendenning stood, causing Amy, who had been stifling a smile, to moan with frustration. "Sir," he said, with crushing courtesy, "I am beholden to you for helping us, and for the warning you have brought. You will forgive, an I leave you."

"Well, I won't." Mr. Falcon waved a dismissing hand, and said airily, " 'Tis not a speck of use your getting all starched up with me, Tio. Used to it. August does it all the time. Besides, ain't told you everything yet. Ah, here is our pretty little maid." He rose to usher the blushing parlourmaid into the room. "Put it here, my pretty. Move that bowl, if you will, Miss Consent. There, now we may be comfortable."

The maid departed, urged on by a sly pinch on her plump person, her squeal turning to a giggle when a handsome douceur was slipped down the front of her blouse. Glendenning met Amy's dancing eyes and lifted his shoulders helplessly. She chuckled, tied the knot on the bandage and gave it a little pat, then turned her attention to the teapot.

Mr. Falcon pressed a glass of wine upon the viscount, telling him he needed it. Glendenning said wryly, "Egad, sir. What further disasters have you to impart?"

Mr. Falcon's bland smile masked the thought that Horatio looked properly wrung out. "I think there's a deal more to your activities these past days than you've told me," he said shrewdly. "What I have to say will keep while you rest for a minute or two after your little—ah, lady's surgery."

Amy took up the plate of sliced currant cake and lemon tarts, carried it to Falcon's chair, and presented it with a curtsy. He patted her cheek, and told her she'd a most fetching way with her lashes. From the corner of her eye she saw Glendenning's frown, and said *sotto voce*, "Best grab a couple quick, Mr. Falcon. His lordship kills people when he turns cross."

Falcon sat straighter. "Eh? What's all this?"

"Nonsense talk," said Glendenning, slanting an irked glance at Amy.

"Was it Farrier?" asked Falcon. "Has that wart come up with you?"

Glendenning drew in his breath sharply and lost all his colour, but his hand was steady as he set his glass aside. "Do you say that Burton Farrier has been asking for me? He was hounding a young gypsy at the races in Epsom, and I snatched his prey from his nasty claws. Threatened to knock him down, as I recall. A wart, indeed."

"A wart it don't do to threaten, you madman! 'Ware of

him, Tio. He's nosing around families suspected to have Jacobite sympathies and—"

Glendenning's eyes narrowed. He asked in a voice of steel, "Has he dared to pester my mama?"

" 'Pon my soul, I hope that was not why she came to us. I'd feared it might be so, but when she started jabbering something about Templeby, I fancied he'd fallen prey to the cents-per-centers. Never say the young fool was *also* out for Prince Charlie? No! Do not answer! I'd as lief not know."

"My brother had nothing whatsoever to do with the Uprising." Glendenning pushed back his chair. "Still, I must go to my mama as fast as possible."

"Commendable, dear boy. But let us be sensible. You cannot rush about England in that repulsive shirt, and we must find you another coat. Also, how d'ye propose to get to Windsor? Have you a coach?"

Glendenning bit his lip.

Amy said with a twinkle, "We've a donkey cart, y'r honour."

CHAPTER IX

The brown coat was a surprisingly good fit, it was a joy to be wearing clean linen again, his buckskins had been well brushed, and he wore a new pair of top-boots. Leaning from the window of the carriage, Glendenning gripped Mr. Falcon's hand, and said fervently that he scarcely knew how to thank him for going to so much trouble in his behalf. "I wish to heaven I'd my purse with me, so I'd not have had to impose. But I shall repay—"

"Pish! I have done so little, dear boy. Our delightful Miss Amy was clever enough to know how to take your measurements, and all my servant had to do was go out and procure suitable apparel. *Vraiment!*"

"What we'd have done without your help, sir, I dare not think. And I have even purloined your coach!"

"I shall have no difficulty in hiring one. Besides, your unpleasant acquaintances may still be seeking you, and they'll not expect to find you in a private carriage with liveried servants."

"You have my heartfelt thanks. Do you wish that your people return the carriage to you at Falcon House? Or at Ashleigh?"

"Heaven forfend I should rusticate in Sussex again! The

Town house, if you please, Tio. Now have done with your thanks! You'd do as much for me or my family, and well I know it. Besides, 'tis I should be thanking you. Your pretty miss will brighten my lonely day, I'm assured." With his cherubic countenance and guileless grin Falcon looked like a beneficent clergyman. He wasn't. Horatio said cautiously, "She's a good little chit, sir. I'd take her with me, but—"

"Take her *with* you?" echoed Falcon, awed. "To Glendenning Abbey? Egad, but you're a braver man than I! Only picture your mama's reaction! And as for Bowers-Malden . . . !" He shuddered. "Ah, but you quiz me, of course. I shall enjoy amusing the pretty, never fear. I'll buy her some decent clothes, take her to your flat, and pass her off as a lady, if—"

"No, sir! I'd sooner she was with someone not remotely connected with all this." The viscount ran his female relations through his mind's eye, and rejected them hurriedly. "It must be a lady who'll not be horrified by some of the things Amy says, yet who will see that she comes to no harm." He frowned, worrying at it, then exclaimed triumphantly, "I have it! My sister's governess—the very person! She's retired to Portsmouth nowadays, and keeps house for her nephew, who's a ship's captain. If you've a piece of paper, sir, I'll give you her direction."

Neville provided a small notepad and a pencil. Having written out the worthy lady's address and again thanked Mr. Falcon for his efforts, the viscount waved as the carriage jolted and started off, sat back on the seat, and with a weary sigh closed his eyes.

If Burton Farrier was haunting the abbey the chances were that he wasn't after Michael at all, but was setting some kind of trap for—

"So you thinks I couldn't be passed off as a lady, does ye?"

Glendenning's eyes flew open as the words were snarled in his ear. Amy's wrathful face was inches away. "Oh, my God!" he moaned. "What the—"

"There ain't no cause to call on the Lord, young man!

Thought you'd be rid of me, didn't ye? Thought as you'd traded me to that—that rascally old rake, in exchange fer this here carriage and yer fancy new—"

"No such thing! How dare you suppose I would— And it has nothing to say to the case, at all events! Where the deuce did you spring from? I'd thought you were safely—"

"Safely dumped into that there gent's hands! And a fine time I'd have had, trying to keep 'em off me for the rest of the night! But you didn't give a button fer that! Anything to be rid o' the worthless gyppo, once she'd served her purpose! Well, I see what he was, quick as quick, so I slipped out and hided under the seat, and you was so eager to be off, you never even noticed!"

She was flushed with wrath, her eyes sparking, her white teeth fairly gnashing. And because, being aware of Neville Falcon's reputation, he had indeed suffered some uneasy qualms, Glendenning said in a calmer voice, "Of course I worried about you, Amy. But I knew you could control Falcon. Lord, anybody could! He's all show and no go most of the time, and a kinder gentleman you'd never wish to—"

"Ah, but what does the likes of *me* know about *gentlemen?* I be only a cheap trollop as you thinks couldn't no ways be 'passed off' as a lady!"

"You are not a trollop," he said angrily. "Nor did Falcon say—"

"Ho, yus he did! And he says as he could imagine yer mama's *reaction*. Swound away, I 'spect, poor old gal, and—"

He seized her by the arms. "The word is 'swoon'—not 'swound.' And my mother is a great lady who would receive you with kindness, so you may stop being silly. You know very well—"

Tears sparkled on her lashes, but she interrupted with hissing fury, "I knows very well I were all right so long as I were cooking and washing and caring for ye, and—"

"And saving my life, and fighting beside me like a regular Trojan." He smiled fondly and wiped a tear from her smooth cheek. "Now pray do not cry. For your own sake you would have been better advised to stay with Falcon, but— Good Gad! What about poor Lot?"

"I told the ostler Mr. Falcon wants him took good care of. You owe the poor moke that much."

"Assuredly. And I've a greater debt. Now do not fly into the boughs, but since you're here I shall take you home with me, and my mama will—"

"Will be *evah* so charmed to meet of her son's fine lady, the gypsy mort," she mocked.

He looked at her tangled hair, grubby blouse, and torn skirt, and hesitated. Mama would be polite and kind, and in a hundred ways Amy, with her fierce pride, would be affronted. He said, "There's a hamlet a few miles up the road. I'm sure we can find a shop, and with the money I borrowed from Falcon I'll buy you new clothes. Never fear, Mistress Consett, you'll look as fine as any fine lady when I present you to the countess."

"Well, I might look it," she muttered sullenly, "But I won't *be* it. She'll know what I is the minute she rests her high and mighty ogles on me."

The thought that his beloved stepmother had "high and mighty ogles" so wrought upon Glendenning that he forgot his worries for a moment, and laughed heartily.

"I don't see what's so funny," said Amy sulkily, drawing as far from him as possible, and glowering out of the window.

"Perhaps not. But when you meet my mama . . ." He chuckled again and, winning no response, said coaxingly, "Don't pout, child. We've so much to be thankful for. We're safe, and—"

"*You're* safe, ye means," she said, rounding on him. "It don't never occur to you that me pal ain't, do it?"

He said ruefully, "Since you are choosing to forget your grammar, I take it you're really overset. But I'm afraid I cannot answer sensibly, because I don't know what 'pal' means. Is a foreign word?"

"Romany, does ye mean?" she retaliated sharply. "Don't be afraid to say it, mate. I ain't ashamed o' what I am!"

"You don't know what you are, so—"

"Well, I ain't too iggerant to know what 'pal' means! Cor! Don't you know nothing?"

He said in his humblest voice, "I have more than my share of ignorance, alas. Enlighten me, Miss Consett, I beg."

"Crumbs! Pal means friend. More'n friend—more like brother; sorta like you took loyal, and faithful, and—and someone what you'd risk yer own skin to help, same as he would for you, and wrapped it all up in three letters. P-a-l."

"Thank you. I'd say it's a jolly good word. Now, what can we do to help Absalom?"

"Nought." She resumed her contemplation of the rain. "He knows what he's about, and he's got your gry, so he'll be all right."

"But I thought you were worrying—"

"And I knowed *you* wasn't."

"Is that why you were so angry with me?"

She shrugged impatiently. "Oh, leave me be!"

Instead, he kept up a steady flow of chatter, trying to make her respond, or to win a smile, but nothing he said could coax her out of her sulks, so that at last he said in exasperation, "If you are so very cross with me, why did you insist upon coming?"

"Reasons . . . And 'sides, when I got in this spanking ready-fer-marriage, I didn't know as you'd turn inside out when yer silly old friend said he'd take me to yer flat. Cor! What a shameful thing *that* would've been fer yer noble lor—"

"And that will be sufficient of your foolishness," he interrupted, losing patience. "In the first place, this ready-for-marriage, as you call it, belongs to Mr. Falcon, and without his kindness in lending it to us we'd have had a far less comfortable ride to Windsor. In the second place, he is neither silly nor old, and if he enjoys to flirt with a pretty girl now and then, he means no harm by it. And in the third place, I didn't want you taken to my flat because—"

"Who cares?" she interrupted rudely. "Not this gypsy mort, so stow yer clack, young man!"

"*I* care! So you may stop talking like a coster-monger, and listen! The reason I—"

"Oh, there was a young coal-heaver, down Brixton way," sang Amy lustily.

"—didn't want you taken to—" shouted Glendenning.

"Who stayed up all night, and slept during the day," shrilled Amy.

"—my flat—" howled Glendenning.

"He liked nothing more than a roll in—"

Glendenning gave a gasp and clapped a hand over her mouth. "Do you want to demoralize Falcon's coachman, you wretch?" he hissed. "Where did you learn that naughty song?"

Amy bit his palm sufficiently hard that he jerked his hand away.

"Well, it weren't from no hoity-toity countess, mate," said she.

"It wasn't enough that I must be dragged through half the clubs in town last night!" Swinging from the saddle, August Falcon stepped ankle deep into a muddy puddle and swore vigorously. An ostler splashed up to commandeer his mount, and he went on, "Why I should have allowed myself to be bamboozled into this forlorn venture, is beyond me! I care nothing for Glendenning and his problems."

Morris gave the ostler instructions, then ducked his head against the wind-driven rain, and hurried to catch up with Falcon. "Any fool knows you're a care-for-nobody," he agreed. "Thing is, old Tio's your second, and the southland ain't exactly littered with bosom bows willing to act for you, so if you want to fight me, we've first got to find him. Besides, must warn him about the Terrier. Only decent thing to do for a friend."

Splashing along the cobblestone path, Falcon shot him a withering look and lengthened his stride. "You speak for yourself, I trust."

"Waste of money," panted Morris, almost running so as to keep up, "to have your chimney swept after . . . the house has burned down."

Having reached the step, Falcon gritted his teeth, came to an abrupt halt, and turned. Blinking through the raindrops he said, "The murky processes of your mind, my good clod, are seldom penetrable, and I shouldn't dignify this one with a comment. But—what in hell have I to do with chimney sweeps?"

"You keep telling everyone you have no friends. Bad business, August. Day may dawn when you need one. You give a shout for help and there's not a friend in the foundry. Then what—"

"Rubbish!" Falcon reached for the door handle. "The day I call on *any* man for help will be a scorching day in December! And don't call me August, blast your hide!"

The door of the Black Galleon tavern was flung open, and a noisy group of gentlemen came out, to pause, groaning, and turn up the capes of their cloaks as they encountered the pouring rain. Holding the door for Falcon, one offered a kindly warning. "Devilish slow inside, old boy. Long wait for a table."

"Is all I needed," grunted Falcon.

The parlour was crowded, the air in the shabby but good-sized dining room wreathed with smoke, fragrant with the smells of ale and cooking, and ringing with talk and laughter.

Morris had to raise his voice to be heard. "Shouldn't stop. We made a late start as it was."

Falcon took off his tricorne and emptied the water from the brim into a dirty tankard. "If we started late, 'twas because, thanks to your blasted persistence, I was unable to get to my bed until three. Furthermore—" He paused as an harassed barmaid was sufficiently diverted by his good looks as to come and take their wet garments.

"There's a party leaving in the corner, sir," she advised, fluttering her lashes at Falcon. "If you gents look sharp, you'll get it."

He slipped a shilling into her hand, and asked with a smile, "Which corner, bright eyes?"

"Alongside the painting." She nodded her head to a table near the fire.

Someone shouted an irate "Millie! What became of our pork pies?"

"Coming!" she howled, and, with a promise to bring them ale as quick as she could, she was gone.

Falcon shouldered his way through the good-natured crowd and commandeered the table, nimbly sidestepping a boozy-looking man who had been reeling about, getting in everyone's way, and who at once whined that he and his friend had "b'n here firs'!"

"Then you should have sat down first," said Falcon carelessly.

The boozy man fussed and fumed and went reeling off, obliging the gathering with his assessment of 'ins'lent puppies.'

Unmoved, Falcon glanced around and saw that Morris had halted and was staring up at the nearby picture. This portrayed a slim young army officer who stood with arms folded and one booted foot nonchalantly crossed over the other. The uniform was magnificent, the sword very much in evidence, and the white horse against which the officer leaned was very fiery of eye, and flowing of mane, its nostrils flaring so that one might almost hear the snort.

"If that ain't just like Morris." The mocking observation came in an undervoice from a large overdressed individual seated with a group of friends at an adjacent table. Falcon turned his head idly. The speaker was about five and thirty, with a belligerent air and a bitter mouth. He had laughed loudly when Falcon commandeered the table, and had met the boozy man's resentful glance with a contemptuous stare and a suggestive easing of his sword in the scabbard. Falcon had judged him a bullying crudity, and a second look gave him no reason to change his initial opinion.

In response to a murmured question from one of his cronies, the large man laughed. "Saw service with him in the Low

Countries. Not worth a damn on the field, but the veriest blockhead off it! Had I not been there to put the sabre in his hand and tell him which way was the enemy, he'd likely have forgot what he was there for. And so shy around the females one might have fancied him straight from the nursery." He laughed again. "I recollect once—" He gave a start as the thong of a whip dropped into his tankard. "What the devil, sir?" he demanded, twisting around in his chair, his face one great scowl.

"I do not understand your question," drawled Falcon. "Pray be more explicit."

"Your damned whip is in my damned ale! Is that explicit enough for you?"

"My apologies. I certainly did not intend to disturb your ale. I'd fancied I aimed at a braying jackass. A mistake, no doubt. The host would certainly not allow such a creature to sit with gentlemen."

There was a concerted gasp.

The bully was a good head taller and two stone heavier than Falcon, and he knew an easy mark when he saw one. His chair scraped back as he sprang to his feet. His hand dropped to the hilt of his sword, and he towered over the slighter man with undisguised menace. "By God, sir!" he said with a ferocious grin, "I'll let some of your blood for that impudence!" Becoming aware of the alien shape of Falcon's eyes, he added, "Whatever you are!"

Falcon drew back his whip, and flicked it fastidiously, caus-ing ale to splash his victim's red velvet coat. "Are you a competent swordsman?" he enquired, making no attempt to rise. "I do not care to waste my time with amateurs."

Accustomed to inspiring terror in those he threatened, the bully was rendered momentarily speechless. "Of all the . . . ," he spluttered, then, "the confounded *gall!* I've sliced up better than you, you dandified curst foreigner! Get on—"

"Ryan!" One of the men at his table had been staring at Falcon, and now jumped up and caught his friend's arm. He spoke rapidly behind his hand. The large man's eyes grew round, and his flush receded, leaving him very pale. He looked at Falcon intently, gave a gulp, and stammered in a far different tone, "I—er— Your pardon, sir, an I offended. I was only funning. Lieutenant Morris is—"

"A splendid fighting man, and a fine gentleman," said Falcon coldly.

"Oh—yes!" With a ghastly grin the bully mumbled, "Yes, indeed! I had not known you was togeth— That is, I wasn't aware he was a friend of yours, sir."

" 'Tis said we may learn something each day we live. Provided we go on living, of course. To which end, I expect you will wish to take your departure? Yes?"

Ten seconds later, another table became vacant.

Falcon watched the retreat thoughtfully, then called above the din, "Hey! Morris!"

Morris started, and came to join him. "Dashed silly thing to do," he remarked, sitting down as two groups scrambled to claim the available table.

Falcon looked at him from the corners of his eyes. "I expect you know what you mean," he said carefully.

"Fellow in the picture," explained Morris. "Shouldn't go about leaning on horses in that fashion. From the look of the brute 'twas ready to rear up. Then where would he have been? I ask you?"

Falcon told him. Succinctly.

"Hum. Well, go on."

"Go on—where?"

"You said 'furthermore.' "

"I did? When? Last year?"

"Just now. Gad, but if that ain't typical of you, Lord Haughty-Snort! 'Tis a rare peacock can remember the egg!' "

Falcon put a hand over his eyes and moaned.

"You said," prompted Morris, "you'd been kept from your bed 'til three, and—"

"Ah, yes. And furthermore, I am at a loss to know why we go to Owen Furlong's country house. Lacking my own keen discernment, Glendenning's life is fairly littered with addlepates he fancies to be his friends. Why trudge all the way to Kent?"

"No, is it?" said Morris, surprised.

Falcon regarded him steadily.

The corner of Morris' mouth twitched. "Thought it was Sussex," he said demurely. "I chose Furlong because he and Tio have been friends forever, and I heard he stood by poor Kit Aynsworth when Kit ran afoul of Colonel Fotheringay. And any fellow who would stick by a friend through Fotheringay is a Trojan!"

"Do you say," said Falcon, sorting the wheat from the chaff, "that we travel through this repellent storm and endure untold hardship for no more substantial reason than that you admire Furlong? Ye Gods!"

Morris pursed up his lips and at length entered a reinforcing, "Sort of man I'd turn to was I in a fix. Thought young Templeby might do the same if he ain't been able to come up with his brother. Wouldn't be surprised if Tio would look for him there. If I'm wrong, I suppose we could try that Minnie fellow. Do you know who he is?"

"Minnie . . . fellow . . . ?"

"Odd sort of name for a gentleman, eh? My thought exactly. But then for the life of me I only understood half of what the lady said."

"*Stupéfiant*," muttered Falcon to the ceiling. "Who is this baffling female, pray tell?"

"You know perfectly well. Lady Bowers-Malden. You heard her say it same as I did. Something to do with mice."

Falcon put back his head and closed his eyes. Opening them after a moment's cogitation, he said, "I think I have it. Truly, I am astounded. Lady Nola said, an I recall, that to ask my father for assistance would be like setting a mouse after the Minotaur."

"That's the fellow!" said Morris triumphantly. "D'you know him?"

Tapping the end of his riding crop against his chin, Falcon answered with his rare and sweet smile, "He just left. But I assure you he'd have been a proper bull in a china shop."

"Rats," said James Morris, disappointed.

———

The Earl of Bowers-Malden had been blessed by two happy marriages. There were times, however, when even so contented a husband suffered moments of exasperation, and on these occasions he had been heard to mutter that when the Good Lord made woman He had lost the recipe half-way through. If his countess was within hearing distance she would invariably riposte with a twinkle that the Good Lord had thereupon *improved* upon the recipe. At this moment, however, feeling big and clumsy and ill at ease in the tiny village shop, Lord Horatio was much inclined to agree with his sire. He scowled at the curtain from beyond which came the murmur of female voices. The dragon of a matron who ran the place had fixed him with such a look when he'd brought Amy into her establishment! He'd felt his face burn, and had scarce known where to look.

Amy had warned him. "She'll suppose ye're trying to make yer new peculiar more respectable," she'd jeered. "What you going to say then?"

In the event, he'd fought to sound like a viscount instead of a shivering schoolboy, and had surprised himself by saying firmly that he wanted Miss Consett garbed as befitted a young lady. Mrs. Wilks, her arms crossed upon a vast bosom that swelled wrathfully, had rested a pitying glance upon Amy, then fixed the Wicked Lecher with a baleful glare and said she was "Just closing."

Quelled, Glendenning had prepared to evacuate, but Amy had saved the day by dropping a curtsy, and saying in her most refined voice that she would be ever so grateful if marm would keep her shop open just for a little while. "I do want my family to be proud of me," she'd said wistfully.

Startled, but at once taking advantage of the indecision that had appeared in Mrs. Wilks' stern eyes, his lordship had put in a remark that there was to be no quibbling over expense. After a moment's hesitation, curiosity and greed had overpowered the upright proprietor. Mrs. Wilks had conducted

Amy to a rear alcove, drawing the curtain closed while regarding the viscount with a glare that clearly bespoke her willingness to deal with him did he dare attempt an entrance.

There had then ensued a flurry of whispers interspersed with occasional Well I never's, Bless my soul's, and Fancy that's. He had shrunk when the curtain was opened just sufficiently for Mrs. Wilks to squeeze past, but instead of recriminations, she had beamed upon him, and begged that he sit and have a cup of tea while he waited. A young girl with a head cold, a thousand freckles, and a painful shyness had been summoned to make tea "for his lordship." Mrs. Wilks had bustled about, gathering up gowns and petticoats, stockings and shoes, ribands, and dainty articles that were hurriedly whisked from sight. These were all conveyed to the sacrosanct precincts behind the curtain, from whence came sounds of stress, giggles, and more whisperings.

At this point the freckled lass sniffed herself into view, carrying a laden tray. She poured his lordship a cup of tea, most of which went into the saucer. His attempt to set her at ease by smiling his friendliest smile and pointing out that he had freckles too, resulted in the lifting of two red-rimmed blue eyes to his face, and an adoring expression that appalled him.

Mrs. Wilks did battle with the curtain again, and rushed past. "Imagine!" she said, returning with her arms full of caps and shawls. "*Poor* little dear! You're a fine Christian man, sir! That you are!" Still beaming, she disappeared around the billowing curtain, leaving Glendenning to indeed imagine—with considerable apprehension—the drama Amy might have concocted for her.

He was finishing his fourth cup of tea when the curtain opened.

"Close your eyes, my lord," commanded Mrs. Wilks.

Since he was fairly sure by now that she did not intend to inflict bodily harm upon him, he obeyed.

A rustling. Then, "You can look, sir," said Amy.

He opened his eyes and almost dropped the cup.

A vision stood before him. A petite, shyly mischievous,

delectably feminine creature, all glowing youth and loveliness from the dainty ruffles of her cap to the hem of her pale pink travelling gown. Her glossy hair had been brushed into fat ringlets that flirted with her shoulders. From under many petticoats a tiny high-heeled shoe was revealed as she held out her skirts and promenaded for him, her velvety dark eyes watching him with something between nervousness and laughter.

The proud proprietor slipped a maroon cloak around Amy's shoulders, and said something, but Glendenning couldn't have told what it was. He was vaguely aware of paying his reckoning, thanking Mrs. Wilks, and ushering Amy to the waiting carriage. The wheels were rolling again, the hooves were pounding, and still he was benumbed. She was exquisite! A rare beauty from the top of her head to the tip of her toes. He'd noticed at the start that she was a lovely creature. He'd not begun to realize just how lovely. Properly dressed, she would take London by storm. She could be groomed, educated—though she had a fair start on her education already, and—

"Love a blooming duck," said Amy. "How do yer birds of paradise ever walk about in these horrid morning-news?"

One of her new shoes shot into the air and landed on the opposite seat.

Glendenning's considerably tattered nerves reacted in the form of a stern reprimand. "No lady," he scolded, "would ever remove her slippers in front of other people. Least of all would she kick them into the air like—like any hoyden."

She was silent for a minute, then her laugh was markedly unrepentant. "Give it up, mate! You won't change Amy Consent by changing what Amy Consett wears. You should've left me back there with old grizzle-guts, 'stead of—"

"There is no cause to be crude. Mrs. Wilks was kind, and—"

"She was kind after I told her a pack of lies. You'd rescued me from the gypsies, I said. You'd been sent by me grieving family to find me and restore me to their loving arms. Cor, what a rasper! And she swallowed the lot. Most people, lordship, is that gullible it's a perishing shame ter slumguzzle 'em."

He said frowningly, "I think 'tis not slumguzzle, Amy. You are obviously of good breeding. If we could discover your true parents, we might—"

"Might what? Make me inter a lady? Marry me to some high-bred gent?" From under her thick lashes, she watched him intently, and added in a rather breathless voice, "Like—like one of yer friends, f'r instance?"

He hesitated. "Certainly we could find you some—some worthy man." He could picture many of his acquaintances did they catch so much as a glimpse of her. It would not be marriage they'd offer, but if she played her cards right, Amy Consett could end up a very wealthy—

"You means if I told all manner o' fibs, some respectable tradesman might be tricked into offering fer me."

"Er—I see no reason why not."

"I might aim so high as a grocer. Or a milliner, maybe?"

He had the sensation that she was very rigid and still, and he said kindly, "Is entirely possible, were you to—ah, be a little more careful with your speech perhaps, and—"

"And cheat and lie and pretend to be a lady. Like you cheat and lie and pretend to be a honourable man?"

He had been staring rather fixedly out of the window, but at this he gave a gasp and jerked around to demand, "What the deuce d'you mean by that?"

She turned also and he saw to his surprise that her face was flushed, her eyes glittering. "I mean that from the first you've picked and snipped and found fault with me. For why? 'Cause I is what I is."

"The devil! You *asked* me to—"

"No pleasing you, was there?" she swept on. "Every chance you got, you rubbed me nose in me iggerance and bad blood."

"I did nothing of the kind! Why, you wretched, ungrateful—"

"Looked down yer perishing nose at me. And at Uncle Ab, what is a honest, God-fearing man what never done no harm to no one. *You!*"

Infuriated, he seized her by the arms. "I suppose *you* didn't filch my purse! Aye, and that poor clod's at the Mop Fair besides! I suppose *you* didn't steal my mare and damn near cause me to get my brains beaten out?"

"There you go," she said, blazingly defiant. "Have at me. I'm just a *common* gypsy. And you're a *noble* Quality cove— when ye're not trying to force me to yer wicked will! And in the very bedroom where I nursed you!" She saw him flinch, and knew the barb had hit home, but she was hopeless and bitterly hurt, and the need to hurt back was so strong that she raged on. "Well, we may be low, Ab and me. We may be coarse folk not worth the likes o' you wiping yer pretty boots on. But I'll tell you what we ain't, lordship. We ain't filthy turncoat *traitors!*"

Even in the gathering dusk she saw all the colour leave Glendenning's face. He released her hurriedly and sat back, staring blankly at the window. After a moment of taut silence, he muttered, "To be loyal to one ideal is inevitably to be traitor to another, Amy."

"Fine talk," she said with something very like a snort. "It don't change the fact ye're a Englishman born and bred, and you betrayed yer king and country. Lor'! What a awful thing!"

His jaw tightened. "You do not understand."

"Hah! Seems t'me like every time gents does something wicked, they say other folks 'don't understand.' Ain't much not to understand about treason."

Goaded, he said, "Charles Stuart is a fine Scottish gentleman. His father was the rightful king—not a foreign prince who—"

"What? Was this German George a evil man, then?"

"I did not say he was evil. But he doesn't want England. He doesn't like England. He refuses to learn our language, and—"

"Not like your Bonnie Prince, eh? Your precious Charlie Stuart who says only the king's got a right to say what happens in Britain. No one else. God told him there mustn't be no parliament, he says. Nor any laws made 'cept what the king makes. And everyone must treat him like he's divine, and do what he—"

He said explosively, "Good God! Who's been teaching you all that stuff?"

"Me books, mate. Me books and me iggerant uncle. But ye knows better, a'course. You knows so much better you went off and turned yer sword 'gainst loyal gents. Or is you going fer to deny it?"

"No. I fought for what I believed best for—"

"For the noble Horatio Clement Laindon, Viscount Glendenning. And what about yer mum and dad? Proud of you, was they?"

He flushed, and said grittily, "If you knew as much as you think you know, Mistress Consett—"

"I know one thing, nobleman. I prigs a cackler now and then, or separates some silly gudgeon from his purse. But I ain't never took no one's life. Specially someone what was fighting for England! I ain't never took the chance I might have to stick a horrid sword into one of me own friends!" She thrust her scornful face under his nose and hissed, "I—ain't—that—low!"

She had cut him on the raw, and his temper flared, sweeping away the restraints of convention and proper behaviour. "You little shrew," he raged, for the first time in his life shaking a woman hard. "How dare you name me traitor? If Prince Charles had won, 'twould be the followers of German George who'd have had that word flung at them! Who'd be hounded and slaughtered even now, and— Ow!"

His grip was steel. Unable to elude it, Amy had turned her head and sunk her teeth into his wrist.

Glendenning jerked his hand back. His eyes narrowed. "That's the second time, and a time too many, my girl!" Wrathfully, he lifted his other hand.

"Go on," she panted. "Hit me! Oh, but you live down to that horrid red hair, you does! A fine Quality you are, to bash a helpless female!"

His anger fled, and left him, once again, appalled by his loss of control. That he, who had always revered women, should have so brutally shaken this fragile creature! That he should have, even for one instant, contemplated boxing her pretty ears! He bowed his head and, deeply ashamed, said brokenly, "God forgive me! I'm as bad as those *chals* of yours. Worse! For I was taught chivalrous behaviour from my cradle. You've every right to . . . to despise me."

He heard a muffled sound and looked up. She was weeping, making no effort to hide her tears, sitting there watching him, with tears slipping unchecked down her lovely face and sobs wracking her.

He felt as if a knife had plunged under his ribs, and he pleaded brokenly, "Don't! Amy, for the love of God don't cry! I cannot bear it!"

He reached out to her, then drew his hand back again, and groaned, "Always, I bring you to tears and unhappiness. You had better have gone with Absalom. He's ten times the gentle-man I am."

Light as a feather, her fingers touched his cheek. "But you—you was—were right . . . l-lordship. I did pr—steal your purse."

"But you gave it back!"

"No I didn't. You got it from Florian. And we took your lovely gry—I mean, horse."

"Absalom did. And you made him bring her back, and you nursed me, and cooked and—and fought so bravely be-side . . ." The words faded and were forgotten, because she was smiling tremulously through her tears, and in her eyes was a tenderness that took his breath away.

"I bit your poor hand, two times," she said with a gulping sob, and taking up the injured member, she pressed it caress-ingly to her cheek.

A great flood of elation swept over him. He knew at last that from their first meeting the spark of love had been growing ever stronger. His heart had whispered of it and he'd refused to hear. He had denied his deepening affection, closed his mind to it, tried to push it away. But still it had grown, quietly, inexorably, wonderfully. And now it was past deny-ing, for it was no longer a whisper, but a shout, a heady joy that filled his entire being so that he was at once ecstatically happy, and awed, and humble.

"Amy," he whispered. "Oh, my lovely, my precious. What a fool I am, not to have known till now!"

He had no need to seize her, for she melted into his embrace. He kissed her tear-wet cheeks, and her brows, and her perfect nose, and he whispered his adoration even as he claimed her lips.

And Amy gave him kiss for kiss, and murmured her own gentle and cherishing words of love.

Outside, the wind was rising, and the rain beat down strongly. But in the carriage, a man and a girl clung together in a haze of bliss, heedless of rain and wind and gathering shadows; shutting out all else but the wonder of this enchanted moment.

At length, resting his cheek against her curls, for her cap had long since fallen off, the viscount asked the question that fond lovers have asked from the beginning of time. "Do you *really* love me, my Amy?"

"Don't you know, dearest? Can you doubt it after the way I've kissed you and—and let you kiss me?"

He kissed her forehead, and she snuggled happily against his crushed cravat. Marvelling at the change in her, he said, "How prettily you speak now."

" 'Twas you taught me, Horatio."

"I thought I had failed miserably. You did so well when first we started, but then you seemed to delight in speaking roughly, as if you didn't want to try any more."

"I know."

"Why?" he persisted, tilting her chin, and running a finger softly along one slim arched brow.

"Reasons . . ."

He chuckled. "What reasons, my heart?"

Sitting up straighter, she answered slowly, "At first, I thought you was just a lazy good-for-nothing rich wastrel. Then you seemed kind, so I thought I'd try and learn a bit from you. Only . . ." She sighed. "You were so gentle with me. So patient, and never complaining no matter how bad off you was. And you never tried to—to maul me about, or take advantage, even when we was alone, night after night."

He said miserably, "But—I did, Amy. I—"

"Only once," she said, quick to defend him. "And even then, you couldn't stop being an honourable gent, and you was—were so ashamed. I could see you was getting to—to like me a bit. To . . . want me. But even then, you treated me with respect. Like I was a real lady—not some gypsy mort—"

He put a hand across her lips and said firmly, "You are not. I know it. We'll find out where you came from, and it will be some good family, I'll warrant!"

"No, Tio." Her smile was tender but very sad. "It's no good to hope fer miracles. We'll never find who I am, or where I come from. There's too many like me. Too many stole childers—I mean—children. And that's why when I began to—to fall in love with you, I was so awful afraid."

He took both her hands and kissed them lingeringly. "Lord knows, I gave you reason. How you can love me, after I have been so blind, and treated you so disgracefully, I shall never understand. But I know at last that to the end of my days I will love you. And that never will I deserve the wondrous, beautiful, tender, courageous lady that is my Amy."

She gazed at him adoringly for a minute, then, reaching up, she took off his wig and ruffled up his hair. "What a fine gent I found to love me. A true blue nobleman. And in spite of the unkind things I said, I do so love your auburn curls."

With a murmur of impatience he tried to pull her to him once more, but she held him off, and said with a tremulous laugh. "You can't never know how much I wish . . . Only—it ain't no use, y'see. I ain't of your world, nor ever could be. And—and you couldn't never step down into mine. That's why I tried to seem even more coarse and—and ig-norant than I be." She shrugged, but her voice was so thready that she could hardly continue. "I fought 'gainst caring for someone I—couldn't never have. I knew—if I let myself love you, 'twould only bring me sorrow. And you too, perhaps. But—but it got too strong for me. I couldn't—" Blinking away tears, she threw herself into his ready arms, and gasped, "Oh, my Tio! I wish I hadn't loved ye so."

A cold finger touched between his shoulder blades and

cruel reality came to taunt him. When he'd lost Dimity Cranford he had thought love would never be his again. But it had
come, and this time he had given his heart to a peerless creature—who was hopelessly ineligible. He set his jaw stubbornly. This was what he'd been seeking all his life. If his lady
was a trifle unpolished, she was also beautiful and valiant and
pure, and he wasn't going to give her up. He said staunchly,
"We'll find a way, my darling girl. Somehow. We'll find a
way."

The carriage rumbled on through the rainy dusk, and the
two inside still clung to each other, although they were silent
now.

Amy's eyes were closed as she hoarded every second of this
blessed nearness; the strength of his arms about her, the dear
clean manly scent of him, the sure knowledge that he loved
her. Memories she would keep for as long as life lasted.

Glendenning's face was grim, his mind engaged in a desperate search for an answer. The answers were there. Starkly
merciless. His father would think he had run mad. Certainly,
he would forbid such a marriage, and though he could not
deny him the title, he could throw him out, cut off all commu-
nication with his family, deny any funds until his own death.
To defy the earl, to take Amy for his wife, would be to lose
all the other people he loved; to lose friends of a lifetime, who
would surely be horrified by such unheard-of behaviour.
Even if his knowledge of architecture would secure him a
position, he and his love would face years of poverty. More,
his disobedience, his refusal to accept the responsibilities of
his birth and heritage, would hurt his father deeply, and cause
him to be shamed before the world. It would grieve his dear
stepmama beyond bearing. And if, by some miracle, Bowers-
Malden relented and sanctioned the marriage, Amy would be
shunned and despised by the *ton*. He knew all too well how
cruel Society could be. Not that there was any need to waste
time considering such a possibility—by no stretch of the imagination would my lord Gregory Clement Laindon permit so
disastrous a marriage, or countenance that a nameless gypsy
girl would someday become Countess of Bowers-Malden.

He could, of course, ask her to become his mistress. He shrank from the prospect. He had heard her at her nightly prayers, and knew how firm were her religious convictions. Almost, he could hear her saying, "I'll die a old maid 'fore I sell meself to any cove who wants to have me without loving me enough to give me his name!" He saw again the bag of onions whizzing at his jaw, and smiled wistfully. So fierce was the pride of his little love, God bless her.

There was only one logical answer: to put her out of his life. Provide for her—buy her a shop, perhaps, and a cottage where she and Absalom could live together in comfort. Put her out of his life . . . Anguished, he kissed the top of her head and hugged her closer.

And he thought achingly, 'Lord, why did you bring her to me, only to part us forever?'

CHAPTER X

The news swept Glendenning Abbey with the speed of a grass fire. Lord Horatio had arrived in somebody else's carriage, and he hadn't come alone, but was carrying a fast asleep lady into the house. A *young* lady! And with the countess and Miss Marguerite in London town! And the earl expected back at any minute! Whatever next?

Thus it was that, as the massive doors were swung open and Glendenning stepped across the threshold with Amy in his arms, he heard the faintest sound, like a muted and collective sigh, and he wondered how many of their small army of servants had gathered where they might view his scandalous behaviour. His jaw tightening, his eyes flashed to the butler. On Darrow's usually imperturbable countenance he caught a glimpse of dismay. It did not occur to him that his recent illness had left its mark on him, and his only partially correct interpretation of that expression sent his brows twitching into his rare frown.

"Miss Consett is fatigued," he said crisply. "She has had a most harrowing experience. I shall want two of our best maids to care for her."

The butler's eyes darted to the steps.

"She brings neither servants nor luggage," said Glendenning in a voice of ice. "Require Mrs. Burnaby to have the Duchess Suite readied at once, if you please. And a fire lit in the hearth."

Darrow inclined his head. "Yes, milord. Perhaps the footmen could carry—"

"No. I shall take her upstairs."

Darrow stood motionless for a second, looking after that resolute figure. A shushing of draperies alerted him to the fact that Mrs. Burnaby was beside him. He turned and sent one round-eyed lackey running for the maids, and the other hurrying to summon the fire boy.

A tall woman, with a graceful carriage and a meticulousness in dress that caused her plain brown gown to appear elegant, the housekeeper ruled her domain with firm but not unkind authority. Just now, her fine hazel eyes were aghast, and she murmured, " 'Pon my soul, Mr. Darrow, he's in a proper rage. Only see how he limps. Whatever do you think . . . ?"

"Trouble, is what I think," said Darrow. "And there'll be more and to spare when the master comes home."

"Which he is liable to do at any minute," she nodded.

"Lord Horatio wants the Duchess Suite for Miss Consett. Best get it ready. Fast."

"The Duchess Suite!" Full of questions and speculation, Mrs. Burnaby knew better than to give voice to either, and after that shocked remark she rustled away, torn between concern and indignation. His lordship looked properly wrung out, true, but he knew very well that the Duchess Suite was reserved for important guests. Not for his new lightskirt!

Striding towards the main staircase, Glendenning was already regretting his quick-tempered high-handedness. Amy weighed very little, but the Duchess Suite was miles away, and his confounded ankle made stairs a nuisance. On the third step, he stumbled.

At once a hand was supporting his elbow. Michael's valet said, "I think you are tired, sir. Permit that we help."

"Gently, then." Glendenning relinquished his burden into the arms of a large and magnificent footman. "Gently. The poor soul is worn out."

He saw by the footman's suddenly round eyes that his words had provided fuel for the scandal, and was too weary to care. Quite unable to keep up, he hobbled after Whittlesey, longing for his own bed, but with no intention of seeking it as yet.

By the time he limped into the luxurious suite, more servants had scurried up the back stairs. Two upstairs maids were flying around the great bed, whipping sheets and blankets about; the fireboy was coaxing a fire into being; a blushful abigail carried in a nightgown, dressing gown and slippers, undoubtedly borrowed from Marguerite; another was lighting candles. The footman stood stolidly with Amy in his arms.

Mrs. Burnaby bustled in. "Oh my, what a lovely creature," she observed, peeping at Amy. With the slightly proprietary manner of one who, having served the family since the viscount was in short coats, did not stand on ceremony, she added, "Now, you really must be off, my lord, and let us care for her."

"Egad," said Glendenning, comprehending fuzzily that he was in a lady's bedchamber. "So I must. You will look after her, Burny?"

"Of course. And you must look after yourself, my lord. You are worn to a shade. I trust you have not been ill?"

"Oh—a little. Nothing to matter. I must see my mother. Is the countess downstairs?"

"Why, no, sir. Lady Nola and Miss Marguerite are both in Town."

"Oh, my God," gasped Glendenning, causing several loyal but worried hearts to beat a little easier. "What's to be done, Burny? Must I go into Windsor for the night? Miss Consett has been entrusted to my care, but we'd no chance to bring a chaperone, and—"

Smiling her relief, the housekeeper said that since Miss Marguerite had left her abigail at home, they would set up a truckle bed, and the girl could sleep in here with Miss Consett, which should satisfy convention, at least for one night.

The viscount hesitated, but suddenly the humour of it

struck him. Whatever, he wondered, would the redoubtable Mrs. Burnaby say if she knew he had spent considerably more than one night alone with Miss Consett, with not a whiff of a chaperone within miles! He rested a last searching glance on the peacefully sleeping face of his beloved, and limped out. Mr. Whittlesey, waiting at the open door, had seen the betraying softening of the drawn features and he exchanged a quick glance with the housekeeper. He had hoped for a minute that they were out of the bog. It appeared that his hopes may have been premature.

Amy had never indulged in the wastefulness of sleeping late. When a distant clock chimed six she awoke to the strange sensation that she was still dreaming. She lay in a bed big enough for five and soft as a cloud. Silken sheets and a quilted pink and white eiderdown covered her, and her head rested on an even prettier pillowcase than the satin one she had prigged from a bazaar last summer. She closed her eyes, but when she opened them she was still in the dream, so she sat up, and pulled back the pink silk bedcurtains. The room was a dream, all by itself. Someone had shared it with her, apparently, because there was a small bed at the foot of her own, which had obviously been slept in.

Unaware that the embroidered and tasselled pull by the bed would summon maids, she got out of bed and wandered about, gazing in awe from one delight to another. Thick rugs were strewn on gleaming floors, the furnishings were white and gold, the walls were hung with a hand-painted paper of pink, mauve, and white, and so exquisite one might chop out bits, she thought, and frame them. The casements stood wide, although the morning was cool and clouds still covered the sun. She hurried over to look out upon a great sweep of gardens and ornamental water, with a park beyond that stretched to the distant hills.

"Cor!" she whispered. "This dream is a bit of all right, it is!"

Dancing over to the wash-stand she poured water from a porcelain pitcher into a bowl so fragile that she dreaded lest she break it. When one dwelt in a dream palace, one must be clean, even if the water was much colder than the stream wherein she usually performed her morning ablutions. She applied soap to sponge and washed bravely.

Afterwards, she went shiveringly in search of clothing, and gingerly opened one of the presses. There hung the gown from Mrs. Wilks' little village shop.

A long time later, she was still sitting on the floor, holding the gown pressed against her. But smells came wafting in through the open windows. Delicious smells of frying bacon and coffee brewing. And instead of sharing whatever time she had with him, she was sitting here, grieving. Uncle Ab would say that was stupid. Dear old Ab. He'd likely led those varmints a proper dance yesterday, and got clean away. But she wondered where he was, and knew he'd be worrying about her. She said a prayer for him, then jumped up and began to brush her hair.

Soon, wearing the pink gown that she would cherish for as long as she lived, she crept into the hall and caught her breath at the splendour of it. She wandered along, edging around carpets too lovely to be stepped upon, and looking about her as she searched for breakfast. Half an hour passed, and she was still wandering. She had seen rooms with red velvet furniture, and rooms with sofas and chairs of blue brocade; gold rooms and cream rooms; and a great big chamber, all scarlet and white, that she'd have thought must be a ballroom, but was evidently a sort of state dining room, for it had a very big table sitting all by itself in the middle of the highly polished floor. It was quite the strangest dining table she'd ever seen, for the top was covered in a fuzzy sort of green stuff with a bunch of white balls huddled in the middle of it. There was a high edge all around the table that would get in the way when you was trying to eat, and most strange of all, there was round holes at each corner of the green cloth, going clear through the table and with little bags hanging under them. She'd stood and puzzled at that table for some time, wondering why the balls was there, and had finally decided they must be for guests to heave at the servants if they was too slow. Going on then, she had been awed by two rooms, one big and one huge, the walls covered from floor to ceiling with crowded bookshelves. Entranced, she had crept in, but she'd heard someone walk past, and, afraid they might think she'd prigged something, she'd hidden under a long thin table until the footsteps receded. Now, she tiptoed back into this wide corridor that seemed to go on forever. Where, oh where was the kitchen? And would she ever find her darling Lordship in this great echoing place?

She turned a corner and, in the middle of another endless corridor, discovered a curving flight of stairs. Very grand. She ran down them, and could hear voices and, distantly, the rattle of dishes. The entrance hall was vast and very beautiful in a royal sort of way, but she mustn't stop to look at all the great mirrors, and the paintings on the ceilings, and the fine but naughty statues, and the vases and bowls of flowers. She skipped along lightly and turning into yet another corridor almost collided with a very big gent who had a rather tired face, and carried a parcel under one arm.

He stopped and stared at her. He wasn't all dressed up fancy like, and he wore a ordinary kind of wig, which was crooked. He must, she decided, be a servant, and a overworked one by the look of him.

"Where's the vittles, mate?" she whispered.

He scowled and looked very angry indeed. "*What?*" he thundered.

Amy jumped to put a hand over his lips. "Crumbs!" she hissed. "D'ye want to wake the lot of 'em? What you getting all beside of yerself fer?" She recollected belatedly where she was, and that she mustn't disgrace her love. Stepping back, she held up one hand to silence him as she straightened her gown. Then, "Does you work here, my good cove?" she enquired with a regal smile.

"No, I do not, madam," growled the Earl of Bowers-Malden, setting aside the gift he had brought from Ireland for his wife. He added with a curl of the lip, "Do you?"

His sarcasm was lost upon Amy. She must, she thought,

have done well, for he had called her "madam." "No, I do not neither," she said, enunciating carefully. But the thought of seeing Tio again was making her too happy to maintain a proper reserve. Her sunny smile dawned. "And it's a good thing," she went on, taking his arm in her friendly way. "Straight, a body could starve to death in here, before he found the fork-and-gaiters." An oddly glazed look came into his eyes, and she bit her lip. Perhaps she'd better talk fancy, at that. "A funny way of gab what I picked up from my second abigail," she explained airily, "meaning pork and taters." And she added, "I'm a—er, sort of guest, you might say. Of Viscount Glendenning. Have you et?"

The earl took a deep breath and a slightly purple hue darkened his face. So Horatio was here, for once. And believing his trusting sire to be safely from home he had dared—had *dared* come slithering into the abbey with his trollop! He'd skin the young dog alive, be damned if—

"Poor old duck," said Amy, peering up at him anxiously. "Ye looks proper gut-foundered."

Reeling, the earl nonetheless managed to declare in tones calculated to freeze Salome in the middle of her dance, that he was neither old nor a duck.

"No, but you better eat, 'cause you do look poorly. It's always the way with big co—men," she imparted, pulling him along with her. "They got to keep their strength up. Don't you worry, mate. I'll see you get fed."

With a muffled snort, the earl pulled free so violently that he cracked his elbow on an armoire chest and had to grip his lips together to keep from swearing.

Amy's arm went around him. "Here, just lean on me. You'll feel better once you got—pop something in yer—your belly."

The earl started a furious rejoinder, but she smiled up at him with such radiance that he experienced the odd sensation that the sun had broken through the clouds and lit this rather gloomy hall. Jove, but she was a pretty little chit. The ridiculous aspects of the situation began to intrigue him. He chuckled and entered the farce. "The breakfast room is over here, miss," he whispered, and opened the door, hoping it was still too early for many servants to be about.

They weren't, but because he had sent a courier on before him, and was expected by eight o'clock, the sideboard had been prepared, and the covered tureens were ready. He ushered Amy inside.

"Here," she said, pausing uncertainly. "You won't get turned off, will you? I mean, is—are you let eat in here?"

"Occasionally, yes," he said. "But thank you for your kind concern. Perhaps you'll allow me to serve you?"

"With what, mate? There ain't nowt to serve."

He grinned, pulled out a chair for her, then crossed to the sideboard and began to dish out eggs and bacon and kidneys and buttered muffins. Placing a full plate before her, he excused himself, went swiftly into the large breakfast parlour and gave an imperative tug on the bell rope. Rejoining Amy a few minutes later, he carried a fragrant pot of coffee which he set beside her. "Now," he said, "we may be comfortable."

"I don't know about comfortable," she said dubiously. "I can't help but feel sorry for 'em, you know, Mr.—What's your name? Me good man," she added, since she was Tio's guest, and must act the part of a nob.

"Gregory," he said, enjoying himself more by the minute. "And yours, ma'am?"

"Miss Consett. You gotta eat more than that! Big cove like you. Better grab some of them—those there pork slices. Don't no one take care of you?"

"Alas, no," he lied, callously disposing of his beloved wife and family, countless relatives and friends, and an army of loyal retainers. He selected a slice of cold pork and conveyed his laden plate to the table. "But—do tell me, why are you sorry for the—er, folks that lives here?"

She threw a glance at the doors and, forgetting her status, leaned closer. "Well, I don't think Horatio likes living here much," she said confidingly. "And I reckon I wouldn't, neither."

Frowning a little, he asked, "Did Lord Glendenning tell you he doesn't like the abbey?"

"No, but it's plain as the nose on yer phiz," she answered, daintily licking jam from her thumb. "His old man's got a proper bad case of the dafts."

Fascinated, he murmured, "Indeed?"

"Must have, poor old gaffer." She waved a piece of bacon at him. "What gent in his right mind would stick pictures up on the ceiling where anyone's going to get a crick in their neck looking at 'em? Unless he didn't like 'em, maybe, only I thought they was quite nice."

At this point the earl, who had choked over his coffee, was obliged to resort to wiping his eyes with his napkin. Amy left her chair to pound him on the back, urge him to drink some water, and enquire with warm solicitude if he was better.

He said gratefully that she was a "kind-hearted creature," and after she had returned to her chair, he asked breathlessly, "What do you suppose caused Bowers-Malden to be short of a sheet? I've heard his son and heir is something of a serpent's tooth. Perhaps he drove the earl to—"

Indignant, she interrupted. "What, Lord Horatio? Stuff! They don't come no finer than Tio." A dreaming look came into her eyes. She sighed wistfully, then realized her companion was staring at her with a rather odd expression. She added hastily, "No, mate. I 'spect it's this house what done it. Give the earl the miseries, I mean. After all, it ain't a proper house, is it? So awful big and lonely." Being a fair-minded girl, she sought about for some redeeming feature, then amended, "Well, I 'spect you could play a good game of bowls in lots of the rooms. But they got the funniest table in their big dining room, with the cloth stuck down and all green and furry, so how they'd ever wash it I don't know. I suppose it's all of a piece, 'cause if they live in places like this it's small wonder most of the Quality's clear off their tibbys!"

Lord Gregory Bowers-Malden threw back his leonine head and roared with laughter.

"You young dog," he growled at his son half an hour later, "how dared you slip your bit o' muslin into the house whilst we was all away? I can well imagine what the servants thought!"

The viscount had been so exhausted when he went to bed that he'd expected to sleep soundly. Thunder had awoken him at two o'clock, however, and between the following storm, his aching ankle, and his many anxieties, he had not slept again. He was still somewhat bemused by the shock of seeing his formidable sire stamp into his bedchamber, but he had never been able to follow the earl's example and act as if the servants were invisible. Turning from his dressing table, he dismissed Whittlesey and took up his wig. When the door had closed behind the valet, he said quietly, "Miss Consett is not a bit o' muslin, sir. Once you meet her—"

"Been chatting with her this thirty minutes and more," boomed the earl, marching over to fling open another casement in the already cool room.

Glendenning held his breath, waiting for the storm.

"She's an entertaining chit," said Bowers-Malden. "The common folk have an innate honesty 'twould behoove us all to emulate. Even so, Glendenning, I—Good God!" Staring at his son's reflected face, he moved closer. "What the deuce has happened t'ye, boy? Never say you went out with that devil Falcon?" One muscular hand touched the viscount's hair very gently. "Caught you in the head, did he? That worthless rogue! I trust you gave as good as you got?"

The smile that accompanied the last words was not quite steady, and to his astonishment Glendenning saw that the freckles, so like his own, which dusted the bridge of his sire's nose, stood out in sharp relief against a sudden pallor. Lady Nola had tried often to convince him that the earl loved him, but he had been very sure his father not only did not give a button for him, but held him in contempt. The fear now so evident in the pale green eyes quite unmanned him, and for an instant he was unable to reply.

Bowers-Malden's hand dropped to his shoulder. "My dear boy," he said in a tone Horatio had not heard for years, "you *are* all right?"

Perhaps because he was so bewildered, Glendenning's slim fingers flew with involuntary and betraying speed to cover his father's hand. Amazement was succeeded by an emotion so deep that even when he could command his voice it was very gruff. "I am quite all right, sir . . . I thank you."

Embarrassment at such a display of affection then seized these two very British gentlemen. Bowers-Malden grunted and took himself to the door and back. Glendenning picked up his wig again, and made an effort to speak lightly. "If you have been chatting with Miss Consett, I'd have thought she would have told you the truth of the matter, sir."

Having recovered his composure, the earl chuckled, and tossed his massive frame into a chair. "She was much too busy giving me her evaluation of this horrid old house, and her assessment of the mental deficiency of most members of the Quality."

Glendenning groaned. "I can well believe it! Sir, pray do not take umbrage. She means not a bit of harm."

"I doubt I have laughed so much in years, nor seen a lovelier little armful. For how long has she been under your protection? You'd have done well to get her instruction in proper behaviour, Horatio, if only for her own sake."

Having adjusted the wig carefully over his scarred head, Glendenning drew a chair closer to his father. If he was very adroit, this might be a perfect opportunity to try and win the old fellow over. "Miss Consett is not under my protection, sir," he began. "At least, not in the way you infer. The fact is that I was set upon in the woods, and she very bravely intervened, and saved my life."

"*What?*" The earl jerked forward, his face flushing darkly. "Have you called in Bow Street? Have you sent hunters after the swine? Hell and the devil confound 'em! That a British peer should be attacked by such vermin!" He sprang up, then sat down again. Breathing hard, his eyes sparking, he demanded, "Tell me the whole."

Glendenning told him considerably less than the whole, fabricating a tale wherein he had chased a pickpocket into the woods and been attacked by more ruffians. Amy's intrepid rescue he did detail, however, sending Bowers-Malden into shattering whoops of laughter.

"By Jupiter, but she's a Trojan," declared the earl, driving his fist onto the arm of the chair with such force his son wondered it did not splinter to fragments. "Lived nearby, did she?"

"Er, yes, sir. With her uncle, who is a most talented artist, and—"

"Is that so? And he let you carry her off, eh? Knew which side his bread was buttered on, and I do not blame the fellow one whit! You owe the gel, Horatio, be damned if y'don't. With some schooling and the right gowns, you'll be able to take her out in public without having to hide your head in a basket. Likely, you'll have to pension her off when you take a bride, though, and that's always a devilish business."

Nerving himself, Glendenning stood. "Sir," he said, "Mistress Amy Consett is the loveliest, the most brave and warm-hearted lady I have ever—"

"She's warm-hearted, all right," interposed the earl with enthusiasm. "D'you know, the chit worried because she fixed it in her pretty head that I don't eat enough. Asked if no one took care of me!" His laugh rumbled out again. "I'm glad to see your ability to select diamonds of the first water ain't deserted you, after all, my boy."

"Thank you, sir. And since you are so anxious that I marry soon—"

"Aha!" Standing also, the earl asked, "Found a suitable lady, have you?"

He looked so eager, his eyes bright with affection. Glendenning's heart sank. He had only just realized that the dear old fellow cared for him. To have to hurt him so soon after that revelation was cruelly hard. He hesitated, trying desperately to find the proper words.

Bowers-Malden noted that hesitancy. His heir was properly tongue-tied. Likely hadn't worked up the courage to fix his interest with his chosen lady. Damme, if his hands weren't trembling, and he looked deuced ill. This was no time to pinch at him. "Never mind, lad," he said kindly. "I've no longer any doubt but that you'll bring home a viscountess who will prove a worthy companion to your mama and Marguerite, and do honour to us all." His son still looked troubled, and he added a reinforcing, "For a while there, you had me worrying lest you might plump for some cit's daughter, or someone even more rankly ineligible, like a—a gel from a flower shop, or even—ha! ha!—a pretty gypsy!" Much amused by this good joke, his clap on the back sent Glendenning staggering.

And it was no use. He just couldn't bring himself to speak the words that would devastate his father. Especially since the unknown menace that the Terrier constituted might very well add to the earl's woes soon enough. With an answering smile, Glendenning decided that he would first resolve Michael's dilemma, whatever it was, and then strive to win Lady Nola's support in the matter of his own romantic difficulties.

The earl declared his intention to call in his man of affairs and set about tracking down the murderous rogues who had attacked his heir. With difficulty Glendenning managed to extricate himself from an immediate involvement in this plan, and at length was able to escape. Bowers-Malden stamped off briskly in the direction of study and secretary, and Glendenning hurried in search of his love.

Lady Nola's personal footman intercepted him as he reached the head of the stairs. "The countess has returned, my lord," he said in a near whisper. "And wishes to see you at once."

Glendenning frowned. Dearly as he loved his stepmother, he was consumed with impatience to see Amy. "Be so good as to tell her ladyship that I will come to her in ten minutes' time."

His attempt to move on was frustrated when the footman sprang to the next step, and faced him with an even more urgent whisper. "My lady is *most* anxious to speak to you, sir. *Before* the earl learns of her arrival."

"Dammit," said Glendenning. "I told you I will come—"

"And Miss Consett is in the gardens with Miss Marguerite," interrupted the footman, the light of desperation in his eyes.

Enraged by such impertinence, Glendenning's frown darkened to the point that the footman shook in his shoes. But that the man should have dared to presume to such a remark argued a real anxiety, and loyalty must not be rewarded with a rebuke. His expression eased, therefore, and with a request that breakfast be brought to Lady Nola's apartments, he changed direction.

Lady Nola looked pale and distraught, but welcomed him formally into her comfortable parlour, then sent her abigail away. No sooner had the door closed behind that devoted retainer than my lady cast herself on Glendenning's chest. "Thank God you have come, Horatio," she gulped tearfully. "I have been at my wits' end, not knowing what to do or—" Drawing back, she exclaimed, "But, my dear, you have been ill, I think?"

He had never seen her in such an agitated state, but he concealed his alarm and leading her to the sofa said calmly, "Nothing of any consequence, and my news will keep. Now tell me what's amiss, m'dear. It is my graceless brother, I presume."

The countess' smile was wan. She told him swiftly of Michael's disastrous fling at the tables, and had just revealed the staggering amount of his indebtedness when her footman returned, followed by maids with two laden trays. The viscount was inwardly relieved because the trouble appeared to be nothing worse than that his brother had run up a disgracefully large gambling debt. While the servants proceeded to lay the table in the window bay, he seized the interval to remark that he had brought a guest with him.

"A Miss Consett, Mama, who chances to be a friend of Katrina Falcon. I came upon her at the scene of an accident last evening. Her maid had been injured, and a physician carried her to his home for treatment. There was no suitable inn at which I could properly leave Miss Consett, so I brought her here for you and Margo to care for." He grinned wryly. "A fine fix I found myself in . . ."

The servants reluctantly finished their task and the footman stood by, prepared to learn more as he waited at table, but Glendenning murmured his thanks and sent them all off.

Staring at him in considerable astonishment, the countess asked as the door closed, "Horatio, was that—"

"A pack of lies," he admitted, smiling as he pulled out a chair for her. "Invented purely for the benefit of the servants. Oh, but I've a deal to tell you! But first, love, you shall enjoy a good breakfast. Or have you already eaten?"

She had not, she admitted. "But I couldn't touch a morsel. Do you eat, Horatio, whilst I finish telling you of this wretched business."

Glendenning slanted a worried glance at her. Lady Nola thoroughly enjoyed her table, and for her to refuse such a tempting display of food when she had not yet breakfasted spoke volumes. He poured her a cup of coffee, then turned his attention to his own meal while her ladyship related the details concerning the Comyn Pin.

"We were so happy," she said, tearing nervously at her handkerchief. "Michael went to offer the pin to Major Trethaway, and—and I thought we were out of it all. Only . . . only then," her voice faltered, "this wretched little serpent of a man came."

The familiar chill was seeping between Glendenning's shoulder blades. He put down his knife. "Burton Farrier," he said softly.

"Yes!" Her worried eyes shot to his face. "Oh, Tio! I am so very frightened!" He reached out to her, and she seized his hand and clung to it, her fingers like ice.

"I fancy you dealt with him beautifully, even so," he said comfortingly. "He teased you about my political persuasions, did he?"

"No. But—but I think he must suspect, because he prosed on about some list of donations made to the Jacobite Cause. Evidently, the list has come to light—not with names, but with the details of items contributed." She heard her stepson's swift intake of breath, and felt his fingers tighten on her own. Scanning his face, which suddenly looked more grim than she could ever remember, her heart fluttered painfully. "Horatio," she whispered. "Do you know if there is—was— such a list?"

By God, but there was! It had been compiled in a well-meant attempt eventually to reward and reimburse the donors, but had it fallen into military hands after the collapse of the Uprising it would have meant sure death for all those named. When he recalled the price that had been paid by the gallant Jacobite couriers who had struggled to deliver that list into safe hands, the viscount's blood ran cold. He had understood that one copy had been destroyed, and that a second list had, at great cost to the couriers, been safely delivered. It was not beyond the realm of possibility, however, that the first list had not been destroyed after all; or that another copy had somehow found its way into the Terrier's hands.

He said, "Even if there were such a list, we did not contribute the Comyn Pin."

"I know. I know. But that revolting creature insists the pin appears on the list, and he implied that if we cannot produce it, he—he will . . ."

"He will have to assume that the rumours about your stepson are perfectly true, and that I donated it to Bonnie Charles? Fudge! The villain is trying to frighten you, m'dear. The pin *cannot* be on the list if we did not donate it."

My lady closed her eyes for an instant. Her voice was thready when she said, "There were—two Comyn Pins, Tio. In the old days, one was worn by the current holder of the title, and the other by the heir. The title died with my father. He bequeathed one pin to me, and the other to my sister Caroline who still, I believe, lives in Edinburgh. It is quite possible that—that Caroline did donate her pin. But I cannot betray her to Farrier, dearest."

"Certainly not."

"So you see," she said miserably, "if we cannot show him ours . . ."

Glendenning drew back. 'That properly drives me to the ropes,' he thought. And he asked, "How did you get rid of him?"

"I told him Michael had taken the pin to a gentleman who might be interested in buying it. My only thought, of course, was to get it back. Farrier went away, saying he would expect

Michael to call on him. When Michael came home, he was so happy, poor darling, because this Major Trethaway *had* accepted the pin as payment in full."

Glendenning said slowly, "I see. Then we must buy it back, Mama."

"Yes, dear. I swallowed my pride and borrowed the rest of the money Michael owed, and he left at once to see Major Trethaway. The next day, Farrier was here again."

"Damn the pest for hounding you so, knowing that my father and I were from home! I fancy he demanded to see my brother?"

"He did, of course. And he—kept at me until at last, I became so confused . . ." She drew a hand across her eyes distractedly.

Raging, Glendenning said fondly, "Do not be in a pucker, Mama. I know you did very well. Lord, but I wish I had been here! I make you my apologies that I was not. I expect you had to tell the pest about Templeby's predicament, eh?"

"I had no choice, Horatio. I could see Farrier didn't believe me, so I had to break my promise to Michael." She looked at her stepson imploringly. "It was a dreadful thing to do, but I—I was sure, under the circumstances, he would understand."

"Most assuredly he would. Did Farrier accept the fact that Michael had traded the pin in lieu of gaming debts?"

"He was angry, but said he would wait, and asked that I send him word immediately Michael returned with the pin."

"Then we've nothing to fear. I shall make good your expense. Michael will have learned a valuable lesson, and— Ah, I see there is something more. Tell me."

" 'Tis just that Michael should have come back long before now. I thought he might have met you somewhere, but I was so worried that I tried to find you. I went to Town, and your friends promised to look for you both. I was sure Michael would be here when I returned. But—" Her hands clenched. "Well, you see, he is not. And we have not much time."

"What? D'you say that wart is holding you to a schedule? I thought you said he promised to wait?"

The countess wet her lips. "He sent a note by messenger, saying he has waited long enough and that he will call here . . . this afternoon!"

Glendenning did not go at once to find Amy. Instead, he made his way from Lady Nola's apartments in the east wing, along the upper hall, around the corner to the north wing, and thence to a sumptuous guest suite.

The suite had been occupied only once in his memory, the guest being a most distinguished eastern gentleman who had offered his own hospitality some years before, while the earl was visiting India. Bowers-Malden was not given to lavish displays, but he had felt deeply beholden to this particular friend, and a suite had been prepared that had been the wonder of the household. Thick rugs had been laid down, fine paintings of exotic Indian landscapes were hung throughout the suite, and the walls and floor of the small parlour had been covered with mosaic tiles. From the servants' chatter Horatio, then eight years old, had gleaned the fascinating information that the guest, who wore very odd clothing, was a Maharajah, and that when he was irked—as often seemed the case—he would retire to the parlour and swear, all by himself, sometimes for thirty minutes at a stretch, and in five different languages.

For a lonely small boy, such talent held enormous fascination. Long after the Maharajah had dispensed splendid gifts to each member of the household, taken his large retinue and gone back into the mystery from whence he had come, Horatio had crept, at least once a week, to the Indian Suite, and especially into the small parlour. With a delicious sense of wickedness, he had practised his own oaths, lowering his boyish voice to what he fancied was an approximation of the Maharajah's tones. The parlour faced north and, with its abundance of tile, was a cold chamber, but it had delighted him on several counts. A faint aroma of incense still hung on the air; the windows overlooked the wilderness area, which extended to the woods, beyond which again, was the River Thames; and, most importantly, nobody ever thought of looking for him there. When the initial fascinations faded, and before Lady Nola came into his life, he had fallen into the habit of retreating to the Indian parlour when hurt or troubled. In later years, he kept his drawing table and his many books on architecture in the quiet rooms, where he could study in a peace quite undisturbed by well-meaning but sometimes suffocating family and servants.

Now, having once again sought his refuge, he sprawled in the comfortable wing chair, deep in thought. There could be no doubt but that Farrier was after him. The business about the Comyn Pin was a trumped-up mockery but, when combined with his suspected Jacobite involvements, it could be used most effectively. If they had a list, and if the pin really did appear on it, they would claim it was the final piece of evidence needed to condemn him.

Only the devil was in it that it wasn't just him. The charge would be High Treason, beyond any doubt, and it would be claimed that he—a traitor to England—had been given sanctuary here. The estates could be confiscated. In addition to himself, his father and Lady Nola would very probably be executed. Perhaps even Michael and Marguerite. His hand tightened on the chair arm, a muffled exclamation escaping him at the thought of such a ghastly development. Even if Farrier's list was forged purely to entrap suspects, who would bother to prove its lack of authenticity at a time when all England seemed obsessed by this frenzy to seek out and destroy Jacobites and Jacobite supporters? No, it was a very real and deadly threat; a threat brought down upon those he loved by his own actions.

There was no point in regretting his decision to fight for the Scottish prince. He had followed his convictions, and it was done and ineradicable. But—why now? Why, after all these months of having believed himself safe, had someone put Terrier Farrier on his trail? Many had suspected him, of course. It was well known that he cried friends with Trevelyan de Villars, who had escaped England half a leap ahead of a troop of dragoons. A particularly unpleasant lieutenant of dragoon guards had damn near caught him with that Jacobite cypher. All those things would be brought out and must add weight to the charges against him. Lord, what a bog!

He drew a hand across his eyes. A little while ago his greatest worry had been how to tell his sire that he loved a rankly ineligible lady. Now, he must face the fact that he had brought the shadow of ruin and death over his entire family.

He jerked out of the chair and paced to the window. The familiar greens of the wilderness area stretched out, serene and beautiful. Two of the spaniels were chasing a ball one of the stableboys threw for them. The skies were pale blue, hung with clouds that moved rapidly, sending shadows racing across the land. In the woods, the trees tossed about, reminding him of other woods, and a valiant lady . . .

To immediately ride out in search of Michael was out of the question. He had no intention of leaving his stepmother to face Burton Farrier alone. Besides, Michael might be on his way home with the Comyn Pin at this very minute. God send he came in time! But if he did not, if he had been unable to get the pin back . . .

Glendenning bowed his head and faced the obvious solution. The ramifications made him horribly aware that he was not a brave man.

CHAPTER XI

Sir Owen Furlong was a tall ex-army officer, whip-cord lean, sufficiently good looking to be sighed over by London's damsels, and much admired by her Bucks and Corinthians. After having been stationed for some years in India, he had sold his commission and at the ripe old age of two and thirty was now thoroughly enjoying what he described as "the quiet life." Quite the man about Town, he was happiest when at his large farm a few miles west of Tunbridge Wells, and delighted to welcome visitors to the spacious and rambling old house.

He was not acquainted with Lieutenant Morris but, moving in the same social circles as Falcon, had encountered him often enough to be aware he could not like him. This had nothing to do with Falcon's mixed birth, or the fact that Sir Owen's lineage was impeccable. Born into one of the most ancient if not one of the richest families in the land, he conducted himself with the quiet assurance of the true aristocrat, a combination that inevitably aroused Falcon's contempt. Aware of this, Sir Owen was puzzled by the late-morning visit. He hid his feelings admirably. Any friend of Tio Glendenning, he declared, was a friend of his. He ushered his guests into a charming withdrawing room with latticed casements, a low, beamed ceiling, comfortable chairs, some splendid marine paintings, and a fire that blazed and crackled merrily on a massive stone hearth.

An old hound heaved itself up from before the fire and padded over to greet the new arrivals. Falcon showed his first sign of enthusiasm, and was diverted from his initial and obvious intention of coming straight to the point.

Morris, having shaken Chaucer's paw when offered, was too polite to at once state their reasons for having come. He accepted the Madeira that was offered, sat beside his host, and complimented him on his home. Sir Owen was only too pleased to respond to such genuine interest. When Falcon concluded his conversation with Chaucer, he was nonplussed to discover the two men chattering like old friends, not about some military campaign which he had been prepared to endure for a second or two, but regarding some feature of the front door.

Looking from one to the other, he said, "Your pardon an I was wool gathering."

"Flea gathering, more like," said Morris *sotto voce.*

Ignoring him, Falcon enquired, "Have you some difficulty with your door, Furlong?"

Amused by the impatience in the handsome features, Furlong said gravely, "I'd not thought so. But Morris is concerned lest it should fall off."

"Fall off?" Falcon stared at Morris incredulously. "Why in the name of all that's wonderful should it fall off? Looks solid as the Rock of Gibraltar to me."

"An you'd had the good manners to join the conversation instead of gossiping with the hound," scolded Morris, "you might have heard. 'When seagulls fly—' "

Falcon jabbed a cautionary finger at him. "Do not. I warn you! Do—*not!*" He turned to find Furlong's blue eyes alight with laughter, and said, "Sir, the reason we are come—"

"It's those iron bands," interjected Morris thoughtfully. "Must weigh a ton."

"And were put there," Falcon said with emphasis, "to

strengthen the blasted door, so it—don't—fall—down! Now that vital matter is clarified, perhaps we can—"

" 'Twould seem to me," Morris persisted, "that the very weight of 'em might cause the door to keel over. Don't mean to be a mustard pot, but I was warning Sir Owen that he'd best take care when he pulls it open. One of these days—"

"My sainted Aunt Clara!" exploded Falcon. "*Will* you cease your idiotic babblings? Furlong, we must ask—"

Furlong saw Morris' mouth opening and, having no desire that bloody murder be perpetrated under his roof, he interposed placatingly, "No, but I am grateful for Morris' interest. I might point out, however, that Tio has gone all through this house, and I feel sure was there any cause for alarm, he'd have warned me of't."

For once mutually baffled, they both stared at him.

Furlong said, "He's a splendid architect. Studied it for years. Were you not aware?"

"Jove," said Morris, impressed. "Is that a fact? Old Tio, eh? D'you hear that, Falcon?"

"Since I am about six feet removed from Sir Owen, I was able to strain my ears sufficiently to catch the gist of his remarks. Does the name Burton Farrier mean anything to you, Furlong?"

Sir Owen's manner became chill. "It means I shall not be at home the next time he calls, I promise you! If you are here in his behalf—"

Falcon uttered an incensed exclamation.

Morris said with rare sharpness, "Do you say the Terrier has been here? Recently?"

"Yesterday. Dashed rum customer, I thought. What is he? Some kind of tax collector?"

"He's a very ugly customer with a sort of roving commission from the Horse Guards to track down Jacobite sympathisers," said Falcon.

"Zounds!" exclaimed Sir Owen, dismayed.

Morris asked anxiously, "Ask you about Glendenning, did he?"

"No! He told me he was trying to run young Templeby to

earth. Good God! You never think he may—" He stopped abruptly.

"We think he's after old Tio," said Morris.

Sir Owen swore. "I'd hoped that trail was cold at last. What does Tio say of it?"

"If we knew, 'twould help," said Falcon. "Glendenning's fallen off the edge of the world, it seems. Lady Bowers-Malden has asked that we try to find him, or find his brother, who appears to have gone haring off after a fellow named Trethaway."

"Harris Trethaway? Claims to be a major?"

"That's the one," said Morris. "Ain't he a major?"

"I don't give a fig whether he's a major or a midshipman," snapped Falcon. "Where can we find the confounded fellow? Do you know?"

"I do, as a matter of fact. Not that I've ever been there, but he's fairly popular in some circles, and I understand he owns a tidy little place in Kent. Not far from Lamberhurst, I think." Sir Owen added apologetically, "I'm afraid I cannot give you a more precise direction, but you'll likely discover it easily enough."

"Then, my apologies, but we must lose no more time." Falcon bent to pat Chaucer, then shook hands with their host. "My thanks, Furlong. You've been most helpful."

Sir Owen gripped Morris' outthrust hand. "I shall expect you to let me know if there's anything I can do. *Anything!* Tio is my very good friend."

He walked with them onto the front steps, and remarked that the wind was coming up. "Looks as if we might have some more rain."

Morris said, "Matter of fact—"

"If it's about the damned door," said Falcon irritably, "have done!"

"Ain't. I was going to ask—you said this major-maybe fellow was quite popular, Sir Owen. Do you say he's—ah, socially acceptable?"

"Oh, yes." Furlong hesitated. "I don't like to speak against a man, but in this case it might—. Well, to be blunt, there are those of us who believe Trethaway is a regular Captain Sharp; not above leading green youngsters into play till they're hopelessly in his debt. I personally think he sometimes uses loaded dice. Told him so to his face—but only got a laugh out of him. On the other hand—'' He shrugged. "Many hold him to be a good enough fellow. Certainly, he's a bruising rider, and a pretty fair all-around sportsman. Poor old Derrydene, for instance, wouldn't hear a word against . . .'' He paused.

Falcon, who had been starting down the steps, fairly whipped around, obviously shocked, and Morris looked stunned.

Furlong said uneasily, "I say! If I've spoken out of turn, I do beg your pardon.''

Staring at Falcon, Morris half-whispered, *"Derrydene!"*

"Well, if that don't beat the Dutch,'' muttered August Falcon.

There were two stone benches at the centre of the abbey maze, but the two people seated there on this bright windy morning occupied only a small part of one of them.

"Are you quite sure you knows your way out of here?'' asked Amy.

"No.'' Glendenning tightened his arms about her. "I mean to keep you a prisoner forever. Those who come after us will refer to you as the Maiden in the Maze. We'll live out our lives here together, and be happy, and nobody will be able to part us. What do you say to that, Mistress Consett?''

She gave a little peal of laughter and leaned her head back against his shoulder, looking up at his smiling face. "And how will I cook your vittles on a old stone bench, lordship?''

He kissed the curl at her temple to which he was particularly attached. "We won't need food. We'll live on love.'' He added ruefully, "We may have to, sweetheart, if my papa throws me out on my noble ear.''

Beginning to tremble, she asked, "For why would he do such a unkind thing?''

"He probably won't. For all his storms and thunderings, he's the best of men. So you had best resign yourself to becoming Amy, Viscountess Glendenning. Good Lord! Whatever will Absalom say? He'll likely disown you for deserting to the Quality."

She did not return his tender smile, but pulled away, and gazed at the tall and neatly trimmed hedges that ringed them in. "Don't say things like that, Tio," she said in a small, shaken voice. "Ye knows it can't never be."

He thought grimly that she might very well be right, but he turned her chin gently, so that she faced him again. "If my father should refuse his consent. And if Fate sends no other— er, stumbling blocks to part us, would you, my darling, be willing to give your precious self into the keeping of a fellow who could offer you, with luck, only a humble cottage? But who loves you . . . to distraction."

She was quite still for a moment, her eyes unreadable. Then, she stood. "No," she said saucily. "But I thanks yer lordship kindly."

He said with quiet dignity, "Pray do not tease, Amy. I am very serious."

"And very dear, my own Quality cove." She leaned to caress his cheek, and he bowed his head to kiss her slender fingers. For those brief few seconds her face reflected a hopeless yearning, but when he looked up, she was watching him solemnly. "It wouldn't do," she said. "Ye knows it. And I knows it."

He sprang to his feet. "Nonsense! We love each other!"

"Yes," she admitted, sighing. "And we shouldn't have let ourselves. I knowed that from the very start and was too weak to—" She saw his frown, and said quickly, "I couldn't live here, Tio. Not in this great palace of a house. I'd fit in like a belly dancer at the vicarage tea! There ain't one of your servants don't talk better'n I do. There ain't one o' yer friends, or their hoity-toity ladies, what wouldn't snigger up their Quality sleeves at Lord Horatio Glendenning, and the gypsy mort he—"

He clapped a hand over her mouth, and pulled her close.

"Do not dare speak in that vulgar way, when you can do so much better! You only say these things because you are foolish enough to think you are beneath—"

"Well, I is! Oh, Tio—I loves ye, but—I *is!* I s'pose it ain't really a matter o' being not good enough 'cause of me birth. God made me, same as He made you. It's more 'cause of your ways. Your life's like—like another world, compared with mine. Don't ye see?" Again, her fingers caressed his cheek, and she pleaded, "Me darling lordship, I'll always remember, and be proud that someone as good, as brave, as wonderful as what you is, stooped to love a gypsy girl. But—"

"Stooped, is it?" He swept her up, returned her to the stone bench, and knelt beside her, hugging her tight, his face buried against the billowing pink gown. "Oh, Amy. You're the one who doesn't see!" He looked up at her then, adoration very clear in his eyes. "When I think of the life you've had to lead, and of how bravely you've faced life, conquered its hardships and terrors. When I see your beautiful self, your goodness, your faith, your never-failing courage. And then I look at the sorry mess I've made of my own life . . . Most beloved of women—I am the one who is unworthy. Not fit to—"

Amy wiped hurriedly at her eyes as there came the sound of hurried footsteps.

"Get up, darling lordship," she whispered urgently, tugging at him.

He did not get up, looking steadily and unashamedly at his half-sister as she came to join them.

Marguerite paused, her heart touched by the picture they presented: the lovely girl, who so obviously had been weeping; the pride, but the shadow of sadness in the face of her brother as he knelt with arms about his beloved. Recovering her aplomb, she said, "Oh, I am so very sorry to have to disturb you. But you must come quickly, Tio. That horrid man is here! And Michael has not yet returned. Poor Mama is so frightened."

When he found her, Lady Nola was indeed frightened. He had sent Amy off with his sister, having asked that they do whatever they might to keep the earl away from this interview.

He strolled into the blue saloon prepared for battle, and con-vinced he had his temper well in hand, but the sight of his step-mother, cool and regal, but with a pale face and hunted eyes, so wrought upon him that it was all he could do not to throw Farrier through the nearest window.

He was at his iciest when the countess performed polite introductions. Inclining his head slightly, but apparently fail-ing to see Mr. Farrier's eagerly outstretched hand, he en-quired how he might be of service.

"No, no, my lord," purred Mr. Farrier. " 'Tis I who am come to be of service to you in a certain . . . most delicate matter."

Glendenning scanned the oily smile and murmured a bored, "Faith, but you overwhelm me. Whatever have I done to inspire such—devotion in a man of your kind?"

The smile broadened. "Why, I am a patriotic citizen, and you, sir, are a peer of the realm."

"Redundant, but true." Standing beside the countess' chair, Glendenning drawled, " 'Tis not required that com-moners remain standing in the presence of a—ah 'peer of the realm,' so you must not be afraid to be seated."

He saw his stepmother's lacy cap quiver slightly at this outrageous condescension, and dropped one hand onto her shoulder.

Farrier's smile was a little fixed, and his hooded eyes glit-tered, but he gave a soft laugh and remarked that his lordship was "too kind." Perching on the edge of a striped satin chair, he folded his hands meekly in his lap, and said, "I am assured that Lady Bowers-Malden has explained matters pertaining to the present whereabouts of the Comyn Pin, and the—shall we say, suspicions harboured in some quarters 'gainst you."

"You must forgive," said Glendenning, returning smile for smile. "I was detained in the country, and have but now returned."

"Last evening," murmured Farrier, rearranging his white hands, and irked because he was now obliged to look up at this arrogant young devil.

"Jupiter! You are well informed. One might almost suppose you to have been spying on me."

"Surely, there is not the need for such drastic steps, my lord? Those methods are, I promise you, reserved only for—traitors."

"Really? I had thought skulkings about and prying into the lives of others had disappeared with Torquemada and his unholy crew."

Farrier spread his hands and shrugged. "Perhaps at the time of the Spanish Inquisition a humble man was obliged to do as his superiors bid, even as now. You will appreciate that, sir, having served in the military."

The lace cap quivered again, but Glendenning chuckled. "You are in error. I have not soldiered for our king."

Like lightning came the riposte. "Either of them?"

Lady Nola said hotly, "How *dare* you imply—"

"No, no, ma'am," said Glendenning. "Is as well that this person come far enough out of his hole to make a cake of himself. I can scarce refer the matter to my solicitors if there has been no more than finicking half-threats and sly innuendo." He strolled closer to Farrier, looking down at him as one might view a repellent insect. " 'Tis clear to see what has held you back in your—career, poor fellow. You are by far too timid. Speak up now. Play or pay. Only—do be very sure before you accuse, for I promise you that a false accusation will land you properly in the suds. Neither my father nor I are quite without influence in Whitehall."

This was perfectly true, but Farrier knew the powers which backed him, and was undaunted. Glendenning saw a secretive grin, and drew his own conclusions. He had hoped to so enrage this slimy creature that he would make a mis-step. He had evidently failed in that. What he did not know was that Farrier was thoroughly enraged. The half-smile on the viscount's lips was so infuriatingly disdainful; the set of the broad shoulders, the proud tilt of the head, the bored manner, all bespoke an aristocratic superiority that made Farrier positively yearn to see my lord's head on a spike atop Temple Bar.

He said silkily, "I could wish my innuendos were without

foundation, sir. It grieves me to find that Lady Bowers-Malden's tale of the Comyn Pin having been sold is without substance."

Lady Nola gasped, her hand flying to her throat.

"Do you know, Farrier, it almost sounds as though you were accusing my mother of lying to you. I trust I am mistaken."

The viscount's voice was quiet, but Farrier saw the gleam in the green eyes, and stood rather hurriedly, as the viscount stepped closer. "How well I comprehend your feelings, my lord. Alas, what I said is perfectly true. I have but now returned from interviewing Major Harris Trethaway. A fine gentleman, who tried to be—ah, kind until I informed him of the gravity of the situation. He then reluctantly admitted that . . ." He paused, and sighed, shaking his head. "I found it difficult to believe, but—"

"Perhaps you would find it easier to believe that I have had enough of your weaselly grin and your posturing, and in five seconds from now will toss you through that window."

Glendenning looked not only capable, but downright eager to do so, and Farrier retreated a step. He said, "Major Harris Trethaway has never even heard of the Comyn Pin! Nor did Michael Templeby offer such an item to him in payment of—"

"That is not true!" cried the countess, white as death.

"Of course it's not true," said Glendenning fiercely. "Please leave us, Mama, so that I can step on this little snake!"

"Stay back!" warned Farrier, taking refuge behind a sofa. "We shall call Trethaway to testify 'gainst—"

"Hell you will! If you're not lying, which I doubt, then this alleged Major Trethaway is! I'll go down there and shake the truth out of the conniving rogue! And if you bother my mother by presenting your slippery carcass on my doorstep before I return—"

"Do not dare to threaten an officer of the king!" shouted Farrier as the viscount advanced. "Unless you can put the Comyn Pin into my hands—"

"Why the deuce," rumbled a new voice from the now open

213

door, "should my son put any blasted needle, pin, or thimble into your hands, fellow? If you came here seeking employment as a seamstress you should have consulted my housekeeper!"

Lady Nola closed her eyes briefly.

Glendenning thought, 'Oh, hell!'

The Earl of Bowers-Malden marched into the room, his face a thundercloud.

Farrier recovered his aplomb and, emerging from behind the sofa, bowed so low that his wig almost dusted the floorboards. "Permit me to introduce myself, my lord," he began unctuously.

"Certainly not. Be off about your business at once. Ah, my lady, I have been searching for you . . . this . . ." The earl interrupted himself to frown, and look from the strain in his wife's eyes to his son's enigmatic countenance. His frown darkening, he turned again to Farrier. "Whoever you are, you have disturbed my wife. I do not permit anyone to do so. Glendenning, why did you allow this person inside?"

"My name is Farrier, my lord. Burton Farrier."

"I wish you joy of it. Good day, sir!" The earl stamped to the bell pull.

"I am here," Farrier went on silkily, "representing General Underhill."

Bowers-Malden's outstretched hand checked. "Are you, by Jupiter! Coming down, is he? Be glad to welcome him. Underhill's a devious fellow at times, but plays a splendid game of picquet. I'd sooner enjoy a halfway proficient chess partner, but they are scarce as hens' teeth, unfortunately. When shall he arrive?"

Slightly bewildered, Farrier said, "The general sent me here on a matter of business, my lord—"

"Which is nothing that need take your time, sir," interposed Glendenning. "I know you are eager to talk with mama, so—"

The earl, who had been looking at Farrier narrowly, lifted one hand. "Farrier . . . I think I have heard that name. You're a bounty hunter or some such damnable thing!"

"No such thing, my lord! I am a special investigator, assigned to the tracking down and unmasking of traitorous Jacobite curs who have invaded every level of our—"

"I do not tolerate bounty hunters in my house," growled the earl, seizing the bell pull and tugging it vigorously. "Leave, or be put out. You may take your choice, sir!"

"It would be exceeding unwise in you to resort to violence before you know the charges that I bring 'gainst Viscount Glendenning," warned Farrier, his voice a trifle shrill.

The earl's steely glance raked his son. "Charges?"

Glendenning said coolly, "This silly fellow demands to see some pin or other, sir. Without it, apparently, I must lose my head."

"Without a *pin?* The fellow's short of a sheet is what it is!"

The doors were flung open and two majestic footmen entered.

"Show this out," said the earl.

The footmen bowed and stood one on each side of the doorway.

"I have the greatest respect for your name and your position in Society, Lord Glendenning," said Farrier, keeping a wary eye on the earl's massive figure. "And because your illustrious parent cries friends with General Underhill, I will stretch a point, and grant you one more day to find your brother. At five o'clock tomorrow afternoon, I shall return with a military escort. If you cannot produce the pin—"

"A pox on your pins!" roared the earl. "Out!"

Farrier's words had alarmed the footmen, and they exchanged uneasy glances as they each seized one of his arms, and dragged him toward the door.

"—at that time," shouted Farrier, struggling and enraged, "you will be conveyed to the Tower and charged with—"

The footmen released him as if he had been white hot, and turned scared faces to the earl.

Glendenning took three quick strides.

Farrier fled, the words "High . . . Treason" echoing after him.

215

The footmen encountered the earl's glare, recovered their wits, and ran.

As the doors closed, Bowers-Malden jerked around, and looked grimly from his son to his wife. "Pray leave us, my lady."

Lady Nola stood. She was deathly pale, but her voice was steady. "No, Gregory. This concerns me, you see."

"An it does," he growled, " 'tis because Glendenning has involved Templeby in his nonsensical starts, no doubt. I had prefer you left, my dear."

She said again, "No, Gregory."

"Very well." He shrugged, and walked over to the hearth. "I await the flower of your inventive mind, my lord."

The viscount knew that the moment of truth was upon him. He did not evade it, but began to speak quietly and firmly and, to an extent, put his father in possession of the facts.

Throughout, the earl stood leaning back against the mantel, arms folded across his mighty chest, his piercing gaze locked on his son's face. Occasionally, a stifled grunt escaped him. Gradually, his complexion darkened but, however outraged, he did not speak.

Glendenning finished, and there was a long taut silence.

Bowers-Malden stood straight. In a hushed voice more deadly than his bull-like roar, he said slowly, "So I was right. Because of your damnable traitorous connivings—because of your lies and cheating and evasions—you have brought death and dishonour to this house!"

Glendenning took a deep breath and gripped his hands tightly, preparing himself for the thundering denunciation; the accusations; perhaps—and understandably—the blows.

Lady Nola went to her husband and took his hand. "Horatio did not tell you all, my dear. 'Twas Michael gambled away the Comyn Pin. Horatio had no part in that. You must not rest all the blame on his shoulders."

The earl looked at her steadily. His high colour had faded, leaving him very pale. He said, "My sweet wife. Always so loyal; so loving. And, as usual, you are perfectly right. The fault lies not with my son—but with myself."

Taken aback, Glendenning protested, "No, sir! How should you be blamed for my—"

Ignoring the interruption, the earl went on, still in that quiet, saddened voice. "I knew what he was. Always, I knew where his sympathies lay. But I closed my eyes. Perhaps, in a way, I was proud because he held such strong convictions, and was man enough to act on them. I lacked his courage, for I should have disowned him long since. I should have realized it might come to this. That he had the power to destroy all those I love."

Glendenning had been prepared for wrath; such quiet resignation from this man whose fierce rages were feared by all, struck him to the heart. A lump came into his throat, choking off any attempt to defend himself.

Lady Nola gave a muffled sob, and the earl took her in his arms. "Surely it will not . . . come to that, Gregory?" she faltered, her frantic eyes searching his face. "Surely . . . they will not kill us? N-Not Marguerite and—and Michael?"

Shattered, Glendenning said brokenly, "As God is my judge, Mama, I *swear* I had no thought to bring such peril upon you! I'll go at once to find Michael, and—"

As if he had not spoken, Bowers-Malden murmured, "If it lies within my power, dear heart, neither you nor your children will suffer. I am not without influence. You may believe I shall use every last iota of it, to protect you."

Lady Nola raised her head from his shoulder, and looked at the viscount. "Horatio." Her hand went out.

Glendenning reached for it, but Bowers-Malden pulled his wife back, as though from contamination.

Looking into his suddenly implacable face, Glendenning pleaded, "Sir, I—I cannot ask that you forgive me. The responsibility is mine. I accept it. But truly, I believed—"

"Your beliefs, my lord," said the earl coldly, "no longer interest me. Your beliefs have destroyed this family, our good name, and all that our ancestors down through the centuries have struggled to achieve. I only hope that if my innocent wife and her children have to pay with their lives for *your* beliefs, you may be satisfied."

217

"No! My God! Don't say that, I beg you! I'll find the pin and bring it back! If 'tis humanly possible, father, I—"

"Do me the favour," said the earl, holding his wife close, "to refrain from reminding me of our relationship for as long as we have left. I doubt you can even begin to guess how bitterly I rue the day you were born."

Glendenning gave a gasp, and shrank away as though he had been struck.

"Come, my love," said the earl tenderly, guiding his stricken wife from the room. At the threshold, he turned back. "Be so kind, sir, as to take your beliefs, and your treachery, and your whore, and leave this house, so that if we must die, at least we can do so with some semblance of decency."

Lady Nola's quiet sobs faded as he led her away.

The room they had left was quiet now. The man who stood there was so silent and still that it was as if he was turned to stone, the only movement being a glittering drop that channeled silently down his haggard face.

The drizzle that had materialised earlier was settling into rain, and a brisk wind blew droplets into the coachman's eyes causing him to swear as he kept the team to a steady canter. Inside the rocking carriage there had been little talk for some time. Cuddled close against the viscount, her arm linked through his, Amy peeped up at him. She could not see his expression, for his head was turned from her as he stared through the rain splashed window.

She squeezed his arm and said gently, "He never meant it, my dearest, you know as he never meant it."

He looked down at her, and she was shocked to see his face so white, his eyes haunted by despair. "Ah—never grieve so!" she cried. "He spoke in anger, and fear for his lady. He'll be wishing he could take the words back this very minute, I shouldn't wonder."

"I would," he said dully. "He meant every word. And he

was right, Amy. I've brought this on him. On them all, may God forgive me!"

"But you never wished them no harm, love," she said, patting his clenched fist. "You was willing to risk yer life, fighting for what ye thought was best fer England. None of us can do no more'n what we thinks is right. Only . . ."

His mouth twisted into a faint smile. "Only . . . ?"

"I can't help thinking, Tio, that—maybe 'twould have been better if ye'd not deceived him so."

He sighed and leaned his head back against the squabs. "I didn't dare tell him. It would have made him a fellow conspirator because, knowing for certain that I'd fought for Prince Charles, he should have reported me to the Horse Guards, and he'd never have done so. It would have worn and worn at him. He's so moral a man, Amy. He holds his word sacred. I couldn't place such a fearful burden on his conscience."

"Of course. I can see that, all right. You done—did just as ye ought, then. Like you always do."

He gave a wry smile and shook his head, but said nothing.

Watching him anxiously, worried by this unfamiliar apathy, she sought about for words of comfort, yet hesitated to intrude on his thoughts.

After a while he muttered, "D'you know, I'm almost relieved it happened. All these months of living with the fear that he might find me out. Of how grieved he would be. Now, at last, it's over."

Fear touched her. She argued, "No, it ain't over! We got to find that pin, lordship! We got to make sure nothing bad comes to your family!"

"It won't. I promise you that."

There was a quiet finality to his words; a determined set to his firm chin that caused her to peer at him anxiously. He said in a lighter voice, "Now do not be worrying, sweetheart. We'll contrive, never doubt it. Lord, but I'd give a lot to have seen your breakfast meeting with my—with Bowers-Malden."

Despite the obvious correction, his whimsical smile reassured her a little. She said, "Good thing you didn't. Ye'd have been proper shocked." She chuckled reminiscently. "Lor', but he's a fierce one. And to think I called him a poor old gaffer and told him he had a bad case of the dafts!"

"You never did!"

"I wouldn't of, if I'd knowed—known who he was. I thought he were a groom or something. I give him a good laugh, but I should've seen right off he was a real gent."

"He is, isn't he?" Glendenning sighed.

She swooped to kiss him, and he asked, "What was that for?"

"For not being cross because of all them things he said."

"How should I dare, when most of what he said was well justified? Only . . . I had no thought to lead my brother astray. I tried never to discuss the Rebellion with him, though I fancy he suspected my involvement in it. I took him to my clubs, of course, and got him admitted. But I've never gone in much for gaming, Amy. I swear he never saw me a heavy loser."

"Well then, ye never set him a bad example, did ye?" She hesitated, then said gently, "Perhaps yer fault was that ye didn't take the trouble to set him a good one."

He nodded. "Very true."

"Still," she went on, "yer brother's a man, ain't he? Old enough to know what's right, I mean. I think your papa didn't really expect as ye'd watch Mr. Templeby's every move. After all, everyone's got to stand on their own trotters, sooner or later. So I wouldn't worry too much about that, love."

Not looking up, he lifted her hand and kissed it wordlessly. Again there was silence until he said in a very low voice, "If he just hadn't forbidden me to ever call him . . . my father. If he hadn't said he—wished I'd never been born." He drew a hand across his eyes, and thus didn't see her horrified expression. She'd been unaware of those bitter words, and she stifled a sob and hugged as much of him as she could, and ached with sympathy.

Pulling himself together, he sat straighter and said firmly, "A fine blancmanger you must think me! Well now, most resourceful lady, enough of pointless regrets. We must move forward, and make a push to outwit Fate, eh?"

"Oh, yes. But—how, Tio?"

"Find my brother. Somehow." He forced away the dread that this might not be possible and said, "I've until five o'-clock tomorrow. Please God it will be time enough."

"Amen," she said fervently. "Where does this here major live? D'you know?"

"I don't." He added with a decidedly grim smile, "But I know a woman who does, so we'll go first to Town."

"Oh. Well, maybe I'll stay in the carriage while you go in." He looked at her, one eyebrow lifting enquiringly. Blushing, she said, "I—er, ain't used to these high-heeled slippers yet, darling Tio."

What she meant, of course, was that she feared lest she disgrace him. He kissed her lingeringly, feeling her mouth responsive under his own, feeling her slight body press eagerly against him. And knowing how unworthy he was of her faith and trust, he said huskily, "How do I deserve you, my brave little love? An you were wise, you'd run fast and far away from me, lest I blight your beautiful life as well."

For answer, she took his drawn face between her hands and said, "In that case, I'm perishing glad I ain't wise. And that'll be quite enough tripe out of you, lordship!"

CHAPTER XII

It was past four o'clock when the coachman, for the fifth time, walked the team around the corner of the ———— quiet street in Bloomsbury. This time, the viscount was waiting on the steps of a neat villa, his cloak drawn close against the rain. The footman scrambled down to open the carriage door. Glendenning called instructions to the coachman, then climbed inside. His cloak and tricorne were wet, and he took them off and threw them on the opposite seat.

Amy said eagerly, "She saw you, then? Did she tell you?"

He put his arm around her and kissed the end of her nose. "Mrs. Alvelley received me. And she told me. Reluctantly, and very little."

Amy's wide eyes were on the kerchief wrapped around his left hand.

He glanced down at it. "I was obliged to give her the choice of telling me what I asked, or of having me go to the authorities and report her for using loaded dice. Thus, her reluctant compliance."

"Clawed you, did she? A proper cat!" She peered out of the window as the carriage clattered around a corner and mud splashed up. "London ain't so big and noisy as what I'd heard."

"This is Bloomsbury, my darling. Far on the outskirts of Town."

She asked hopefully, "Shall we go through May Fair, then?"

"I'm sorry, no. I instructed the coachman to skirt the more travelled roads and avoid traffic. We are going to the east now, to London Bridge, and thence across the River to Southwark, and—"

"London Bridge!" She gave a squeal of delight and clapped her hands. "Oh, how I wish it weren't raining, but—!" Guilt overspread her animated face, and she put a hand over her lips. "What a silly I be! As if this weren't a matter of life and death, and here I act like a foolish child! Only, all my life I've heard about London Town, and I've never seen it, Tio. But I ai—is not forgetting the fix we're in, honest I ain't, so don't be vexed, please, dear lordship?"

He kissed her fondly. "How could I be vexed when you shine like a ray of sunlight through this ugly business?"

Breathless, she pulled away at last, and again turned her fascinated gaze to the window. "Only look at all the carriages and waggons! Why do the folks live so close together, I wonder? It is not so pretty here, is it? What they do with all the trees? Where does we go after we cross the bridge?"

"Into Kent. A long and tiresome drive for you, I'm afraid. All I could pry out of the wretched woman was that Tretha-way owns a house somewhere near the Wells. 'Tis going to be a rainy night, and will likely be dusk before we arrive, but I cannot stop, love. I'll settle you into a comfortable hostelry until I've run down Trethaway, and call for you when—"

"Oh, yus you won't!" said Amy indignantly, her careful accent coming to grief. "You ain't going after no viper like that all alone, young man!"

He laughed into her militant eyes. "I take it you envision a pitched battle. But having neither blunderbuss nor cooking pot, most beloved and daintiest of warriors, what shall you fight with?"

A flash of petticoats, a glimpse of a shapely limb and a red satin garter, and her knife was glittering under his nose. Her dark eyes sparkled. She said, "And won't they be surprised when they find I is not a gentle and perlite lady o' quality, but a gypsy lass which knows to help her man in a shining-bright!"

Deeply moved, he marvelled at her courage. Faced with danger, there was no shivering dread for Amy Consett; no whimpering. She set her dauntless, dimpled chin, and took her dagger into her resolute hand. And she would back him, all right. To the last, she'd stand beside him. It must not come to that, of course, but to know how faithful and steadfast was her love was balm to his grief. Bowing his head, he kissed her hand, so that she cried out for fear he would cut himself.

He looked up at her, and said, "If we come through this safely, my Amy, how very proud I shall be to make you my wife." And he thought 'But if we cannot come through safely, my little love, I shall make very sure that you are not dragged down with me!'

They travelled at breakneck speed now and, despite the rain, made excellent time. Even so, it was dusk when the carriage approached Tunbridge Wells. Glendenning gazed at the passing countryside with eyes that saw little of winding lanes edged by dripping hedgerows, or cottages and scattered farms where the warm glow of lamplight spoke of families gathered cosily together. All his thoughts turned on his own family. He could not get the echo of his father's bitter words out of his mind. He could see with wrenching clarity Lady Nola's tears, and could picture her present state of mind. Poor mama. Torn between her love for her husband and her love for his errant heir.

Amy stirred in his arms and yawned sleepily, and her hand came up to caress his cheek. "You look so tired, darling lordship. Wasn't you able to snatch a little kip? Ye'd oughta—"

The carriage lurched. Shouts. The door was torn open, and a familiar voice cried, "Good Gad, Tio! What we've been through in your behalf, and here you lounge, frippering about with a—"

"Falcon!" gasped the viscount, staring disbelievingly at the very damp young Corinthian who clambered into the coach.

"And me," said Morris, climbing in after him with a flurry of raindrops. "How de do, ma'am? I must—" His honest eyes widened appreciatively. "By Jove!"

Bewildered, Glendenning demanded, "What d'ye mean? What have you been through in my behalf?"

The coachman opened the trap and peered in at them. "We've tied the gents' hacks on behind, melord. Shall I keep on?"

"Yes. Er—yes." The trap shut, and he said, "Jamie, will you please explain what this is all about?"

Morris hesitated, then nodded to Amy, his face solemn.

"Oh, Lord," exclaimed Glendenning. "Your pardon, ma'am. May I present Mr. August Falcon and Lieutenant James Morris? Gentlemen—Miss Consett. My betrothed."

Amy saw astonishment come into one rather guileless face, and a faint amusement dawn on the other, which was so handsome as to make a girl's knees weaken.

"My congratulations, Glendenning," drawled Falcon.

"Oh. Yes. Er—jolly good, what?" mumbled Morris, turning very red.

"It's all a fudge," said Amy, with a shy smile. "I is not betrothed to no one."

Morris' eyes became even rounder at this artless speech.

Falcon looked at Glendenning thoughtfully. "Where in the devil have you been all this time?"

Morris observed, "You look awful, dear boy. Sorry, but there 'tis."

The viscount said, "It's a long tale that we can sort out later. Now, will you please tell me why you are here?"

Despite some interruptions from Morris, Falcon contrived to explain. When he finished, Glendenning said, "Then you've discovered where Trethaway lives! 'Pon my soul, I do not know how to thank you! To have gone to so much trouble for me!"

"Do not be deluding yourself," said Falcon. "I am here only because"—he slanted an oblique glance at Amy's wondering face—"I need you to act for me. Even so, I think we are entitled to hear why you saw fit to disappear these two weeks."

"Yes, of course. But first—how on earth did you find us?"

"Luck, dear boy," said Morris, scarcely able to tear his eyes from Amy. "We was heading back up to Windsor, to see if you'd gone home, and—"

"And if you do not wish to be recognised," drawled Falcon, "you should not jaunter about in a carriage with your crest on the panel. Do I mistake it, or are you also here to see Tretha-way?"

"You don't mistake it. 'Tis vital I see both that bas—er, rogue, and my brother."

"Won't do it," said Morris. "We called at Trethaway's house not an hour since. He's gone. Hopped the twig, I shouldn't wonder. Likely one leap ahead of the constable, for he's a bounder from what I hear."

Watching Glendenning's worn face anxiously, Amy slipped her hand through his arm, and smiled encouragement.

"Did you learn where he is gone?" he asked in a controlled voice.

Morris looked severe. "His people said he was off to Portsmouth to take ship for Italy. 'Twill be no great loss to Eng—"

"My God!" exclaimed Glendenning, frantic. "Then we must stop him! When does he sail?"

"With the morning tide, I believe," said Falcon. "But I promise you, your brother ain't with him. Trethaway's man said there had been no visitors for several days."

"But Michael *must* have gone there! He took funds to buy back— Oh, Lord, you don't know!" The viscount ran a hand across his brow distractedly, then said, "That nail, Farrier, claims that the Comyn Pin was donated to the Jacobite Cause! And—"

"Hmm," said Falcon. "I recall my father mentioning once that your stepmama was a Comyn."

"Jupiter!" Morris shook his head. "Shouldn't have donated the lady's pin, Tio! Very bad business!"

"He didn't donate it," said Amy defensively. "His brother sold it."

"To cover some—debts," said Glendenning. "He didn't know it was on the Jacobite list—if it is, which I doubt! The thing is that I must prove 'tis still in our possession. I've to show it to Farrier by tomorrow afternoon, or—" He shrugged, wordlessly.

Morris and Falcon looked at each other.

Morris said, "Best tell him the rest."

Again, Falcon glanced at Amy, then said, "Owen Furlong says Trethaway cried friends—"

"With Sir Louis Derrydene!" finished Morris.

Glendenning stared, thunderstruck. "Derrydene!" he whispered. "Then, 'tis very probable that this Major Trethaway is in fact . . ."

"One of the League of Jewelled Men," said Morris.

The fire leapt and crackled up the chimney of the private parlour, the clock on the mantelpiece ticked away the seconds, and the rising wind drove rain in occasional busy chatterings against the casements of the small inn. The three young men gathered about the fire were silent, however. Glendenning had taken a bedchamber for Amy, partly because he wanted her to have a few minutes to rest and refresh herself before they resumed their quest. She suspected that the men desired to hold a small council of war and would be able to talk freely without her presence. What she did not suspect was that there were things to be discussed which they were forbidden to speak of to anyone outside their own very select group. Several minutes had passed since Glendenning finished his terse account of what had befallen him during these two weeks. He had not spared himself; his voice becoming not altogether steady as he spoke of the nightmarish confrontation with his father.

Morris was first to break the silence. Not looking at Glendenning, he muttered sympathetically, "What a devilish fix to have landed in."

"In more ways than one," murmured Falcon.

Glendenning's eyes flashed. He snapped, "If you refer to my betrothal—"

Falcon waved a languid hand. "Miss Consett is one of the fairest Fairs these eyes ever beheld." He turned his head to meet the blaze of Glendenning's anger. "To that extent, certainly, I congratulate you."

"If you *dare*—if you *dare* suppose her to be beneath—"

Morris leaned forward and interrupted placatingly, "Do not gratify him, my dear fellow. You know that he delights to be a thorn in the flesh of anybody he encounters. 'Tis for no one—save perhaps your own family—to comment on such a personal matter as the lady you choose for your wife."

Perhaps because he was under such a great strain, Glendenning said wildly, "Comment and be damned! She's an angel! I've told you that she saved my life—how bravely she fought, God bless her! How can you think anything save that *I* am the one who is unworthy?"

"Never doubted it for an instant," said Falcon.

Morris laughed, and Glendenning's ferocity eased a little.

"Anyone must be blind not to see that the lady is a veritable diamond." Falcon finished wickedly, "In the rough."

Glendenning was on his feet in a swift pounce. "Stand up, damn you!"

"So that you may knock me down? Certainly not. Why invite me to comment? Did you assume I would say only that which would please you?"

Glendenning glared at him, but his innate honesty could not deny the truth of those sardonic words, and he sat down again.

"A baby starling can stretch its mouth very wide," sighed Morris, "but rarely says anything sensible."

" 'Twould afford *me* enormous pleasure to confound the *ton* by doing just as you propose to do," said Falcon. "But . . ."

"That—is—enough!" said Glendenning through clenched teeth.

"True," Falcon acknowledged. "The 'buts' are obvious."

Morris suggested helpfully, "You can always call him out, you know, Tio. After me, of course."

"To expedite which eagerly anticipated event," said Falcon, "might we perhaps devote some thought to what we're going to do next?"

Glendenning drew a hand across his eyes. "Yes, of course. What a fool I am!"

"No, no," said Morris kindly. "Nerves tied up in knots, is all. Understandable—damned if it ain't. You're in a proper vise, dear boy, and we must get you out of it—somehow. Don't know how. Wish I did. But you may be sure I'll stick by you."

"If you say you will march to the block with a man who has only himself to blame for his present peril—you're a blithering fool," sneered Falcon. "Which should surprise none, of course."

Glendenning's jaw set, and his fists clenched, but he said in a voice of ice, "I mean to make damned certain that *no one* accompanies me to the axe, Falcon. But I thank you for your loyalty, Jamie."

Morris suppressed a shudder at the thought that so splendid a fellow as Glendenning should meet such a ghastly fate. To hide his consternation, he stood and, walking to the door, held it open invitingly. "Adieu, Lord Haughty-Snort. Scamper back to Town, and forget you ever knew us. Tio won't name you as having shielded a Jacobite, so do not be shivering in your boots."

"Your generosity is equalled only by the dimness of your wits," jeered Falcon. "Do you not yet realize there's a deal more to this than the fact of Glendenning's misplaced loyalty to the Stuarts?"

Morris closed the door, and said with a grin, "I think what he tries not to say, Tio, is that he's with you."

"We are all with him," said Falcon. "If only in the interests of self-preservation."

Glendenning said sombrely, "You really think the League of Jewelled Men wove this beastly web?"

"*Assurément!* Can you doubt it?"

"Well, I can, if Tio cannot," declared Morris, returning to his chair.

"You would!" The slim hand holding Falcon's wineglass gestured impatiently. "Make an attempt to use your heads, gentlemen. We know that Sir Louis Derrydene helped engineer the tragedy that damn near ruined the house of Rossiter. We know that Gideon Rossiter found the lapis figure of a jewelled man in Derrydene's home, and we have other clues that established Derrydene as having been a member of the League. We believe that because he failed to completely destroy Sir Mark Rossiter, Derrydene was executed by the League and his death passed off as suicide. Now, we find that this same villain was bosom bow to a murky individual calling himself Major Harris Trethaway. And that Trethaway has manipulated Glendenning's brother into giving him a piece of antique jewellery now purported to have been donated to the Jacobite Cause. Glendenning cannot prove his innocence without the Comyn Pin, and Trethaway has conveniently left the country. Good God! Is it not plain? This entire ugly business is a scheme of the League!"

Glendenning said, "But—why? To take personal vengeance on me because I was one of those opposing them in the Rossiter fiasco? 'Twould have to be a murderous group indeed deliberately to plot the execution of my entire family when they could simply have me killed."

"Besides," put in Morris, "I'd think that whatever they're up to would keep them sufficiently busy. To go to all the trouble to stage such an elaborate revenge don't seem very likely."

"Not if 'tis only a matter of revenge," murmured Falcon thoughtfully. "The question becomes—do they scheme to kill two birds with one stone?"

Glendenning said, "Gideon Rossiter believes they plot 'gainst England. Do you say they've a grudge 'gainst my father as well?"

Falcon shrugged and with his rare grin said, "Bowers-Malden is not the most amiable of men."

Fighting against betraying the pang that transfixed him each time he thought of his sire, Glendenning said, "To my knowledge he doesn't even know of the existence of the League of Jewelled Men."

"In company with most of England," said Morris glumly. "I wonder what the deuce they *are* about."

Falcon murmured, "Perchance we can come at it. Let's see now, exactly what have we thus far?"

Glendenning said slowly, "A burned-out shipyard. A fraudulent trading company. A great estate seized for debt." His head jerked up. "Good God! Are they after the Abbey, then?" He answered himself impatiently, "No, what fustian! 'Tis entailed."

"Unless," said Falcon, "it should become property of the Crown—due to treason on the part of its owner."

Glendenning exclaimed, "Yes, by Jove! In which case 'twould likely be sold!"

Morris said eagerly, "As the Rossiter's Promontory Point estate was sold!"

His eyes brilliant, Falcon said, "Neither of which could ever have been purchased had not their rightful owners first been disgraced and ruined! Jupiter!"

"But why in the name of creation would they go to such lengths?" said Glendenning. "There are other estates that *could* be purchased. Why all the chicanery?"

Pondering this, they were silent until Falcon muttered, "Should we perhaps consider those involved? Two highly respected, powerful men, much in the public eye. Sir Mark Rossiter. The Earl of Bowers-Malden."

"And coming on top of that ghastly scandal involving Lord Merriam," began Morris.

Glendenning shook his head. "A quite different matter, Jamie. Merriam was caught cheating at cards, and shot himself. How should that . . ." He paused, frowning.

"Just so," Falcon murmured. "I've no love for England's bluebloods—my own being so vastly inferior—but I'll own to having judged Harlow Merriam to be the last man to cheat—at anything."

"M'father would agree with you, August," said Morris,

apparently forgetting Falcon's objection to the use of his Christian name. "Served with Merriam in the East India fleet. That was before he became a peer, of course. Merriam, I mean."

Glendenning said, "I believe Merriam was—"

Amy opened the door, and they all stood. She had tidied her hair and looked neat and fresh and enchantingly pretty as she smiled at them, her gaze lingering on the tenderness in Glendenning's eyes. "I'm sorry to interrupt, gents," she said.

The viscount crossed to take her hand, and murmur that he was far from sorry.

"The thing is," she said, "that your coachman says the horses are ready now, Tio. We can go on."

Morris said, "To Portsmouth? An we ride hard we can reach there by dawn. But your lady . . ."

"Goes with me," said Glendenning, to Amy's obvious delight. "Only—first, I must stop at Trethaway's house."

Falcon sighed. "We told you—"

"I know." Glendenning's jaw set stubbornly. "Even so—I will stop there."

"Then 'tis as well I told the cook to pack us a picnic hamper," said Amy, twinkling at them.

"Jove! What a treasure you've found, Glendenning," said Morris fervently.

Falcon took up Amy's hand and kissed it with easy grace. "Ma'am, your slave."

She laughed. "What a rasper!" and then, as she saw Morris' jaw drop, she added hurriedly, "Ye can both hop— I mean ride in the coach with us. Is that all right, lordship? We can tie their horses on behind."

Not giving a button what they thought, Glendenning said, "Anything you want is all right, my dearest."

"Did you ask 'em to put in some cold chicken, ma'am?" asked Morris holding the door open for her.

Amy had indeed requested that cold chicken be added to the hamper, and, trying to ignore the dark shadow that hung over them, they enjoyed their supper as the carriage once again rolled down the darkening country lanes.

"Glendenning has been telling us of your exploits, Miss Consett," said Falcon, reaching for a crusty roll and a slice of cheese.

Amy hesitated.

Glancing at her, he asked, "Do I offend?"

"Oh, no," she said brightly. "I just dunno what that jaw-breaker— I mean, I think you're very nice."

He stared at her. "Nice . . . ?"

"You don't know him, Miss Consett," warned Morris around a chicken leg.

"Well, I don't, a'course," she admitted. "But he's a fine handsome co— gent. I never see such glims— I—er, I mean eyes," she added, with a guilty glance at the viscount.

Falcon wiped his fingers fastidiously, and drawled, "Perhaps you find their shape displeasing?"

"What? Oh, no. I did notice, a'course. But I'm too well breeded to say anything." Unaware of the bomb she had tossed into the suddenly quiet coach, she laughed her lilting laugh and leant forward to pat Falcon's knee. "I ain't really, mate. No use pretending, lordship love. I ain't well breeded at all. What I meant was I never see eyes that colour before. I thought they was black at first. I 'spect they really set the ladies a'swooning, eh?"

His breath held in check, Glendenning thought, 'Let him dare give her one of his damned sardonic set-downs!'

August Falcon put back his handsome head and laughed as he had not laughed for many a day. "Do you know, Glendenning," he said breathlessly, "you don't deserve her! Be dashed if you do! Have you any sisters, dear ma'am?"

She sighed, and said in a suddenly wistful voice, "I don't know. Have you?"

"Yes, I'm proud to say."

"One of the most beautiful ladies in England," said Morris, also wistfully.

"I ain't surprised," she said, and peeping up at Glendenning, very conscious of how drawn he looked, she said with a dimple, "I wonder you didn't fall in love with her, Tio."

"He didn't," sighed Morris. "I did."

"Ooh," she exclaimed, before Falcon could utter the crushing remark he had ready. "I think as we're in Owler country."

Glendenning peered through the dusk at dimly seen wooded slopes, and echoed curiously, "Owler country?"

"Smugglers," she nodded. "Folks what work at the dark o' the moon, like the owl. Ab's brother's one of 'em, and a fine living he's made of it. Though a bit chancy, y'know." She frowned thoughtfully. "I wonder if . . ."

Falcon pulled on the check string, and shouted, "Stop here, coachman!"

The carriage jerked to a stop, the footman swung open the door and let down the steps. Glendenning jumped out, scanning the good-sized house set back from the lane in a grove of trees. Amy reached for his hand, but he said quietly, "Wait here, my love. I'll just—"

"I'm coming," she announced determinedly.

"No! It might be risky. Stay with her, please Morris."

Morris murmured an uneasy acquiescence, and Amy sighed, and sat down again.

Their cloaks blowing in the wind, Glendenning and Falcon walked quickly across the muddy lane.

The cottage was in complete darkness; not a gleam of light to be seen, nor a wisp of smoke from any chimney. The only other sign of human habitation came from a glowing window atop a rise at least half a mile distant.

Falcon said, "Deserted. Come. We must ride hard are we to reach Portsmouth in time."

"I know." Glendenning pounded on the knocker. "But I mean to get inside."

His second thunderous assault on the door produced no more result than had the first. Not a sound came from within the house.

Falcon said irritably, "We waste time!"

"Ride then," said Glendenning. "I tell you I'm going inside."

"If you mean to break in—"

"Since they refuse to answer the door, I see no other way."

"And how if they're waiting to blow your head off? They'd be perfectly justified, you looby."

"Then I must hope their aim is poor." Proceeding around the darkened house, testing windows, Glendenning said, "If I'm right, the League wants me alive—to be duly arrested and tried for High Treason." He reached up, and shoved. "Aha! This one is not locked!"

"For the simple reason," pointed out Falcon, eyeing the small round window high in the front wall, "that no one, save a small child perhaps, could climb through the stupid thing!"

"I could," said Amy.

Glendenning swore, and whipped around. Amy stood there, Morris beside her. "I couldn't stop her, Tio," he said shamefacedly. "She threatened to scream if I tried to hold her."

"Wretched girl," said the viscount, harassed. "Now I must carry you back! Falcon—break the damn door down!"

"And have the village constable after us? No. I thank you!" Amy danced away from Glendenning's reaching hand. "He's right. There's likely riding officers out. There always is on dark nights. For the Owlers."

"Yes, by Jove," said Morris, with an uneasy glance around. "And m'father would have my ears was I taken in charge for breaking and entering! Lose my commission too, I shouldn't wonder. Best give it up, Tio. House locked up tighter'n any drum."

"Dammit! No! I tell you I'll— My God! Amy! What are you doing?"

"Taking off me pretty gown, and me petticoats," she said blithely. "Cannot wriggle through no windows wearing ten ells of muslin!"

"If ever I heard of—"

"I know. No lady worth the name would do such a wicked thing. Well, I ain't a lady, dear lordship. Now if you gents will turn yer naughty eyes away . . ."

Laughing softly, Falcon at once turned his back, Morris having already averted his horrified eyes. Glendenning groaned, but followed suit.

After a moment and some hard breathing, Amy said, "There! Now—I'll have to be boosted up, Tio."

"I'll find a ladder," offered Falcon.

"No need, Mr. August," she said airily. "My lordship will give me a leg-up."

Glendenning argued, "I cannot boost you up, with my back turned."

"Right. So it must be you alone, Tio. Come now, ye've seen a lady in her chemise before, I 'spect. 'Sides, it's nice and dark."

He took her in his arms, and could not refrain from kissing her swiftly. Very conscious of the supple and scantily clad young body pressed so close against him, he murmured in feverish anxiety, "You have your knife, dearest?"

"Yes. Up!"

"You'll be very careful?"

" 'Course. Come *on!*"

And so, torn by fear for her, spurred by need, he lifted her until she was able to grasp the sill. "A bit more, love," she hissed.

How inestimably more fragile she looked in just her dainty chemise. And, Lord, but how he loved her! Praying for her safety, he seized her ankles and lifted.

A wriggle, a squeak, a last glimpse of an enticingly rounded little bottom, and she was gone.

"Oh—God!" he moaned.

"Shouldn't have let her do such a thing," said Morris. "Shocking!"

"To say the least of it," agreed Falcon with a chuckle. "Zounds, but how my dear grandmama would have admired your Miss Amy! Are we permitted to turn around, my lord?"

"She's inside." Glendenning gathered up gown and petticoats. "If either of you *ever* breathe a word of this!"

Falcon sighed. "Alas, I collect we cannot, in honour. But I shall tell my grandchildren, I warn you! And if—"

A crash from inside.

Glendenning's heart jumped into his mouth, and he was up the steps in a flash. Before he could batter down the door, there came the sound of bolts being drawn, a key turning in the lock, and the door was opened a crack. An imperious hand appeared. "Me dress, please Lordship," said Amy.

With a sigh of relief, he passed the garments to her. "What happened? Are you all right?"

"I knocked over a table full of gimcracks," she said, retreating behind the opening door. "Now I'm going to pop into this little room here, and make meself decent, while you gents look round. I don't see nothing, Lordship, but there's someone here."

Hurrying into a small dim hall, Glendenning checked, and whispered sharply, "What d'you mean? Did you hear talk?"

"No," she answered from behind the door. "But I heard something. Take care, dearest."

"Probably a cat," suggested Morris. "Fond of cats."

Falcon drawled, "How fascinating."

Moving swift and silently, Glendenning prowled about. The house was deathly still. He strained his ears, but although the stairs creaked slightly when he trod up them, he heard no other sound. And yet, like Amy, he sensed that they were not alone in the house. Passing from a narrow hall into a bedchamber, he could distinguish very little. He found a candelabrum, luckily with a tinder box beside it. "As well be hung for a sheep as a lamb," he muttered, and lit a single candle. The objects in the room sprang into view. A large canopied bed, strewn with garments; drawers still standing open; boots and shoes scattered about. He crossed to a closed door and entered a well-appointed dressing room, as untidy as the bedchamber. Somebody had left in a tearing hurry, that was clear, but—

A scuffling sound caused him to tilt his head. Moving farther into the small room, he listened intently. Again, it came—a strange, stealthy sound, seeming to originate under the floor.

He hurried into the hall, almost colliding with Morris, and wasn't surprised when the Lieutenant whispered that he'd heard "something odd."

They went downstairs. Falcon stood in a large and over-furnished dining room. He held one finger to his lips as they joined him. The scuffling sound was followed by a muffled bump.

Emerging from a cupboard, Amy hissed, "D'ye hear it, Tio?"

He nodded. "It was clearer in the upstairs bedchamber. This way."

The room directly below the bedchamber proved to have a locked door. There was no sign of a key. Glendenning handed the candle to Amy, motioned the others back, then kicked hard. After two more kicks, the door splintered and flew open.

Amy held the candle high, revealing a small book room. "Oh, my Lor'!" she cried. "Tio!"

Glendenning was already running to the man who lay with ankles securely bound and hands tied around the leg of a sturdy reference table. Despite his bonds, the captive was struggling feebly. Glendenning dropped to his knees and wrestled with the neckcloth that had served as a gag, and Amy came swiftly to hold the candle high, and offer her little knife.

The light shone on a young face, deathly white where it was not streaked with dried blood. Glendenning raised him tenderly, and the powdered, dreadfully splattered head rolled back against his shoulder.

"Hello, halfling," said the viscount, his eyes glinting with wrath as he took in the bruises and torn lips, the pain in the hazel eyes.

"Tio . . . ?" Michael Templeby's voice was a croak. He tried to reach up as Amy released his wrists, but the rope had bitten so deeply that his hands were useless. "Thank God . . . you came! That—bastard took . . . the Comyn—"

"I know. Easy, now. We'll get you up and—"

"No! Must—must tell you!" The words faded.

Falcon passed a glass of brandy to Glendenning. "Courtesy of departed swine."

Morris came up with a dripping towel, and Amy took it and began to bathe Templeby's battered face. "Poor boy," she said kindly. "Oh, but they have hurt him, Tio. Look how he's been beaten!"

The viscount held the glass to his brother's lips. His voice harsh, he said, "I only thank God he is alive."

Falcon muttered, "I wonder why."

"This will sting a trifle," said Glendenning. "But try to get some down, Michael."

Templeby swallowed, and choked gaspingly, but seemed to rally a little. Again he tried to lift his hand, and Glendenning took it and held it firmly. Clinging to him, his brother groaned, "I am so sorry . . . so very *sorry*! I fought . . . them, but . . . too many. I'll tell Papa! I'll—"

Tears sparkled in his eyes, and Glendenning smiled and said with a gentleness he was far from feeling, "Hush, lad. We'll make it right, never fear."

"My fault!" moaned Templeby in an agony of remorse. "Absolute . . . gullible fool . . . but I swear, Tio . . . I never meant to—"

"Of course you didn't. Don't scourge yourself so. We all make mistakes—Lord knows I've got you beat in that pasture! Just tell us, if you can. It was Trethaway, of course? His servants told my friends he's off to Portsmouth and will take ship for Italy—yes?"

Templeby's eyes were losing focus. He half-whispered, "No. I heard them . . . talking when they thought I was . . . senseless. Told—told servants . . ." His head sagged.

Glendenning took up the wet towel and bathed his brother's face again. "I'm sorry, but you must tell us, Michael. Wake up, lad! What did he say?"

The dazed eyes blinked up at him, the brows knit in a painful concentration. "Something about . . . Squire somebody."

Glendenning heard Morris' muffled exclamation, then he bent lower to catch his brother's faint words. "Not Portsmouth, Tio. Dover. Sails . . . dawn tide . . . I'll confess . . . I'll tell Papa . . . all my fault . . . So . . ." And with a weary sigh he lay very still.

Amy gripped Glendenning's shoulder. "Poor boy! Tio—he's not . . . ?"

"No. Lend me a hand here, Morris. We'll put him on the sofa in the withdrawing room. Do you pull the curtains, Amy, and Falcon, light some more candles, please."

They carried the unconscious man along the hall and deposited him carefully on the sofa.

Glendenning straightened and stood for a moment looking down at that motionless figure. He touched the tumbled hair gently, then turned a bleak face to the three who watched him.

Falcon said, "Not much doubt now. But I doubt Trethaway is the Squire."

"He may not be their leader, but he's in that murderous League up to his neck. I'm going after him."

Morris nodded. "The carriage?"

"No." The viscount turned to Amy and put his hands on her shoulders.

Her smile tremulous, she said, "Ye wants me to stay with yer poor brother."

"He is in sore need of your skills just now, my love."

"Nonsense," said Falcon. "Mistress Amy cannot be left here with only a wounded man to her protection! Some of Trethaway's people might come back!"

Glendenning looked at him levelly. "This is High Treason. I'll not blame you an you stay clear."

"Blame me! I rate a medal for standing by you to this moment! And had your friend Gideon Rossiter seen fit to give me proper warning two months since, I'd not be sharing your bog."

Morris said indignantly, "Two months ago Ross didn't even know there was such a thing as the League of Jewelled Men! How the deuce could he guess what it would come to?"

"I doubt any of us can guess what it *will* come to. Especially you, Sir Gudgeon." Falcon turned back to Glendenning. Despite all this grumbling, his eyes blazed and there was an air of barely suppressed excitement about him. "I suppose you expect me to ride with you?"

"No. I would hope you could stay with my lady, but—"

Perversely affronted, Falcon said with a black scowl, "I can out-shoot, out-fight, and out-think our military pea brain with my—"

"Of all the puffed up, arrogant—" snorted Morris.

"Love a duck," exclaimed Amy. "And they say women talk! While you three nitter at each other, Major-Maybe is likely hopping onto his boat! I can look after meself and this poor boy. Go!"

Falcon met Glendenning's steady gaze and, comprehending why he had been chosen to stay, shrugged, and muttered sulkily that he hoped he would not be hanged for protecting a lady.

"I'll ride with you, Tio," offered Morris. "You may count on me."

"Sir Launcelot," said Falcon.

Glendenning said, "There are no words to properly thank any of you. I swear upon my honour, you will not be implicated in my treasonable past."

"When a man is put to the question—" began Falcon, then he caught Amy's eye and turned away. "Come and look at this, Morris!"

Morris crossed to his side.

Glendenning pulled Amy to her feet, and led her to the door, his arm tight around her. She clung to him, then lifted her face, and he kissed her hard. Removing sufficient funds to cover his expenses, he gave her his purse. "When you think my brother well enough, will you take him back to the inn, my darling? He'll likely want to go home, but please keep him down here until I send for you both."

She looked frightened. "Bean't ye coming back this way, then?"

"I doubt it. If I get the pin from that hound, I'll have to ride like fury to reach the Abbey in time." He cradled her face in his hands. "Whatever happens—I love you more than I ever dreamed possible. Will you believe that, lovely one?"

"Yes, but . . ." Her hands flew around his neck. Trembling,

she said, "Tio I got a un-brave feeling all over! What will you do if—if you can't get it back?"

He smiled down at her, then kissed her again and, with his lips against hers, whispered, "Love you forever."

CHAPTER XIII

Swinging into Falcon's saddle, Glendenning glanced once at the cottage and the candlelit window against which was the silhouette of a small and very still lady. Then, he turned to Morris, already mounted and waiting.

"I mean to ride hard, Jamie. It is already nigh ten o'clock. You're quite sure . . . ?"

"We've at least five and forty miles to go," said Morris. "I'm ready, Tio."

"Are you? Any pistols in your saddle holster?"

"Aye." There was a note of surprise in the word. "D'ye think—"

"I think they wanted me to find Michael, and then go haring off to Portsmouth. With luck, they won't be expecting us at Dover, but there's no denying they're a dangerous crew, so be ready for an ambush. God speed!"

They were away at a canter, and the race had begun. Skirting the dark mass of the forest they rode ever south and east through the blustery night. The rain ceased, then came down again, harder than before, the wind driving it so that the drops stung their faces. They passed few travellers; an occasional Portsmouth Machine rumbled by with a rapid pounding of sixteen hooves, a spray of mud, a shout from the coachman;

sometimes another rider would loom up, flash past, and disappear into the darkness again. Once, both horses neighed and shied in fright as a stray cow appeared in the middle of the lane, and Glendenning, his thoughts on the outcome of this venture, was almost thrown.

After that, he tried not to dwell on the what-might-have-been, or on the terrible what-might-be. But Amy's sweet face persistently crept into his mind. A score of images rose up: her vibrant joy in the early mornings; her intense concentration as she tended his hurts, or sewed his torn shirt, or sliced vegetables, or worked at her chairback. The mental picture of her ghostly rescue brought a sad smile to his mouth, so that Morris, catching a glimpse of him in the light from a church window, wondered. A moment later, the viscount's thoughts were on his parting from the earl, and it was as well the darkness hid his expression.

The darkness and the foul weather made it hard going, and periodically Glendenning slowed for the sake of the horses. The time lost chafed at his nerves, but with iron control he fought the panicked urge to gallop without pause. There was little talk between the two men, even when they slowed and conversation was possible. Morris could well imagine his friend's state of mind, but in his heart he feared that their desperate journey was doomed to failure and, being unable to find any sincere words of encouragement, he kept silent. He had slept soundly until quite late that morning, but the wind was a relentless enemy, the rain was cold, and as the miles slipped past, he began to tire. If Glendenning was weary, he gave no sign of it, and kept to a gruelling pace. Little wonder, thought Morris. He set his jaw and determined to say nothing that would slow them, but he was relieved when distant lights began to twinkle through the rain. Soon, they were thundering into the yard of a neat tavern. Glendenning's shout of "House—ho!" brought an ostler running, set three dogs to barking, and awoke a bright rectangle of lamplight against the night as the tavern door was swung open.

Dismounting, Morris instructed the ostler as to the care of

their mounts, while Glendenning went inside to arrange for the hire of new ones.

He stepped into another world; a bright, warm, and cosy parlour. In response to his request, a maid scurried off to fetch coffee. The host came, beaming, and allowed as how it was a "nasty night." Fortunately, he maintained a good stable and the viscount was able to obtain fresh and allegedly spirited hacks with no difficulty.

Morris arrived, and for the few minutes required for the horses to be saddled up, the two men adjourned to the glowing hearth and drank their coffee.

Morris peered at his friend anxiously. Gad, but Tio looked as if he carried the weight of the world on his shoulders.

Glendenning saw that concerned stare, and said with a smile, "I'm a dour dog tonight. My apologies, Jamie. You cannot know how grateful I am that you ride with me."

Morris grinned. "In a day or two we'll be laughing at all this, old fellow. Set a lamp under an earthenware pitcher, and the light can't shine through, y'know."

It was as well, thought Glendenning, that Falcon hadn't heard that one! He said, "And you really think we'll find the light in this business, do you?"

"Certain of it," said Morris bracingly. "In despite this miserable weather, we've covered nigh twenty miles already, and 'tis only half past eleven o'clock. Plenty of time, dear boy! We'll be in old Dover town hours before dawn!"

Half an hour later his optimism was severely shaken. The host's instructions on a route that would "lop a good ten mile" off their journey proved quite accurate. Unhappily, the persistent rain had transformed the "quiet stream" he described into a raging flood that had swept away the only bridge. Unable to find dry ground, and proceeding cautiously in the darkness, they found themselves struggling through ever more treacherous mud.

Seething with frustration, Glendenning halted. Sheet lightning on the horizon lit low-hanging clouds and briefly illumined a bleak and level landscape of low shrubs and long drooping grasses. "Hell and the devil!" he raged. "I think we've landed ourselves in Romney Marsh!"

Dismayed, Morris said, "Can we get out?"

"We *must* get out!"

Within a very few minutes, however, the horses were floundering in stirrup-deep water, cold as ice, and treacherous with trailing reeds. More by luck than good judgment, they eventually reached firmer ground, but the animals were still hock deep in mud, and the riders were soaked to the skin. Above the voice of the wind and the hissing rain, Morris discerned another sound, low but ominous. "Hold up, Tio," he shouted.

Another glare of lightning showed the same bleak landscape, but Glendenning was appalled to catch a glimpse of tumbling waters ahead. If they'd stumbled into that fast-moving flood there'd have been no reaching Dover for either of them. "Thank God for your ears, Jamie!" He dismounted stiffly, unhappily reminded of every bruise he'd taken during the battle at Absalom's cellar. "We'll have to go by shank's mare," he said, trying not to sound as despairing as he felt.

Morris' voice was almost too cheerful. "Is there another road, d'ye think, my pippin?"

"I know there's a road out of Rye that follows the coast for some distance before it cuts across the marsh to—Hythe, I think. But it's a devilish rough track and will take us miles out of our way. If we could but see the stars, I'd have some idea of where north lies and we could hope to come quickly out of this. As it is, we may well be turning due east, deeper into the marsh!" He bit his lip, and thought 'God forbid!' but started off, treading with care and leading his mount. "Stay close, Jamie," he called. "And pray!"

After what seemed hours of toil, he was very weary, chilled to the bone, his legs numbed, and he doubted they had progressed a mile, but when he'd been a hunted fugitive he had learned how much a man may endure and still keep trying, and he struggled on doggedly. There was little doubt now but that they were moving towards the coast. If only he'd not snatched at the innkeeper's suggestion of a short cut! He smiled wryly. He could call up half a hundred 'if only's,' and good old Morris would likely have as many homilies to answer them.

Turning wearily, he peered into the driving rain. "How are you, Jamie?"

The answer came jerkily through chattering teeth. "Perfectly fit, d-dear boy!"

"Jove, what a Trojan you are! A fine bog I've led you into! If ever we—"

He tripped, and fell heavily, landing with bruising force on the hands he threw out to break his fall. His knee hit hard and painfully, and he swore as he pushed himself up. His knee had hit—*hard?* Holding his breath, not daring to hope, he groped about, then gave a triumphant shout. "Jamie! We've come to a road!" He clambered to his feet and hugged Morris exuberantly. "God be praised! We'll be able to ride again!"

"J-j-jolly g-good," panted Morris.

Mounting up, Glendenning reined around. "We'll have to go slowly, else we're liable to miss the— Jamie?"

Morris was still hauling himself into the saddle. "Bit s-s-stiff, T-Tio," he stammered. "Now—which way?"

It was a good question. The lightning was almost continuous, and by that heavenly glow they were able to catch frequent glimpses of the more level surface of the road, but there was not a sign of other travellers, and no least indication of where they were. They both decided to go in the direction the horses were now facing, and started off once more.

To ride without having to wade through mud and reeds was a vast improvement, but the wind was rising, buffeting so strongly at times that the horses were staggered. If this weather held, luck might be with them after all, for the ship would likely not leave the Tidal Basin until the wind dropped.

An indefinite time later, Morris gave a hoarse shout. A dim light glowed ahead. His heart leaping, Glendenning urged his mount to a fast trot. He could see the darker loom of a small house, and a lantern bobbing about. He rode up to a low wall, and gave a hail.

A startled exclamation, and the lantern swung toward him.

Surprisingly, a woman's voice cried, "Bless me soul! Ye never come off the marsh, sir? I'd not a'thought man nor beast would venture that road on such a perishing night!"

Shivering convulsively, Glendenning nonetheless felt a soaring elation. They'd done it! Somehow, they'd made their way across the marshes to the outskirts of Hythe! "We're not here by choice, ma'am, I promise you," he said. "But—we're here! That's the important thing. Can you direct me to the best road to Folkestone?"

"Folkestone? Why, sir, that do be beyond Hythe! And you and your friend all over mud and so—"

A colder hand than his own was clutching Glendenning's heart. Scarcely daring to ask, he interrupted, "Is this not Hythe, ma'am?"

"Bless yer—no, sir! This be my man's farm, and I'd be snug 'twixt the sheets if it hadn't been that some of they silly sheep got out of the pen. Hythe's 'way up in Romney Marsh!"

Glendenning's voice sounded far away in his own ears when he said, "I had thought we *were* in Romney Marsh."

"Oh, poor gentleman! Ye're in *Denge* Marsh. But if ye keep on a few miles ye'll come to Rye, and—"

"Rye!" The viscount's shoulders slumped. Instead of riding to the northeast they were headed southwest! Once again they had travelled miles out of their way!

"Zur . . . ?" The voice seemed to echo, but the hand that shook him was persistent.

Glendenning opened his eyes and peered stupidly at the square, bronzed face hanging over him.

"Ye said as Oi wuz to wake ye at four," said the man in a broad Kentish accent. "And four it do be."

The viscount's mind began to fit pieces together. The rain had ceased shortly after they'd left the farmhouse in Denge Marsh. Providentially, the high winds had blown the clouds away allowing a three-quarter moon to escape and light the soggy landscape, so that they'd been able to follow the road with less fear of stumbling into the mud again. Despite cold and fatigue, they'd plodded on doggedly and shortly before three o'clock had reached this small inn just south of Folkestone. To dismount had required a major effort, and the sleepy ostler's suggestion of a hot toddy and a soft feather bed had been well nigh irresistible. From Folkestone they could reach Dover in an hour, but Glendenning, grimly aware that he might then have to turn about and gallop for Windsor, knew also that although he'd enjoyed little sleep the previous night, and was bone weary, he dare not stop to rest. Poor Morris had been slumped against his mount's neck in a deep sleep, and had come down from the saddle in a rush when Glendenning tried to wake him. Deeply remorseful, he had only then recollected that two months earlier Morris had been sent home to recuperate from wounds suffered in the War of the Austrian Succession. It had been the deciding factor. He'd half-carried his exhausted friend into the warm parlour of the Black Sheep, and bespoken two rooms.

Now, he pushed back the blankets and asked if a horse was saddled.

"They'll be ready when ye gets down to the yard, zur. I bringed ye some hot water and a razor, and me old lady got most o' the mud off yer boots, but they're still something damp, surely."

"My friend is unwell, I don't want him wakened." Glendenning pulled his topboots on, and began to shave quickly with the none-too-sharp razor. "How is the weather? Shall any craft be able to set sail, d'ye think?"

The man pursed up his lips. "Wind be summat fierce, zur. Was ye meaning here? Or upalong to Dover?"

The razor arrested, Glendenning glanced at him. "Is there a difference?"

"Open sea hereabouts, zur. Dover do have the big Harbour and a'many shippings, and with the wind in this quarter . . . No, sur. Them as had to sail quick-loike 'smorning, put their ships into our cove early yestiday when weather started to blow up."

249

"Do you say that there *will* be some sailings today, but that they'll be from here?"

"So Oi do rackon, zur. Less'n it blows up a full gale, loike."

Glendenning sent him off with an order for coffee and toast. His coat and cloak had, to an extent, been dried by the fire, but his wig would have benefitted from comb and tongs and his tricorne looked sadly wilted. Untroubled by such minor concerns, he hurried downstairs. The enticing smells of coffee and burning logs hung on the air. Lamps were glowing in the parlour, and a fire was already licking up the chimney. He went to the low latticed casements and peered into a blustery darkness with just a finger of lighter grey outlining the eastern horizon. Leaning on the sill, he wondered if it was possible that their disastrous journey had actually been a godsend: if they had all unknowingly come to the very spot at which Trethaway might be forced to embark. Such luck seemed unlikely but, by Jupiter, he'd make damned sure of it before he rode one mile toward Dover!

The rattle of china brought him around from the window. "Blast!" he exclaimed.

Morris sat by the fire, mug in one hand, and a thick slice of toast in the other. He turned to the viscount with a pale face but a bright smile, and waved the toast. "Help yourself, old sportsman."

Glendenning said quietly, "I'm a sorry dolt, Morris. I'd selfishly forgot you're still recuperating. If you had but spoken up last night—"

"Spoken up about what? We're here, are we not?" Morris sneezed, and coffee splashed. Setting the mug aside, he reached for his handkerchief and blew his nose. "Plenty of time, too," he wheezed, taking up his mug again. "Doubt there'll be any sailings 'til the wind drops."

"Not from Dover, at all events." Glendenning gulped some coffee and bit into the savoury buttered toast. "But the host tells me that some vessels have put into a cove near here, so as to be able to sail with the morning tide."

Morris stared at him. "Have they, by Jove! Then— perhaps . . . ?"

"Exactly so." Another swallow of coffee and he started to the door, toast in hand. "I'll come back as soon as I learn—"

Morris jumped up. "Be damned if I don't think you're trying to turn me off," he said indignantly. "Well, you won't do it, and so I tell you!"

Glendenning's arguments were well taken, and quite wasted. When he rode out, James Morris was beside him.

The wind was stronger, sending their cloaks flying, bending treetops, and filling the air with leaves and debris that caused the horses to dance nervously. The clean tang of the sea was strong in the damp air, and soon the two men could hear the boom of waves breaking against the offshore rocks. Following the tavern keeper's directions, they rode along a narrow track that wound downwards until, by the slowly increasing light, they could distinguish the gleam of the waters of Dover Strait. It was still too dark to see the beach, but bobbing lanterns could be distinguished to the east where great ships rode uneasily at anchor. They went on, eyes and ears straining, until a voice hailed, and a seaman stepped out in front of them. "Ahoy, there! You be the gents for Calais?"

Morris roared a sneeze, which the sailor evidently interpreted as a denial.

Glendenning said, "We were to meet the rest of our party hereabouts, but mayhap we're early—or they've postponed sailing."

"There is some gents farther up the beach, sir. Where ye bound?"

"Italy, eventually," said Glendenning.

"Ar, and going to Paris first, I hear. That'll be them, then. Waiting to board the frigate for Le Havre. She's a fine ship and if I knows her captain there won't be no postponing for this blow! A good voyage to you, sirs."

They threw him a coin, and moved on. When they were out of earshot, Glendenning murmured, "Sounds promising, Jamie, but I think we'll play least-in-sight, just in case."

They rode in amongst some shrubs and low trees where they dismounted and tethered the horses. Moving on, they circled inland for a short way. The sky was dark grey now, visibility improving to the point that they could see the darker loom of Folkestone's hills. Below them a break in the cliffs led down to the cove. Glendenning halted, listening intently, his eyes trying to pierce the gloom, but he could see no one. They went down slowly and with great caution, until Morris tugged at Glendenning's sleeve and hissed, "Listen!" They both paused, ears straining. At first the viscount heard only the many voices of the wind, but then came the sound of a man whistling. And the melody set his pulses racing with excitement, for it was that ancient marching song called Lillibulero.

Morris whispered urgently, "Did you not tell me that Miss Amy's uncle heard a gentleman humming that tune?"

"Aye! One of the men who brought the jewelled ruby figure into Mr. Shumaker's shop to be repaired!" Elated, he said, "We've found 'em, Jamie! By heaven—we've found 'em! And the bastards are part of the League—never doubt it! Come on! And keep your pistol handy!"

They crept on and, rounding a great upthrusting rock, were suddenly within yards of their quarry: three men standing close together, facing the stormy seas, their cloaks billowing, and one breaking off that repeated whistling to exclaim, "There she is! There's the longboat!"

A very large individual with a coarse, guttural voice sounded less enthused. "I don't like the sea, Major, sir. Least of all on a morning like this here. Can't I stay—"

"No, imbecile. We've had our orders."

The whistler, more stockily built, said dryly, "Those orders did not include your taking the pin out of England, Harris."

Glendenning's hand clamped tightly onto Morris' arm.

The first man, who must be Harris Trethaway, laughed. "I was told to get it from that young fool Templeby, and to lure his brother far from Windsor, both of which I've done very neatly. As to destroying the pin—why should I be so wasteful? The Squire may have no further need of it, but there's a rascal in Paris will give me a small fortune for it. I shall open an elegant gaming house in Italy. You'll hold equal shares, dear coz, and Camber and I will live a life of luxury in the sunshine, out of sight and out of mind.''

The whistler grumbled, "You take a desperate chance. And dammitall, so do I! You were ordered to destroy the curst pin! If you weren't my cousin—God help us if the Squire ever finds out! You know how merciless he can be."

"How shall he find out? The only ones who know I didn't destroy it are you two. We'll all be rich, and whatever his schemes may be— Speaking of which, do you know what they are?''

Glendenning, who had been inching forward, pistol in hand, halted abruptly, breath held in check as he awaited the response to that question. When it came, it was emphatic.

"If I did, 'twould be more than my life is worth to divulge it! Only the holders of the jewelled men know the full details.'' A pause, then he added in a guarded voice, "Or think they do.''

Trethaway asked curiously, "What d'ye mean by that? Are they being played false?''

Another pause. Then, "We deal with powerful men, Harris. Men of great wealth and vaunting ambition. In my experience, the schemes expounded by such fanatics often prove in the end to bear little resemblance to what was initially proposed, and those who follow are apt to find themselves committed to plots they would have backed away from had they known— But, there—pay me no heed. 'Tis likely no more than my own gloomy imagining.''

"Even so, I'm not sorry I am on the outer fringes of your mighty League. And you may be pleased to know that if their schemes should fail—''

In that instant some pebbles rolled past Glendenning's boot. Lightning fast, he jerked around, but before he could even warn Morris, a cord was about his throat, strangling him. Dark shapes rushed to batter him down. He fought back even as he struggled in vain for breath. He heard grunts and curses and more blows smashed at him. The blood roared in his ears. His eyes were dimming. His last anguished thought was that he had failed his family . . .

"... in the devil he could have found us ..."

"... she didn't know! and ... another soul!"

"If I hadn't hired these bullies, just in case ..."

"... almost to shore! ... no time to ..."

The voices seemed to drift near and then fade away again. It was hard to breathe, and Lord, but he hurt; he must be bruised all over. He tried to think where he was. Not in the woods with Amy, for the smell of the sea was in his nostrils ... Amy! He managed to force his eyes open. Strangely, although he thought he must have lost consciousness, he didn't seem to be lying down. A gaunt, wolfish face with a thin trap of a mouth and hard grey eyes materialised before him.

"The—pseudo major ... I presume," he said faintly.

"But not a pseudo victor." Trethaway's smile was unpleasant. "I must own you have astounded me. How in the name of all creation you could have come up with me here, is past belief. Who betrayed us?"

Glendenning managed a grin. "Nobody with whom you are ... in the least acquainted." He glanced about and discovered that he sat leaning against a tree, his arms pulled back and his wrists tied behind the trunk.

"Observe, my lord hero," said Trethaway, pointing to the side.

Two words were chalked in bold letters on the surface of the rock that loomed ahead. CHÂTIMENT UN!

Glendenning said contemptuously, "A message from your master?"

"Only part of it." Trethaway grinned. "The rest is over there."

Turning his aching head, Glendenning smothered a gasp.

Morris lay face down nearby. He was not tied and, horrifyingly, there was no sign of life. After a stunned minute, the viscount looked up again.

Trethaway chuckled. "So that is what is meant by 'a speaking glance.' "

"Damn you! Have you killed him?"

"Lord knows, and it don't matter either way. He is of no importance. Do you know, Glendenning, I cannot say I'm sorry you came. I shall delight in knowing you will watch my departure. I've had a score to settle with your family for years! You don't know why, I see. Your top-lofty sire was one of the men who blackballed me at the Cocoa Tree." He scowled darkly. "Made it impossible for me to get into any of the best clubs. I'd never served him a bad turn. He did it purely out of his damned arrogance!"

"Not at all. He likely thought you a blackguard. As usual, his judgment was impeccable."

Trethaway's lips twisted into a snarl. He drew back his fist, then paused, a cunning look coming into his face. He took a small leather case from his waistcoat pocket, opened the lid, and held the Comyn Pin tantalizingly in front of the viscount's eyes. "Look, your lordship," he jeered. "We up anchor within the hour. From here you will have a clear view as I sail into a bright future, taking with me the only hope you had of saving your wretched family. Ah, that makes you sweat, does it? Think on it, dear old boy. Think of the questioning they will inflict upon your mother . . . your innocent sister . . . your stupid brother . . . Think of the rope you have put about their necks. Think of their screams when the axe—"

Glendenning swore, and struggled against the ropes until he could feel blood slipping down his hands. "You accursed . . . bastard . . . ," he panted. "If your Squire is as—as highly placed as I believe . . . you may think of *his* face when I tell my questioners . . . where you've gone, and that you've taken the pin with—"

A shout from the beach cut off his words. "Major! They're coming in!"

An instant longer Trethaway stood in frowning thought. Then he replaced the case in his pocket. "They will not listen to you," he said with a shrug. "And at all events, the Squire likely won't care so long as you come by your just deserts.

Still, I shall leave you a token of my esteem." He kicked out hard, and chuckled as Glendenning's face twisted with pain. Striding down the path, he called blithely, "Adieu, traitor! Your friends will think twice before they ever again interfere with the business of the League of Jewelled Men."

Glendenning's wrists were raw, but he struggled desperately to escape. Perhaps there was still a chance. If he could free himself and hire a fast boat, he might catch that murderous rogue. It felt as though he'd been tied with leathers, rather than rope. Likely, they'd cut the reins from one of the horses. Certainly, however he fought, the knots weren't weakening, and his arms had been forced back so tightly against the tree that his efforts were very restricted. Breathless, he leaned his head back, thinking. Perhaps there was another way. He was tied near the base of the tree, but the trunk narrowed as it soared higher. Gritting his teeth, he tried to push himself upward. At first his efforts seemed fruitless, but he persisted doggedly, refusing to let the pain beat him, cursing aloud in anguish, the sweat trickling into his eyes. After a while, the constant effort and the unnatural position made his arms ache so that he could hardly bear to continue. He paused for a minute, to catch his breath and nerve himself to start again. And this time, with his first try his arms seemed to move a little. "Excelsior!" he gasped and, shoving with his feet, he strove until his arms moved again, and then again, inch by jerking inch. Gradually, the strain on his arms lessened, and at length he was able to battle his way to his feet.

Panting but triumphant, he muttered, "Now, thank God, I'll have more leverage!" A moment later, he groaned an anguished "Blast!" as a splintered piece of bark gouged his arm. The jagged edges, protruding beside him, reminded him of the broken branch he'd landed on when he was thrown in the woods. That had been sharp enough to pierce his boot. If this was as lethal, he might at least be able to jam it into the knots that held him. He strained and tugged, and at last his wrists were over the outthrusting bark. Groping, testing, pulling, he felt the knot catch at last. The leather was coming free! Another minute or two . . .

He glanced seaward. A longboat was lurching across the tumbling grey water. He stood as if frozen, watching helplessly.

The skies were brightening to dawn now. Trethaway, seated in the stern of the longboat, was clearly distinguishable, turning to wave a mocking farewell, and flourishing the case that held the Comyn Pin.

In that same moment, beyond him, the majestic frigate was swept up on a great black wall of water. The sailors stopped rowing, their shrill cries rising above the howl of the wind as the monstrous wave rushed upon them. Trethaway whipped around, and half stood in the extremity of his terror. An instant, the wave towered over the longboat. Then, Glendenning had a brief glimpse of oars tossed like matchsticks, of arms and legs flailing, and the longboat hurtling into the air, end over end. The horrifying scene was blotted out as the wave raced on to thunder against the clusters of rocks, sending great columns of spray high into the air. When its fury had subsided the only things to be seen between shore and frigate were a few splintered oars, some oilcloth capes, and what looked to be a gentleman's tricorne.

A sobbing groan was torn from Glendenning. The Comyn Pin could never be recovered now. His last faint hope was gone.

The apothecary was a fussy little man with a high-pitched voice, a perpetual sniff, and the manner of someone whose presence is anxiously awaited elsewhere. Despite these affectations, he stood at the table in the private parlour of the Black Sheep, and bandaged the viscount's lacerated wrists with swift efficiency. He ignored his patient's questions, however, vouchsafing instead the information that three bodies had been washed up from the sunken longboat; all seafaring men. "Should never have attempted to row to shore in such weather. But I fancy when gentlemen drop sufficient gold into a captain's hands . . ." He glared at Glendenning accusingly.

"I am sorry for the tragedy," said the viscount. "But why does my friend not regain consciousness? On the cliff he revived for a minute or two, and you said the blow to the head did not look to be of a serious nature."

"The fact that he regained consciousness for so short a time is a very bad sign. Besides which, although it grieves me to own it, I am but a mortal man, and mistakes can be made. The last unfortunate I thought to have sustained no serious injury, died the following day. Of a heart seizure."

"The devil!" exclaimed Glendenning, paling. "Do you say Lieutenant Morris—"

"I say he took no serious hurt. I also say he was evidently severely wounded at some fairly recent date, and has not recovered sufficiently to have gone jauntering about through a stormy night, getting himself soaked to the skin and thoroughly exhausted. If you are his friend, sir," he added, with another of his accusing upward glances, "I wonder you did not deter him from such a scatterbrained course of action."

'A fine friend I am,' thought Glendenning, and said, "I wish to God I had! But regrets will pay no toll now. An he has rest and good care, will he—"

"He *might* be lucky enough to escape the pneumonia. I doubt it. Were you robbed of all your possessions?"

Divining the reason for such a question, Glendenning also wondered why nothing had been taken. "Fortunately, my purse was in my saddlebags," he lied, adding dryly, "Never fear. You will be paid."

"Good. I've donated a small fortune to young bucks who get themselves knocked up because they've not the sense to—"

"Are you finished? I'd like to go up and see him."

Irritated, the apothecary renewed his denunciation while securing the bandage.

"Enough," said Glendenning, one hand lifting authoritatively. "Your philosophizing delays me, and I've to be in Windsor by four o'clock."

The apothecary's tight mouth sagged. "You're—*mad!*" he gasped unequivocally. "You should be laid down upon your bed for a day or two. Besides, 'tis half-past ten now, and it must be eighty miles at least to—"

He spoke to empty air. Tossing a guinea onto the parlour table, Glendenning limped to the stairs.

Morris lay very still in the small darkened bedchamber. Walking softly to the bed, Glendenning looked down at him. "Poor old fellow," he murmured. "The blight that is Glendenning caught you up well and truly!"

"Now, now, sir," put in a quiet voice. "Doan't ye be blaming of yourself."

A very stout little lady extricated herself from the chair by the fire and came to smile at him comfortingly. "I be Mrs. Goodstone, and a foreigner in these parts, being as I were born in Sussex. But I wed Goodstone twenty years agone, and I know the folk hereabouts well enough to know why gents risk the marshes on stormy nights. If Owlers bring the riding officers here, they've no call to worrit. Goodstone and me, we've a fine cellar and no questions asked."

So she thought he was a Free Trader. His heart heavy, Glendenning wished that were so. Lord knows it would be a lighter burden than the bitter one he carried. He returned her smile and assured her that no excisemen were after him. "The thing is, I've urgent business that won't wait, and have no choice but to leave my friend here. He must have the best of care and attention. I'll pay in advance for tomorrow, and send people after him."

" 'Lor' bless ye, sir. He'll have the best we got, I promise you. You go along—though you'd be a sight better off to keep to your room. It appears to me like you could do with some sleep yourself, sir."

Glendenning thanked her, asked for pen and paper, and these being provided, wrote a brief note.

Jamie—
You are the best of men and, owing you so much, I must now desert you here, and ask yet more of you.
Please see that Miss Consett is taken to Tony

Farrar's home. It is called The Palfreys, and is
located near Romsey, in Sussex.

Dimity, Lady Farrar, will care for her.

Tell her to remember always what I said when
we parted.

My humble thanks. God bless you.

Tio

He folded the note and left it on the table, under Morris'
watch.

Outside, the wind drove clouds across the pale sky, and
from the east came the constant booming of the surf. An
ostler led out his horse. The animal looked rested and eager
to run. Patting the warm neck, Glendenning muttered,
"You'll get your chance, my lad."

He rode northeast to Folkestone, and from there took the
Tonbridge Road, but traffic impeded his progress and, whenever he dared, he cut across country at the gallop. The rain
began again. The wind buffeted horse and man, and the
muddy roads were treacherous, but he pushed on relentlessly.
When the horse was too tired to gallop, he stopped and hired
a fresh mount. The lack of sleep began to tell, and by noon he
was fighting a fatigue that increased with every mile. Many
travellers on that stormy day looked wonderingly at the man
who rode at such reckless speed. One irate gentleman opened
his carriage window as the viscount raced beside him, and
bellowed that he was a heedless young fool who might spare
a thought for his horse, if not for himself!

Glendenning did not even hear him. His mind was closed to
everything but this race against time. This race he must not
lose, even though death would meet him at the finish.

CHAPTER XIV

The Earl of Bowers-Malden tried not to hear the tall case clock strike four. Seated in the vast withdrawing room, he felt, for the first time in his life, small and powerless. He tightened his arm about his wife, and said gently, "You are very composed, my love."

Lady Nola did not move her head from his shoulder. She said in a far-away voice, "I am quite terrified, Gregory. For . . . for the children, you know."

The dreadful prospect of the fate that awaited them loomed again in all its horror. His dear wife. Marguerite's youthful loveliness. Michael's fine young manhood. He was not a man who prayed often, but he prayed now, silently, intensely. 'Dear God—don't let it happen. *Please*, Lord! Don't let them suffer shame, torture, dismemberment, to pay for my own son's reckless folly.' He said with an effort, "I would have thought Marguerite might have kept with us this—this last hour."

Lady Nola uttered a muffled sob, and clung to him. "Oh, my love! Perhaps Horatio—"

"No! Do not speak his name! I'll not have—"

There was a commotion in the hall. Agitated voices, and the sound of hurrying footsteps. Farrier! How like that merciless hound to be early! Well, he'd not find the Laindons weeping and whimpering before—

Darrow sounded frantic. "Sir—*no*! I beg of you! Do not go in—"

He *begged* . . . ? Bristling, the earl stood.

The door burst open. Coated with mud, his eyes red-rimmed and sunken, his face a mask of exhaustion, my lord Glendenning reeled into the room.

With a muffled imprecation the earl stamped forward. "*Damn* you, sir! How *dare* you set foot in my house?"

The countess stood also, and said brokenly, "Tio! Oh, my dear, were you able to get it back?"

"I tried, Mama. God knows, I tried! But—"

Concealing his own brief and now shattered hopes, the earl thundered, "Of course he didn't get it back! Had you really expected such a care-for-nobody to rescue us? Egad, but you're a dreamer, madam! *Out*, my lord! Or must I throw you out myself? By God, but I *shall*!"

So spent that he could hardly stand, Glendenning gripped a chairback. "Trethaway is drowned, but . . . took the pin with him. I must . . . must speak to you alone, sir."

The earl said nothing, but his lips drew back in a snarl, and he advanced purposefully.

Glendenning sank to one knee.

Lady Nola uttered a muffled sob.

The earl, taken aback, said, "You may well grovel!"

Glendenning looked up at him and his mouth twitched into a rueful smile. He said faintly, "Purely . . . involuntary, I'm afraid, sir."

The earl grunted, and marched to the bell pull.

"I could not bring you the—the Comyn Pin," said Glendenning. "But I've brought you the way out of this. I—implore that you hear me. Fa— my lord, when I've done, you can . . . throw me out. But first, if you care for your wife and her children, you *must* see me . . . alone."

Bowers-Malden paused. There could be no doubt but that Glendenning had been through some kind of hell. The ruffles fell back from the hand he held out revealing that the wrist was bandaged, and there was a look of abject humility in his eyes. Too late for that, of course. But, whatever else, he'd come back. He was man enough not to have run to save his own skin. Drawing a bitter consolation from that fact, he growled, "You may steal two minutes of the few I've left to share with my dear ones. Lady Nola, if Michael has returned pray desire him and Marguerite to come to us." He added implacably, "When Lord Glendenning has left this room."

The viscount sighed and started to drag himself to his feet.

The countess looked helplessly from one to the other of these men she loved. Then, with her handkerchief pressed to her lips, she left them.

Glendenning's struggle to stand drained his remaining strength, and he could get no farther than a footstool. His head seemed to weigh a ton, but he managed somehow to bring it up. A glass of brandy was being thrust at him.

Beyond it, the earl's face was sternly contemptuous. Glendenning took the glass with a hand that shook, and the powerful brandy burned away some of the crushing weariness. "I found Templeby, sir. He was injured, but not seriously, I think. I have arranged that he not come here."

He spoke with quiet steadiness, and suddenly, to see him thus, muddied, and too exhausted to stand, so wrought upon the earl that he was obliged to turn away. He walked to a nearby table and took up a rare paperweight. Examining it, but with not the slightest notion of what he held, he said, "I shall hope he has the good sense to obey you, in which case one of us, at least, may be spared. I granted you this interview, Glendenning, only because you had sufficient backbone to come back and face your punishment with the rest of us. Now—"

Quite aware of how his sire hated to be interrupted, the viscount interrupted. "Well, that's it, isn't it, sir?" He fought his way to his feet. "The punishment must be mine. Only."

The earl's hand tightened upon his paperweight. "Your sense of responsibility is apt, if several years late in dawning. Has this wondrous new comprehension also inspired you with the solution?"

"I should think that would be obvious, sir."

His eyes fixed upon the object that now dug deep into his palm, Bowers-Malden said, "You mean to confess your guilt to Farrier?"

"If I thought that would serve, I'd not have come back here. It won't. He would still claim that you had shielded me."

The earl's leonine head lifted slowly. He met his son's eyes, and for an instant felt so sick that he was unable to speak. Then he said in a voice that shook, "Do you . . . dare . . . to saddle me with—with—"

Glendenning saw horror in the strong face of this man he loved, and he started forward instinctively, but drew back. "It still wants forty minutes to five o'clock. I have sent word, in your name, to Hilary Broadbent, desiring that he bring a troop here at once. He should arrive in ten minutes. You must denounce me the instant he comes. With luck, Farrier won't reach—"

"Luck . . . ?" Bowers-Malden's face was white. The paper-weight thudded to the floor. "*Luck?*" he whispered. "Do you call it *luck* that . . . that a father must . . . send his only son to a traitor's hideous—to public execution and—and—" Unable to continue, he covered his eyes with a trembling hand.

Glendenning staggered to his side and, daring his wrath, gripped his shoulder. "Sir, you *must*! Only your public repudiation of me, your demand that I be arrested for treason, will save all—all those—" His voice broke, and suddenly he was blinded by tears. He gulped, "Those I . . . love."

Bowers-Malden uttered a travesty of his bull-like roar, and shoved his son from him. "If you loved me you'd not have— You'd not ask—" But the boy was right. It was their only chance. One death. Or five. But God in heaven! He searched his son's eyes and found sorrow, but also unflinching resolution, and he croaked, "*Damn* you, Horatio! How *can* you expect . . . ? How can I . . . ?" He jerked away, tore out his handkerchief, and buried his face in it.

Glendenning drew his sleeve across his own eyes, thus leaving a streak of mud to betray him. Despite his efforts to keep his voice under control, it faltered as he said, "I am not by any stretch of the imagination a hero, sir. I'd most happily give every penny I own, every bit of my inheritance, not to—to have to pay the price of my . . . sins; not to have placed you in so terrible a quandary. But there is no other way. You must know, fa—er, sir, that if you do *not* denounce me, I will die as surely—only with the terrible grief of knowing I have dragged you all to the axe with me. I beg of you, spare me that shame, at least. I shall meet my Maker with enough on my conscience!"

The earl turned a stricken face, and shook his head wordlessly.

Desperate, Glendenning said, "If there was any other way, do you think I would resort to this? There *is* no other way. This is our one hope! *I* have brought this nightmare down upon us, and *I* must take the consequences. You *cannot* allow our innocent ladies to suffer. Sir—if you now hand me over—"

"Even were I—prepared to—to take such a step, that hound Farrier would claim he'd already accused you, and that I was only denouncing you now to try and save the rest of my family."

"I expect he will say exactly that. But you are a powerful man with many influential friends, and he knows it. You can maintain that you'd never believed my guilt, but now you know the truth, and therefore disown me, and hand me over to—to the king's justice. I think they will be unable then to accuse you of shielding a traitor, nor—"

His words were cut off as the case clock chimed the half-hour.

It was like the knell of doom.

For an instant the two men stood mute and stricken, gazing at each other.

The misery in his father's eyes wrung Glendenning's heart. He said, "Sir, you will have to be very fierce and outraged. You doubtless already loathe and—and despise me, but if—by some miracle—you still have some vestige of affection for me, you must not allow Hilary to suspect it. One thing in our favour is that he knows I have always been so in awe of you."

Bowers-Malden jerked his head away.

The time was racing, and they must do this before Farrier arrived, or they were lost! Glendenning urged, "Think, sir, of all the times I've disappointed you; told you what were half-truths, at best. Think of the time I've spent studying architecture, when you would so much have preferred that I take my seat in the House, and interest myself in politics; of how often I've stayed away for months, when Mama had—hoped—" His voice shredded. He thought, agonized, 'Oh, God! If I could but have that time back! If only I'd come home more often, and—'

Through his despair and remorse, he heard running footsteps. The door burst open. Darrow, looking terrified, gasped, "My lord! M-Major Broadbent, and a troop!"

Bowers-Malden said hoarsely, "Show the major into the morning room, if you please."

The door closed.

Glendenning's bones seemed to be melting. He crossed to the sideboard, but when he tried to pour the brandy it splashed until the earl's hand came to take the decanter from him. Bowers-Malden poured two glasses. Offering one to his son, he growled, "Drink it down. You need it."

Glendenning obeyed. False courage, but it gave him strength. He returned the glass to the silver tray. 'Don't let him see what a coward you are!' he told himself. 'Give the poor old fellow a small vestige of pride in you!' He managed somehow to smile. God, but he was cold. So cold. Fear was an awful thing. He'd not been afraid on the battlefield, but now . . . "I'd best go and tidy up, sir. Can't have old Hilary thinking I've galloped here to—"

"To sacrifice yourself?"

Glendenning blinked, and bit his lip. He put out his hand tentatively. "Sir—would you please . . . could you, d'you think, bear to shake my hand, before . . . ?"

"Fiend seize you!" Bowers-Malden's eyes glittered with tears. "I'd like to—murder you!" His arms went out, and crushed his son to him. He said a choking, "Horatio . . . ! Oh, my dear boy . . . God bless you!"

Glendenning gulped, "Papa. I've always . . . I hope you know how much I—"

Another minute and he'd weep like a woman. He wrenched away, strode as rapidly as he was able to the back stairs, and climbed for the last time towards his suite.

In the room he had left, the Earl of Bowers-Malden turned a ravaged face from the open door and stared down at the glass in his hand. He lifted it to his lips—not to drink, but to kiss the glass. Then, with ineffable sadness, he hurled it to shatter in the hearth.

He felt very weary now; drained, and tired, and old.

And it would not do!

He wiped his handkerchief across his eyes, then drew a deep breath. Squaring his shoulders, he walked into the hall to find young Hilary Broadbent.

And to condemn his son and heir to the slow torment of a traitor's death.

The morning room was a pleasant and airy apartment, being blessed with many long windows that overlooked the ornamental water. On the light blue walls were hung fine paintings, all gently pastoral, and several pieces of Monsieur Pelletier's gilded Louis XIV furniture added grace to their charming setting. It was a room to lift the spirits and chase away gloom, yet when Bowers-Malden entered on this grey and stormy day, he had the distinct impression he had stepped into Bedlam.

Hilary Broadbent, dashing in military scarlet, was chattering gaily with a flushed and unusually vivacious Marguerite, and Michael—whom Horatio had evidently failed to keep away—was attempting to engage Corporal Willhays in conversation. Willhays, a shy young man for whom Broadbent entertained high hopes, looked uncomfortable and not a little bewildered; emotions the earl shared.

They were unaware of his arrival and, for one brief moment he stood in the doorway, watching them. Templeby looked wan, but not much the worse for whatever injury he had suffered. Likely the boy knew of the impending tragedy, though he was talking brightly enough. Incomprehensibly, Marguerite fairly sparkled. Small wonder Broadbent appeared entranced. The young major had been a frequent visitor of late. If Lady Nola was right in believing that he cherished a *tendre* for Marguerite, he would soon face a most difficult moment.

It was a moment he himself dare no longer delay.

Clenching his hands until the nails bit into his palms, the earl cleared his throat. Usually, that resonant sound silenced a room in a wink. On this nightmare afternoon, the effect was less dramatic. Broadbent's head turned at once, and he stood straighter, smiling at the earl over Marguerite's shoulder. Corporal Willhays came to attention and looked even more uncomfortable. To his lordship's astonishment, however, neither Templeby nor Marguerite appeared to have heard him, and both went on talking animatedly.

He walked into the room, and cut through the flow with a harsh, "Good afternoon, Broadbent."

"At your service, my lord," said the major, with a crisp military bow.

"Papa!" All smiles, Marguerite ran to slip her arm through his. "I have just been telling Major Broadbent that he must be sure to come to us for the boat races next month. If his military duties will permit, of course. 'Twould be so nice if he could persuade his mama to come also, do you not think, sir?" And without pausing to allow her astonished stepfather to comment, she rushed on with unprecedented loquacity, "You and my mother are well acquainted with Lady Broadbent, and I am sure Mama would like it of all things. Do you not agree, Michael?"

"No doubt," the earl interposed, wondering how she could possibly chatter so foolishly under these terrible circumstances. "But I have urgent—"

"With what am I to agree?" Templeby turned from his conversation with the sergeant to direct a tolerant smile at his sister. "Some feminine nonsensicality, I'll wager, eh Margo?

You have sisters, Broadbent. Are you also bedevilled with constant demands to take 'em to balls and routs and all manner of entertainments? I vow that last month alone . . ." And he went on in this vein, listing the numerous events to which he had been required to escort his sister, many of which his mystified stepfather knew very well Marguerite had not attended, and several of whose existence he had not even been aware.

"You are ill-used, I dare swear," he said, breaking into this surfeit of verbiage. "But I must require you to—"

"No, no, dearest Papa," trilled Marguerite, squeezing his arm and interrupting with a rudeness she had never before shown him, or anyone else. "I protest I cannot permit my brother to so unjustly defame—"

"Enough!" It had been borne in upon the earl that all this chit-chat was a deliberate attempt to circumvent his purpose. They must then be aware of his purpose, poor children, and Lord knows, he could not blame them for seeking to divert him. Indeed, nothing would give him more pleasure than to abandon his heartbreaking mission. But the clock was ticking remorselessly. At any instant that repellent spy Burton Farrier would arrive, in which case Horatio's dear life would be sacrificed to no purpose. Not dreaming how distraught he looked, he barked, "Leave us, if you please. I have something to say to Major Broadbent that—"

Marguerite's face crumpled. "Oh, now you are cross," she wailed, and throwing herself into his arms, sobbing, hissed into his ear, "Do not! There is still hope! Do not!"

Still hope? The earl glanced at the clock on the mantelpiece. It wanted ten minutes to five o'clock. By Jupiter, but there was not still hope! Nor very much time left! His attempt to detach his stepdaughter became quite a struggle, and he had to use more strength than he would have liked to escape her clinging arms.

Templeby said sharply, "Papa, she meant no harm. I wish you will not—"

"Be still!" snapped the earl. "I know what you both are about, and you shall not stop me. Broadbent!"

—————

269

The major's comely face had become increasingly troubled. For some time he had held a deep and secret admiration for the lovely Miss Templeby. He also had reason to be suspicious of her stepbrother's political allegiance, and had prayed that if the blow should fall, he might be far away at the time. When the message had reached him at the barracks, he'd entertained the deepest misgivings, which had been lulled by the apparent light-heartedness of the Templebys. Now, the earl's obvious distress, Miss Templeby's sudden deathly pallor, and her brother's strained expression, awoke his earlier unease. Above all else, however, he was a soldier, and he put his own feelings aside.

His face stern, he stepped forward. "Yes, my lord? I believe you sent word that you had something of gravest import to convey to me . . ."

With a strange sense of discovery, Glendenning looked about him as he came down the main staircase. He had always scorned this house, his love of architecture inevitably causing him to deplore the lack of graceful lines and the sheer immensity of the old pile; the expense necessary to maintain it properly; the inefficiency of its floor plan; the impossibility of keeping it adequately heated in winter; the miles of walking required of the servants to deliver food from the kitchens to the various dining rooms. Only now, when it was so soon to vanish from his ken, did he realize how much a part of his life it was. His hand on the rail was a caress; his eyes lingered wistfully on the bishop's chair at the foot of the stairs that never had stood quite straight since he'd hurtled into it, aged seven, having achieved a truly magnificent rate of speed while sliding down the banister.

He turned towards the withdrawing room, trying to walk steadily, though fear made his knees weak and shaky. So many dear memories rushed to meet him that he began to think he must be a very stupid man never to have properly appreciated them. There was the painting their ball had sent crashing down one rainy afternoon when—against all regulations—he'd been teaching Michael how to play cricket in the great hall. Here was the portrait of Ephraim Laindon who, at the tender age of fourteen, had sailed with Drake against the might of the Spanish Armada, and gone on to win fame and fortune for his naval exploits. Lady Nola had used to guide him along the various portraits of his forbears, and tell him glowing tales of their achievements. He shrank from the realization that his own portrait would never serve as an inspiration to youthful Laindons in years to—

Horses! Many horses on the drivepath!

He rushed to the nearest window. A coach was drawing up at the foot of the steps, preceded by two dragoons, another riding on each side, and with two more bringing up the rear. The door was swung open, the steps let down, and Burton Farrier climbed out.

Glendenning leaned there, one hand against the wall. In a few minutes he would be marched out to that coach, his hands tied behind him with the traditional silken cord, en route to the Tower. He must not think beyond that. He must get to the withdrawing room before his courage failed him. By now, Papa would have denounced him to poor Hilary Broadbent, who would then become yet another victim. He took his hand down. The palm was wet, and he could feel the cold sweat of terror beading on his temples. Despising his cowardice, he walked on, his thoughts turning to his beloved. He would never see that darling, valiant soul again, for God send she would not come to see him publicly mutilated and decapitated.

He could hear Darrow at the front doors, and the distant purring voice of Burton Farrier. A wave of dizziness swept him. If he could only run! If he could only escape this death that would be so beyond words hideous! But he could not run. He was the only one who could save his family.

He reached the withdrawing room. The door stood partially open. For just a second he stood utterly still. Then, with his shoulders well back and his head high and proud, he went in. His vision seemed a little blurred, but he saw the earl and

271

Hilary facing each other. Hilary looked so stern, and Papa—poor dear man, how ghastly white he was. A muffled sob drew his gaze to the side. Margo was clasped in Michael's arms. Damnation! He hadn't wanted Michael here! There was no telling what the young hothead would do. Lady Nola was not present. He wondered anxiously if the strain had caused her to become ill, but then thought his father had probably contrived to spare her the spectacle of accusation and arrest.

"There!" cried the earl hoarsely, pointing at his son. "It is my painful duty, Major, to—"

Burton Farrier demanded harshly, "Why are you here, Broadbent?"

Stunned, Glendenning was shoved to one side.

"He is here," said Bowers-Malden in a croak of a voice, "because I sent for him so as to—"

Paralysed with shock, Glendenning thought, 'My God in heaven! *He hasn't done it!* What the *hell* has he been about all this time?' They were doomed, then! They all were doomed!

"Why you sent for him is of no importance now, sir." This was a very different man from the purringly obsequious individual Glendenning had met at the Mop Fair. Burton Farrier's face was a mask of triumph. In response to his authoritative gesture, two troopers marched up to range themselves one on each side of Glendenning.

"A moment," snapped Broadbent, "Lord Bowers-Malden, I must demand that you tell me why—"

"The matter is out of his lordship's hands," said Farrier. "I am here in my capacity of special investigator for General Samuel Underhill of the Horse Guards, and my authority takes precedence over yours, Major." He walked closer to smile gleefully at the viscount. "Horatio Clement Laindon, Lord Glendenning, since you have failed to produce the Comyn Pin, I now arrest you in the king's name, on a charge of High Treason!"

Glendenning flashed a glance at the earl. His father's anguished eyes were fixed upon him, and the powerful hands spread in a gesture that was a silent acknowledgment of failure.

His worst fears realised, Broadbent stared in horror at the accused. Glendenning was paper white, but when he spoke his voice was quite steady.

"My father sent for Major Broadbent so as to—"

"I'm not surprised." Thrusting his chin under Glendenning's nose, Farrier almost crowed with satisfaction. "But the time for calling in the military so as to save his own skin is long past!"

This vindictive speech brought the full ramifications home to Broadbent. This festering little bounty hunter would now be able to accuse them all! Bowers-Malden, Marguerite, the countess, Templeby, they all would die for having given sanctuary to a traitor! His mind reeling, he said haughtily, "What the deuce you're about, Farrier, I cannot pretend to know. But you'll arrest nobody without I see some evidence of treason!"

An instant, Farrier stared at him, his eyes narrowed and angry. Then he glanced at Marguerite, still clasping her brother's arm. He purred, "Perhaps your presence here has a logic I'd not previously perceived, Major. That can be looked into later. Meanwhile, I am only too pleased to accommodate your—er, interest in the unhappy details. Lady Nola Bowers-Malden was born a Comyn. A Scottish clan. She inherited the Comyn Pin, a plaid pin of great antiquity. By some strange chance, that same pin is contained in a list of valuables that were donated to the cause of the Pretender, Charles Stuart. In spite of the widespread belief that Lord Horatio Glendenning was in sympathy with the Jacobite Cause, and may even have fought for Prince Charles, my superiors hesitated to accuse a peer of so heinous a crime. He was given ample time therefore in which to produce the Comyn Pin, and thus prove his innocence." He folded his hands benignly. "That time, sir, has now run out."

Glendenning said, "The pin was mislaid, Major. Years since. We have tried to find it, but—"

Farrier laughed derisively.

Broadbent's heart sank. They had him, then. Poor old Tio.

In the face of such a charge, there was not a thing he could do to help.

"Mislaid," smirked Farrier. "Such a convenient happenstance. And would you not suppose that so valuable an object would have been sought, and a great hue and cry raised at the time?" His tone hardened. "Come now, Lord Glendenning. You are fairly caught, and have also ensured the arrest of your family, since—"

"No!" Glendenning said ringingly, "Not one single member of my family had the least knowledge of—"

"So here you are, lordship! I been looking and looking all over this great big place fer ye!"

Shock hit the viscount with the power of a physical blow. Whirling about, he whispered "Amy!"

She came tripping into the room, looking lovely but rather vulgar in a gown of cherry satin, two necklaces about her white throat, and her powdered hair swept into a very high and elaborate style and interlaced with a wide cherry satin riband liberally sprinkled with gems.

"What ye all standing about fer?" she asked, in what the viscount called her coster-monger voice, her bright gaze scanning the occupants who watched her with admiration, curiosity, or amusement.

"Young woman," began Farrier officiously, "You will be best advised to have nothing to do with—"

Amy let out a shriek. "Ow! It's that horrid gent what frightened me at the Mop Fair! Tio!" she ran towards him, arms outstretched. "Don't let him—Whoops!"

The unfamiliar high heels conspired against her, and she fell headlong. Springing to catch her up, Horatio felt her warm arms close around his neck and cling tight. Loudly imploring his protection from "that horrid old gent," she whispered against his ear, "Make a fuss 'cause I've prigged yer ma's jewels."

"No!" he muttered, ostensibly comforting her. "Stay clear of this!"

Echoing his sentiments, Farrier snapped, "Keep away from him, girl! Broadbent—arrest—"

"Cor!" exclaimed Amy, pulling away from the viscount. "You got no call to arrest me, you ain't! I never did no such thing!"

Her eyes, a little narrowed, glinted at him. He realised that whatever her scheme, she would carry it through alone if he refused to help, and so he entered her drama, saying with pseudo-anger, "I did not say you stole them. I only said—"

"Ye said I shouldn't of prigged 'em. And if you'd like to know about it, me lord, I didn't."

A trooper started toward Glendenning. Amy lifted a hand that sparkled with diamonds. "Just one minute, me good man," she said loftily. "I borrered a couple of sparklers from yer ma, lordship, only to show yer how nice they look on me. Never meaning to keep 'em, mind. And I'd have asked her 'cept she wasn't there to ask. The rest, I sorta . . . found." On the word, her eyes sparkled with mischief. She giggled, and spun around, spreading her skirts, only to again trip, and sit on the floor with a bump and a generous revelation of dainty ankles. Undismayed, she said laughingly, "And if I say so me own self, they looks proper lovely! Don't you agree, mate?"

Despite the fact that the excess of jewellry was very vulgar indeed, she was a bewitching sight, and the troopers grinned their appreciation.

Farrier, not in the least appreciative, snarled, "You men— get that woman out of here! Broadbent, I demand that you do your duty and place these people under—"

Lady Nola came into the room, and said in her resonant voice, "Miss Consett, you forget yourself! Stand up at once!"

Glendenning's eyes flashed to his stepmother. She was a little pale, but her head was high, her manner regal and re-flecting no more than shocked disapproval.

Struggling with the trooper who was trying to help her to her feet, Amy trilled audibly that he was "a naughty boy!" then gave a squeal as the riband in her hair was dislodged. It fell to the floor scattering adornments. "Now see what you been and gone and done," she wailed. "If any of 'em broke, it ain't my fault, melady!"

Marguerite screamed, "*Mama!* Look!" Her trembling hand

pointed to a large brooch that flashed and sparkled on the rug.

"Good heavens!" gasped her ladyship, starting forward. "It is my pin! Gregory! See! 'Tis the Comyn Pin!"

Dazed, the earl moved to take up the jewel.

Another hand was before his own. Farrier snatched up the pin and glared down at it. "Nonsense! This is not your pin! It cannot possibly—"

"Why can't it possibly be my mother's pin?" demanded Glendenning, baffled, but striving. "I'd be most interested to hear the reasons for your so positive denial, sir."

"Would you!" Farrier was tearing at the pocket of his coat. "I leave nothing to chance, my lord! 'Tis the secret of my success. For instance, I fancy you never dreamed that I might bring with me a detailed drawing of the Comyn Pin!"

Glendenning's heart sank, for wherever his adored gypsy had found the brooch, it most definitely could not be theirs, whereby her own precious life was now at risk.

Farrier spread a folded paper on the nearest table, and sent a triumphant grin at Glendenning. "Now you will all see the folly of trying to deceive an expert!"

Curious, although he knew there was no hope, the earl strode to peer over his shoulder.

"Miss Consett," said Lady Nola, annoyed, "where did you get that brooch?"

"I never done nothing wrong," wailed Amy. "I found it on an old doll, ma'am. 'Twas all dirty, but I liked it, so I give it a bit of a polish and it come up nice. But I never prigged it, so there was no call fer ye to bring all these nice soldiers to take a poor girl to prison!"

Straightening, the earl growled, "Well, Farrier? Well? It is identical, of course. I demand you apologize for your dastardly behaviour!"

Glendenning swayed slightly, and was obliged to steady himself against a chair.

"Not so!" Baffled, his face pale and twitching, Farrier shrilled furiously, "It is a fake! A fraud! I don't know how you—"

A bull-like roar interrupted him. "Do you say, sir,"

boomed the earl, the epitome of outraged majesty, "that this is *not* my wife's family pin? I invite you to look, sir, at the archaic symbols! Exactly as described on your drawing. Note, if you are capable of judging, the excellence of the stones! Do you suppose, sir, that we found ourselves a—a magician, who conjured up a copy? Hogwash, sir! Poppycock! I wish I might meet such a wizard!"

Glendenning thought numbly, 'He is a little bit of a wizard . . .'

"It is a fake, I say," shouted Farrier, rage overcoming discretion. "I know for a fact that the Comyn Pin—" He stopped abruptly.

Glendenning murmured, "Hoist by your own petard, Terrier?"

A glare of frustrated fury was levelled at him.

Broadbent, very sure there was more to this than met the eye, marched over to commandeer the pin and make his own comparison with the sketch.

"You may. You may th-think . . . ," spluttered Farrier all but incoherent.

"I shall tell my friend General Underhill exactly what I think, sir," roared the earl. "You come here during my absence, threaten my wife, frighten my daughter, impute all manner of evil to my son, and all because of some damnfool *list*—which, incidentally, I have never seen and I begin to doubt anyone else has! Now, when we show you proof positive of Lord Glendenning's innocence, instead of admitting your error like a gentleman, you gobble threats and more accusations. I *think*, sir, that this entire ugly business has been nothing more nor less than a diabolical scheme to discredit Glendenning, or to take vengeance upon me for some perverse reason. Or did you hope perhaps to win yourself more fame and notoriety? I do not scruple to say, sir, that if I had a reputation like yours, I'd be more wishful to bury it under the rug than to draw attention to it!"

Farrier looked like a wolf at bay, but before he could speak, Broadbent handed the pin to the earl.

"I remember seeing this years ago, sir. It looks the same to me, but we can assuredly have it authenticated."

"We will do so," said the earl. "And I'd also like to have a copy of this alleged Jacobite list authenticated, to which end, Farrier, you may tell General Underhill I shall instruct my solicitors to call upon him."

Thwarted, Farrier managed to pull himself together. He snarled, "You will waste your time, sir, for the list is a State secret!" His hand shot for the pin. "I'll take this for evidence 'gainst—"

The earl did not bother to deflect that darting hand. He simply lifted its owner aside. "You will take nothing, sir, but your odious self, sir, and your foul repute, sir—from my house. NOW!"

The final word vibrated the windows.

There was a faint scurrying sound in the hall, as the small crowd of servants gathered there, scattered.

His lips twitching, Major Broadbent said, "We will escort you, Mr. Farrier."

To have suffered the unspeakable indignity of being swept off his feet and replaced as though he were a naughty child caused Burton Farrier to become nigh purple with humiliation. Speechless, he jerked his head from one to the other of those present, as though marking each for some future and fearful retribution. Then, horribly aware that several troopers were barely able to suppress their mirth, he gulped and stamped his way from the scene of his first major defeat.

CHAPTER XV

The withdrawing room was relatively quiet now and, the earl having demanded a full accounting, Michael Templeby, seated on a sofa beside his mother, was finishing his part of the tale. He had held nothing back, and was grateful that there had, as yet, been no major explosions.

"And so," he said, "after Tio and Morris left, and I felt a—er, bit more the thing, we went off looking for some Owlers. Amy—I mean, Miss Consett, and Falcon, and I. By Jove, sir," he interrupted himself, swinging around to smile at his stepfather, his face still aglow with the relief that marked them all, "that Falcon's a peculiar sort of fellow, do you not think?"

Bowers-Malden stood with his back to the hearth, still finding it hard to credit that they were all here, safe and unharmed in their own home, when by rights they should be on a journey to the executioner. He shrugged. "He's a splendid-looking man, but one can scarce expect a half-breed to behave as a proper British gentleman should."

From the deep chair a little removed from the others, the viscount said quietly, "He grudged each moment spent in helping us, I grant you. But he helped just the same. I doubt we could have managed without him."

There was a brief and rather awkward pause. After the

departure of Burton Farrier and his military escort, their over-wrought nerves had reacted in an emotional outpouring of joy and shared embraces. The countess, openly weeping, had de-manded quiet while she offered up a fervent prayer of grati-tude. Not one of them had been able to restrain tears. During the subsequent confusion Amy had slipped away, and Glen-denning had retreated more and more into the background. He had not spoken for some time, and his words seemed to hang against the silence.

Templeby said hurriedly, "Oh, yes, indeed. I didn't mean to sound ungrateful. Lord knows, I bless you all for what you've done for me."

Marguerite, her chair close beside the earl's, asked, "Where is Mr. Falcon? I wish he had come in so we could have prop-erly thanked him."

"I doubt he'd have allowed you to do so," replied her brother. "He cannot abide the niceties of polite behaviour, and would likely cut you off, saying it was a dead bore and that he should never have allowed himself to become involved with such a set of silly gudgeons. At all events, he no sooner discovered that I was able to be up and about, than he went rushing off after Tio and Morris."

Glendenning's head had been nodding, but at this he jerked awake and asked sharply, "Falcon went to Dover?"

"Yes. Said he had to see you didn't fall into a muddle, because you must second him in a duel. Do they really mean to fight?"

"They say they do." Glendenning frowned. "Certainly Jamie Morris is in no case to fight anyone for a while. If Falcon does come up with him, he'll be fairly gnashing his teeth to find he must wait again."

The earl said testily, "Never mind about Falcon. Go on, Michael. What's all this about Owlers?"

"Well, sir, it seems Miss Amy thought her uncle might have taken refuge with them when he got away from the varmints who were chasing him. So she persuaded us to go in search of them, and a dashed murky business it was, I can tell you! Creeping into forest hideaways, and caves and the like at dead of night. And when we did come up with them, be dashed if ever I saw such a set of rum customers." He laughed. "In more ways than one!"

"Perhaps they were, Mr. Templeby. But we found Uncle Absalom, just the same, didn't we?"

The viscount shook off weariness and was on his feet at once, and the other gentlemen stood as Amy came into the room. She had discarded her borrowed finery, and brushed the powder from her hair, and the cherry dress emphasized her dark beauty. She seemed, thought the earl, as he had thought once before, to bring sunshine into the room with her. His eyes flashed to his son.

The adoration on Glendenning's face was very obvious and, returning his gaze, Amy blushed betrayingly. She turned away, beckoning to the man who hesitated in the hall. "Come on, Uncle Ab."

Absalom sidled in. He looked fierce and belligerent, but his steps were halting, and there was about him the air of one who is poised for instant flight.

Glendenning limped forward. "So it *was* you, Ab!" Seizing the older man's hand, he wrung it heartily. "You saved my life—my family! How may I ever thank you?"

The countess and Marguerite hurried to add their own praise and thanks. Absalom tried in vain to retreat. Glendenning gripped his arm. "No. I will not let you run away. You must stay to be properly—"

"I done it for my Amy," declared Absalom, trying to hide behind Glendenning as the earl also bore down on him. "Ain't no need fer ye all to go making a whale out of a minnow! I'll tell ye straight out, I got no love for you Quality lot! England would be a sight better off if ye was all—"

"You done it, Ab," inserted Amy quickly. "That's what counts."

"And 'twas a masterly piece of work," said the earl, coming forward again, having halted momentarily in the face of Consett's odd behaviour. "Do me the honour of shaking my hand, sir!"

"We-ell," muttered Absalom. "If that's the way of it . . ."

He thrust out a hand, then gave a squawk as the countess suddenly swooped to press a kiss on his tanned cheek. "Don't ye *never* . . . do that!" he gasped, looking ready to faint.

"You dear, wonderful man," she said earnestly. "Without your great talent, my dear son would be under sentence of death at this very moment."

"As would we all," grunted the earl.

They closed in around Consett, full of questions and admiration, plying him with brandy and cakes until he was quite surrounded and beginning to find this not quite so unpleasant as he'd supposed.

The viscount led Amy to a far windowseat. "Beloved," he murmured, pressing a kiss on her hand. "Oh, my dear! I thought I would never see your adorable face again."

"And look as if you can scarcely see it now, darling lord-ship." She touched his cheek, quick to have heard the break in his voice, and to see that his red-rimmed eyes were glittering suspiciously. "My poor love, you're proper knocked up. I 'spect ye've had no sleep, and you're limping again. Is it that ankle?"

"The late Major Trethaway—er, leaned on it a trifle. With his boot."

"*What?*" The earl had wandered to them. "That filthy swine kicked you? The devil you say! You gave as good as you got, I hope?"

A rueful smile crept into Glendenning's eyes. "I'd been clubbed, and was down, and tied to a tree at the time, sir."

"By the lord Harry! What an unmitigated scoundrel he must have been! I wish to heaven I'd had the chance to take my horsewhip to him!"

Glendenning had so hoped for a quiet word with his love. Stifling a sigh, he murmured, "He won't be kicking anyone else, sir."

The earl nodded. "Fellow drowned, you said? Now I want to hear about that, Horatio, among other things! And as for you, young lady, there's a deal I want to know about you and your—er, uncle. How in the world you smuggled him in here, for instance. And how he was able to copy that accursed pin in such a short space, and—"

"And that he is a masterly chess player, melord?" said Amy pertly.

The earl caught his breath, and his eyes lit up. "Begad! You don't mean it? Then we shall not let him escape! Hey! Consett . . . !" With an imperative gesture he returned to the chattering group by the fireplace.

Amy chuckled, and turned to her love. "There. Now we can—" The words died away. Fatigue had at last overmastered Glendenning. He sagged against the window, fast asleep. Watching him, Amy was seized by a deep tenderness. With one fingertip, she touched the haggard cheek, the black shadows under his closed eyes, the weary, drooping mouth. "Poor lordship. Ye've paid the price, my dearie."

His eyes half opened, then closed again.

She bent and kissed his brow gently, and whispered, "And so have I . . ."

Leaning back against the pillows, Glendenning stirred sugar into his coffee. He had been so soundly asleep yesterday evening that they'd had to half carry him to his bed. He'd slept the clock around, awakening to find his bedchamber bright with late afternoon sunlight and to find also that he was ravenously hungry for breakfast. He had been finishing that breakfast, and lost in contemplation of the nightmare that had so nearly ended in tragedy, when August Falcon had strolled in, drawn up a chair, and demanded to be informed of developments. He had refused refreshments, but in the course of Glendenning's account had made several forays into the covered dishes the footman had left on the bedside table.

"Then you've no doubt it was all contrived by our nefarious League," he said when Glendenning was giving a brief description of having come upon Trethaway atop the cliffs.

"No possible doubt." The viscount paused, and said

gravely, "Trethaway had printed *châtiment un* on that damned rock."

"Had he, by Jupiter!" Falcon appropriated another slice of bacon, then leaned back and settled his booted feet on the bed once more. "Charming fellow, your friend Trethaway."

"Mmm," said Glendenning thoughtfully. "At least, I think 'twas Trethaway. Though it might, I suppose, have been the Lillibulero fellow."

The bacon arrested in midair, Falcon looked up. "The— what?"

"No. The who. And why on earth you refuse to let me order you another tray, instead of—"

"You may order trays to your heart's content. I, however, not being hungry, shall not eat whatever they may hold." Falcon popped the bacon into his mouth and wiped his fingers on the sheet. "Meanwhile, pray enlarge upon your fascinating 'who.'"

The viscount took a swallow of his coffee, edged a plate of crumpets toward Falcon, and recounted what he and Morris had overheard.

"Truly a case of being in the wrong place at the right time," said the "not hungry" Falcon around a crumpet. "How they must yearn to have our heads. And damn near got yours! But still, they failed." A faint grin curved his mouth. "They won't like that. D'you think we should trot to the Metropolis and advise the great man at Whitehall?"

Glendenning said dryly, "Farrier works for Underhill."

"Well, yes. But— Good God! You never think . . . ?"

"I think that there can be little doubt but that the League of Jewelled Men is much larger and more powerful than we'd assumed. Which being the case, they could very well have members in high places. I do not mean to criticize, my dear fellow, but you are dripping butter all over the rug."

Falcon, who deplored untidiness, was aghast, and hurriedly used Glendenning's napkin in an attempt to rectify matters. Standing then, he said impatiently, "What a block you are! There's a general officer in Whitehall who might be implicated in some damnable scheme 'gainst England,

and you pinch at me because I spill a little butter! What the deuce are we to do?"

Glendenning sighed. "I have barely escaped the ghastly fate of being directly to blame for the shameful deaths of my entire family. I have been ambushed and beaten and come within a whisker of handing my own stupid head to that wart, Farrier. I have also, God be praised, found the lady I mean to make my wife, and I long to see her. For several days—at least—I refuse to even think of the League of Jewelled Men, damn their dirty hides!"

"Hum." Falcon sat down again. "Whereby I am, I take it, *de trop.*"

"Decidedly *de trop*. However, I am so grateful for my reprieve that I cannot quarrel with anyone today. You may finish the crumpet to which you are apparently committed, although—" He stopped, frowning.

Glancing at him, Falcon said, "You have remembered something."

"Yes. Something the Lillibulero Man said to Trethaway. He suspected that the masterminds of the League may actually be planning something even more dastardly than whatever was their original scheme. He called them fanatics, and I'd the impression he was disturbed by what might lie ahead. Trethaway asked him if they—the rank and file members—were being played false."

"Ominous, to say the least of't, unless it leads to dissension in the ranks. And you were unable to identify this Lillibulero Man? Either of you?"

"Morris had been knocked out of time at that point. I really thought the poor fellow was dead. Did he not tell you?"

"Lieutenant Morris was too busy chortling in his infantile fashion that you and he had 'done the thing' whilst I'd been lollygagging about with Miss Consett." He scowled darkly. "I'd no sooner arrived at that confounded inn than the clod was tossing his repellent homilies at me. Gad, Tio! How you can endure him is past all understanding."

Glendenning's lips quirked, but he asked gravely, "Then you are come to arrange your meeting, is that it?"

"Eh? Oh—yes. Of course. These crumpets would be the better for some of that jam. Thank you." Concentrating on jam and crumpet, Falcon drawled, "I'll own I was also curious to see if you'd rushed here to offer yourself up for execution." From under his lashes, the dark eyes watched Glendenning obliquely. "As you evidently intended."

"In which case," the viscount evaded, "you'd have been obliged to find another second. Is Jamie well enough to fight?"

"He is so well that I must lose no time in rushing back to Town. I've no doubt he is already annoying my unfortunate sister. Besides which, an I fail to keep an eye on the Rossiter female—"

Glendenning asked with a lift of the brows, "Do you refer to Gwendolyn?"

"Is there another? Oh, Lord! Never say so!" Upon being assured there was only one Miss Rossiter, Falcon mopped his brow. "You may smile, Tio, but the wretched creature delights to cut up my peace, and fairly haunts Falcon House. I mean to tell Katrina to find a less argumentative friend! Much more of Miss Rossiter's interference, and Apollo will be useless!"

"Gwendolyn argues with Apollo?" asked Glendenning innocently.

Falcon gave him an irked look. "Our meeting is set for next Monday, though the others will have to be approached, of course. Is that convenient for you? Be very sure, if you please. Damned if I propose to suffer through another put-off."

Glendenning assured him that he had no objections. And watching the door close behind him, thought, 'Barring more disasters.'

Half an hour later he was shaved and dressed, and Whittlesey was assisting him with his coat, when the earl came into the room and with a gesture dismissed the valet.

Glendenning stood, his stomach twisting into knots. Much of yesterday afternoon was a confused muddle in his mind, but he knew his volatile parent well enough to be prepared for a change of heart.

His face enigmatic, the earl stared at him. Clearing his

throat, he said gruffly, "Well, sir? We brushed through that fiasco. Are you satisfied?"

"I would say rather, that I am most humbly grateful, sir. Though I cannot expect you will ever forgive me."

The earl marched straight at him, clapped him on the back, then stamped on to gaze out of the window, and said a little unsteadily, "Had you not found your pretty gypsy, we would all have perished, Horatio."

"I am very aware, sir."

"Are you also aware that her alleged 'uncle' is a positive genius?" Turning back into the room, hands clasped behind him, the earl went on, "I've not enjoyed a game of chess so much in years! Lady Nola and Marguerite hid him in the Indian Suite, and brought everything he needed to design the spurious Comyn Pin, did you know it? They ruined your grandmama's ruby ring; your great grandmama's tiara; and Lord knows what else in the process! Those rascally women! And, Zounds! what a splendid craftsman Consett is! How he mastered the carvings on the piece, to say nothing of creating it in so short a space is little short of incredible. I dare to think his work will pass muster even if 'tis subjected to examination by real experts. I mean to make ample provision for him. If his exquisite niece had not decided you might not be able to retrieve the real pin, and had she not found her uncle and brought him here . . ." He pursed his lips, his eyes very grim. "Well, we can but see she is well recompensed. You must ensure that, my boy."

"I mean to do more than that, sir. In fact, I intend to wed her."

The earl's jaw dropped. "You mean to—*what?* Have you lost your wits? The lass is a beauty, and I'll own we've a debt to her we're never like to repay. But—a common gypsy to be the future Countess of Bowers-Malden? Pshaw! You surely cannot suppose I would ever agree to such a disaster?"

Glendenning walked to face him. "I love her, sir. With all my heart. And I dare to hope she returns my affection. No— please do not say she is not good *ton*. Her birth is unknown,

I admit, but certainly she was stolen. 'Tis very possible her family may rival our own.''

"Flim flam! You've no least chance of proving such an unlikely circumstance and must accept her as she is, not as you wish she might be! Horatio, be sensible, lad. She is an enchanting minx, but a minx nonetheless, who would disgrace you a hundred times a day! You'd be bored with her in a week, irritated with her in a month, and ready to strangle her in a year! And can you not foresee what the *ton* would do to the poor child? For *her* sake, if not for your own, give up this impossible piece of chivalry!"

The viscount said with a slow smile, "No, do you think it that, sir? It is not, I promise you. Amy is more than enchanting. She has a fine mind that darts about like any butterfly, and is full of curiosity and eagerness to learn. Most of the young ladies of Quality whom I meet at social events would, I feel sure, bore me, even as you say. I mean no unkindness, and do not doubt they are gentle and kind. But they have not a thought among them that goes beyond gossip and fashion and parties. When I am with Amy, I see something I have seen all my life—and she imbues it with magic, so that I find I've never really seen it at all. She is as lovely as she is exasperating; her nature is generous; she is kind, but also fiercely independent; and certainly she can be outrageous. I suspect we will have some lively quarrels, but as to my becoming bored with her—never! My life will be busy, I acknowledge, for 'twill be a struggle to keep up with her interests and, perhaps, to keep her from some shocking exploit or other. I think, sir, that you are right, and the *ton* may scorn her. I hope they will grow to love her. I know I do, and always will. If it distresses you, I shall take her far away. My apologies for making such a speech, but . . ." A wistfulness came into his green eyes. He said tentatively, "Whatever your decision, I pray you do not mean to forbid that I name you my father?"

It occurred to the earl that he had missed something: that somewhere he had failed to see that his son was not a foolish fribble after all, but a man he could be proud to have sired, and that if the viscount's political persuasions were ill-judged, they had nonetheless been followed with commendable courage and loyalty. His heart swelled with affection, to hide which, he said grumpily, "If Michael were my own flesh and blood, by Jupiter, I'd be tempted! But I'll have no gypsy caravans around the ornamental water, Horatio, and so I warn you!"

Speechless, Glendenning blinked at him.

The earl held out his hand regally. "Go on with you," he growled. "If you will persist in this tomfoolery!"

His son dropped to one knee. The earl's hand was dutifully kissed, and a radiant grin was levelled at him. Then the door was flung open, and the viscount all but ran along the hall.

Lady Nola was quiet for a long time, and Glendenning's apprehension deepened. He shifted uneasily in his chair, and said at last, "Mama—you *do* like her?"

Her eyes turned from their contemplation of the fragrant bowl of sweet peas on her parlour table. Looking at him gravely, she said, "I think she is a *rara avis*, Horatio. But she is no fool. And she would be very foolish to marry you."

Relieved, he said, "If she should be so foolish, Mama, will you give us your blessing?" He saw her small frown and added quickly, "My father voiced all the arguments I am sure you must feel, but he has agreed."

"An I do not give you my blessing, shall you give her up?"

He stood, walked to the window, and came back to stand before her. " 'Twould grieve me to marry 'gainst your wishes. But—no, ma'am. I'll not give her up."

She nodded. "Then I suppose you must have your gypsy, my love. Almost, I have lost you. I really could not bear to do so again."

There was only Absalom to see now, and Absalom might be the most difficult of all. But, striding rapidly across the courtyard, Glendenning's heart was so light he felt he might have floated. The nightmares were done at last. Now came the joy, the love, the great and so undeserved happiness.

The old house looked quite beautiful at this golden hour. It was surprising, in fact, that after all the rain so few people were out here enjoying this balmy late afternoon. Not so much as a gardener to be seen. The only person he really wanted to see, of course, was Miss Amy Consett, and, Lord, but he longed to see her! He'd not be surprised to find her awaiting him in the great hall. With luck, Absalom would be with her, and he could petition the dear old fellow for her hand. Amy was willing, of course. A little scared, perhaps, but she would not refuse him. Would she? His rapid stride faltered slightly.

'I couldn't live here, Tio . . . Your life's like another world, compared with mine.' Her voice was so clear it was almost as if she stood beside him.

He began to walk faster.

He had a blurred memory of her kissing him as he'd fallen asleep in the withdrawing room yesterday. And of a sadness in her eyes.

He reached the great hall, almost running. It was deserted, save for a lackey who swung open the door for him.

Turning on the man, he said, "Have you seen Miss Consett?"

"She was with Miss Templeby, my lord."

Glendenning sprinted up the stairs.

The lackey's voice floated after him. "This morning . . ."

Marguerite was not in her room, and her abigail said she believed her mistress was showing Miss Consett and Mr. Consett about the grounds.

Somewhat reassured, Glendenning hurried to the window, but he could not discern the faintest splash of colour that might be a lady's gown, nor, in fact, any sign of life, save for a solitary peacock. Returning to the hall, he went first to his own, then to his brother's suite, both of which were empty. The absence of servants was beginning to alarm him. They were always about. The confounded house fairly crawled with them. But it was stupid to be so afraid. She wouldn't leave him? She wouldn't run away?

He raced to the stairs again, tore down them, and went outside. And never dreamed how many eyes watched him.

The sun was going down when he returned to the house, and by now, terror had him in its grip. Almost the first person he saw was Whittlesey, coming slowly down the stairs. The man looked startled, and backed away as Glendenning took the stairs two at a time, and stopped in front of him.

"Tell me," said the viscount grittily. "You know. You all know. That's why everyone is avoiding me like the plague! Where is Miss Consett?"

"Sir, 'tis not my place—"

"Don't be roaring at yer man, milor'. He don't know nought." Absalom stood on the landing, surprisingly distinguished in a simple brown habit, though his wig was as untidy as ever.

With a sigh of relief, Whittlesey escaped.

"Thank the Lord!" Glendenning hurried up to the landing. "Absalom, I've been unable to find her. She's teasing me, the saucy scamp, is that it?"

Consett couldn't help but feel sorry for the man who scanned him with such desperate intensity, but, "Run off," he said, not softening the blow. He saw the lean features become very white, and added, "Well, you mighta knowed she would. Yer brother's gone after her. Won't find her. If my Amy don't want to be found, she won't be found, and she didn't want no part o' being a Quality mort. What's more, I don't—" He stopped, perforce, as Glendenning seized him by the throat.

"Where has she run? Tell me, or by God, I'll—"

"Are you run quite mad, Glendenning?" The earl ran to wrench at his son's arm. "Let Mr. Consett go at once! Damme! Let go, I say! This man is a guest in my house!"

"Amy has disappeared, and this rogue won't tell me—"

"Rogue, is it! You've a damnably short memory! Only hours since, Mr. Consett saved all our necks! I would suggest that you make him a profound apology, sir!"

His father's powerful hands and the voice of reason broke through the viscount's maddened fury. His fingers relaxed their grip, and he stepped back.

Clutching his throat, Consett advised in a fierce croak that he wouldn't tell such a madman where his niece was if he knew—which he didn't.

"She's got herself lost is all," declared the earl. "Where's that fool of a butler? Ah—there you are, Darrow! Have all the staff out at once! Miss Consett is lost somewhere. I want the house and grounds searched!"

The butler hurried off. Shaking his head, Consett followed.

The earl lowered his voice, "Pay no heed to what he said, Horatio. He's a good man, but a revolutionary, I fancy. Likely don't like the notion of his niece marrying into the Quality. I'll wager there's nothing more to this than that your lady's found a quiet place to sit in peace and get her thoughts sorted out. Very sensible. Just be easy, m'boy. We'll find her, never fear."

But they did not find her.

At dusk, Glendenning swung into Flame's saddle, the earl watching him glumly.

"You're a fool not to wait until morning. Templeby's not yet back, and may well have come up with her. Even if he has not, what can you hope to accomplish at this hour?"

"I only know I must try, sir."

"Then try in the morning! I shall call in special constables. She can't have gone far, and—"

"She is *alone*, sir! I daren't wait another second, much less till morning!"

"But—"

Horatio bent lower, gripping his father's hand strongly. "Papa, I beg you—get word to Morris, and August Falcon. They'll help, I know it. I'm going to her—er, cottage in the woods. It's near Epsom. If she's not there, I'll try Mimosa Lodge. Kadenworthy may have seen her."

"But, Tio," pleaded the earl, using his son's abhorred nickname in this moment of distress, "it don't make sense to—"

"If anything should go wrong, sir, go to Gideon Rossiter. He'll explain."

"Wrong? Now see here Horatio—is there something more to—"

But Glendenning was already riding out.

CHAPTER XVI

More than three weeks passed before Glendenning again crossed into Berkshire. Thunder was bumping down the clouds, and he pulled his cloak higher about his ears, ducking his head when a gust of wind drove rain into his eyes. Another grey day, as these past three days had been grey. He sighed wearily. A fitting return home, perhaps.

Despite his determination to devote years, if need be, to the search, he'd been sure he would find his love within a very short time. He knew so many of her haunts; surely, she could not for long escape him. Yet this was the twenty-fourth day, and he had found not so much as a trace of her.

He had reached Absalom's cellar at about noon the day after leaving home. He'd approached the ruins very cautiously, and watched for a good quarter hour before venturing from the trees. And he'd known by the time he went inside that she was not there. The League had been there, however. The shelves once so neatly stocked had been ransacked, glass and chinaware smashed, the contents of pots and cans strewn over the floor in a wave of senseless destruction that ants were doing their best to tidy up. A small pile of ashes and some scorched pages were all that remained of Absalom's peerless sketches and notes. The painting Amy had so treasured had been slashed with a knife, and the frame smashed. Bedding had been piled in the centre of the kitchen and set alight. Apparently, the hunters had ridden away, assuming the cellar would burn to the ground, but the fire had gone out after most of the bedding and the table was consumed.

To see such devastation had wracked Glendenning and, wandering through the wreckage, coming upon bits and pieces of items that had been cherished by Amy, brought memories too painful to be prolonged, so that he'd ridden out very soon.

From the ruins he'd gone straight to Mimosa Lodge, but Kadenworthy was at his hunting box in Yorkshire. His gentle aunt, troubled by the viscount's distraught manner, had pressed him to stay for tea and, failing, had said apologetically that her nephew was not expected to return until the weekend.

Leaving the Lodge, he'd ridden to Epsom, and then Reigate, and he'd spent the rest of that day and the next scanning an endless succession of faces, searching narrow alleys and busy thoroughfares, prowling the crowded marketplace and the yards of inns and taverns, and enquiring of ostlers or pedlars or rag-and-bone men if they'd seen her. Some knew her, but none had encountered her for weeks. Hour succeeded hour, but until far into the evenings he persevered. The following day he rode to a fair. The next was devoted to a bazaar, and the next to a race meeting. Thus, the days slipped away as he wandered the Down country wherever people might congregate, sure each time that she would be here—she *had* to be somewhere in the throng, *this* would be the day he would find her. When night forced him to abandon his efforts, he refused to be discouraged, but after a few hours' sleep, was up at dawn and off to another village or town, or summertime festivity.

At the end of the first week, he thought he'd found her. In Godalming he learned there was to be a mill next afternoon in the fields outside Dorking, the combatants sufficiently well-known pugilists to attract a crowd. He'd set out before dawn, riding northeastward, and gradually becoming part of a great noisy company, all heading with eager expectancy for the scene of combat. It was the very kind of crowd where Amy might decide to do a little "prigging," or perhaps try to sell some pretty thing she had made. Reaching the site, he'd left Flame at a makeshift livery while he prowled. His heart had leapt when he'd spotted a slender gypsy lass with a scarlet scarf around her thick dark hair, and a provocative way of walking that had convinced him his long search was ended at last. Shoving his way through the crowd he'd come up with her, seized her by the shoulders and whirled her around, shouting an exultant, "Sweetheart!" But the startled face turned to him had nothing of Amy's beauty. The features were coarse; the eyes, bold and calculating, had swiftly taken his measure, resulting in an inviting smile as she swayed to him. The brawny farmhand beside her, however, had viewed this infringement in a far different light. The viscount's polite apology had been refused with wrath and violence. The pleased crowd had enjoyed an extra mill. The altercation had been short but sharp, and Glendenning had gone his way with a split lip, his ears ringing with the admiration of the spectators, and the vituperations of the disappointed gypsy girl, who knelt beside her champion, clutching the guinea the viscount had offered, and shrieking a profane assessment of his character.

Since then, he had lost count of the miles he'd tramped. His days had deteriorated into a dreary procession of faces and figures, of hope that sprang only to prove vain, of a growing despair that must be fought lest it defeat him. Worst of all, fear had become his constant companion. His darling Amy was beautiful and brave, but she was all alone. What if some of the *chals* found her? What if she'd been kidnapped by the Squire's animals, as they had tried to do before? Haunted by such terrors, he found it hard to sleep at night, and often woke from such ghastly nightmares that he dreaded to sleep again.

As one week blended into the next, worry and lack of sleep began to undermine his spirits. If there had been just a crumb of encouragement, if only one person had seen her, or heard of her, he could have kept hope alive. But when, after all this time he'd discovered no trace, out of sheer desperation his thoughts turned towards home. It was, he told himself, quite possible that Michael had found her the very night of his own departure. Perhaps, while he wasted time searching the south country, August or Jamie had already brought her safely back to the Abbey.

So it was that on this afternoon of clouds and rain and the sullen grumbling of thunder, he came again to the Abbey and turned Flame towards the stable block.

"His lordship's come!" A rush of feet followed that youthful howl, and two stableboys were beaming up at him, and shyly welcoming him home.

Glendenning smiled, praying they would say "Miss Consett's back, sir!" But they did not, and because he so dreaded the answer, he dared not voice the all-important question, and asked only if his brother was at the Abbey.

At once their faces became solemn. Mr. Templeby had been here, they reported, but had gone off again.

Glendenning asked that his saddlebags be brought up to the house, and made his way through the downpour. The skies were even darker now, and lightning zigzagged against the low-hanging clouds. The following thunder was still distant, but they were probably in for a stormy night. An ill omen, he thought wretchedly, then pulled his head up. Be damned to omens! This was just his first try. Next time, he'd rope in Michael and, with luck, Jamie and Falcon as well, unless they'd fought their— He halted, with a guilty gasp. Once again he'd completely forgotten the duel, and his promise to Falcon! Lord, but the man would be more like to murder than to help him!

Starting for the door that led into the west wing, he felt a hand on his arm. The stableboy had followed with his saddlebags, and now touched his brow respectfully and said that there had been some trouble with the thresholds, and would his lordship please to use the main entrance. Sure enough, Glendenning saw that makeshift barriers had been erected to block the various outer doors. "Joy!" he muttered, and started the long haul across the courtyard. Lost in thought, he forgot the boy behind him until lightning flashed again, and he heard a startled exclamation. "Here, I'll take those," he said, reaching for the saddlebags. "No need for both of us to drown."

The boy protested staunchly, but Glendenning took his burden and sent him splashing off.

He had expected that one of the lackeys would come to his rescue with an umbrella, but the front doors remained closed until he was reaching for the handle, at which point they were swung open.

Darrow, ever imperturbable, bowed and welcomed him as if he'd left an hour since. A lackey hurried to take the saddlebags. A hovering footman relieved him of cloak, and whip; another took his gloves and tricorne. Making off with their burdens, they all looked so cool and efficient and non-committal.

"Is the earl at—" began Glendenning.

"Horatio!" Lady Nola came down the stairs and held out her hands to him. "Thank heaven you are come home, my dear!" she said, drawing him towards the west wing. "Did you learn anything of her?"

Such a simple question, but with such terrible implications. Amy wasn't safe, then; she wasn't here. He had braced himself for such news, but the reality was still crushing. He shook his head, and asked, "Has there been no word at all, Mama? I'd thought perhaps Michael—or Falcon might have—"

"Falcon!" she exclaimed, looking irked. "Do not even mention that wretched creature, Tio! He came here breathing fire and smoke, as usual. Something about a promise you'd made and—"

"Blast his stupid duels," he exploded. "Oh—your pardon, ma'am." He drew a hand across his brow distractedly. "I had hoped, you see . . . but—"

"Even so," she said with a disapproving air, "there is no call for language, and— My heavens! Your father particularly wished me to join him at four o'clock, and I am late." She started off.

"Mama—wait! Please. I must talk to—"

"Yes, dear. Later on," she called over her shoulder. "Do you go on up, and I shall come to you directly."

He stared after her. There had been no embrace, no real anxiety about Amy, no sympathy with his own grief. It was unlike Mama to be impervious to another person's suffering. Furthermore, neither his father nor Marguerite had come to hear whatever news he might have. He felt hurt and betrayed, and started towards the stairs, head down and his heart like lead. Probably, they still blamed him for their recent ordeal. That was understandable, after all. And none of them really approved of his lady, nor guessed how much this meant to him. Perhaps they had never loved as deeply as he loved, so that each hour of not knowing, of growing terror, was worse than the last. Perhaps they had never missed someone so much that it was an unceasing ache of the heart. Dear God, if only she was well, and not—

"Pray have a care, your lordship, else you will surely bump into me."

The young voice was soft and cultured and musical. A friend of Margo's, thought Glendenning dully. Too weary to move fast, he murmured an apology and stepped to the side of the stair. The lady did not pass, and he lifted his head slowly.

He saw a jewelled slipper peeping from beneath the scalloped hem of a pink and white striped underdress. The paniers were of deeper pink satin, the tiny waist contained by a stomacher that spread gradually to reveal pearls glowing on a creamy expanse of bosom. He saw at last an exquisitely lovely face, with a patch trembling beside ruddy lips, and framed by powdered and upswept curls. She stood there, watching him and plying a fan in one small hand. And her great dark eyes held an indescribable tenderness.

Shock, added to fatigue and despair, proved too much. Glendenning's eyes blurred, and he groped blindly for the rail.

A flutter of draperies. Warm arms about his neck. Tears, blinding him. And he was sitting down, hugging her close, trying to talk sensibly, but able to do no more than to whisper her name, over and over again, and know that he was behaving like a fool, and not care.

The flames that flickered on the hearth provided the only light in the book room, and the earl, standing by the mantel gazing down at those flames, kicked a log absently, and muttered, "We had best go to them now."

" 'Twill take more than thirty seconds for Horatio to recover from the shock," his wife argued. "How I kept from telling him when I saw the despair in his eyes, poor boy, I shall never know. Tell me what you mean to do, sir."

He looked troubled. "I know what I *should* do. For both their sakes."

Lady Nola said musingly. "One seldom sees a great love. I think I have now seen one."

"Oh, do you!" he said, indignant.

"I meant," she amended, hiding a smile, "a love as passionately offered—on both sides."

"If you are saying, madam, that you have never offered such a—a depth of affection to your unfortunate spouse—"

She raised her head and looked at him squarely. "I do not say that at all. But—I *have* sometimes wondered, Gregory, if you offered because you really cared for me. Or because you liked me—"

"*Liked* you madam," he roared.

"And you knew I loved Horatio," she finished.

"Of all the cock and bull— Of all the— By *Gad*, madam wife, but I should wash out your mouth with strong soap!"

Lady Nola chuckled. "Now there is a declaration of love, if ever I heard one!"

"And here is another declaration, m'dear," he said, his resonance much diminished. "You know dashed well how much I— Er, that is to say— Well—deuce take it, Nola! How I'd go on—without you . . . ! Which has nothing to say to the case, because you *do* know it, and you merely mouth all this rubbish to turn my thoughts. The plain and unvarnished truth is, that he warned me he meant to marry the chit. And she's pretty, and sweetly natured, and a bright little thing—but I still hoped that, especially after this separation . . ." He sighed.

"But that is precisely why Amy insisted upon it. To give him time to change his mind. Do you now mean to withdraw your consent? I think you will lose him, Gregory. 'Twould take more than mortal man to part them."

"I know it. Well, I never did understand him. Lord knows, I tried. But, of late I have come to realize . . . how much— Oh, dash it all! What I am trying to say—"

"You are trying to say that you cannot bear the thought of him walking out of your life. No more can I."

He came to sit beside her and take her hand. "My lady, what will come of it? Consett! I never heard of such a family, and nor did anyone else. Tio will be a laughing-stock! We *all* will be laughing-stocks!"

"Instead of merely being corpses, shamefully put to death and with our heads on Temple Bar."

He gave a gasp and pulled her into his arms. "Dear God! Do not remind me!"

"I think we must never forget it, Gregory." She kissed his cheek and settled back with his arm still comfortably around her. "But this may not be the disaster you envision. Amy is a darling child. Certainly she has good blood in her, and though we may never discover her true name, I've a notion she may very well become the rage."

"The rage? A nameless gypsy? When half of London's matchmaking mamas had it in mind *their* very eligible daughters were destined to become Viscountess Glendenning? They'll crucify the poor chit!"

The countess' eyes took on a martial look. "Not whilst I am by, they will not! Furthermore, I shall enlist the aid of all my friends. Phyllida Gurnard, especially. And if I can snare her grandmama—"

"Phyllida . . . hmm. Born a Dunster, wasn't she? Thaddeus Briley's sister? Then the grandmother is the dowager Lady Mount-Durward, eh? A proper dragon! You'll have some formidable allies, my dear!"

"I hope I may persuade them. Amy looks divinely when she is nicely dressed, and she exudes warmth and gaiety. 'Twill not be the first time a commoner has married into a great house, although we may have to conjure up some tale of her having been stolen from a branch of a very good family."

"A broken branch," he said glumly.

She chuckled. "No, that can be done, I think. Cheer up, my dear. We are alive and all together. Perhaps more together than ever we have been."

"Hmm."

"And besides, the gel learns so very fast, you know. In just these few days I have taught her a great deal. Her speech is much improved, and she doesn't use nearly as many—er, vulgar expressions."

He said with a stifled sigh, "And she did save us. That I own."

"She did indeed. Furthermore, although she very obviously worships him, she is no weakling, and will handle his starts nicely. And besides," added the countess with enthusiasm, "she's a good sort and a rare mort, and I don't doubt he still means to make her his trouble-and-strife!"

The jaw of her noble spouse dropped. "God bless my soul!" he gasped.

Held fast on her beloved's lap, joying in the feel of his arms so close about her, Amy said brokenly, "If that ain't just like you, Tio! I worked so hard and . . . and tried to be a lady for ye. And what must you do but collapse at the—the very sight of me!"

"But where in the world were you?" Glendenning stroked her cheek as if he could not believe he really held her. "I've searched and searched, and—and worried so."

"Poor lordship." Gently, she wiped the tears from his cheeks. "Small wonder you almost fainted, and only look at how thin you are! Haven't you been—"

"Never mind all that fustian! Why did you run away? Don't you know what I've gone through?"

"I runned off 'cause . . ." Her lashes swept down; she said

haltingly, "Because I loved you too much to let you marry me out of gratitude 'cause—"

"*Gratitude!* Did it never occur to you that I loved you too? That I'd have wanted to wed you even if you hadn't formed the habit of saving my life?"

"Yes, but—you got a station in life that— Tio, dear, I couldn't bear to think that . . . someday you might be ashamed of—"

He put a stop to that speech by taking her face between his hands and raining kisses on her brow, her cheeks, her eager mouth, and saying between these hungry embraces, "My foolish little love . . . My darling, darling girl . . . If you knew how much I adore you . . . How grateful I am that . . . you're safe . . . God! I've near run mad! . . . Who found you? . . . When? . . . Where?"

She laughed breathlessly. "I came back my own self, and I crept in before everybody was up, and hid in that tiled room you like so much. It made me feel nearer to you, to see all your books and things. I didn't mean to come back. Not never. I meant to be strong, but—I found out that I couldn't keep away and—and still go on living. I knew I'd rather be— your fancy piece than—"

She was, of course, again interrupted, and then Glendenning said sternly, "You may disabuse your mind of that stuff, for you are not going to be any such thing! Who found you?"

"Margo's abigail. Next morning, it was. And then Margo came, and I made her promise not to send after you. Not for a bit. And next day August Falcon came and he went off with your brother, trying to find me. And then Jamie came with your friend Captain Rossiter, and *they* went to look for me. And I know it was naughty, but I wanted to give you time to think—just in case."

Another interruption. Then, Glendenning said, "You scamp! All time I was worrying myself into a panic!"

"Poor darling Lordship. But your dear stepmama and your sister were teaching me how to walk, and dress, and talk right. Which I'm too happy to do just now. And—oh, Tio, my own

Quality gent, do you like me now that I'm trying to be a lady for—"

He crushed her so close that she gasped, and he kissed her until she could not breathe. And as he held her dear and tight against his heart, it seemed to him that he heard a great sigh that came from nowhere, and from everywhere. And he wondered how many of their faithful servants had watched this very publicly conducted love scene.

From the corner of his eye, he glimpsed his parents coming slowly across the hall towards them. Smiling.

With a shocking lack of restraint, and betraying not the slightest evidence of contrition for having been caught in such abandoned behaviour, Horatio Clement Laindon, Viscount Glendenning, proudly kissed his love again.

EPILOGUE

Long after midnight on the seventh of July, 1748, the vast ballroom of Falcon House glowed with candle-light.

A round table had been placed in the centre of the floor, and five young men were seated around it.

A long silence was broken as August Falcon said irately, "Be damned if I mean to be bound by the oath we gave Underhill! The fact that Burton Farrier works for him and did his possible to have Glendenning's head lopped, tells a story I like not at all."

"We have no proof of treachery," argued Morris. "The general might simply have acted on what he believed to be—er—"

"My treasonable conduct," interjected Glendenning calmly.

"Sorry, Tio," said Morris. "But—'tis possible, y'know. And at all events, we could have made our own investigations without informing the general. But by allowing Furlong to know of the existence of the League we break our given word, and a gentleman's word is—"

"Is so much fustian, if 'tis given to the wrong party," snapped Falcon. "If you wish to leave, Morris—by all means—"

"Easy, Falcon." Gideon Rossiter, seated at the table beside him, turned to Morris with a smile in his grey eyes. "I think we must take into account, Jamie, that Burton Farrier very obviously knew that the Comyn Pin accompanied Trethaway to the bottom of the Dover Strait."

Falcon said impatiently, "Besides, the very existence of his Jacobite list is suspect, in my opinion."

"I must agree, gentlemen," put in Furlong. "I know for a fact that there were two such lists. The first was indeed destroyed, and the second safely delivered."

They all stared at him in amazement. Morris opened his mouth to comment, met Falcon's eyes, and closed it again.

"I think," said Glendenning with a grin, "we had best not ask how you came by that information, Owen. I'd understood the list to be just that—a simple record of who gave and what they gave. This business of two lists, one with items numbered, and the second with names, is quite new to me. Has anyone here knowledge of it?"

Furlong said slowly, "The first two were as you described. The third, if it does exist, must be of recent date."

"Oh, I expect it exists. And was probably manufactured by Farrier purely to trap Glendenning." Falcon added grudgingly, "Still, I am forced to agree with Morris. For the life of me I don't see what Furlong has to do with this unpleasant business."

Once again, all eyes turned to Sir Owen. He said, "I asked Tio to put in a good word for me because, although I know very little, I suspect a good deal. And I may also be a victim of the League." He frowned, and hesitated before continuing in a lower voice, "You are probably not aware that a marriage contract existed between myself and Miss Henrietta Albertson."

Rossiter said sharply, "Admiral Albertson's daughter?"

"The lady was a passenger aboard a ship that foundered off Beachy Head about eighteen months ago, wasn't she?" asked Glendenning.

Sir Owen nodded.

"Oh, Gad!" exclaimed Morris. "I am very sorry, Furlong."

"Thank you. I'll not pretend a deep attachment to the lady, for I was abroad for many years, as you know, and I scarcely knew her. Even so, we were childhood friends, and she was a gentle and lovely creature. We had discussed our marriage by letter, but I was still abroad when the admiral was accused. Henrietta was devoted to him. She would not have been on that ship save that when her father was sentenced, the shock was more than she could sustain, and her health became so impaired that her brother sent her out to Italy for the milder climate." He stared at one hand that gripped the arm of his chair. "When Falcon and Morris came to see me, trying to find young Templeby, I sensed there was a good deal more to the tale than I'd been told."

"Furlong met me at White's," put in Glendenning. "We fell to discussing the business of Lord Merriam, and the Albertson case, and between us formed a few conclusions."

"Which they brought to me," said Gideon Rossiter. "When we connected those two instances of fine gentlemen ruined, and their estates confiscated, we could not but notice a similarity. I felt that Sir Owen had a right to join us. Lord knows, if this League is only half as powerful as I suspect, we will need help. If you wish to put it to a vote, however . . ."

Only Lieutenant Morris desired that a vote be taken and, seeing that he was outnumbered, he withdrew his objections and said in his amiable way that they had best "get on with it."

Rossiter said, "In that case, Sir Owen, you should know that we believe the League of Jewelled Men to be dedicated to some mischief harmful to England. And that the destruction and imprisonment of Admiral Albertson, the disgrace and apparent suicide of Lord Merriam, my own family's ruin, are bound up in the business. Glendenning's near brush with tragedy adds yet another piece to the puzzle."

Falcon muttered, "Yes, but if there is a connection, what is it?"

"The acquisition of some extreme valuable property?" suggested Furlong thoughtfully.

"We thought of that," said Morris. "But, as Tio said, there's lots of fine estates to be had, without resorting to such elaborate dramatics as ruining admirals, disgracing diplomats, wiping out vast enterprises, murdering an entire family."

"If their aim is to cut down and disgrace some of England's finest men," said Rossiter, "they're certainly achieving it!"

Furlong leaned forward. "Gentlemen, you all know a deal more of this League than I, but—is it possible that it was these *particular* estates that were desired? And that the only way of acquiring them was to break the entail by having them confiscated?"

"If that were so," said Glendenning, "what do they want them for?"

Falcon, whose quizzing glass was tracing an invisible figure eight on the table, murmured, "Might be interesting to see who buys 'em."

"Stuff!" said Morris. "Don't make sense. Rudi Bracksby bought Promontory Point, and a better man don't draw breath!"

Looking at him from under his brows, Falcon said, "Your sentiments, Morris. For myself, I never liked the man."

"Lord! Who *do* you like? 'The wheat may turn gold in the sheath, but a hasty scythe can—' "

"My—*God!*" howled Falcon at the ceiling.

There was laughter. Then, Glendenning said, "Very well. Let us assume, firstly, that certain great estates are being pirated. And, secondly, that several highly placed gentlemen, formerly much respected, have been deliberately disgraced and ruined. Is there anything else significant that we are missing?"

"D'you know," said Rossiter musingly, " 'tis probably pure coincidence, but some incidents involved shipping—have you noticed? My father's shipyards, for instance; that damned fraudulent trading company; Admiral Albertson."

Morris nodded. "And Furlong's painting."

"Furlong's . . . *painting?*" echoed Falcon, staring at him. "What in the name of Hades has a *painting* to do with the League of Jewelled Men?"

" 'Tis a very fine marine," said Morris defensively. "And if you—"

Glendenning interpolated sharply, "What is it, Owen?"

Furlong, who had paled a little, said, "Good God! I hope, nothing! But Morris is perfectly right. It *is* a very fine marine. A painting of my brother's ship. He captains an East Indiaman. My father owns shares in the Company!"

"So did mine," said Rossiter. "And I chance to know that Rudi Bracksby is one of the larger investors."

Glendenning said, "All of which may mean nothing. Many rich men own shares in companies and enterprises, but their lives don't touch. However, it seems to me we're entitled to raise a cheer, for we've a sight more to go on, now. We can watch General Underhill—just in case. We can be alert for any new scandal involving a great house. We can find out who is buying up these seized estates."

"And we can guard those we love," put in Falcon. "Don't forget Trethaway's message. *Châtiment un.* If you were the *first* to be chastised, the obvious implication is that more punishment is in store, and any one of us may be next. Or our families, and—"

"Jupiter!" interrupted Morris, his eyes ablaze with excitement. "We *are* forgetting something! The Lillibulero man, Tio!"

Glendenning said, "Good God! You're right! He is Trethaway's *cousin*! Can we but find him, we've found a member of the League!"

"That should be simple enough," said Morris.

Falcon yawned. "Or would be, if Trethaway was the scoundrel's real name—which I doubt."

Morris gave him a disgusted look. "If anyone can stamp a fellow's cheer right back down his throat . . ."

" 'Twould seem to me," said Sir Owen encouragingly, "that every least detail is important."

Falcon grunted. "In that case, I shall add a probably inconsequential detail. When Morris and I went to see that jade expert in Windsor, he mentioned that the figures he'd appraised—two of the jewelled men, Furlong—were identical in all save weight. One was, he thought, slightly heavier."

"It might, as you say, be inconsequential," agreed Glendenning. "But Mr. Consett told me that when the two gentlemen took the broken ruby figure to the jeweller, they insisted the repairs must be completed so that there was not the *slightest* variance from its original weight and measurements."

Puzzled, Furlong said, "Yet if the weights of the various figures vary slightly, why should it be vital that the repairs be so exact?"

There was a pause, as they all pondered.

"We could sit here all night, making absurd guesses," muttered Falcon.

"True." Rossiter stood. "Even so, I think we are entitled to our cheer. We have made progress, and forewarned is fore armed. I, for one, mean to fight the bastards, however, and wherever, I may." He put his right hand palm down on the table. "Gentlemen? Are you with me?"

They all came to their feet. One by one each man placed his hand over the others and joined in a solemn vow to do all they might to circumvent and expose the machinations of the infamous League of Jewelled Men.